The
LOST
GLEN

The

LOST
GLEN

NEIL GUNN

RICHARD DREW PUBLISHING LTD

Glasgow

First published 1932
by The Porpoise Press, Edinburgh

This edition first published 1985
by Richard Drew Publishing Ltd
6 Clairmont Gardens, Glasgow G3 7LW

The publisher acknowledges
the financial assistance
of the Scottish Arts Council
in the publication of this book

British Library Cataloguing in Publication Data

Gunn, Neil M.
  The lost glen.
  I. Title
  823'.912[F]   PR6013.U64

  ISBN 0 86267 139 6
  ISBN 0 86267 138 8 Pbk

Printed in Great Britain by
Blantyre Printing & Binding Co. Ltd.

FOREWORD

NEIL GUNN enjoyed a creative life that lasted almost thirty years. In the late 1920s and 1930s he was closely associated with a literary renaissance movement that had turned its back firmly on a form of writing that had depicted Scotland as an idyllic rural retreat in favour of interpreting and describing Scottish life as it was. Gunn's first novel, *The Grey Coast,* was very much in the spirit of this renaissance; *Morning Tide,* the second novel to be published, was very different, being an 'impressionistic' book containing a magnificent vision of childhood. It was an instant success and won Gunn much acclaim, and a book award. He was encouraged by his publisher to build on this success by producing another book in similar vein. He refused and persisted in trying to persuade his publisher to publish a book that had appeared in serial form in 1929 — an 'angry young man's book' that went to the core of problems facing his native Highlands. The publisher was persuaded, and in 1932 *The Lost Glen* made its appearance.

The book itself is obviously of historical interest in that it describes Gunn's own parish in the difficult years between the wars. To that extent it is an historical novel. But when Gunn writes, 'This land was too old. Scarred and silent, it was settling down into decay. The burden of its story had become too great to carry. . . .', it is clear that he has more on his mind than describing a declining community at a particular moment in time. His deep concern is for what has been 'lost' and the passing of a way of life that enshrined certain values and beliefs. To this extent the book still has relevance to any community suffering from exposure to alien values.

To explore his theme of cultural collision and its effects, Gunn uses two characters, a local man, Ewan MacLeod, who had to return from university in disgrace, and a retired colonel who finds it possible to live comfortably on his pension at the village hotel. Both men are in a sense alienated from the community. The Colonel in self-imposed exile reacts to his position by bullying the locals, whom he thinks he understands. Because of his failure, Ewan is something of a spiritual outcast. He has not lived up to the Scottish ideal of a 'lad o' pairts'. Unlike another 'failure', Joseph Conrad's Lord Jim, Ewan does not flee but stays. 'To clear out was too easy. It evaded vision. It evaded everything. And vision can never be evaded.' Ewan's vision concerns his own landscape, from which his own salvation has to come, but his earlier spiritual ardour turns into a terrible irony. He moves through the book as a kind of village Hamlet, whose broodings illuminate so vividly the predicament in which his community finds itself. The predicament is all important. 'The Colonel and himself were chance figures in a drama that affected the very earth under his feet.'

The idea of loss in the book's title points to one of Gunn's great themes — that of man's relationship to his past. Unlike Sir Walter Scott, who feared the irrational darkness of man's past, Gunn sees the source of man's being as a heart, not of darkness, but of light. He adds to the quest for innocence pursued by great minds throughout the ages a belief that his own Celtic and pre-Celtic civilizations had something that was worth reaching back for. He sought, 'not a revival of the old, but the old carried forward, evolved into the new'. The finding of *The Lost Glen* has meaning for us all.

DAIRMID GUNN
Edinburgh, 1985

PART ONE

CHAPTER ONE

I

EWAN MACLEOD was aware that his disgrace was known before the bus drew up by the small post office a hundred yards short of the hotel. The usual waiting group all looked at the outcast student, the older ones secretively, but the youngsters with a stare. His father, large and slow-moving, stepped forward with a small smile:

'Well, Ewan, is it you?' They shook hands. 'Let me carry that for you.'

'Oh no,' replied Ewan, 'it's quite light.'

'You've got home again,' said Alan Ross, who was a great friend of his father. He was a thick-set man with a grey-black, bushy beard, a low-toned voice, and a quick glance. His shoulders hunched upward in an odd warmth.

Several greeted him. Ewan said 'Yes' to them, smiling, his dark eyes flashing here and there, the faintest colour beneath his skin, all in a way that might be mistaken for a natural touch of friendly embarrassment. In fact, it was surprising to them how normal he was about the whole affair. Eyes, when they could, peered at him with inhuman penetration, for he personated so much in the way of

9

monstrous behaviour. So that later in any one of the little croft houses, a man might say quietly, ' I saw Ewan Macleod coming off the bus to-night.' The woman would glance up quickly, asking, ' What did he look like ? ' And the man would answer, ' Oh, just as usual.'

The man's words would hang themselves in the silence. Then perhaps the woman would say, ' It's his poor mother I'm thinking of.' Or if she was another kind of woman she might say, ' I don't know how he has the face to come home! Bringing disgrace on his parents. He must be a bad rascal! ' And she would get into a heat about it and her virtue would be hurt and could not remain silent, as though it had all happened to herself. And another woman might say, ' Well, she had always great ideas, and her brother had the money which he earned where he did. Little good of it has come to them, seemingly.' And so every house would live under the shadow of Ewan's return. At length the man would go out and lean against a door-jamb or a gable-end, and stare into the darkening silence, and after a time would say to himself, ' *Thighearna*, if I had been him, I think I would have stayed away altogether.' And there would be in his heart a dark and uneasy condemnation.

Meantime Ewan and his father had started along the road towards the hotel, everyone looking after them. ' There'll be a sad home down there this night,' one old man said. And a younger man muttered half-laughing, ' *Dhé*, I wouldn't care to be in his boots! '

The little boys and girls heard this, and stared

10

after Ewan and his father, their mouths slightly open.

When they caught each other's eyes, their faces twisted in a self-conscious way. But as they didn't laugh, the boys' bodies twisted also a little grotesquely, and then two or three of them started running away at a great speed till they came to rest all of a sudden on a grassy knoll near the cliffs. 'Yon's Ewan back!' They stared at the sea, their faces smiling in an arrested awe. Then they began tumbling about the knoll. It was much as though they had overheard some man cursing and daring God to strike him dead. It excited them deeply, and every now and then they would pause and gaze in that smiling half-daring way, their eyes glistening.

The road rose slowly to the hotel, which with its white walls dominated this part of the world. It was an irregular building, for the original rectangle of stone had been added to, until now there were several chimney-shafts and out-flung back premises, the whole set against a flattish mound of twisted pines. The main gable was to the road, and the long front looked upon a deep glen.

As Ewan and his father approached this gable, which was on their left, they acknowledged several friendly greetings, but did not have to stop to speak. It was all a very delicate affair . . . until they saw Colonel Hicks stroll over to the roadside, smoking his cigar. The Colonel regarded them directly.

' Evening, John.'

' Good evening, sir,' replied Ewan's father.

But the Colonel's whole business was to look on this young fellow. His face was drawn to a harsh restraint. Clearly Colonel Hicks could have said something to the point. His jacket, tightly buttoned about his full body, gave him a menacing dignity.

Ewan's father hesitated awkwardly. As Ewan averted his look, which had suddenly become constrained and hostile, he saw his young sister Jean stand out from the kitchen premises and wave to him. He raised an arm, saluting Jean, and turned away. His father hesitated a moment, conscious of a sudden darkening on the Colonel's face. Then he followed his son.

They turned their backs to the road and their faces to the sea, for a short cut led them along the crest of the valley and by croft dykes until the path went down steeply in grassy steps to the cleft in the rocks where their home was.

' What's Jean doing at the hotel ? ' Ewan asked.

' She's just started work there,' replied his father, ' but she comes home at nights.'

A dryness flicked Ewan's face.

' I'll take it now from you,' said his father, and grasped the old Gladstone bag.

' It's not heavy,' said Ewan.

' Neither it is,' said his father, surprised. ' How's that ? I thought you would have some of your books in it.'

' No,' said Ewan, ' I left them all behind in the lodgings.'

His father paused and looked at him. Ewan saw the dreadful hope in his eyes. Their faces gathered the bleak whitening that comes off the bone.

' Did you ? ' his father asked, huskily.

Ewan turned his face to the valley.

' I left them all addressed to Uncle Will,' he said.

There was a still moment. ' Of course,' nodded his father, ' you would,' and he went on, carrying the bag. Ewan coming behind him on the narrow path, gazed now and then at his back, at the movement of his shoulders, at the head lifted against the sea.

When they were about to descend the steep slope, his father paused, and without looking at Ewan, said:

' Your mother is upset.'

' Yes,' murmured Ewan.

' She feels it—pretty bad.' His father lowered his eyes and regarded his left hand, moving the thumb over the finger-tips slowly.

Ewan did not answer.

His father looked at him and saw that his face was deathly pale and his forehead glistening. Then he looked at the sea.

For seconds their bodies remained stiff as if beyond their power to move. A moment of piercing divination came to Ewan wherein he saw their twin bodies caught up against a fateful eternity, not dark, but faintly silvered, like the far and utter loneliness of the sea.

' We'd better be going down,' said his father, and started, Ewan following him.

His father was perhaps no taller than himself, but he had a bigger frame, moved more slowly, and his eyes which were blue under dark hair had a more reflective steadiness. They would rarely be stirred or cursed by Ewan's sensitive passions; but, given time, they might set sea and land in their place, and men against them in a just proportion.

13

As they stepped down, Ewan had the wintry freedom of being unobserved, and now and then as he cast a look at familiar places, at croft houses on the opposite slope, at the old curvings of the stream, at the two-plank bridge, his expression flickered bleakly. And once his eyes lingered on a house high up and to the left on the lip of a corrie where Colin McKinnon lived with his daughter Mary. His face was cold and worn, and when it smiled it had the secretive look of the outcast, strengthened with a sardonic understanding. Against the pallor of his skin his brown eyes appeared black and his lashes heavily shaded. With his damp forehead he looked ghastly and ill.

At that moment it seemed fitting that his home should be cut off from all the others. Here was its blue-slated mottled roof, the little plateau it stood on where the glen narrowed upon the sea, and no life moving about it. It was familiar and yet strange like a remote memory of a house come upon in the valley of a dream.

And now here he was walking from the brae-foot to its white gable-end with his mind empty of all thought, as if the whole thing were taking place in vacancy. Only the faintest tremoring ran over his flesh and centred in a melting way in his chest. As they came in line with the front of the house, Ewan saw little Annabel's face snatch inward from the door. He smiled and began to breathe heavily, his lips flattening against his teeth before being licked by his tongue.

As they passed the window he felt his body against it.

His father went in first with the bag. The bag

14

bumped a little against the short narrow passage. They were in the kitchen. 'I'll put the bag here,' said his father, as he stooped to one side and left Ewan to face his mother.

The daylight was thinning and already within the kitchen with its one small window there was a faint gloom. Within this gloom the flat pale cast of his mother's face seemed heightened in a way that left Ewan gazing at it, for he saw, what he had never quite observed before, the resemblance it bore to the face of her brother William. There was the same fixity, the same curious rigidity of condemnation, except that in her case instead of being combative it had a deadly calm.

She was standing by her chair near the fireplace, her body short and stout, her strong hair drawn straight back. She made no move to meet him. His head drooped and he looked aside.

'Come in,' she said in a voice that was level, almost indifferent.

What a welcome when he had returned before, what a bustling!

He walked into the kitchen, turning his shoulder to her.

'Sit down there,' said his father.

'I'm all right,' he answered, moving about, looking at things on the shelves.

'Sit down and we'll get a cup of tea,' said his father. 'You must be hungry.'

'Oh, I'm all right,' said Ewan.

His mother swung out the steaming kettle on the crook and filled the teapot. Everything was in readiness.

'Where's Annabel?' his father asked.

No one answered.

'Annabel!' called his father, and waited. 'I wonder where she can have gone to?'

His wife paid no attention whatever. The tea was ready.

'You can sit down,' she said. Then after a moment she called in a loud, dead voice, 'Annabel!'

There was a stir in the gloom by the back door.

'You can come in,' said her mother with flat, unconscious irony.

Annabel entered, wriggling and shy. Her face had her father's blue eyes, but her hair was almost fair, and blue and fair were alive in a perpetual sensitive flight. Her affections were so vivid that she was very attractive. She was eleven years old.

She stole into her chair and did not look at Ewan, her hands gripping tight under the table and drawing her shoulders together and her head downward.

Ewan did not speak to her.

No one spoke.

The father, because he was uncomfortable, ate in a large way. 'Footch, the tea is hot,' he said openly, and poured it into his saucer.

No one else had a word to say. The mother refrained from eating, neither ostentatiously nor unobtrusively. She simply did not eat. She stirred her tea in a deliberate way as if she were thinking about it, or about something else, or about nothing.

Annabel had put a piece of bread in her mouth, and it was so dry that it kept tickling the roof of her mouth in a strange ridged way. Once it tickled her so much that she nearly vomited.

Ewan stretched out his knife, cut a shaving of butter, and began to spread it on a piece of oatcake.

The flicker and flap of the peat flame became noisy in the kitchen. The mother drew a deep breath that tremored. They all heard it loudly.

Action became heavy and slow. A hand went out in a way that was secretly and intolerably observed.

All at once Annabel burst into tears, and getting hurriedly to her feet rushed sobbing from the kitchen.

' Annabel! ' called her mother sternly.

Ewan muttered an excuse, got up, and walked out. After he closed the front door behind him, he stood still. So it was like that! The bitterness amused his face. The eyebrows lowered measuringly upon eyes that gleamed with a light that the features trapped. He heard his parents' voices uprise and he walked away. He had no desire to overhear what they had to say. None.

He walked past the window and along to where a path descended steeply by the inner end of the rock that was the foundation of the green flat on which their house stood. The rock was twenty feet high, and soon he walked out from it the few paces to the stream which just here left its heavily bouldered course to spread itself upon a narrow beach of small, clean pebbles. Across the stream, the land rose again steeply but irregularly so that the little creek was roughly an indented half-circle, not a hundred yards across from outermost sea-rock to sea-rock. To the left, a flat spit, slowly submerging itself, acted as a jetty. At the inner end of this spit his father's boat was drawn up on the pebbles, a rope from her head being tied round a great stone. To the left again of the boat and close into the hill was a tarred shed, in front of which were one or two grey lobster creels and odds and ends of gear, with two oars rising by the side of the shed and leaning their blades against the hill, which was very steep and all green grass. Across the inlet were no grassy slopes, the creviced rock rising sheer and dark. From the shed, the near chimney of the house could just be seen.

Ewan crossed the stream on the boulders that divided its last effort at a pool from the surrender of the beach, and so avoided the crunching pebbles.

The sea had a strange effect on him, lifting his loneliness to loneliness more complete. Its remote silvered light was cold and sterile, utterly without emotion. . . . How beckoning its farness! And deep; immense and deep.

Its breath came about him as he leaned against the boat ; a tang that made the flesh shiver in the negation of emotion. How clean! how exquisite! And how cold!

Nothing mattered. Stared at, the sea forever moved without moving; it crawled on and was there. Far off, success was drowned and defeat was a spent murmur. The ultimate sea.

Within it, however, sound, like a choked human whimper; against the rocks. . . . Again, but close in; and all at once his heart jumped for it was beside him. He moved round the boat. Annabel got up and fled beyond the shed. He started to follow her and paused, his expression bleaker than the sea's.

She was running away from him, terrified. . . . Poor Annabel, she must have had a bad few days after Uncle Will's letter had arrived. How, forgotten, she would have been tortured, creeping down here and perhaps praying passionately to God! He had once overheard her pray for a doll round in the little cove at low tide. When she had come out afterwards (he had slipped away) she had looked self-conscious, as if daylight were not quite the right time to pray to God, and to do it in a cave was even more wrong. He had never forgotten that innocent look of guilt, and he had only once seen it again, on the face of a student girl who had just been passionately kissed for the first time and might equally well have been in illicit communion with Heaven.

Ewan's expression, as he hesitated, listening, grew soft in disillusion. Blood sentiment touched him and his lips came apart in half-wistful irony. He started for the shed, stepping lightly, but did not surprise Annabel, who darted off before he rounded it. He raced a few steps, for he had her now between the sea and himself, but all at once pulled up dead and shouted in a hoarse voice: ' Annabel, stop! '

She fluttered on the very rock-edge. His heart was racing sickeningly. ' Annabel! ' raked his throat.

She stood looking back at him, her chin down-drooping, gathered into herself, but in some mysterious way conscious of her power.

' Annabel,' he pleaded, ' come here.'

She did not move. As her head drooped farther, her face became almost completely hidden. ' All right,' he said, in a certain indifferent voice, and walked slowly away and disappeared from her sight round the shed, when he immediately drew up.

He waited there a long time, listening, his whole

body intensely alive, his eyes glistening, like one who had waked out of a drugged dream.

At last he could wait no longer and pursing his lips as if to whistle, he walked casually round the shed.

Annabel had not moved, but her body had drooped more and she was quietly crying. Intuition told him that he could now walk up to her and that she would not stir or try to avoid him.

' Annabel,' he said softly, ' why are you crying ? ' He laid a hand upon her, but her body kept hard. ' Annabel, don't you like me ? ' He drew her up against him. He sat down and took her on his knees, gathered her with an arm. ' Annabel, little Annabel,' he murmured. Then all at once the crown of her head came from against the pit of his chest and she clung to him, her nervous hands gripping at his clothes. She wept passionately, clutching at him in fistfuls. She burrowed into him. She could not get far enough in. She choked her mouth against him. And all the time he smoothed her hair with one hand, while the other held her close, murmuring odd sounds, looking over her passionate little head at the sea, until, grind his teeth as he might, his eyes filled, the sea wavered, and drooping his head to her hair he kissed her.

She felt this new and awful affection. It caught her where she was lost and brought her back. Her face crushed upward and she saw that his eyes were wet. For one shining moment her look remained wide. Nor did he try to avoid it, but into his own expression brought a smiling disillusion, letting it pass insensibly into a brotherly attitude of amusement, wherein he faintly and archly mocked her.

20

He saw her devotion glow. She read his face to its last character, to the twist of his lips that twisted her heart. She could not believe her fortune, and after gripping him fiercely wriggled from his hands and sped away on the excess of emotion.

The experience was one of wonder. Such family affection was never indulged in. Ewan stared out to sea a trifle ashamed, annoyed with himself for his wet eyes. Here he was, the victim, the scorned, the martyr, whose heart could never more be moved, near weeping over a little sister, aged eleven!

Emotion faded. His smiling face grew grey. But, unknown to him, light remained in its uplifted look.

2

The experience with little Annabel affected him within the next few hours in many ways. She was the opposite of the intellectual and rational processes pursued in his studies. To everything that had been ' high ' in his pursuit of divinity, to steadfastness, to the subjugation of the flesh, to the asceticism of the spirit, she was—the emotion that he had experienced was—the temptation of weakness, of all those vague associations connected with man's fall. Not so much the fall bodily as mental. The spirit losing grip on itself, permitting the athletic grouping of its cardinal beliefs to fall asunder within the high-walled city.

Colour and warmth and affection without measure, without order; the completely irrational, the betrayal: called the sin, the snare. Even little Annabel was a flame. . . .

As darkness fell on the sea, his body grew cold, and, deserted, felt for the flame.

But another took Annabel's place. The shy flash of Mary McKinnon's stormy eyes, the grown, moulding body.... The look that came on his face held more of guilt than Annabel's when it had come out of the cave or the student girl's when it had for the first time been passionately kissed.

In a moment he realised it and his satire grew bleak—and slowly challenging.

What were these forces of austerity and success but a cold, infernal pride. Let them defeat him and cast him out, he could see through and beyond. . . .

This warmth and sweetness—penetrating to the core of life. Life became beautiful before it. And the very earth caught its glow—the green and the blue, mountain wings in a rush of air—until understanding became profound.

Thought sent Mary out of his arms and left her in his heart.

Mary and himself, in this glen or another, the mornings, the evenings, with one or two neighbours like his father and Colin McKinnon and Alan Ross, and the young men not eaten by ambition, with their wives and children, flying children like Annabel, all alive like flames.

True, the vision again, as it had haunted him on that dreadful last night in Edinburgh; but looking at it coolly could he honestly say that there was any other that lured him more ?

Thought entered his heart and Mary went out before it.

Speculation beat its fierce hawk-wings, ranging

the ages. Christ and Gautama and Tolstoi—the leaders of humanity had all searched back for the lost glen of their vision, breaking, as a first step, the shackles of personal ambition and material success. That was the *fact*. The vision of what they searched for was greater than any vision they had ever had. And that word ' shackles '—why ? Because the spirit is held, is conditioned, by what the body strives for. Had he not seen it everywhere from professors who would be ' teachers ' to a student like Lothian who despised only certain forms of success but would excel ruthlessly in whatever province he decided to work ? Had he not seen it very clearly in the case of his uncle ? His uncle was an admirable man not only in the eyes of the world but in the eyes of the Church. Out of ' nothing,' he had ' worked himself up '—from a ' lowest rung ' into a ' pillar of the Church.' Modern civilisation in its highest manifestation. The exceptional man, the flower of his age. That wasn't exaggeration : it was the simple truth.

Even his uncle's barman must concentrate on his job if he wants to get on, concentrate on it far more earnestly and far longer than on wife and child and home or social life. If he doesn't, then sooner or later he will get sacked and slowly but surely ' go under.' Apart from the exception, that is the inevitable course. It was the course his uncle had adopted in Ewan's case. There had been no enquiry into why Ewan had had these students in his room, what forces and ideas had been moving him, what humanity meant to him, what he meant to himself— that last and most inscrutable of all enigmas.

23

Not that Ewan reasoned all this out step by step before that glooming sea. He had reasoned it all out so frequently that almost at any moment his mind could assume the viewpoint of the conclusion . . . and see it—and himself—in the thin cold light of the land of rejection. Touched now by a vanishing warmth of Mary.

But he could never find the solution that abided in that exquisite land of denial. Always the ironic moment came, as it came now, pointing its jeering thought at the striving of the visionary.

Make-believe! It was a terrible and blasting irony . . . wordless, because he had no curses.

He stood on the rocky spit, his figure dark against the night sea, then turned and came past the boat-house, crossed the stepping-stones and went up under the rock on which his home stood.

But not up to his home, where his mother would no doubt be sitting brooding or, worse, going about the kitchen in that awful silence. How she had wanted him to 'get on'! Oh, dumb heaven, how dumb your canopy to her now! Her son *despised and rejected*. . . .

The awful association gripped him like a blasphemy. As its first sharp rigour faded, he looked sideways at a moving self-importance so insignificant and impotent that it was laughable. A dark-drifting figure, its thought circling and bumping like a blinded moth. That was about the true extent of it! His body cooled to a whipped strength.

He followed the path that went up by the stream until it joined the main road beside the stone bridge.

He knew what was drawing him in this direction,

24

as though the momentary warmth of Annabel's body was still against him. Not that there was any chance of meeting Mary McKinnon.

He would see to that.

By devious ways, however, and with cunning, he worked steadily up the hillside towards Colin McKinnon's cottage, pausing and listening, squatting when footsteps came, but going on with an ever-increasing fixity and almost fierceness of intention. The smell of the earth, the close contact with it, entered his blood. He sweated and breathed deeply. A feeling of relief and secret exhilaration touched him. Turning once, he saw the hotel with its lights on the crest opposite. Colonel Hicks, with glass at elbow, was probably telling someone of the young pup who had sold his parents and had had the brass face to come home again!

Some of the Colonel's intolerance was released in Ewan. He sensed the man physically, smelt his cool superiority and assurance, and wanted to come at him darkly in a ruthless way. Something evil in the thought, secretive and of the night, squeezed Ewan's mind in a cruel sweetness. He threw it off at once and went on, warily enough to elude an army, with an added vigour. Nor did he permit the usual up-thrust of self-mockery. Why should he ? Too much thought had made him a figure of indecision. Too much Christian idealism had made him live outside the world of men. The Colonel never had any indecision. Not for a moment. Ewan saw the face that had condemned him crush beneath his hands— then pulled himself up. In a moment Christian idealism looked at him with weary, sad eyes, that were his own eyes, smiling in a bitter, weary way. And in another moment the Colonel faded from his mind, because here was the light of Colin McKinnon's cottage.

Colin had always been his friend. Colin had taught him the chanter whole evenings through. The last year or two he had not seen so much of Colin and even less of Mary. And now—he could see neither of them.

It was a new experience to lean there against the hay-stack with the hole in its side watching his friend's house. The light in the cream blind was motionless and no shadow touched it. After he had stared at it for a long time, its stillness grew enchanted in a way that was sad and detached and inimical. Under the burden of it, little by little his senses ached. Life behind the motionless yellow blind was motionless too, like the head of an upright man bent over a righteous book . . . and the figure of a girl knitting with such unbreathing care that even her needles did not click, while now and then from under motionless eyebrows eyes secretly lifted and watched . . . without knowing it.

Colin and Mary, so far removed from him, that he could conceive Colin reading in a book with a Sabbath calm!

True, Colin might repudiate him. But if he walked right up and knocked on the door now, how well he knew that Colin wouldn't! . . . And yet . . . supposing Colin did ? As he would be bound to, in a way. Not an obvious way; hardly even with an obvious restraint. But still with that invisible veil of difference. For he would never question Ewan.

And Ewan could never tell. A man may not justify himself to his friend. Not openly, anyhow, or directly. Perhaps . . . yes . . . in some moment of withdrawn intimacy that time and place hold as in an evening light, when the tones of speech become impersonal as the accents of a poem, and only the telling face moves in its remembering grief or bitterness.

But now, at this moment. . . . Ewan's face moved in a slow satire. A debauched youth caught in a drinking orgy and thrown over by his own uncle. Drinking . . . and, no doubt, whatever usually went therewith. Wine and women!

Not that that in itself would in the profoundest sense matter to Colin. What Colin would despise him for most was not carrying his undertaking through. There was something mean about his defeat, and weak. A hidden pride would never have allowed it. Something worthless at the core, turning soft and rotten. Not the fine, secret Gaelic temper.

Yes, Colin, too, wanted success, but not so much the open success of the others—of, for example, his mother—as the hidden unyieldingness of the spirit that is like a sheathed blade.

Colin would not forgive him, could not, because the moment would come in the far reaches of his mind when he would despise him, that terrible moment of clarity which he, Ewan, knew so well. For Ewan had betrayed something more than himself. And not to many is the awful power of betrayal given. To less and less in this ancient land. Therefore how jealously must the few guard it! The secret of the heather ale! . . . hardly even a parable for the secret of the hidden steel.

As he gazed at the blinded window Ewan had a clairvoyance of intuition that saw his spirit stand naked—and shiver in the crystal light—and wither.

It was the profoundest intuition he had ever had, the most destroying. And the clarity was the purer for the ultimate truth that whatever he may have betrayed in the fight, he had not betrayed the secret spirit. Colin would never know that. A last tonic thrust that left the steel in his heart.

Then his mind sank.

His body came to with a violent shiver, and before thought could attack again, he walked away from the hay-stack. Almost at once he was aware at a few paces of a figure coming up the path towards him. It stopped, as he stopped. They knew each other through the darkness. As he started, she started.

' Good evening,' he said to her.

' Good evening.'

' I was going for a bit of a stroll,' he explained.

' Oh yes,' she answered.

Her voice was distant and poised in a shy brightness. It drove everything out of his mind.

' Were you in seeing father ? ' she asked.

' No,' he replied, ' I wasn't in.'

She was carrying a parcel by the string. It swung round in her hand and her body pivoted slightly also. Ewan's body swayed from one foot to the other.

' Are you coming in ? ' she asked.

' No—thanks,' he answered.

Their bodies moved again in the silence.

' Well, I think I'll go in,' she said.

He had nothing to answer this time, and as she walked past him his flesh flushed to her nearness so that he gulped and choked a little; then started on his own way blindly, blindly smiling and filling his lungs to bursting point with air. His heart got skewered by a quick pain, so that all at once he could not breathe past a certain point. He stopped, gripping at his breast, and, looking back, saw the door open and close.

This cramp of his was amusing. He sat down and tested for it carefully. In a very short time it was quite gone. However—ah, hang it, he was tired, tired. He threw himself flat, his face into the grass, into the earth.

3

Late that night, Ewan's father went down under the rock. It was very dark, but for that matter he could find his way blind-fold. The pebbles crunched under his feet as he crossed over to the other side and felt his way to the boat. His hand, outstretched, touched the gunnel and gripped it. Then he stood very still, listening.

After a minute he left the boat and went up to the shed. Entering, he pulled the door carefully shut behind him. After listening again, he struck a match, and in its light peered around. His eyes glistened, jumping hither and thither in a furtive way totally unlike them. The features, too, were drawn in an anxiety that all the time hearkened for the minutest sound.

The match burnt out. He trod on its red ember, and, outside again, latched the door. The night came against him darker than ever. He had not heard the sea before, for it was calm weather, but now the water lip-lapped, choked, and swirled back in invisible gurgling eddies. There was one very pronounced eddy low on the spit. He went towards it. The whole sea brimmed to his feet, choked and fell back, the water spinning over the shallow rock-edge . . . where suddenly he saw a pale patch the size of a man's face. His heart stopped as he stooped to peer—when the odd reflection vanished.

Upright again, he looked seaward, then turned to the black shed, along the farther side of which he groped with hands and feet. He came back to the front of the shed, and stood hearkening. All at once his voice came harsh and unnatural:

' Are you there, Ewan ? '

He listened to his voice and to the silence.

Leaving the shed, he went back over the crying pebbles and up under the rock. He hesitated for a time near the footbridge then went back to the house. His wife looked up at him as he entered, the cool, large air of the night about him. His shoulder to her, he said:

' It's very dark about the shore.'

She did not speak and after a moment he glanced at her. She was knitting evenly, her face pale and set. She would not give in, he thought, though she had to sit there forever.

Something in the dour unyieldingness angered him. The clock struck eleven. She looked up at it:

' It's high time he was home.'

Her husband pulled out his pipe and lit it. Then he sat down and took off his cap. He smoked slowly and fully. But after a very short time he got to his feet again and put on his cap, drawing at his pipe more heavily than ever. He hesitated at mid-floor and said:

' This is a strange house.'

She paid no attention to him, and his large, slow body made for the door, which he pulled quietly behind him.

She lifted her head and, hearing stifled sobbing sounds up above, went to the foot of the stairs that were steep as a ladder, and called:

' Will you go to sleep there ? '

No one answered.

' Do you hear me ? ' she called.

' It's Annabel,' said Jean's voice dourly.

' Well, tell her if she doesn't stop it I'll come up to her.'

She listened a moment longer partly to hear but partly because she was now near the front door, which at last she had to open.

The night met her like a black wall. She thrust her head into it, then drew back and closed the door.

As she came into the kitchen, she paused for a moment by the table, her knuckles bearing heavily upon it.

It's very dark about the shore.

She went slowly and sat down and gathered up her knitting.

Her husband, who was now crossing the bridge, was angry with her. And the more he got divorced from her, the more he sought the secret companion-

ableness of his son. For there was in her to-night—
had been in her for a week—some of the dour, hard
spirit of her own people. Her face became flat in
its discontent and in colour like the prickled skin on
a plate of cold porridge. She would hold to that
attitude, even should her son do away with himself.

The last thought swathed itself darkly. His
heart constricted in him as he started up the river
path, and his head turned to each side and listened.
There was a small night wind which moved in a flat
of rushes on his right. A curlew called overhead,
the long tremulous cry travelling swiftly inland with
the bird itself, tidings from the sea. Rain—or
storm. . . . He disliked the sound of it, and already
it was dying out afar off as if within death's closing
mouth.

What moved his wife was this: she had done
the whole thing, she and her family—represented
by her brother William. The Macleods had not
a haepenny, and, in any case, could hardly understand a sacrifice for learning! She had got round
William. And William had the satisfaction, the
sanctimonious satisfaction, of educating a Macleod, or, at least, of starting to educate him and
then—breaking him. Well, well, it was a pity
perhaps that Ewan did not go through with it
when he was at it—but, damn them for having
broken the boy and driven him—out into the dark
—like this. . . .

His step firmed. His body moved strong and
unyielding. If this man were driven to vengeance
his hands would come together slow but deathly sure.

He caught at footsteps and stopped.

' Is that you, Ewan ? '

' Yes.' The footsteps approached.

' We were wondering where you were,' said his father.

' I was out about,' replied Ewan.

' Oh yes,' said his father.

They could hardly see each other and stood there in a moment's penetrating intimacy.

' Well, we'll go home,' said his father. ' Your mother was getting anxious.'

And all at once Ewan knew with a strange and dark surprise that they had conceived the thought that he might do away with himself.

When his father remarked that one could hardly see the road, he agreed, but he was really walking within this new thought. It at once set him aside and lifted him up. It had a veiled importance and attraction. With the body absolutely weary, annihilation was another name for sleep. It had never hitherto come before him, not anyhow face to face. . . .

' Were you in anywhere ? ' asked his father.

' No.' And Ewan followed his father's train of thought until it asked:

' What were you doing ? '

' Oh, I had a bit of a walk.'

His father was friendly. Ewan could feel the warmth in his voice; at the first word had heard the relief that yet was no more than an easing of the breath. But between them, the shadow of his defeat; and this new strange thought of suicide. He felt shy and would have walked away from this man now if he could. Yet they were held together by a bond darker than the darkest thought. He was a youth within the circle of his father's being, as if tied by a cord to his father's loins. His father was a grown man, like Colin: the final arbiters of that secret spirit which he had betrayed.

The wind whispered in the flat of rushes; the planks across the stream echoed their footsteps.

' Are you hungry ? ' his father asked.

' No,' said Ewan definitely. ' I don't want anything.'

His father opened the door and entered.

' Come in,' he said aloud and companionably.

As Ewan entered the kitchen his mother looked up at him. But his eyes, blinking in the light, found a chair, upon which he sat down.

' It's very late,' said his mother.

Lifting a leg on to his knee, he began to unlace a shoe, faintly smiling at her tone. When his mother's eyes lowered to her knitting he looked at her, the squat upright body, the prickled face, the strong hair caught straight back so that it seemed to be pulling at the temples. His smile faded out at a mouth corner. He stood up in his socks, hesitated a moment, then without a word turned to go.

' Have you a light ? ' asked his father.

' Doesn't matter,' muttered Ewan as he went out of the kitchen, hearing behind him his father's voice, ' Is there a candle ? ' and his mother's flat reply, ' There's a candle in the room.'

He did not light the candle.

It was cool to lie full stretch between the sheets and hear the sea again, the sea about the rocks . . . about his youth. Had he ever heard it quite

34

silent? . . . Never. Always that faint murmur . . . lifting its sea-shell upon the ear of the night. How lonely and exquisite to be finally cast out, with nothing any more to hold to, to hope for. To be purged of every relationship, to be left bare. In the Gaelic poem, the girl said, abandoning herself to her betrayer:

' *You have taken east, and you have taken west from me,*
  You have taken from me the path before and the path
    behind me,
  You have taken moon, and you have taken sun from me,
  And great is my fear that you have taken God from me! '

4

As he lay on his bed an odd detachment came upon him and for the first time in four days and nights, the emotions of that last fatal night in his Edinburgh lodging could be tranquilly remembered. Though he had foreseen then the reception he would get on his return, he had not foreseen the decision he would come to this night, without effort, without even conscious thought, and yet with finality. He knew exactly what he was going to do to-morrow.

Through the clear relief of this he was even able to look back with a certain curiosity. The whole evening in Edinburgh could be felt as in the flashing past of upstanding posts, but it could be seen too at any point in detail. The first point was probably the appearance of the landlady ushering in the two extra students. The entry might have been deliberately timed to pick up Lothian's oaths. How shocked the withered old woman had been! She

35

had kept gazing at him, Ewan, until he had had to say, ' Thank you, Miss Bryce.' They all turned and looked at the haggard witchlike face, with its profound disapproval. It started mumbling. ' Thank you, Miss Bryce,' he had said to her again, but in a way there could be no mistaking. And she had gone out.

This cold dismissal of her—a new experience in itself—had released him, and any reluctance there might have been to use the bottle of wine which Lothian had produced from a pocket, calmly disappeared.

Lothian was, of course, at the root of the whole evening. With his slight, fair, neatly dressed appearance, he had that crisp assurance which was so very effective. Being a medical helped him. And when the others had ragged him because he had been the only one who had got a mere d.p. (duly performed) passmark, he had let them have it.

It was the first time that he, Ewan, had ever offered to celebrate examination results, and the purchasing of the bottle of port, which the five of them had been drinking up to this point, had cost him much thought, and as though the others felt this in some way— for he was, besides, the only one of them ' of the cloth '—it produced in them a heightened, reckless gaiety.

Lothian's attack on the first-class man had been characteristically sweeping: an imitator, a swot (he had declared), a coward frightened to death that he would break his reputation and so given to sweating at exam. time—all through the night—that the bedsheets. . . . Whereat Munro had got so hurriedly

to his feet that the chair overbalanced backwards and
he had landed on the floor with a loud crash.

The gaiety increased. But when at last Ewan
was called upon for his speech, an odd momentary
silence had touched them, as though in an inexplicable way the whole evening hung on something in
him, which was, as it were, the ghost at their heart !

He had supported Lothian. Facts and laws had
to be known precisely and he assumed that Lothian
was not against these as such. He would put
Lothian's attitude into a question: Why should a
man who swots up facts out of a book be considered a
higher type than, say, a man who sails a boat ?   Or
why should a man who does the counting at a desk
be considered more important than the man who
made the things that are counted ? Not imitators so
much, perhaps, as by-products of the doers. . . .
When he had finished he had turned to Lothian, ' Is
that your point ? '

' Exactly,' said Lothian, watching him. ' Won't
you finish your wine ? '

He had hesitated a moment. . . . ' Even if it is
contrary to my ideas ! ' and emptied his glass.

But Lothian's mind was not satisfied. The wine,
too, was carrying him beyond the first stage of
artificial brilliance. There was something he wanted
to be at. He tried to shut up Munro who, as a football ' blue,' was beginning to tackle rather obstreper-
ously. ' Let us have another drink ! ' he cried.

This had brought Ewan uncertainly to his feet,
whereupon in a moment he saw the amazing thing
happen in Lothian's mind. Lothian suddenly
wanted to be at him, to tear the veil from the smiling,

37

dark, damned Highland fellow ! The desire for the torturer's satisfaction was in his eyes ! And yet certainly, up to that moment, Lothian had had nothing but the friendliest and most generous feelings towards him. And even now he had to turn on another, shouting, ' Baird, you're a blasted metaphysical fool ! Your wits gather wool in a damned fog ! ' At which moment the door had opened and the landlady had ushered in the two new guests.

When at last she had gone, one of the newcomers said to Lothian, ' I say, Lothian, you were fairly going it.'

' Wass I ? ' enquired Lothian, raising his eyebrows. The assumption of the other's West Highland accent was a piercing mockery to which the newcomer, MacTaggart, responded with a smile that only succeeded in showing its instant venom. But Munro rocked on the couch, spluttering, 'Lothian's squiffed. He's tighto. Know what he was trying to make out ? ' He got to his feet and staggered slightly, and so drew all minds, laughing, upon himself.

The port, however, had begun to have quite a real effect upon their unpractised stomachs. As time went on, each became conscious that he might have to give himself away, and so began to talk and laugh the louder, to banish the possibility of squeamish surrender. Through the thick blue haze their faces jerked and laughed. In the end Munro began to sing—and, of all things in such company, a Gaelic air. But clearly he could not think of any other and he had to sing. The last defiant thing he could do. And when the cushion bowled him over, he sat up again, singing all the time, singing for dear life, his face turning slightly green.

The uproar steepened. Lothian, the finished Lowlander, desired it to be known that he detested that ' maudlin Celtic-fringe muck.' Munro never heard him, but in a revealing moment Ewan knew that the remark had been meant for MacTaggart and himself, the sensitive Gaels !   And Lothian was only too well aware that MacTaggart preferred to suppress his Gaelic origins !

He, Ewan, had turned on Lothian and smiled. Lothian had seemed unable to remove his eyes.   A naked, penetrating moment—from which Lothian had swung round and shouted above the hubbub:

' Shut up, Munro, you Hielant b— ! '

Whereupon, as at a signal, the door had swung open and Uncle William had stood on the threshold.

That compact awful body with the small eyes that looked all the smaller for being wide open in the pale fleshy face with its clipped grey beard !   The effect had been startling enough for them all.   But for Ewan there had entered—the executioner.

Even the silence had caught something from that grey dreadful doom, until Munro, slewing round from his position on the floor, stared—and belched loudly.

For Ewan the crushed mirth had been agony. But Uncle Will had soon silenced that.   He had left nothing unsaid.   Nothing.   Ewan's poverty, his mother's ambition to have her son in God's pulpit, his own money for the purpose: the whole thing blisteringly, with a wrath in restraint that could plainly have lashed them all with its scorpions.

It had all meant, of course, that his uncle had got him at last. As a godly man he would naturally have shown anger in any case; but here was perfect justification for the open flowering of their secret enmity; he could now rake up and blot out. And in his desperate fight for appearances, he, Ewan, had felt himself look anything but penitent, had caught indeed at his reserve, at the old fatal reticence which had introduced so early in their relations the poison of suspicion.

Even when Lothian had stepped forward and with superb courtesy had begun, ' I am sorry, sir, that you should have witnessed this scene. Mr. Macleod here is not to blame for it. It is I who took this wine and these men— ' he had been impelled to interrupt him: ' One moment, Lothian. Please remember you are my guest.' And Lothian had winced as if he had been struck.

Uncle Will might have been struck too, judging by the fierce quickening in him, and violence might have followed, had not Munro chosen the moment to be sick, opulently and on the carpet. The horrible business in that blue atmosphere provided Uncle Will with his obliterating climax: 'And you'll go back to your vomit! That's what *you'll* do! ' The door crashed loudly behind him.

Whereafter he had felt quite cool, smiling before these fellows. He had felt not so much cool as in some unearthly way liberated, as if he had moved out of himself or shed something. He had gone over at once to Munro and caught his shoulder. ' It's all right, Munro.' Bent down and tried to lift him up.

Munro, who knew more intimately than the others what it all meant, had flopped and burst into tears. The others had come round helpfully; all anxious to do something to wipe out the moment. And when Munro beat the floor fiercely with his hands, shouting through his tears, ' O God! O God! ' they had laughed, relieved, and finally cleaned up the mess with handkerchiefs. He had seen them all out, calling cheerful farewells, in good form, and returned to his room, when all at once his body began to tremble.

He had listened for the landlady and then gone into the dark lavatory; got down on his knees but soon found he could not be sick. The straining brought a cold sweat to his forehead, and he came back into the room. His landlady was there, sniffing for fire about the oilcloth floor with a pinched intense concern.

He had told her it was only a burnt handkerchief. But her face with its misery of condemnation excited him and an inward warmth crept in a flush over his brain so that he had sat down heavily.

She said, ' It was an awful night.'

The tumblers clinked, her fingers going deep into them. The image came before him of mouths drinking from those places where her black-seamed fingers went. She wetly sniffed. She was excited too; a gentle repressed creature, a withered maiden. He had been such a nice young man—studying for the Church. You wouldn't know you had him in the house—that mannerly and quiet. ' Good morning, Miss Bryce.' ' Good night, Miss Bryce.' Her shrewish misery could reach the verge of tears. For

41

she had something to say. Oh she had something
to say. And she said:
  ' Your uncle heard it all. He was in an awful state.'
The glasses trembled and clinked. Her knuckle-
knobs shook. ' He said to me—as he was going out—
that, that he wouldn't be responsible—any more.'
  ' I see.'
  ' He asked me what you owed. I told you you
did not owe me anything until the day after to-
morrow. He paid that.'
  ' Oh.'
  There never could be tears in her dried body.
Only misery and damp sniffings to the brain. She
hesitated at the door, wrung with ineffectiveness.
Suddenly, however, she threw him a searching and
surprising look. Then she passed out.
  He had got up at once and started about the room
again. Finally he had got his cap and headed for the
Blackford Hill.
  When, hours later, he had got back to his room,
he had felt his body purged. Its exhaustion would
bring on sleep at once.
  But it didn't. His wakefulness had become
abnormally acute. It had sharpened to a point
where he had cried, ' *Oh-h . . . what will they say at
home ?* ' Had gripped the bedclothes and drowned
his mind in violence.

  So that night of unspeakable torment had begun.
  For up to this point there had been at the back of
his mind, wordless but there, the conviction that
what had happened, being an end of all the human
relations in his life, meant that he would, could, never

42

more go back home. It had meant that he had to 'clear out.' Although he had been condemned, he had also in this new sense been freed.

But immediately he admitted this freedom to himself its sustaining influence became suspect. To 'clear out'—was such a manly gesture! Simple, sweeping, positively splendid in its brave decision!

The irony of this had developed a curious disintegrating power. It penetrated the mockery till it saw between the flesh and the bone, drew away the flesh from the dry bone.

To clear out was too easy. It evaded vision. It evaded everything. And vision can never be evaded. Like a flame it had burned everything away to the final truth and left him staring at that. For it was not that he would sit on some roadside of the world and think of his mother and father and homefolk and what was said of him, and the gloom, and the way his mother would close up; it's not that he would see all this in a silent malignant growth of shame shadowing his old home to the far-off darkening of death; not that he could not stand against these, if need be, though his heart died in him for sorrow of it: but that deeper, profounder still, the evasion would blast that final core of integrity that was himself, the white core before which the flesh shivers in exaltation and fear.

For not to betray that core is always to suffer martyrdom. There is no other way out.

Whatever happened to him after, *he would first have to go home*.

How his mind had risen into an exquisite apprehension of just suffering! He had felt his face as he walked his road grow white and quicken, the air cold upon its lifted look. The road went on and down . . . and there was his home.

Ah, but he would go out when the darkness came. . . . To Colin McKinnon's ? Mary . . .

As Mary McKinnon's face with its dark stormy eyes had flashed before him, all his high martyrdom had crumpled and he had turned over and smashed his face into the pillow.

Bitterness had got crushed out of his body's contortions like a poisonous sweat. When at last he had thrown himself on his back, consciousness was little more than a trembling mist that at any moment might lift and pass.

It did not pass, however ; it steadied and cleared; and presently his uncle's face had uprisen, broad flat crown to tapering chin-whisker. The flesh was full; strong sparse grey hairs stubbed the cheek bones; its unrelenting expression never wavered.

A murderous hatred of it had obsessed him as he gazed at it.

Yet even at that moment he saw what was in it of righteousness. For his uncle had worked himself up from a barman to be the owner of a pub in a slum, and now believed that this had not been his choice but his fate. He had the mind for higher things. But even if he were classed with sinners and God were against him, yet would he be all the juster on that account. . . . Without issue, he had been prepared to make an offering of this child of his sister. And the child by an evasive quality in him had slowly raised doubt and, thrusting out of that, a chill bitter enmity. To-night he had probably learned to his satisfaction why the child could never open out his secret mind!

From that face he had turned away on his pillow, for there was no charity in its unyieldingness, none —no more than in God's face. His spirit had cried out that charity was only in Christ's face, in the kind understanding eyes of Christ, in that look before which one's soul rose up glad and flushing.

That's why he had been drifting away from the dogmatists and the theologians and their text-books. Oh, he knew the impulsive soul had to be disciplined. Youth had always wanted to break away, to rebel, to fly into—chaos. He was no exception. A tiny entity. He knew that, for the love of exquisite learning was somewhere in the marrow. Not boastful learning, or learning for its own sake, but learning for its amber honey.

But honey in the end—not dust.

Not dust, O God, or our throats choke and we die. Not righteousness of the publican, not uprightness, not any of the virtues—none of them. They are too hard, too obvious, too iron-clasped to be chalices for the spirit.

To be first—we worship that—everywhere. And it wasn't enough. Ah, not only that, it missed the whole point, it missed the essence, the honey of the world's delight, the fragrance of the spirit's flower. It was too easy, too boastful, too ravenous of time. It licked up the spirit and left the husk —for the acclamation of the multitude. It was wrong. It wrung the heart of the world till its spirit fainted.

Feeling his own spirit faint, he had sat up in bed to

45

recapture it.   He had looked about him in the dark room and presently found himself hearkening to the odd bits of furniture.   The furniture listened back, still and dark-looming, and no sound was made.   No sound in the room, no sound outside the room . . . and far beyond to utmost boundaries, to the sky, no sound. . . .

From a great distance came back into focus the field of his mind . . . slowly gathering the green of grass, the tumble of the sea; gathering colour and shape, the sweep of a mountain, the bright acres of the crofts.   Figures became recognisable; they moved slowly, as if time were a benediction and space the wind-swept playground of thought.

This might be reality extended into the dream, the colours intensified, the humans endowed with wisdom and lit eyes.   But its pattern was abiding, its essence true, and its truth desirable.

This had come upon him with a calm and ineffable certainty.

He had known then that it had been at the back of his mind always as an unconscious standard.   Against it had been measured lecturers and publicans and class divisions and success, without effort of his will.   The hard, the brilliant, the pushing . . . were in that ultimate place the gestures of bad manners.   Bad manners because insensitive, and given to measuring matter against and over spirit.   As if anything between two human beings can interest but the gesture of the spirit.   There is nothing else but the spirit that looks through the eyes and moves the body as wind moves a tree.   The very phrase 'bad manners' is in itself so insensitive that one would avoid it, while meeting eyes glance and smile in a faint embarrassment.

Nor was that refining it too far. For such sensitiveness meant not less strength but more. Driven far enough, it turned an edge of steel, razor-thin, without mercy. He could penetrate his uncle with an insight so clear that it was cold and destructive. He could destroy him with his hands, knowing no emotion beyond the sustained constriction of his own body. . . .

His emotion had overwhelmed him again, until once more the vision cleared.

His father, out in the open, sun and wind and land and sea. Night with lonely friendly lights in the darkness. Colin McKinnon playing ' The Lost Glen,' so that the darkness becomes an ache and the glen extends to a universe set with stars. That emotion of space, how impersonal and how quivering sweet! The first shudder before art; man's shudder before God's art. And no man may know God, any more than he may know art, until he is alone.

Was not that the place that his race had come out of ? And was it not the spirit that his race had forever been concerned with ? Not matter, not grubbing, not success, not ' getting on,' but the play and the sparkle of the spirit in music and fun and work in the open and—poverty ? No, not poverty, any more than Christ's poverty, or Socrates'. And even if frugality in these latter days had become too frugal, whose fault was that ? The land of the Gael, the shore-haunts of the Norseman—what held them now ?

47

Why was that great spirit in eclipse and passing—
with here a slum-world congested like men in a pub,
his uncle's face behind them, that unwavering face,
rising ghost-menacing above a dark movement of
infernal heads?

Sometimes he had hinted as much—and been
laughed at. Lothian dismissed the 'pretty-pretty
antiquated tosh.' Baird had drawn a parallel to the
'poetry of escape.' They could not see the awful
spiritual principle and its eternal significance.

The 'poetry of escape'—that leads to martyrdom!

Within the grandeur that was Rome, Christ's
'poetry of escape'—that led to crucifixion. Within
the greatness that was Greece, Socrates' white core
of integrity—that led to the poison bowl.

With an awful virginity he had seen the thought
of Christ and of Socrates with a finality too profound
to bear. These last years he had moved within the
white verge of Christ's mind. Not that he had ever
become familiar with Christ. He had never even
prayed to Him direct. He had looked from afar at
the picture of The Last Supper. How could one
approach Him? How dared one—ask? To inter-
cede, to beg . . . how self-important. Yet now and
then, in a tranced moment, he had seen Christ as it
were at a little distance coming down by a ripe
cornfield, plucking an ear or two; and when he had
seen Him, without turning his head he would whisper
quickly to a friend, 'Look, there's Christ.' And
they would both grow shy, but hold to their way with
beating hearts.

Until at last his vision had got exhausted also and
all his body streamed away from his eyes, from the

dark bony rounds of his eye-sockets. Even when he lay perfectly still, it streamed away. Quiescence and sinking would no more come upon him. The alternation of convulsion and calm had got broken. His mind was getting broken, its circling parts moving out and out . . .

*   *   *   *   *   *   *

Lying here in his bed at home, the murmur of the night sea in his ears, Ewan refused to remember any more. The experience had been too intense. There were moments when his body had been burned away and his spirit had attained an utter clairvoyance. Too terrible now. So terrible that already its crisis was behind him, its white purity, and he was drawing away—drawing away from his youth. . . . It was as well that he had gone through it; better that he had fought these four days homeward (the humiliation of them he never wished to call to mind). The fight comforted him, lying here in bed, listening to the sea in the windless night; made his to-morrow's decision not only inevitable but friendly. Listening, he fell into a profound sleep.

CHAPTER TWO

I

WHEN he awoke, the knowledge that this was his
last day at home, that when the night came he
would secretly walk away to return no more, gave
the morning a strange brightness.

Immediately after porridge, he went to sea with his
father who wanted white fish for the hotel and bait
for some lobster creels, which he was to set in the
evening.

As they swung at anchor, each working a handline
up and down with fingers sensitive to strike, his
confidence increased. It suffused him with a sense
of pleasure. He felt at ease in his father's company
and was hardly surprised at the sound of his own
voice as it came hanging already to a memoried
note.

'I would like to tell you about Uncle Will and
how it happened,' he said.

'Would you?' asked his father quietly as he drew
in his line rapidly, hand over hand, over the gunnel
of the boat, his face to the horizon.

'That's the best one yet,' observed Ewan.

'I believe it is,' agreed his father as he took the
hook out of the fish. Then he dropped his line over

50

the side again and they went on working up and down.

'I knew a lot of fellows there at college,' proceeded Ewan in a pleasant tone. 'I played the first year in the football team. Uncle Will, when he got to know of it. . . . I dropped out of that. I knew a lot of the fellows—many of them from the north, like Munro from Dornoch, Dave Sutherland from Wick, and one or two from Thurso. . . . It's a difficult thing to accept hospitality—and never to return it. There was one fellow there—his name was Lothian—a very nice fellow, and generous—very generous. He had a bit of style with him. His people were well-to-do. In the end I hated taking anything from him, or going anywhere with him or any of them. I suppose pride wouldn't let me tell them I was poor as all that.'

'It would not,' said his father, striking strongly.

'I lived pretty carefully. I never took a tram if I could help it. I had no pleasure in spending any of the money. I saved every haepenny. The idea began to grow in me that I would pay back Uncle Will at the earliest moment. I started saving in real earnest. He never really cared for me. And when I spent a week-end with him—I had nothing to say. I felt awkward. He used to look at me and ask abrupt questions. I would feel myself growing red, as though I were guilty. I dreaded these week-ends. They choked me. His ideas were so very rigid. And then one week-end—I think I have him!' concluded Ewan, and began hauling in rapidly.

Thus he went on to tell his father of the bottle he had decided to buy to celebrate their success; and of how Lothian had brought another in. He told the whole tale very much as it happened, entering into detail; for once he got going he found now a curious fascination in describing the scene. He spoke simply but with a glow in his eyes. The boat rose and fell on the long waves of the sea.

'William,' said his father, 'was a man that never struck me much. He was not.' His right hand whipped up with some violence. 'I think I have him this time,' he judged, and landed a fine cod.

'Our luck is in!' said Ewan.

'So that was all there was to it,' remarked his father, fishing again. 'I thought as much.'

Ewan saw the arid expression on his father's face. His father's blue eyes were dry and bleak, his mouth slightly puckered. He was fishing with deadly precision.

Ewan smiled to himself and felt his flesh grow warm. Somehow here not only one's mind but one's body grew large. His vision had been right! There was so much space, and clean wind, and far horizons. Nothing little or petty or mean. No enclosing walls and dogmas deadly and doubtful. Here was freedom, liberation. Not the freedom that meant licence. The very contrary. Look at his father's movements: the sensitive listening of his mind, his bodily alertness, the cool control. . . upon the slow heave of the sea.

Manhood came upon one here in the freshness of the morning. Here, too, food was being produced—the most important part of the whole economic scheme. All that was left to complete man was that thought should be engaged. Ah, and there was something else too—that sense of well-being which is akin to the glow of creation, is indeed creation's very self and moment. This moment, now.

When they landed they were rather silent and moved slowly about the stones, taking the lines out, the fish, and hauling the boat up with a friendly ' Heave! ' They lingered, saying a word now and then, walking up to the shed and back, until his father at last remarked, ' Well, I suppose we'd better go up.' There was nothing else for it.

They had drawn so near to each other that as they went under the rock Ewan felt a little shy of his father. He could have lingered with him about that shore, on that sea, until time died out. He could even see working within the silence of his father's mind the deadly resentment against William. But it would have to remain dumb. One could not get a fellow like William on that sea in a small boat. For he was in a pub, very successful, ordering the making and breaking of lives . . . the flower of his age.

Nor did his father speak throughout the mid-day meal beyond the necessary word or two, as though he did not care now what silence there might be.

After the meal, outside the back door, Ewan said to him :

' I'll take the fish up to the hotel.'

' No,' said his father, ' I'll take them.'

' But I can take them.'

' No.' His father was quite firm.

Then Ewan understood that his father would not let him be seen carrying fish to the hotel. It would be too early an indignity for him before the people. Ewan smiled bleakly.

' I'll take them all the same,' he said.

' Your father will take them,' said his mother's voice flatly behind them.

Neither of them turned round. Ewan stooped and caught the string which held the fish.

' I won't be long,' he said.

' All right,' said his father.

' I don't want you to go with them,' ordered his mother. ' There's been enough—' She paused, and all at once re-entered the house.

Ewan half-turned his face to his father, but did not look at him, and then walked off. His father looked about on the ground.

Ewan's mind became a cold blank as he climbed the hillside; sometimes the coldness touched his face to an arid humour. He ran into Alastair bàn, who was nearly his own age, a gay, fair-haired youth, who greeted him, however, with a slightly exaggerated merriment.

They chuckled and laughed together—and separated before a silent moment came. They were friends from childhood. And the meeting was uncomfortable for Alastair who, of course, could make no reference to what had happened, nor even show that he was aware of it other than by the delicacy with which he avoided it.

As he crossed the main road, Ewan encountered Donald MacCrimmon, who was delighted and surprised to see him. ' Bless me, Ewan, is it yourself ? And carrying up the fish, too,' he added, ' for your father! '

He was a middle-sized man, quick-muscled, with an etched vivid face. His hazel eyes looked and shifted. He spoke for the most part with a nervous rapidity.

He was very dark; and even all the darker for the grey hair here and there. His nervous energy indeed denied him his fifty years and made him the natural companion to many a joke. No one else would, on the spur of the moment, have quite hit off the phrase 'for your father.' That year he had become Colonel Hicks's gillie.

Even as they greeted each other, Ewan saw Colonel Hicks approaching from the direction of the post office. 'Better get rid of the fish. See you again,' he said to Donald, and went round to the back premises where he encountered the kitchen-maid who used to be in his own class at school.

She met him frankly, with a friendly smile. She had always been cheerful, her dark eyes given to lighting up a trifle recklessly. Full-bodied, she had something attractive and warming in her glance, and he stood talking and smiling. He felt in rather a reckless mood himself. No one knew that this was his last day.

'So you didn't like the church,' said Molly roundly, and winded him.

He felt his face go red and looked at his hands. She did it so well, too, with such uncaring amusement and a tone of challenging equality. Her sidelong glance turned away to the tub into which he had put the fish. 'You can wash your hands there,' she said, pointing to the tap.

As he washed his hands, he was aware of her eyes on him.

'How do you like being here?' he asked.

'All right,' she said. 'Colonel Hicks comes round to feed the cat.'

He laughed. She held him out a towel. As he took it, he looked at her, his eyes sparkling.

She met his expression with the same friendly challenge and said outright:

' I don't blame you.'

' Thanks.'

' No need to be sarcastic.'

' I'm not.'

' Well, anyway, they talk such rubbish,' she said. He laughed. ' Where's Jean ? '

' She was here a minute ago. Will I get her ? '

' Oh no. It's all right. I was just wondering.'

He hesitated, the smile flashing in his eyes.

' Well . . . so long ! '

' So long, Ewan ! ' she cried cheerfully.

Unmoving, she watched him pass the window. Her eyes became thoughtful. Then something of regret or denial passed over them and she shrugged—and turned on the tap as Jean came in.

' Ewan was here with the fish and asking for you.'

' Was he ? ' asked Jean, and after hesitating a moment went out at the back door. She returned, saying, ' He's out of sight.' And stood still.

' We'll clean the fish,' said Molly.

As Jean put on her apron, Molly gave her a side-long glance. Jean was sixteen, pale and dark, like a gipsy; and her expression was reticent, even dour, as if there was a fire smothered in her somewhere. Her hair was always slightly untidy and a wing of it was inclined to fall over a brow. Molly lifted her eyes from her and looked sombrely out of the window for a time. All at once she got briskly busy.

The hotel proprietor was in the bar door at the back of the premises as Ewan passed. He was a ponderous slow man with a drooping, quiet manner and a ragged moustache. Without smiling, he said in a soft, almost confidential voice, ' Well, Ewan.' Ewan greeted him with a cheerful nod and held to his way.

Just before the main road crossed the stone bridge, he turned to his left up the glen to Torbuie. The ground on either side sloped fairly steeply and was wooded in irregular patches of hazel and birch. Trees also lined the stream, hanging over boulders, and hiding many of the small, dark pools. He did not want to go home for a few hours. It would then be time to go out with his father to set the lobster creels. After that they would come back and have something to eat. It would be dark when he would go to his room and wrap into a bundle the one or two things he required. He would leave a note for his father. ' I'm off to try my luck in the world.' Something light like that. No need to be solemn about it. . . . Though it might be a temptation to say, ' Off to try my luck in the world. I won't come back this time. So don't be anxious.' By the morning he would have put in twenty odd miles easily— cutting straight inland and south. He possessed the sound sum of seven shillings and fivepence. That had got to work his passage to Glasgow. First town, Helmsdale. Nothing there—fishing derelict. The map of Scotland spread itself before his eye. His face took on a dry expression. But he would reach Glasgow all right in time—and take a ship. No— not to the colonies! And his aim would be—success. He would ' get on ' !

His flesh gathered tremorings of excitement. Deep in his heart he knew that he had never been cut out for this sort of thing. He could see it all clearly, could map it out, but whenever he looked too closely his imagination shuddered. It was nothing to have to fight at once. But to have to go on fighting day after day, year after year, toughening, blasting, cursing . . . letting go . . . denying himself, fulfilling nothing. . . . It was arid, that. Arid; not even martyrdom! Sheer negation. To fulfil the material triumph of ' getting on ' !

His face drew to a smile over which the wind passed coldly. The wind was rising and the sky darkening. It wasn't going to be much of a night for the mountain-track! The trees darkened too, and the water, but in an intimate way, with a sort of inner glow that drew the eyes to them and through them back into remote memories. His nostrils flexed of their own accord and caught an elusive fragrance that was only half of the earth. He looked up and down the hillsides, where the trees swayed, buds sore-swollen upon their wintry twigs, and where elbows of the earth stuck out, boulder-warts here and there upon a dark-brown pelt.

This land was too old. Scarred and silent, it was settling down into decay. The burden of its story had become too great to carry. . . . Yet all its body could in a moment become a watching face, saturnine and appraising. He kept it company for three miles, till it fell back from him and, as its final enigmatic expression, exposed in a wide strath the hamlet of Torbuie.

A huddle of grey houses, straw-thatched, lying to the earth with an aged decrepitude that humped their backs. Seven of them all told. No life stirred urgently, nor cry of child. An old man came to a gable-end and, his shoulders hunched, stood looking towards Ewan. A middle-aged man ploughed slowly in a field. Far away as Ewan could see stood a dark pine plantation against a hill, with smoke rising above it. The smoke came from the many chimneys of Sronlairg Lodge, where Colin McKinnon had been head keeper until Mr. Denver acquired this residence of a Mackay laird as his autumn box. Between the American and the hotel-keeper the glen to-day ran its ancient course. Ewan's eyes fell on the houses that now seemed to be huddling for warmth, and all at once he saw them mean and wretched, and understood that they were dying, thin-blooded and miserable; they would never more be warm in all time, and the spirit shunned them as it always shunned death.

They became like places in a vision, rather than actually stared at; and even when he turned his back on them and went down the glen again, his inward eye beheld the old man watch him out of sight then go inside and say to his wife, ' I saw some one but could not make out who he was. He stood looking across at me for a long time; then he went away.' The woman would listen to this. ' I wonder who it could be,' she would think aloud; ' what was he like ? ' ' I don't know,' and the old man, seated and with one hand to the fire from habit, would stare out through the window. ' That was a queer thing for any one to do,' his wife would murmur. ' Yes,' and the old man would gaze until the eyes shed their curiosity and grew vacant as the glass.

It was not that the spirit was dead but that it had passed. There no longer was any meaning in living there. How terrible, how awful, the slow movement of time, with its grey sterile hand! O God! thought Ewan. And the invocation seared his mind.

He hid his mind in what had been friendly and fresh and full of labour and leisure and happiness; the old music, the games, the fierce passions, the fights, the stir, the excitement, the loneliness, the grey mists, the sun, the sea; life centred on itself, young life fierce or glowing or dreamy, but life, with belief in its time and place.

As he neared the bridge he observed coming up the glen road towards him a youth and a girl. As they drew near he saw that they were his sister Jean and Ronnie McAndrew, son of the head keeper who had taken Colin's place at Sronlairg. Ronnie, who was at the secondary school in Thurso, was home for the Easter holidays. He was fair-faced, slim, and sensitive-mannered. His eyes glanced and his skin grew rich as, smiling, he tried to look unconcerned. Jean's eyebrows on the other hand lowered over eyes that had a sort of awkward, lambent glow. They looked as if they were caught in a companionship which they were aware would be misunderstood. Whereas, well, it was just the merest chance that here they were walking on, and on, like this. . . . Ewan smiled, said 'Hallo, Ronnie!' And Ronnie answered, 'Hallo!' his eyes glancing at Ewan's face and glancing away, like a young stag trying to hold his own. Jean did not look at her brother at all.

Ewan passed on, the smile growing reflective and humoured. He remembered once when he had come back from Thurso himself, hanging about the bridge, and meeting Mary (whom he had spied leaving her house), and walking with her up the glen. How his heart had swung round inside him, while he had searched for gay and bright things to say! Almost distressed he had felt as though it weren't such a great thing after all; yet fascinated and disturbed beyond his secret dreams. Indeed, after that first walk was over, it haunted him; how it haunted and tormented him!

As he came to the bridge, he observed two men upon it: old Angie Sutherland of the croft below the schoolhouse and Alan Ross. He had to stop and speak to them. They were quiet and friendly, regarding him in a way that took him for granted, as if he were one of themselves and had no history. ' It looks as if it might be a dirty night,' said Alan.

How well they can do it! he reflected, as he walked away, their released thought in his shoulder blades.

By the time he came to the footbridge he caught the funnel of wind from the sea. The glen sheltered them from the nor'-westerly wind that was blowing outside. He heard the booming in the rocks. The afternoon was sinking quickly. It would be dark early to-night. He caught a glimpse of his father moving on the foreshore and went down to him.

As he came round the rock, his father was standing beyond the boat, looking out to sea. Ewan drew up, as though a force had come against him.

His father was different from the other men in the place, even though one or two of them, like Alan Ross, had when young gone as hired hands to the East Coast herring fishing. But the glen was in spirit a settlement of landsmen, the old Celtic stock that is of the land rather than the sea. But his father had in his spirit that something extra of the moving deeps. Not that that meant any restless or vivid quality in him. Indeed it was as if the sea soothed him, and in the coldest weather, heaving out there, he could fish for hours. His croft had now been handed over almost entirely to Alan Ross, for whom he laboured in the season, getting milk and produce in exchange.

But it was a stormy and treacherous coast, not naturally adapted to breed seamen. His father had got so used to judging the sea's moods that something of their darkness was sometimes observable in himself, not moodily, but as a silence in which there was a steely sparkle as of light in a jaggle of blue-green water. His large frame, too, could take on a broad steadiness, that, seen against the sea, gave him, to a moment of emotional vision, a quiet, heroic loneliness.

Ewan went on. His father turned, hearing his footsteps, and said, 'Well, Ewan, you've got back.' How smooth and friendly the tone, how companionable! Ewan warmed under it, felt himself cut off with this man from the mean land, from eyes that pierced the back, and tongues that were 'generous.'

Cut off from all that, into this pocket of the sea, the sea that cleansed. Listen to it along the rocks. Over against the dark face, a spout of foam. The waves swinging past, with here and there a white smother, a lifted mane.

'I'm afraid,' said his father thoughtfully, 'it's going to blow.'

'You think we shouldn't chance it?' All at once

62

Ewan wanted to chance it more than anything else on earth. It came over him in a strong, reckless craving.

'It's getting just a bit beyond us, I think.'

'You have the creels ready?'

'Yes.'

They stood silent, looking to sea.

'It's a pity,' muttered Ewan.

'It's the pull back,' said his father. 'There's the Black Rock out round the corner there; then there's the rocks off Cladach. That's the main places. But the pull back from Cladach—against that.'

'I'd take an oar, of course.'

'I know. But it's not weaker the wind is getting.'

'Didn't you once,' suggested Ewan, 'when it came to the worst, beach on the Cladach sand?'

'I did,' said his father. 'But I'm never going to do it again, if I can help it. No.'

They stood silent. Then the father turned away, but, happening to lift his eyes, caught sight of the ridge of his home. He paused, looking at it a moment, then quietly faced about. If they did not go to sea, they would have to go up there.

'Do you think it's getting worse?' he asked, hesitantly.

'I don't think so,' said Ewan, turning his eyes away.

'The creels are all ready and baited,' said his father. Ewan became strangely conscious of the silence. Then his father's voice fell:

'We'll chance it.'

For a moment, Ewan could not move, as if the decision had been taken out of their hands. He threw a secretive glance over his shoulder at the ridge

63

of the roof, before following his father to the black shed. There was a darkling triumph in that glance and a veiled awe.

' It'll be no time,' said his father, ' before the darkness will come down upon us.'

5

As they drew out of the creek, they saw Annabel standing by the little wall between the house and the rock-edge. Her features were indistinguishable, curiously pale. One hand was at her mouth.

Ewan had the bow oar, and as he watched Annabel something moved in his heart. He raised a hand and gave her a wave.

Her head drooped lower.

' She feels things too much,' said his father.

Ewan, who thought his father had not seen her, was stirred by the voice. His mind lightened in quick understanding. She did feel too much. He smiled, and just as they were going out of sight waved a hand again. But the little face did not move. It was the last thing they both saw, before their minds were given wholly to the sea, which was now fairly lively under a wind blowing out of a dark and closing nor'-west.

' Looks dirty,' said his father.

A rising hiss of wind blew spindrift into their faces from the crest they had broken. The sea darkened. They were travelling quickly, pulling a long steady stroke, the oars creaking against the thole-pins.

Ewan could now see that the weather had a hungry snarl in it. It was not anything like roused, and nosed about in snufflings of short temper, in quick violences. It was treacherous and left one wary and uplifted.

Already it was spouting on the Black Rock, an irregular outcrop the size of the floor of a large room. Soon the white spray would be sweeping right over it. The cliffs on their left were booming although the sea was running past them. No craft would have a chance against these walls! How they would crack and toss back, to catch again and splinter! Ewan's lips came off his teeth in a measuring smile. Good luck to them! The lips came slowly together and the smile faded in a lean fighting challenge.

Gradually he gave himself over to the sea and the rising storm. Such an exhilaration came upon him as he had not known for years. His body glowed to its last cell. Every muscle quivered, eager and sensitive. His eyes, cleansed, flashed and penetrated. The lean challenge grew full of light and the beginnings of laughter. And there his father, the quiet strong body, bending forward, dipping the oars, swaying back, without effort, as if he were hardly pulling at all, but all the time thinking out the chances, his face to the nor'-west, holding all the chances within his judgment, soundly and surely.

A deep affection moved Ewan, a warm companionship. How splendid it was to be here with him, with this father of his! How sure and quiet he was! Not glowing in any way, but quiet and rock-sure. Ewan eyed the rocks, then turned his glance on the wave-crests that curled and hissed and smoked in the gusts. His teeth showed laughing. Rocks and waves—look at them!

And the nor'-west closing nearer and blacker; the waves deepening, losing colour, darkening, spent bubbles seething when their craft clove through.

... Rooms and corridors and rooms ... bookshelves ... a hissing gas-jet. ... Outside, dark-jacketed people, myriads of them ... crushing and rushing ... great arc lamps. ... *Drown them, swish-sh, the engulfing water over them!* ...

'Hold!' said his father, who thereupon pulled against Ewan's oar, and so they came into the slack water behind the rocks off Cladach beach.

'It's going to be a real dirty night,' his father said, leaning over his oar a moment and turning his head. His glance flickered and held, 'You're looking better already, boy.'

The pallor had all gone. The strained student look, the veiled expression, the restraint—gone also. Cheeks whipped red, eyes glistening, a tongue licking stung lips.

Ewan stretched himself, easing his body, a half-embarrassed smile acknowledging his father's expression.

'It's fine out here,' he said.

His father turned his look away. 'Well, as to that, we'll have to hurry—if we can do it at all.' He shifted his oar. 'Back her in a bit.'

Working both oars, Ewan followed his father's directions. When they had put down three creels, his father said, 'That will do. And now we'll go home.'

'Aren't you going down— '

'No. You wait!'

And when they stood into the weather again, Ewan saw what his father meant.

He thought they were never going to pull away from these rocks. This was a very different thing from running before the wind. His body that had felt so alive and strong was now light and unbalanced and tugged at the oar-end without weight. The water became hard and resisted the oar-blade so that the wood bent and would hardly sweep through.

Little by little, however, they crept away from the Cladach rocks. It would only be a matter of time and sticking it, Ewan thought. But very soon he began to doubt this. His wrists got numb. The muscles of his arms lost all resiliency, so that his hands yoked to the oar and pulled straight-armed. Then a moment came when, half missing his stroke, the bow of the boat swung round the least bit, where-upon the wind caught it and though Ewan's whole body lifted off the seat and strained to its utmost, the boat turned still more. In no time she was nearly broadside on, with his father holding water. By the time they had straightened up again, they had lost way.

' Are you tired ? ' called his father.

' No,' cried Ewan.

' It's going to be a real dirty night.'

The wind blew through Ewan's clothes. Spots of rain stung his neck. The blackness, lowering, approached from the nor'-west. His father was now guiding the rowing, and once or twice cunningly gave his son an easy minute by taking the wind a point or two on the off bow.

On the peak of the wind-wave they hung on their oars; as it passed they pulled through and made way. Ewan's whole body was now rising and twisting on the oar. His father in front could not see him. He did not care what signs of distress he showed so long as he got weight into his stroke. The oar was brutal and unwieldy. The sea was like iron. Ewan's breath hissed, his face drawn and implacable. He did not mind the sea, the danger; did not mind death itself; nothing mattered now but the supreme need for keeping his oar going and fighting through. The strength of his body must have been filched from him, but not his spirit. Not that! . . . Not it! should he drop dead.

'How are you now?' cried his father.

'Fine!'

'Here it comes!'

They held on.

His body began to wriggle. His spirit whipped it, lashed it.

The sea streamed away white-capped and broke on the Cladach rocks. Streaming away before his eyes, rushing on and on, darkening, tumultuous, the wind hissing and lashing, driving them on, whipping them to froth, darkness on its low rushing wings.

The sea gave birth to its own fury.

The rocks held.

A wave split on their bow, its waters meeting in Ewan's back.

'Can you hold on?' called his father.

'Yes!' shouted Ewan.

His body wriggled at the oar-end. His spirit began to lash it too violently, because into his spirit had crept the thin, loathsome worm of fear. Fear that this accursed, most accursed, utterly futile spent weakling's body of his would cave in. That man should reduce his body to this was a betrayal, was

68

more humiliating, bitter-tasted, than wormwood of death. O God, it was humiliating, humiliating! . . .

There he was nearly breaking down, giving way! The worm, the worm of fear, with its filthy ooze upon his betrayed body.

His gasping face drew lean as a curse . . . that might collapse on tears.

Worse and worse, the verge of tears—the eyeballs stung—O God—the oar would not—it would not come through—not through—

'Here's the Black Rock. Can you hold on ?'

'Yes!'

They drew abreast of the Black Rock. They lay abreast of it through time. They would never separate from it. Never. Not until they let go utterly. . . .

His father took the wind's weight.

'Ease you a little!' he cried.

Perceptibly they moved off and up, his father now pulling all his great strength.

After a time his voice rose:

'We'll have to stand out a little. Two hundred more yards.'

She came about a couple of points and immediately Ewan got her weight. The respite had let him gather himself. Two hundred yards. They would do it yet! But her weight—ah, her weight—and she was swinging round. He couldn't keep her head up. The wind was too strong. She was swinging right round. She was beating him. They were nearly broadside on. O Almighty God, give me—give me strength. . . . They have taken my strength from me—oh, God!

'Steady!' called his father. 'A little yet!'

The Black Rock, with its low surfaces, was now directly below them. They were nearly broadside on to it.

His father smartly shipped his oar and turning in his seat got his hands one about with Ewan's.

'That's you, boy!' he called.

Ewan's blood surged with warmth for his father. His spirit rose within him like a great cry, shame and love in the cry.

'Look out!' yelled his father, seeing it coming.

The wind hit them in a solid wall, drove them before it like driftwood. Their oar hit on a submerged shelf and was thrust violently out of their hands. Their boat was carried on to the shelf. The wall of the gust tore past; the wave fell back; before they could get to their feet, the keel grated, their boat turned over, and they were emptied into the sea.

Ewan rose through the swinging foam-strewn water. He could not breathe. He had sucked salt froth to his lungs. The choking agony left his lungs like to burst. He must reach the rock in a moment. In a moment. All his congested face was like to burst. He 'crawled' blindly. Only three yards. The lifting wave . . . and he gripped the rock. The wave left him. He scrambled a further yard and lay on his stomach. Air got to his lungs in exquisite agony. Already he was forcing himself to his knees. On hands and knees he gasped, head hanging, mouth spewing open. Then he staggered to his feet, turned and faced the storm, swaying, gasping harshly, eyes wide and wild.

There was no sign of his father anywhere.

The storm streamed over the low rocks, smashed and spouted in blinding curtains. He caught a glimpse of the boat, full to the gunnels, drifting rapidly down wind, then lost her in the near gloom. They had hit on the outermost point.

A voice croaked. The voice was trying to shout, 'Father!' All round the platform of rock he staggered, croaking 'Father! Father!' When he fell, he scrambled onward on hands and knees, before getting to his feet again. Always to his feet, swaying, staggering round. A madness of urgency possessed him. 'Father! Father!'

The sea was beating him; the monstrous accursed sea was tearing—tearing everything out of him. Everything. His whole breast and heart by the roots. 'Father!' Ah, dear God, spare his father! Spare him! Throw him up now—now—here—at this spot —now—

The sea gave up nothing. And once by a superb treachery it nearly got him. In a rocky recess a black head bobbed and disappeared. He lunged for it, slipped, and went down through clinging tangle-weed. The head had been a broad tangle-frond upswept for a moment.

As he scrambled up, the sea threw him from his hold and sucked him back. The second time it was touch and go. And if he had gone he would never have come back.

He knew that as he lay gulping on the rock. He knew it—and did not care. The storm threshed over him. He lay there without moving, his forehead on his arms. When he got to his feet again, urgency had died in him.

71

His face was drawn. The lips came off the teeth. He met the storm's eye; did a last round of the rock.

His father was drowned.

He came to rest on the middle of the rock, his back on the wind, staring down the maddened seas. His mind was growing smooth. A wide calm was coming upon it. A fatal serenity.

He turned to face the storm in a last defiance— and saw a lantern light move in the creek, out from the boathouse. He stared at it for a long time, his expression quickening again. That would be his mother. His mind had made itself up to death, and now the torment of life came back into him.

He turned from it and looked down the seas. The wind threw him off his balance. A white sheet swept him. He faced round. The light was there, waiting.

He hesitated still, then began undressing. As his fingers went to his throat his teeth rattled. He stood naked, blood at hands and knees. His eye measured the water in a sterile smile. Then he watched his chance and went clean in by the head.

6

Ewan's mother came back to the slipway with the lantern. Annabel pressed close beside her. Neither of them spoke. They knew that no boat could live out there. She thought to herself, ' They will run ashore at Cladach.'

She would send Annabel up to Alan Ross's and tell him. He would know what to do. She herself would wait here.

She would wait here—to make sure.

She had better send Annabel at once.

' Annabel— '

Annabel screamed and clutched into her mother, digging her hands into her mother's thighs. She screamed till the terror in her voice broke harsh and abject.

Her mother forcibly held her away.

' Look! ' screamed Annabel.

There was motion in the slack water near them. A black head with no face was coming slowly, slowly, to their feet. Her mother watched it. The head revolved as it touched the low spit, and a naked body crawled up, curved half erect, swayed, then fell with a thud on its side. The lantern light gleamed on its face.

It was her son, Ewan, come back to her alone.

PART TWO

CHAPTER ONE

I

As Clare Marlowe stepped from the rattling old runabout on to the upward track, the hill wind came about her face. In a slight thoroughbred gesture her head went up, her slim body drew taller, and with mouth closed and nostrils dilating she sucked in the heather fragrance till her lungs choked. Poised on the moment's ecstasy, she turned round to overlook the land beneath her and the far sea beyond— and caught the fair-haired hotel chauffeur tip her black-haired hotel gillie a certain sort of wink, whereupon he swung round dangerously and rattled off. For seconds, quietly composed, she stood gazing at the distant sea, let her eyes fall from it to wander over heather and mountain-side and horizon-peak, before she turned again and pursued the upward track. The gillie, following with the fishing gear, studied her ankles and back and head-poise with a dark twist of appreciation.

She went lightly, swayingly, so that her footfall was scarcely heard; too lightly, with no grip; elusively as though in character with the frail, convalescent pallor of her face. She had the look of one recovering from an illness, and when next she paused

77

and turned, her slim breast could be seen panting, her level blue eyes shining, her cheeks delicately flushed. Respectfully he turned from her towards the sea, awaiting her pleasure. He felt rather than heard her move off, and with game bag, rod, and net, he followed.

The track, slanting round the breast of a hill, met in a hollow the small burn from Lochdhu. The trickle of water formed a series of tiny pools with miniature falls or hidden runnels between. Stunted birch and hazel, bracken clumps, old bushy heather, with now and then an invigorating whiff of bog myrtle. It took her a little time to trace to its source the myrtle scent. When at last she squeezed the leaves and sniffed her fingers, her eyes sparkled afresh. Plainly she had made a discovery that evoked old ideas or images. Interestedly she regarded the slender withies with their green, aromatic leaves. So this was bog myrtle. And here and there, so that one might have passed them by, these wild flowers. Trefoil, tormentil, red bell-heather, butterwort, milkwort. She might have asked her gillie if he knew what they were. She didn't ask him. For a long time she stood by one round pool watching beetles skate. When the pool grew quiet she broke a tiny piece off the bog myrtle twig she carried and dropping it skilfully sent them miraculously skating again.

The path followed the burnside directly upward. By the time she came to the crest she was frankly winded and sat down.

'Have we much further to go?' She turned to him directly and smiled.

' No,' he answered, politely looking away, ' you'll see the loch in a few steps.'

' Good.' And she gave herself to the view, which from this point was magnificent. The wind blew steadily and, though the sky was overcast, fanned the face with a fresh warmth. Very soft it felt, like a petal between finger-tips. Reflective finger-tips touched her cheeks. Eyes steadied on the far sea, glimmered. North-west to north, to the Arctic. A grey haze for horizon, for the illimitable. Space vast and quiet and strong. The breasts of the hills about her with the sea strip yonder like a shining doorstep to the uttermost. Magnificent the sweep of the spirit from the grey Arctic to the still, dark mountains, to the far cones hazed in purple, south-west to west. Hazed sky, too, high overhead; and passing from peak to sea, through corrie and heather and myrtle, the wind, the soft, warm August wind. Yet for all its breadth and sentinel grandeur, this land was in some curious way intimate and known of the spirit that swept and bathed. She would find out all the human names it bore too, but not of this gillie now, who had caught a wink and buried it in the peatbog of his face. So she lingered, in no hurry; and while she sat there her gillie stood. He would keep on standing there until she elected to move on again. She turned a quizzical look on his patient, polite back. He stirred, and muttering, ' I'll go on and get the boat ready,' walked quietly past her.

She sat on, the world faintly lightening from the passing of his dark presence, faintly emptying, so that involuntarily she thought of him and the obliging likeable, fair-haired young man who had winked.

79

There had been that between them, that eye-flick of a common humanity, reaching out to the humoured possibilities of all love-making flesh. Impertinent, a trifle lewd. Yet hardly impertinent because not meant to be seen. Secretive . . . but there.

She got up and felt herself walking lightly as though the wine of the hills had touched her blood, and heather-scented plumes her unprotected skin. How deliciously responsive the convalescent body to this great old earth! Sensitive as a magnetic needle; how wise she had been to head north!

One month—one whole month—until her veins would be full of the wine. No thought. No care. A giving way to it. Complete licence! To get filled, charged . . . she hesitated over ' debauched ' and her cool blue eyes lit in a measuring smile. Then London again, her private secretaryship and her high secret ambitions! She suddenly saw the loch, Loch-dhu, and its face was rippled in dark laughter.

It pulled her up. Of all she had yet seen it struck her as being the most intimate, as if she were stumbling on some lost experience out of time and place. Which, when she had drawn breath, was interestingly ridiculous, for she had never before been in Scotland. There was a grandmotherly connection, to be sure, but then that was the sort of joke cabinet ministers made when addressing Scotch audiences. She knew that sort of joke, for her under-secretary (her chief!) was near enough full rank to make life exciting. Yet the loch was dark, and here on its face the wind ran in the darker flush of just audible sound. Half sitting on the bow of the boat with legs ashore was her gillie, waiting patiently, rod up. She went towards the boat with the sensation of all this having happened before. As she drew near she said:

' I'm afraid it won't be very interesting for you. I have never fished before.'

' It would be as well to have a few practice casts.'

He took off the cast of flies, ran out several yards of line, and made a simple throw or two on the heather. ' Like that,' he said, and handed her the rod.

She flicked the nine-foot split-cane wide and large.

' Permit me.' He held the rod just over her hands. ' Like this.' He flicked it back and forward with his wrists.

' Oh, I see ! '

He stood aside and watched her while she coiled the line round her neck. She laughed. It seemed so stupid of her.

' It takes a little time,' he encouraged. ' You are whipping the rod too quickly. The line must get time to come back before it will go out.'

His gillie's voice was respectful; his manner, while sensitive, was firm. There was strength in his brown hands and lean face. His eyes when they had looked directly at her, which had only been once, were somewhere between moss brown and peat black. He was quite thirty, she judged. She herself was twenty-six. On the whole she was rather astonished that she could not flick the few yards of thin line with anything like certainty. The point would persist in whipping down to the heather, and when she tried to keep it up the line came about her ears. Then she became rather annoyed at herself, gave her mind earnestly to the business, and succeeded tolerably.

When at last they were afloat, with the dark water lapping and glucking, the loch took on a new aspect. As he pulled along shore she dipped a hand in the water. In its coolness was a soft warmth. She found herself trying to feel it between her fingers as though it were an elusive skin. She gazed over the side. Impenetrable, black as night. And warm, caressing.

' We'll try a drift from here.'

She did not succeed at once, but when he had shipped his oars and come beside her and shown her how to take advantage of the wind without letting it stick the flies all over her cardigan, she began to make some headway. It was a perfect fishing day and presently a trout rose. It took the fly and spat it out.

' You were too slow. You must strike,' he said.

' Was it at my line ? ' She held the rod with the flies streaming in the air and looked at him. Clearly she had never until that moment realised that she might catch a fish. The idea seemed rather to startle her. Her face came all alive in a rigid way.

He explained shortly why, as trout won't swallow what they don't like, it is necessary, immediately they catch the fly, to strike upward so that the hook may be driven home.

' Oh,' she said, and turned away and looked at her flies and at the water. She made no move for seconds. The boat drifted on. Suddenly she started fishing again, and as they were nearing the end of their drift, hooked a trout. Sitting close behind her, he instructed her properly. She did not speak except once to insist, ' But my point *is* up.' He caught the butt and tilted it towards her. ' Like that,' he said. Then he got the net and landed the trout which was all of six ounces.

The trout fascinated her. It yawned twice and lay still. He put it in the bailer, which he shoved under the stern seat, and got quickly back to his oars. They were nearly ashore. 'Reel in and get hold of your flies,' he ordered. She obeyed, and sat thoughtfully before him as he pulled across the loch. In the next drift she got nothing, but in the third she caught two. She asked no questions, did not speak at all. By lunch time she had five.

'The time has gone quickly,' she remarked and drew a long thin breath.

'A moment, please.' He leaped ashore and beached the boat in a smart run.

She half-reached for his half-offered arm and jumped. 'That was very pleasant.'

He brought out her small lunch basket. Then lifting the game bag, he walked away out of sight. She stood looking at the place where he had disappeared for quite a time.

2

She sat down to her lunch with a smile. Getting into it! And the rather thin wine was refreshing. The chicken sandwiches had not too much taste, yet gathered a moist palatableness as they were munched. The dark water rippled away off, and the faint motion of the boat was in her head. The wind had at last got through her skin, leaving a glowing sensation all about her body. The red spots of the trout, the darting trout, exotic spots, swam behind her eyes.

83

The sensation of being bodily unwashed held a rich languor. ' Slightly savage,' she thought to the dark water, and made noises with the mouthfuls of sandwich. Then she cleansed her mouth with the wine and looked about her—and again at the place where he had disappeared.

The heather was soft where she had stretched herself, and when she closed her eyes the lulling motion of the boat was more real than ever. ' Drugged,' she thought, with a delightful feeling of being half curled towards a central warmth. But the smile in her thought had not strength enough to reach her face which, now that her eyes were shut, seemed more of a frail convalescent texture than ever, though touched to a note of purity rather than greyness. In her smooth brow was quiet and self-possession, invaded by fine fair hair. Her body gave a small unconscious snuggle and she fell asleep.

The first thing she met on awakening was his eyes. They were directly above her, for he was stooping in the act of settling her burberry about her body.

' I thought you'd get the cold,' he said, stepping back without confusion.

She took a moment, then sat up and shook back her hair.

' Oh,' she said; and then, ' thanks! ' and finally, ' have I been asleep ? '

' Not much more than an hour.'

She smiled, and gave a quick little shiver, her teeth clicking. ' It is a bit cold.' She stood up. ' Though not really, is it ? ' and turned her face to the wind and felt it. He was walking back to the boat.

84

She hesitated on reaching the boat, but in the end went aboard without remark.

' How long have we to wait for the car ? '

' About three hours.' He stopped rowing and turned the boat broadside on. She unloosed the tail fly, and after a little was fishing with some show of energy and interest, as if her mind were suddenly made up to it. But it was that hour in the afternoon when loch trout often mysteriously disappear, and though she got a couple of small rises, she touched nothing. But she was now warm again, and when at last she hooked a trout it played itself quite well.

Then, later, a drift proved exciting. Working the oars quietly, he took her cross wind so that her tail fly came within a yard or two of a line of reeds off the lee shore. Her first fish was a good half pound and fought gamely. The second was bigger and flashed a strong, reddish under-body. Twice it leapt clean out of the water. Excitement trembled in the arm that kept the point up. Her desire to capture this fine fellow became urgent. All her senses got focussed in this desire.

' Try and keep him from the reeds,' he warned, and began to pull very gently away from the grey tentacles. The lust of capture increased in her. ' Don't let him under the boat! ' he said sharply, and manœuvred the boat too quickly. She lost her balance and sat down heavily on the stern seat, leaving the line fluttering loosely about her head. When she got to her feet again the strain was still on. He eyed it for a moment. She was caught under the boat.

He bent over the side and found the bob fly fast in the planking. There was no tail fly—but he did not disclose the fact.

' I'm sorry,' he said.

' It's not gone ? ' she asked blankly.

' Yes.' He took the rod from her and laid it down. As he bent to the oars, he added, ' I should not have altered the boat's course.'

' And why did you ? '

' Because I saw the trout was going to pass under the stern in spite of you. When they come down with the wind boring deep like that it's not easy to command them.'

' If I had been a real fisherman, you mean.'

' You fish better for a first day than any lady I have been with.'

' Oh. That's very kind of you.'

' No, ma'm,' he said, and for a fraction of a second the polite form of address arrested her and she glanced at him. His eyes were looking past her down wind and held no particular expression. Her eyelids just perceptibly lowered in a flicker of dry amusement. She looked over the stern and dipped her fingers in the water. It was more soft and caressing than ever. The amusement passed out in a smile at the water, leaving a quite inexplicable something of satire as the lees of thought. Then she straightened up, cast about her, her head in its characteristic gesture rising clear and steadying to the wind in a frontal expression of calm, rather distinguished assurance. No word was spoken until they reached the windward shore.

86

' I think that's about enough for to-day,' she decided. Whereupon he lay on his oars again and beached smartly.

While he was taking down the rod, she examined the trout for quite a time. Lifting her head, she had a roving look at the background of hills, and a lingering stare for the dark water rippling on and on. Then she turned and walked slowly round by the loch edge until she struck the gravelly outlet. A final look at the water revealed it running on as before, on and on. With a sense of snapping an intimate dark attraction, she turned her back on it and took the path down by the little pools. But the loch went with her in a vague bemusement . . . of the wind and the motion of the boat . . . some vague thing else which brought a faint smile in about a tendency to stare into amused vacancy. The skating beetles were there, were regarded detachedly. The myrtle scent . . . she paused and inhaled a slow deep breath, her eyes to the bright step of the sea. Reflective finger-tips stripped some leaves and crushed them and rolled them until the green juice stained the skin. She stared at the finger-tips, smiled, and feeling for her handkerchief wiped them ineffectively. The mused feeling was pleasant and full of an under surge of well-being, of growth; like sap stirring under warm rain. And behind this hypnotism of the mind something dark and running on and connected with bodily growth and health. To think is to define. . . . No one should think here: they should grow—grow deep and rich—and dark. When she reached the roadside, she sat down, conscious that she might have thought definitely had she desired. She stretched her arms and lay back.

Sluggish and warm her body. Divinely soft. She heard her gillie's footsteps but paid no heed. From a deep breath, ' Oom-m-m,' she sighed out on a long, fainting monotone . . . and wondered lazily if he heard, and slowly smiled, and sat up. He was walking down the road towards the bend where he could command the car's approach. She lay back again. This sense of being swung between earth and heaven was too delightful for interference. Like being swung in a god's hammock. Why not God's hammock? Why not? Dear God, we forget You. With our little gods and our merry-go-rounds and our hectic dancings and dressings and schemings, we forget You. Your eyes like the hill loch and Your breath honey-fragrant, and Your space—space to swing-g-g. . . . Oom-m-m. . . .

The rattle of the old Ford penetrated her final wordless communion with a God whom she created with the sense of creating a splendid manly fairy-tale. The fair-haired driver kept eyes front this time, very respectful.

They trundled home at a rather breakneck speed, and the surface was rough. A couple of straggling crofts came into view. The cottages were right on the roadside, and in a ditch an old milch cow grazed, attended by a barefoot youngster and collie dog. The driver's knowledge of the incalculable was uncanny or else he took a lot for granted. One or two hens took off on flailing wings. She would mention this to him. Surely, of all places on earth, there was no need for speed here; particularly this sort of speed. Perhaps it was their only excitement, their dressings and dancings and schemings! An old man sat at a gable-end holding on to a child of some fifteen months. She swept by them like a goddess in a black chariot. They would remain with their eyes like that, looking and looking, until tethered youth would once more get its fist out of its mouth and stutter frenziedly at the old earth.

The car drew up on the noisy shingle before the front entrance to the hotel. The driver jumped to open the door.

' Didn't you come rather quickly ? ' she asked.

' Yes, ma'm; but I've got to be at Lochanathar for the Colonel at six sharp.'

' Oh.' She looked at him. ' And it would hardly do to be late ? '

' No.' They both smiled as she turned away. From the perfectly simple way he had offered his excuse, it was plain that a certain attitude towards her uncle, Colonel Hicks, was become second nature to those amongst whom he now passed most of his life. But what had really been troubling her mind for the last mile was this business of giving her gillie a tip. She wanted to start well and yet not overdo it. A preliminary propitiation.

' Thanks very much for my lesson. I hope I shan't be such a trouble again.' She smiled frankly and unobtrusively slipped him a folded pound note. Ewan Macleod touched his cap.

' Thank you, ma'm.'

She felt very relieved as she walked away. It seemed all right. Altogether this tipping business, unless one knew exactly, was rather difficult. These Highlanders looked such—such gentlemen. Her smile did not fade in dry amusement, as she was

89

genuinely relieved at having brought so splendid a day to such a satisfactory conclusion.

3

When Ewan had attended to the fishing tackle and had had a lazy smoke, he went along to the general store beyond the post office where he bought a small present for his mother out of his windfall.

As he returned towards the hotel garage, he ran into Donald MacCrimmon, the Colonel's gillie, who was fiery eyed and full of quick action, which meant that he had had a drink or that the Colonel had been getting at him.

' How goes it, Donald ? '

' Oh, fine,' snapped Donald, ' fine ! '

Ewan laughed.

' The old boy been standing his hand ? '

' Damn me,' said Donald, ' sure as death he will drive me to stand him my foot, so he will! '

' Tut, tut, Donald! Curb your wrath.'

' Curb my— ' Donald stuttered lewdly, and threw a quick glance about him.

There was always a snap about Donald, an alert, challenging manner, a sort of Gaelic quicksilver, ever throwing him open to teasing attack. He was the Colonel's favourite butt, his gillie and court jester. On an odd night, Colonel Hicks, for the benefit of some new acquaintance, would hunt out Donald, give him a drink, and proceed to run down the Highlands. Donald's anxiety for Gaeldom and for the Colonel's feelings begat a lingual dexterity that was vastly amusing. The Colonel would wink at his drinking friend. 'You're talking a lot of rot, Donald!' 'I may be talking a lot of rot, Colonel, but if you go the length of saying—' and so on, until the Colonel would at last shout, 'That's enough!' But Donald would go on talking until finally there was nothing left for it but to kick him out.

Donald smartly wound up the line he had been drying.

'What went wrong?' asked Ewan.

'What always goes wrong—when you're out with the like of yon! He got into a trout that was two pounds if he was an ounce. The biggest I ever saw on Lochanather. The trout began jumping. He got frightened he would lose him. When the trout came near the boat he put too much strain on, pulling him to the surface. I told him to let him go because he wasn't played out yet. He shouted to me to net him. "Net him, damn you!" And then when I did put the net under, he kept the strain on!'

'So you scooped up with the net and lost him?'

'What else! If he had slackened his line, as I told him, the trout would have sunk into the net all right.'

'Of course. And what did he say when you told him?'

'He threw the rod in my face.'

Ewan laughed.

'What happened then?'

Donald's expression grew rich with an awful humour. 'He was enough to frighten anyone. Boy, he was terrible! Then we had a whole hour to wait for the car. And, to cap all, Alastair bàn had a puncture!'

'O lord!'

' It was nothing to laugh at, believe you me.' And Donald nodded with some importance.

' Come on round, then, and have one with me.'

After treating Donald in the bar, Ewan continued round the back premises towards an out-kitchen where he knew that his sister, Jean, would by this time be cleaning the trout which she would have removed from their show trays in the entrance hall. He was thinking of the passages between Donald and the hotel-keeper, who in his slow-speaking, soft voice thought that he would not have Donald criticising his guests!

In Donald's anger at the Colonel there was that amusing streak of the meretricious! Ewan's eyes glimmered sardonically. Donald knew himself warring with a Sasunnach Colonel! He was aware of a certain personal licence, a certain greatness in the strife. He felt himself storming the heights with the wind blowing through his hair—like his verses about the Heights of Alma! He was a great man, Donald! . . . And the humour of it, there was something great about Donald, something in his spirit like quicksilver, something trickling through from the last squeezings of his tribe. But against the overlordship of the Colonel, Donald's agility was the agility of a weathercock—up in the air and seeking out the way the wind lay! Amusing! Against the Colonel! . . . Ewan's eyes narrowed involuntarily upon his thought as he turned and stepped quietly to the door—and suddenly saw the Colonel in the flesh.

His sister Jean was standing by a deal bench, a tray of trout and a washing sink before her, and beside her, come presumably to inspect the trout, stood Colonel Hicks. Ewan paused as he saw the Colonel's expression. The Colonel was looking sideways at Jean, at her neck and bent head. The excitement of attraction flushed his face to a lusty smile and his arm went round her waist. Jean gave a quick struggle and, half-turning, saw her brother. The Colonel also saw him—and stared at him, his brows gathering. Then as if what he had been doing to Jean was a trifling affair naturally within his province, his imperious look turned once more upon the trout, lingered a moment, a flick of anger urging it apparently to deal with this prying fellow. His face darkening, he removed himself from them back through the inner door.

Ewan stood quite still, lean features grown leaner as though they had been cut by a whip. Jean emptied the tray of trout in the sink. Her face was flushed in a dour embarrassed way and a loosened wing of black hair fell over her brows. Without looking at her brother, she said:

'I made some tea for you.' Her voice was husky and petulant. An untidiness about her face, a gipsy richness.

'Oh, I don't know,' said Ewan lightly. 'I'm late. I think I'll get home.'

'It's all ready.' Her voice thickened. In the petulance was perverse appeal. He felt her near tears, as if something more than the Colonel's recent gallantry was in her mind, something to which it was but the trigger.

'No, I think I'll get home. Mother will be looking for me. I've something to do. Good-night.

93

See you in the morning.' And he turned and went out.

His face pinched and his lips tightened. He stood at the corner of the projecting out-kitchen, eyes slitted and glinting. A lean, dark evil in an eagle face. A hand came up like a claw, closed noisily, then returned to the trousers pocket. The mouth gave way in a slow twist. He hung a moment, then strolled into the bar.

The hotel-keeper came to the inner door and glanced at Ewan, a carving iron in his hand and a white apron round his waist.

' Well, Ewan ? '

His drooping reddish moustache and heavy features hung motionless about his considering eyes. One should know that this dinner hour was not the time. . . .

' Bottle of Johnny Walker,' said Ewan. ' Sorry to trouble you.'

John McAlpine, entering, stooped beneath the counter and coming erect again placed a tissue-wrapped bottle of whisky before Ewan. While gathering the silver, he said:

' You'll not be forgetting that you're booked for to-morrow ? '

Ewan chuckled.

' That's all right. As they say, what's a bottle of Johnny Walker amongst one! ' His eyes met the innkeeper's searching look, baffling it; so that the carving iron was forgotten for a moment, and quietly rounding the bar, John McAlpine went to the outside window to steal a glance after the man with the bottle. . . . Seemed to be starting off in the direction of his home right enough. But that was nothing to go by. Why hadn't he bought the bottle when he was in before ? Probably he wouldn't be wanting Donald to see. . . . The hotel-keeper returned thoughtfully to his carving.

As Ewan, rounding the gable-end, opened up the front entrance on his left, he was aware of a figure in the doorway, and was walking steadily past without looking, when a voice he had been with all day, called, ' Ewan ! '

He stopped, turned round, touched his cap, and, perceiving his presence was awaited, walked up to the door. His fishing pupil had a light wrap about her shoulders and, bathed and dinner-dressed, looked palely radiant, her cool eyes translucent with rather excited interest, as though their smile might readily take wings of humoured laughter.

' Oh, Ewan, by the way, we have been discussing to-morrow's beats. I can have Lochdhu again. Will that be all right ? '

' Very good, ma'm.' He touched his cap and quietly turned on his heel.

She looked after him. The amusement in her eyes faded to speculation. He did not appear exactly delighted. Thoughtfully she went back to the lounge.

4

When Ewan crossed the stone bridge the daylight was still strong. He hesitated, looking about him, then climbed the bank on his left hand and going along a few paces entered a thicket of stunted brown birch, where he sat down and drew the bottle from his pocket. He read the label through the tissue paper, smoothed and twisted the paper round and round, and returned the bottle to his pocket. Lying back, he stared down through the withies.

Presently his face lost its conscious expression and rising up from beneath came the pattern of its still life. Seven years had made sure of the permanent lines. The smooth uncertainties had firmed in bone ridges, and the smoother skin had run to etched shallows. Nothing was blurred now; little or nothing vague. The face was thin and tanned. The fine bone of the nose could almost be felt under the skin.

That youth's pallor of dream, of aspiration, of the spiritual, that restless seeking and surge, had changed or gone. The loneliness, the belief, and the torment. The world had narrowed. The high imagery had faded. And the permanent pattern was bone. The jaws, too, had found their line, and as the front teeth bit now on a grass stem, the line firmed in a remorseless way. . . . Yet up into the staring face the old ghost rose and, caught by the remorseless line, grew featured and ironic.

The eyes glittered as they stared, and sometimes a lid flicked and measured unconsciously.

Until the face broke and came alive. Sitting up, Ewan looked about him, his lips parting as though ready to mock any one who had been watching. There was no one, however, and drawing a slow breath, he settled back against the slope, his hands behind his head.

There was no hurry. The question of time had been solved long ago. Besides, the single whisky he had had with Donald let his flesh lie smoothly. His stomach was curled up within him, and because of it the evening caught a thin golden note, faintly cold. This note could be heard more clearly with the eyes closed. . . .

His eyes opened wide, and without moving he gazed through the screen of withies at Jean going up the glen road beyond the burn.

The evening had gathered a slight dusk. Jean's face looked paler than it had done in the kitchen, more moody and strained, and she appeared to be expecting someone or trying to avoid someone. Once or twice she threw a sidelong glance in a furtive way.

She was out of sight in a few yards and he was scouting noiselessly along through the stunted birches. He saw her back for a moment, and then she was gone altogether.

He lay down and wondered what on earth she could be up to, his face growing curiously still, his mouth slightly open, as if he were listening. There was an odd strained smile on his face as if an inaudible thing were being very nearly overheard.

His mouth closed and he looked hither and thither, the smile hardening in his eyes, self-conscious and uncomfortable.

Damn, what could she be up to ?

Her face, pale and furtive, came before him again. He had felt uncertain about her for some time, as though she had something on her mind. And not only that—or more than that . . . But her face, it suggested—what did it suggest ? Her woman's face.

Dark, gipsy, troubled . . . a sort of rich dourness, a smothered fire. Attractive—*in that way*.

His eyes flashed among the withies. A hand began plucking fistfuls of grass. The Colonel—

He got up. He could not let the Colonel enter his mind. To live with any ease, a mind must have certain taboos. If it need not be rigid about them, it at least must have the right to enforce them at will. Otherwise life could become malignant and intolerable. He had gone into the withies to put his mind at ease. To find ease, and in the darkening to go up to Colin McKinnon's with the whisky. He had not been to Colin's for a long time.

Before emerging from the withies, he sat down again and let himself stare across towards the glen road. But it was not long before he had to recognise what he was doing. He was watching . . . the way from the hotel.

He arose at once and climbing upwards struck the cart road leading to Colin's. Occasionally he turned round to survey the valley. But in this he no longer deceived himself, and when he saw what gleamed more brightly than a cigarette-tip coming down the steep road from the hotel, he paused. The Colonel smoked nothing but cigars.

He went on at once. Here was an instance for the need of enforcing a taboo. Otherwise how easy to let the mind grow malignant! At sight of the glowing cigar-tip his whole mind had turned over in him and his body had gripped like a fist! In a moment!

Laughable. As if Jean hadn't a perfect right to fulfil her own life in her own way. And in a flash he knew it wasn't that. What got him was the Colonel's power and assurance, the natural way he assumed mastery over what he called ' the natives.' Jean to

98

him was like a dancing girl to a Sultan. There was no moral question at all. To his equals the Colonel was the gentleman, smiling and courteous. He had seen him at it!

Ewan hissed a note or two. Really! As if Jean in any case would allow the Colonel to. . . . It showed the lengths to which brotherly thought could go! If the Colonel attempted anything of the sort, he would simply and sheerly knife him.

A laugh rose within him and humour from it spread on his face. His body, released, became light and began to climb readily. This brought him nearer to Colin's without having to think about where he was going. He rather hung on to his humour as if there were some faintly exciting irony still to be caught and examined. Indeed by the time he approached the byre end of the house, the Colonel was little more than a detached speculation, which one grew amused at, vaguely.

For at last there was no doubting the voice. It was quite real and came out through the byre door and was Mary's. She was milking in the byre and crooning to herself.

When a woman has a golden voice and sings with great art, the song can yet be borne. But when the same woman croons to herself a tune out of the heart of her race, then she is moving forces beyond her art's knowing or caring. Motherhood and child-hood, of the one and the many, with all the passions that have gone to their making, and the memories drawn off. With no more why or wherefore than exist love and life and death.

This fatal note caught Ewan. His heart flushed

within his shivering flesh. Longing uprose and buried its head. Into the night faded desire as it curled within his breast. And then up through this voice of the race came the singer's own voice, in three notes that grew rich, spreading out—and sank.

His whole being sharpened to an edge of violence. His emotion became insupportable.

But the voice held him easily, and already the momentary conscious or subconscious uprising of the singer's feeling had passed into a memory poignant beyond any memory of tragedy. The age-old spell had him; white magic within the dark door. White —like her face, her hands—inside through the dark door in the gloom. . . . His eyes gleamed, his breath became a torment. . . .

The front door of the house opened and Colin, her father, came out, smoking heavily, to take the air. Ewan walked towards him. Colin paused.

' Is it yourself, Ewan ? '

' Yes.'

' God bless me, it's good to see you.' His easy voice thickened with welcome.

' I heard your pipes last night,' Ewan said.

' You did ? '

' Yes.' His secret emotion fell from him and he rose clear. ' That's one thing you'll never know,' he said, smiling, ' what your pipes sound like across a glen.'

' It's maybe as well.'

' Or you might walk off after the sound ? '

' Ay, and catch it and put it in a boxie, like a gramophone.' This was the odd talk that Colin liked, and he blew out the smoke with an amused emphasis.

He was a man of middle size and well knit. In the gloom his hair was quite dark and his sixty years had gathered a certain simplicity that lay coiled and at ease as an adder lies in the sun. His head went up and he looked through the gathering night across the valley to the pale distant hotel lights and the blurred whiteness that was the hotel walls. The whole view quickened a trifle under Ewan's presence.

'Perhaps they'll have gramophones there too, heaven knows,' murmured Ewan.

The talk drifted upon imagining what the glen would be like, should they 'come back.' They decided that only those would come back from the beyond who liked it and then it would be paradise.

The hollow of the glen rose up into the air on dim wings, hovering at the level of their eyes, and ever in the quietness seeming to heel over and fall afar off where the faint sound was of the sea in the rocks.

They were laughing away to themselves when Mary came out of the byre carrying a white pitcher.

'Hallo!' called Ewan.

She returned his greeting, scarcely pausing as she went on into the house with the milk. The air from her passing came in an eddy about him.

By the time they reached the kitchen-living-room, Mary had disappeared through an inner door to back premises.

'Sit down,' said Colin.

When Colin turned round from lighting his pipe at the fire, he saw Ewan putting his tissue-wrapped bottle of whisky on the kitchen dresser and glancing along the wall-shelves for a cork-screw.

'Lord, it's getting rusted!' said Ewan, examining

the steel screw. Then he tore off the capsule and extracted the cork.

' Goodness, boy,' said Colin, ' what have you been up to at all ? '

' Why shouldn't I ? ' replied Ewan. ' It's the wine of the country.'

' Eh! ' said Colin, glimmering. ' But it's dear. It's a ransom. You shouldn't— '

' Ransom is the word,' suggested Ewan.

Colin looked at him.

' Our own drink,' said Ewan, his spirits sparkling as they rose, ' is sold into bondage. Only sometimes the rich are kind, are kind, sometimes the rich are kind. Where are your glasses, man ? '

' Mary! '

' What is it ? ' came Mary's voice.

' It's two tumblers,' replied her father. ' Where are they ? '

' On the dresser there.'

' It's blind we are, Mary! ' called Ewan.

' You'll want water,' came Mary's voice, receding.

' The water's in it,' shouted her father, ' and it's dear water at that. Hold, boy! Hold! '

They toasted each other in their native tongue, and then lit their pipes with paper spills, smacking rapidly in the friendliest way.

The kitchen was bright and cosy. The hunting trophies gleamed high on the papered walls. A stag's royal head was guard over the door to the back premises. An old clock with a figured face swung its deliberate pendulum on the mantelshelf. A huge steel engraving of Landseer stags ; a calendared maiden with rich bosom half hid in flowers ; framed photographs. On the middle of the dresser a mass of candytuft billowed out of an ancient soup tureen.

Colin's clearing of his throat when the spirit had passed was pleasanter than a joke. And then the turn of his head, the friendliness:

' You were surely in luck's way.'

' I was.' Ewan was in excellent form. ' She was English.'

' They have the money, the English.'

' I don't know that she has very much money; only the joke was she didn't know what to give me.'

' She would be frightened to offer you a small tip! '

' Yes. They all know we expect a good one. She gave me a pound.'

' Did she though ? '

' She did.'

' She wouldn't know about the fishing.'

' Not a thing.'

' Is she an old one ? '

' Not so old as I am myself.'

' You're telling me that ? Did she do anything at the fishing ? It was a good day for it. Where were you ? '

' Up at Lochdhu. The day was all right and they were on the take. She got a few.'

' She would be pleased at that.'

' I think she was.'

' She'll be the sort that doesn't show ? '

' In a way—yes. It was amusing when she got into the first one.'

' I'm sure.'

' I could see that she went to the fishing without really thinking that she might catch fish. A sort of outing—the thing to do. But when she saw the trout lying dead there in the boat—you know the fine red spots they have on Lochdhu—she didn't know whether she liked fishing or not.'

' She's like that, is she ? '

' Well, no—not exactly. She'll go on fishing.'

' I see.'

Ewan stretched himself in a restless leisure.

' It's after London. She's healthy but run down. And all this place is strange to her.'

' Yes,' nodded Colin. The whisky and the companionship were warming him, and the day's light gossip was interesting and full of delightful ease. ' Who is she ? '

' I believe she came up alone.'

Colin lifted an enquiring look, almost as if it were part of the game.

And Ewan took a slow pull at his glass. ' She has an uncle here—Colonel Hicks,' and he set his glass carefully on the floor beside him. Then he raised a half-smiling counter.

Colin's look hardened. ' I didn't think he had a living soul belonging him,' he said quietly.

Ewan threw a searching glimmer across Colin's eyes.

Time hung a moment.

' Is she—what is she like ? '

' No, she's not like the Colonel.'

' He's a queer man yon,' reflected Colin judicially.

Ewan was interested in Colin's judicial tone. It was such a delicate withdrawal! He waited.

' Tell me this,' said Colin. ' What keeps him staying up here nearly the whole year round ? '

104

'How should I know?' smiled Ewan. 'Only there is this about it. He has here what he was no doubt used to out East: he has command over folk. He can drink and do what he likes and always come out on top. It's a nice position to be in.'

'I see,' nodded Colin. 'But couldn't he have that amongst his own people?'

'He might—if he had the money. But even then he wouldn't have the same freedom to let himself go. He might lose caste there. But not here. He's not merely good enough for us: he's too good.'

'I suppose that's it,' nodded Colin.

Ewan waited, poised.

'And not having the money he couldn't keep up the style down south. Quite so.' Colin was thoughtful.

Ewan had to repress his chuckle.

'But what, I wonder, brought him here?' enquired Colin.

'Probably because half of him is Scotch—and it's difficult to keep the disreputable part hidden. That's why he knows us so well.'

'I have heard something like that,' replied Colin, 'but I thought it was a joke meaning that the half that was Scotch was only Scotch whisky.'

Ewan laughed outright. 'It's both. A double Scotch, in fact.'

'So it's true then, that his mother was Scotch?'

'She was, I believe, what is called an Anglo-Scot,' and he stole a look at Colin.

'I see,' said Colin agreeably.

'I have even heard,' remarked Ewan, 'that she was one of those who have love put on them by the Highlands.'

'Quite so,' nodded Colin. 'That's very interesting.'

'Isn't it?'

'And what part of the Highlands did she come from, did you say?'

'London.'

'I see,' said Colin. 'So that's the connection. I often wondered where it came in. So her son has come to finish his days amongst us.'

'He has. Yes. He has returned to his natives once more. Donald fairly caught it to-day.'

'Did he?'

Ewan related the incident of the two pound trout and the rod chucked in Donald's face. 'I saw a small fleck of blood on his chin.'

Through his pipe-smoke, Colin's eyeballs glistened in their amusement.

'He's the lad, Donald,' he mused.

Ewan watched him. Colin moved restlessly.

'What about a tune on the pipes?' suggested Ewan.

'What do you say yourself? Only the bag is a bit hard.'

'Then we have the very stuff for her,' and Ewan caught the whisky bottle.

Colin got to his feet. As he brought the pipes from the parlour, Mary came in.

Perhaps it was shyness that gave her fresh, dark beauty an air of pride. Not so much pride as wilfulness, a country wilfulness not quite sure of itself. A flash of the wild swept by dark wings. And in the wild, black berries. Ewan caught the light from her glancing eyes.

106

'Here we're at it!' he said.

'Oh, that!' Her smile coloured and her teeth gleamed a moment.

Her father looked up.

'We're giving the old bag a dram.' He was full of sly humour. She turned up the wick of the lamp a bit higher. As her face came near the lamp globe, the flush seemed to glow inwardly, her eyes to radiate light self-consciously, stormily. Almost wet the lashes looked, one or two of the hairs seeming to stick together.

'After the whisky,' said Ewan, 'the bag gives the chanter the smell of its breath and drives it clean mad.'

'Will the smell start with the bag?' she wondered.

Colin looked up from his task.

'It's never where it starts, lassie—but how it ends. You remember that.'

'We'll see how it ends,' covered Ewan, 'in a minute.'

And in a little while Colin blew through the naked reeds. 'They'll do,' he said, getting to his feet.

But on the flat knoll outside the piping was of little account. Colin excused himself by saying that he could never play well after a glass of whisky. And when they sat by the well, Ewan started talking in a merry, reckless way, almost as if he were anxious to run ahead of himself or of some dark thing inside him. To Colin's 'What's great pipe music, then?' he delivered something in the nature of an oration, finishing up, 'Laments and warlike strains and that sort of tribal stuff—we're away back in the delightful tribal stage. We have never evolved beyond that. We're living on a dead past like ravens on a dead sheep. When the sheep is completely rotten we too shall pass. Did you never get the smell, Colin, on the hill wind ? '

' What smell is that ? '

Ewan laughed. ' This reminds me of that appeal in the paper the other day.'

' What appeal was that ? ' asked Colin.

' By these ardent fellows who want to put up a tablet.'

' I didn't notice. Where ? '

' In the Isle of Mist—to commemorate the most famous of all the piping colleges! ' Ewan swayed once more. ' Our great and glorious " Cause " in a nutshell: PUT UP A TABLET.'

' What's wrong with that ? ' asked Colin.

' Oh, there's nothing wrong with that, not a damn thing! That's the joke.' Laughter is invigorating. ' Come on, Colin: *The Lost Glen*.'

' No, then,' said Colin; ' not to-night.'

' What's wrong with to-night ? '

' It's a fine night,' said Colin, easing his collar band, ' and a cool air.'

Ewan laughed once more.

When they returned to the house, Mary glanced at his face. He would not sit down. When she turned away, he shot a look at her back. ' Good night! ' he called gaily. Colin accompanied him to the door.

5

On the way home, Ewan was in excellent humour. ' Well oiled! ' he murmured. His feet landed on the rough surface without jarring impact, their abandon airy and adept. He hadn't felt so enlivened for long enough. ' It's a fine night—and a cool air! ' Hang it, it would make an ass laugh the way Colin got like that, quiet and casual, when touched! ' Fine night! ' What did Lothian say the O.T.C. sang at camp? ' My name is Sammy Hall, damn your eyes. I've only got one— ' Oh curse the loose stones that rolled away from airy fairy feet. There the hotel lights. The Highland ship of state, Colonel Hicks in command. The white blaze of his portholes. He anyhow hadn't got Sammy Hall's trouble! What did that decent old Edinburgh W.S. suffer from when he was run in for his interest in young girls?— enlarged what's-its-name. Oh, laughable.

But out of Ewan's underthought the Colonel was swelling to a gargantuan figure that soon menaced the glen like a storm-cloud, the brows steep, the face implacable, the mouth closed by jaws that held. The body, buttoned tight, curved to a black cylinder of thunder. This figure reached over Ewan and shut out the skies, so that he was under its shadow, as was the earth about him, and the glen, and the water hushed and running in the hollows. Ewan's eyelids flicked and the Colonel stood back into himself, his tubby body holding all the menace of that inflated vision, the face unyielding in which superiority sat so strongly entrenched that even in its menace there was contempt. It was the face a man must smash—or crawl before. And Ewan felt his world crawl before it, the very earth and boulders lying down, the water forever slipping away.

Ewan was drunk enough to believe that there was a profound reality in this antithesis, that the Colonel

109

and himself were chance figures in a drama that affected the very earth under his feet. Being chance figures, they did not matter; were indeed figures of melodrama. But none the less did the earth await the outcome of their secret strife, as if they stood for an ultimate conquest or defeat.

Yet to suggest to the Colonel that there was such *strife!* O lord, how amusing! No wonder that the earth grew sleek!

Ewan stepped on its hide with extra abandon, stumbled, caught himself up and swore with a bitter intensity.

In a moment, from being exhilarated, his mind grew dark and unpleasant. The exhilaration had been artificial. He had been blowing it up. He could not get used to swearing or to coarse raking thoughts. That was the truth. They left a dark taste of despair. They meant nothing. They were futile and blotted out his mind. Yet one needed them, needed their 'escape.' From what? . . .

Ewan stared at the thought—past it into himself— and saw a being that would quietly and efficiently murder. He felt this being—sensitive and dark and proud—and ruthless. To destroy with the hands and then wipe them—as the swordsman wiped his blade—with fastidious indifference.

At the image he smiled, growing weary. The burn ran on his right. Hang it, he was played out. Whisky on an empty stomach—and now the effects fading.

As he crossed the two-plank bridge, he looked over a shoulder towards the sea. He heard it but could not see it. It was dark down in the hollow. And the sound of the sea seemed remote and passing outward.

As he came on the rock, he saw his house against the sky. There was a light in the kitchen window. He had never come home yet and found the light not there.

The house and his mother and Annabel. Keeping them he could keep no other. And would keep no other. Melodrama had it in the end! Always.

CHAPTER TWO

I

W<small>HEN</small> Colonel Hicks left Jean to her brother in the out-kitchen, he went to the sideboard in the dining-room and brought out his own whisky bottle with its beribboned clinking monogram. Having poured himself a stiff one, he raised his head and caught his face in the mirror. He looked at it a moment with attention, at the severity gloomed with annoyance. The skin was tanned, with a faint wash of purple just beginning to show through a fullness here and there. This fullness that might some day run to pouches now held the features to a steady strength. In this face the eyes were small but blue-green, clear, and alive, and at the moment shone intolerantly. The hair was grey with no least suggestion of baldness. It was combed neatly back in a way that left the upper part of the brow smooth and intelligent like an impress from far public-school days. The Colonel was sixty-four.

He withdrew his eyes without any alteration in their expression and stooping again lifted out his own soda-syphon. He swallowed his drink without taking the glass from his lips, then returning bottle and syphon to their own compartment, left the dining-room and went upstairs to dress.

On his chair he sat a moment thoughtful and motionless, before beginning to take off boots and stockings.

Each foot fell with a thud, four toes stuck together and white, the big toe reddish-purple and apart. He waggled all his toes, then lifted his eyes from them and, again motionless, decided that that fellow Ewan was damned insolent. Like a dark flush Ewan's past swept his mind. He had never been able to stomach him. Behind his quietness he was so pretentious and cunning. His face at the door had been so—so—hm! The Colonel did not even think of Jean.

When he got to the bathroom he found it locked. He shook the knob firmly and as he retired decided that the splashings were made by lawyer Stansfield. The fellow shaved there, if he wasn't mistaken. He must say something to McAlpine about this. It was happening too often. As if he weren't late enough at least to find the bathroom disengaged!

His bare legs stumped the room, the toilet ware on the wash-stand and the door of the wardrobe clicking and creaking as he crossed certain spots on the floor. A current of air fanned his legs coldly. He listened at the door, his brows gathering, then turned into the room and started walking up and down again. His restraint began to lag behind his anger. The aimless walking maddened him. An oath came explosively. The bathroom door clicked, and as he got into the corridor he saw the retreating jazz dressing wrap of one of the Miss Sandersons, her reddish ankles twinkling beneath. She threw a swift look back as she vanished into her bedroom.

Presently through the hiss of the bath-taps Colonel Hicks heard approaching the unmistakable footsteps of Mr. Stansfield. The knob rattled firmly; the footsteps retreated. Very leisurely, with luxury of puffings and gruntings, the Colonel proceeded to the not unpleasant task of washing away the day's stains.

He met Mr. Stansfield as he came out.

' Hullo, Stansfield—not dressed yet ? '

' No,' said Stansfield tonelessly.

The Colonel entered his room and began to dress with some satisfaction and, remembering the occasion, not a little care.

The occasion was the company of his niece, Clare Marlowe, who was awaiting him in the lounge, which was half glass-porch and half entrance-hall.

He greeted her charmingly, his body neatly braced in its dark jacket. Had she had a good day ? Yes, she had had a splendid day. Her eyes were full of light:

' Did you see the trout I caught ? '

' I did. I asked specially when I came in—and went through and had a look at them. Not at all bad—for a beginner ! '

' Oh, you needn't mock me. I shall surprise you yet.'

' I don't doubt it. Not for a moment.'

' And if you'd seen the one I lost ! '

' Ah ! ' said the Colonel, and chuckled richly. ' There is certainly hope for you now ! '

' No, but it's true, really. You ask Ewan. And see how quickly I'm developing the fisherman's selfishness ! Tell me, had you a good day ? '

' No,' said the Colonel, as they found chairs. ' As

114

a matter of fact I had a very bad day. However . . .'
His lips pursed and he gave a dismissive shrug.

His voice, at its usual pitch, penetrated the small
lounge. The three Glasgow Sanderson ladies were
inclined to speak in undertones, and the newly-
married young couple, birds of passage, in the far
angle of the glass porch, had their faces to the hills.

The Colonel was hardly even disturbed by the
day's misadventures. After his long residence in the
North, he found again in his niece the lost virtues of
quality and breeding. In the presence of her quiet,
distinguished air and voice, the others were common,
the Sanderson women being beneath consideration.
The Colonel warmed to his niece. His neatly
brushed hair left his courteous forehead more intelligent than ever. He was proud of this glimmering
young woman, not only for her own sake but for his.
She made it so clear where he belonged. And now
she wanted to know how he had had such a bad day.

He would rather have avoided the subject, yet
there was in it too a certain attraction, for he had a
singular knowledge of his surroundings and their
people. 'You don't know Donald, my gillie,' he said.

'Didn't I see him this morning?'

'Yes. I said you don't know him.'

'Oh.' She smiled too. 'What did he do?'

'You mean what didn't he do? As it so happened
I was particularly anxious to land a trout I hooked,
a big fellow about three pounds. Nothing half so
big ever been seen before on Lochanathar. Well, he
missed him.'

'How do you mean?'

'Missed him with the net. Scooped up—like

that—missed the trout, fouled the cast, and— ' The Colonel snapped imaginary gut.

' What hard luck! But surely a gillie should know how to net a trout ? '

' Quite,' said the Colonel with an enigmatic air.

Clare was trying to penetrate this, when Alfred Stansfield, a man of forty-five to fifty, entered uprightly, his *Times* under his arm. His greying hair was neatly brushed over his ears, his face weathered and firm, his body tall and with an unhurried confident movement. He acknowledged Clare to whom he had previously been introduced, and took a chair by the glass front for the light.

' What luck, Stansfield ? ' asked the Colonel.

' Pretty fair, thanks.' He lowered the paper to his knees. ' I hope you had a good opening day, Miss Marlowe ? '

' Splendid, thanks. I enjoyed it immensely.' She half turned. ' And caught some trout.'

' Good. Macleod knows about fishing.'

It took a moment to fix Macleod to Ewan.

' Ah—yes. And Mr. McAlpine says I may have Lochdhu to-morrow.' She paused. ' That is, if I'm not— '

' No,' smiled Stansfield, and his eyes found a merry gleam. ' I don't think anyone will grudge you Lochdhu.'

' How ? Is it . . . ? '

' It's all right really,' he said plainly; ' quite a lot of trout in it, but for some reason they rarely run to any weight.'

' Oh, and I have just been telling how I lost a monster! '

' Ah, bad luck! '

Just as the Colonel was about to speak the dinner bell went.

The Colonel and his niece had their small table by the double window. Stansfield sat alone well back in the room and against a wall where he was not disturbed. He rarely spoke unless directly addressed. The three Sandersons had their corner—a white-haired, pleasant-faced, elderly lady, a thin, raffish woman about forty, fair and full of merriment and a Kelvinside-English accent (a source of considerable amusement to the Colonel), and an anaemic-looking girl emerging from her teens, with a languid manner, a short red tartan kilt, and a pale eye which fell away slowly from a man's face (the combination of hill and sea air, together with the bracing austerity of the heights, was supposed to be doing her good). Six persons sat at a corner table; a young widow (to whom the Colonel had for a time been gallant) in the party of a well-conditioned man and his wife with their son who wore public-school colours, and the young married couple who had arrived in a two-seater. At another table an artist and his wife were discussing the fishing with two jolly young men with whom they played bridge at night and who owned a sports two-seater which they tortured into all sorts of hill-climbing feats (they had penetrated to the shores of Lochdhu by an obliterated cart track). A final table was occupied by three quiet-mannered sportsmen, whose talk showed an intimate knowledge of most Scots fishing hotels; they were about to move on after a three-weeks' trial of Ardnacloich.

Of all this company, Colonel Hicks and Stansfield

117

were the only old-timers. Stansfield was a London solicitor, and though his month was as fixed as the summer sun, and more dependable in its habits, it was at the best but an isolated event compared with the Colonel's now almost continuous residence. It was the Colonel who had had the big, old, solid dining-room table displaced by the small private tables, with the commanding position of the window as his headquarters.

To this table he now gravely ushered Clare.

Presently a half-bottle of wine was brought. Having read the label, she looked across at her uncle. She had arrived in time for dinner last night, and had happened to mention claret. McAlpine reported he had run out of it. The Colonel said to Clare that he had probably never had it. She had laughed.

' But how kind of you! ' she now exclaimed.

' It's a pleasure.'

It was. It was an excellent pleasure. ' You'll forgive me if I stick to my own. It's the only thing one can be quite sure of here.'

Clare glanced with interest at the silver monogram. She enjoyed her meal, talking quietly and appreciatively. Already there were sluggish stirrings of a new vitality.

The Colonel finally raised his eyebrows. Coffee in the lounge ?

' Yes,' she assented readily, and, preceding her uncle, felt that they would not be disturbed.

' This is delightful,' she sighed, as she let her head fall back and her hands droop over the chair-arms.

The Colonel had a pleasant weakness for young

women. Life at that moment grew rich for him. No, she would not smoke.

'Quite right, my dear.' He thought of the pale Sandersonian affair in the red kilt. 'This smoking amongst certain women—just getting a bit too much.' He lit a black juicy cheroot and as he stretched back, the wickerwork fondly protested. 'So you enjoyed your day?' He crossed his legs.

'I did—immensely—more than I can say.' She spoke with an earnestness that trailed off into a lingering smile. 'I still see that loch; and the wind—it's all about my body. I feel drowsed.'

'You'll sleep to-night.'

'I know I shall. And I haven't been sleeping too well.'

'No. But we'll buck you up here. That's what you've come for. We mayn't have much—'

'Ah, but you have. Indeed I wonder if you haven't everything.'

The Colonel smiled in a certain way. Here he was on his own ground; had indeed such special knowledge that he could afford to be tolerant. 'You don't know very much about it, I'm afraid, but a month of it should do you no harm.'

'I'm sure it won't,' she said lightly. 'And I'll tell them when I go back that they need not waste any pity on you.'

Her innocent words might have been a whip severing gaiety from silence. The Colonel slowly drew himself back from contemplation of the silence, the better to let his voice come round and penetrating, 'Oh, they *pity* me, do they?'

119

' No,' said Clare, with innocence so casual that it was superb. Her eyes appeared to glimmer in a far reminiscence. But the Colonel was not deceived. He had a genius for the dark laceration.

' I didn't know they exactly *pitied* me,' he said. ' I may have had my own ideas as to what they thought. But it never struck me that they—ah—*pitied* me.' It was the sort of joke that one could enjoy. He even withdrew his cigar to have a good look at it.

Clare's eyes moved in her head until the Colonel was secretly focussed, then moved away.

' I didn't mean anything like that at all, of course,' she said, with the lazy smile that implied her uncle was having a game. ' Although, as you know, they think that everyone who isn't doing what they're doing is to be pitied! '

' I know.' The Colonel nodded. ' I am aware exactly of what they think. Exactly. Quite.' The humour in his tone was like a creeping wind.

Clare lifted her wrap about her shoulders. ' I'm sure what they think doesn't matter,' she said in good-humoured dismissal. ' Indeed,' she added, ' you would be surprised to know what they think about me! '

' At least it's nice,' responded the Colonel, ' to be a sinner in such company.'

Clare's smile lit up. ' At least that's clever of you.'

His chair creaked. He blew smoke. Clare saw that the subject, which she had so unfortunately raised, fascinated him. His chance stroke of wit, too, excited him. But his normal methods of approach were forthright, and now his lips pressed together as if they could no longer find anything to say that would not be too much. Altogether it was an uncomfortable moment. A certain sympathy towards letting him unburden himself moved generously in Clare. There always had been in him something quick-tempered, tormented; in a sense, jealous. But this was hardly the place or the time. Besides, he was really going too far. As he perfectly well knew, many retired men like himself, with no more money, contrived to live down south. She summoned the slow magnanimous smile that comes out of a woman's wisdom.

'And, in any case, you aren't quite fair to them, poor people!'

'Amn't I?'

Clare, smiling still, leaned back, and, turning her head, looked out through the glass upon the hillside of crofts across the valley, her eyes lingering on the view and showing no slightest sign of personal stress.

'Anyhow, they don't matter,' he said suddenly.

'No,' she murmured almost gravely, and turning from her contemplation of the view, finished her coffee. 'That was quite nice,' she said, lifting a bright face. 'They do you rather well here, don't they?'

'Might be worse, I suppose.' The Colonel gulped the last of his coffee. It was easy, he supposed internally, to dismiss the subject.

'But I think they do do you well,' she insisted, bent on reviving the pleasant note.

But he could at least counter this. 'I'm afraid what they do do, they've been driven to.'

'Surely not as bad as that?'

'You think not?' He almost smiled. 'They have about as much initiative as—as a mule.' That it wasn't quite the perfect comparison brought a gleam to his eyes. He went on, 'When I came here first there were little more than four walls and four bedrooms. And there would never have been more if McAlpine had been left to it. The wing with our bathroom, the old rackety Ford, a number of the fishing lochs—I had to drive him to get 'em. And now he has to come trooping in to get my advice on any da— on—everything.'

'Really. I had no idea you had made the place.'

He dismissed the remark. 'It was their laziness got me. Wanted to lounge about in their poverty.' His tone was curiously concentrated.

'They don't look like that, do they?'

'Take it from me—you'll never know what they look like.'

His tone compelled her glance. In the gleam in his eyes she caught something not so much sarcastic as malign. It affected her like a shocking and intimate revelation. She lowered her head. The enchanted world she had moved in all day slid away from her and left her silent.

The Colonel had more to say. 'Behind their laziness, they're cunning. There's something in them that's crooked. But that's only the beginning of it.' Clearly the depth of his knowledge was beyond sounding. There had come, too, into his voice with these words an abrupt, husky note of conspiracy. Clare felt drawn by it, attracted despite herself. It was all a horrible exaggeration, of course, brought

about by her unfortunate reference to those who
' pitied ' him, so that he was merely finding here an
outlet for his private humour. Or was it she herself
who was over-responsive, because of her day's exquisite impressions, impressions like secret flowers
that would shiver when any sort of serpent slid
through ?

' But take the gillie I had to-day. Ewan—Ewan
Macleod, is it ? ' she asked impersonally.

' Yes. I know him too.' The Colonel remembered the insolent look in the kitchen.

Clare waited, her eyes on the croft houses, lying
still in the first smother of dusk.

' What about him ? ' she had to ask.

' Oh, nothing much. Only that in addition he's
a bit of a rotter.'

Clare's face turned slowly with wide-open eyes.

' Really ? '

' Yes.' The Colonel's humour drew taut. ' All
right as a gillie. Supposed to be pretty good at
teaching a woman to throw a line.'

' Yes, I can say he's good at that! '

' But otherwise,' and the Colonel's teeth fixed in
the cigar and the lips curled away. Then he removed
the cigar and looked at it. He said suddenly: ' He
thinks such a damned lot of himself. If I were a
fellow like that I'd have cleared out and hidden
myself for good.'

' Oh,' murmured Clare.

' His father—a fisherman-crofter down there. His
mother—sort of thing you sometimes find here—
aspiring to get a son through the university. University career, y'know.' The humour of it was

123

worth restraint. ' He gave them a university career all right! '

The far evening quiet touched Clare's spirit to a suspense of listening. The evening listened. The wind had completely fallen. The deepening dusk was like shadow from the slow meeting of wings of silence, imponderable, above their world, folding. The Colonel chewed his cigar. The juice ran about his gums with tonic astringency.

' So he didn't make good at the university ? ' came Clare's detached voice.

' No, he didn't! ' The Colonel's short laugh was oiled with the cigar juice. ' His mother has a brother who runs a pub in some slum in Edinburgh. A very religious man. He said he would put Ewan through the university if he would go in for the Church. They are much given to the Church here,' remarked the Colonel.

' He didn't graduate ? '

' One night this religious publican cut off supplies, after your gillie had used them for about two years.'

' Why ? '

' He discovered how the young man lived. It was not according to the teaching of the holy Scotch Church.'

' In what way ? '

The Colonel hesitated.

' You mean he was loose—drink an' that ? ' suggested Clare.

The Colonel met her look.

' I suppose others have gone that way. But did you ever know of anyone who, after being kicked out like that, bringing disgrace on his parents—after all that—came back home. To a small poverty-hole like this. What ? They say his mother has never gone over her doorstep since.'

Clare's face came curiously alive.

' Really ? ' she said, watching the Colonel.

' And that's not all.' As he nodded, the Colonel's neck thickened. Then he crushed his cigar-stub in the ash-tray and took another from his case. Clare saw his sucking mouth in the match spurts. The cigar glowing, his eyebrows lifted again, disclosing the eyes and leaving the upright furrows above the nose with their suggestion of imperious temper. ' No,' puffed the Colonel, ' that's not all.'

Clare waited. The Colonel took a careless look around the empty lounge.

' We don't say anything about this. Only—it was odd, to say the least. When he came back from the university he went to sea with his father. One night in a storm his mother found him naked on the beach, but of his father and the boat—no sign—gone.'

' But— ' stammered Clare, fascinated.

' Anyway, he managed to save himself,' and the Colonel's expression closed.

2

The following morning Donald MacCrimmon came on Jean in the back premises.

' Is he not up yet ? ' he asked.

' I think he's up,' answered Jean, ' but he hasn't come down for breakfast.'

Donald stood in the doorway looking at her, his face alive with a half-humorous, half-irritable expression.

' He's the damnedest one,' he said.

' Now Donald! ' She smiled faintly but without looking at him.

He was never quite sure of her. There was a secret life behind her eyes that teased him, and about her clothes, her hair, a suggestion of untidiness that attracted like a warm overspilling of life; a suppressed life—that usually gave the skin an odd glow, a gipsy moodiness. This morning, however, Donald noted a faint discoloration of the skin here and there, and the inner glow seemed dead. He thought in his own mind that she was unwell, yet there was a haggard something more in it than that, as if she had stared long at a point fixed and dreadful and had forgotten how to sleep.

A certain movement of her head made him aware of his silence.

' Here's the best part of the morning gone. What's the good of going out now ? ' he declared.

' Did he say he was going ? '

' I wouldn't mind if he had only said it.'

She half smiled again.

' Was he late going to bed ? ' he asked, after a moment.

' How could I know ? '

' If you didn't know you might have heard him,' he suggested. ' It wouldn't be that difficult to hear him sometimes.'

She lifted her head as though she had caught a step approaching from within, then went on with her potato-peeling.

' I doubt if there's to be any fishing for you to-day.'

126

'That's fine,' returned Donald, blustering comic-
ally. 'I'll be having a holiday to myself. It's the
grand weather for it.' He withdrew his eyes from
her.

She gazed at him.

'I could do with a holiday,' he rushed on. 'I
could do with a good long one.'

'What would you do with it?'

'If I had the power to do what I liked with it,' he
answered, assuming his precise 'English' tone, 'I
would make the Colonel my gillie.'

The potato slipped out of her hand.

'I would say to him,' proceeded Donald, 'when
he didn't net a trout, I would say, what the— '

'Go on!' said the Colonel from the doorway
behind.

'Beg pardon, sir,' muttered Donald, blood darkening his face.

'Let us hear exactly how you would put it,' the
Colonel encouraged him.

'I couldn't put it—before ladies,' blustered Donald, affecting a half-laugh.

After an astonished moment, the Colonel's throat
gave way.

'What's that?'

'Just a joke, sir.' And Donald slid out through
the door and backed away a yard or two, with the
least possible appearance of either backing or sliding.
The Colonel followed him.

'A joke, eh?'

'Yes, sir.'

The Colonel laughed. 'You're an absolute jack-
ass!'

' I may be all that,' Donald replied. ' Everyone is entitled to his opinion. You can— '

' Will you shut up ? '

' There's no law to make a man shut up,' Donald declared. ' A man may be poor but he can open his mouth. Besides that, I have been waiting for you all the morning.' In spite of his words, his tone contrived to be propitiating.

They had both paused.

' So you thought, after the exhibition you gave yesterday, that I would trust you with a net again.'

' Well, you said— '

But the Colonel's look stopped him. Then the Colonel exploded him with a word and turned away.

Donald drew himself up.

' You can go to hell with you,' he muttered harshly —in Gaelic. The Colonel looked back at him; but Donald, head up, was marching into the garage.

There was no one in the outkitchen as the Colonel passed the open door. He continued round the hotel and entered at the front door, fully awake and ready for his breakfast. Several times he chuckled as he chewed the succulent bacon. *' Before ladies!'* It was rich!

Donald, his clown and jester, could be relied upon. The thought amused the Colonel at odd moments. Without him, life would be stale. He pottered about in pleasant and aimless fashion, yet was never at his ease for long because of something ever ready to prick him. An interview with McAlpine was a cheerful break. He informed McAlpine, apropos of his lack of claret, that his cellar was a disgrace. All sorts of wines would have to be laid down, not in a miserly one or two but in dozens.

' Yes,' said McAlpine.

The Colonel regarded his meek expression and knew that the yes meant that he wouldn't think about it just yet. The soft, flabby face so like a woman's, the drooping moustache, the mild manner—how clearly they could be read!

The Colonel had an excellent ten minutes, finishing up, ' Yes, I know, it's *your* money,' then withdrew his penetrating look and turned round and left him.

Except for the Sandersons, he was alone for lunch. To a ' Good-day ' from the oldest, he bowed, courtly and cold.

Thereafter his restlessness set him off on a walk. His humour kept pricking him on. It had even interfered with his sleep in the first part of the night. The truth was, he realised, that Clare's advent had upset him, had jogged him out of his groove. It brought back *them* too vividly. They pitied him now. A good joke that!

There were times in bed when the maddening joke had created fantasies of revenge. In the close night he had sweated, turning futilely. Already he was out of touch, out of class. By her reticence, by her consideration for him, in a thousand trivial ways, she had made him feel his ostracism, without her being in the least aware of it, without his being aware of any definite attitude or act himself. It was well into the morning before he had fallen asleep, and when the knock came to his door he dismissed it with a spent anger.

Now as he went down the road to the stone bridge he felt fresher, but the aftermath of the night was behind his thought and found outlet in his attitude to the life about him.

The Colonel reckoned he knew that life. His position gave him a peculiar insight. Donald he could see through to his last shift. The evasiveness that tried to have a proud front, the speech that went on and on blowing him up, his whole air of being independent, of being a gentleman even though he was a gillie, of being important, the effort at manners positively—' before ladies! ' . . .

Colonel Hicks got the satisfaction that comes from all penetration. Seeing what he believed so many of them pretended to be and how their position thwarted that pretension appealed to him particularly, gave him a perverted pleasure. He searched for it, and no shift of hotelkeeper or gillie or crofter but could be read by him. When he met a man who accepted his position humbly, he secretly despised him. He wanted the ' gentleman,' the fiery or evasive humours that could be pierced or cowed.

This baiting was the only game of intelligence left to the Colonel, and out of it he often extracted much mirth. Sometimes, too, it sharpened his wits to a demoniac degree, and in a following moment his pleasure would receive its rich overflow in an imperious gesture or, even better, in physical violence. A royal clean sweep!

Much of which was no doubt understandable enough, if not indeed inevitable, once it was recognised that the Colonel was a voluntary outcast from his own class through his own particular brand of independence. All the evasions that moved his 'natives' were already by a profound intuition in himself. In them, he was, as it were, continually coming up against himself. The game (this thing in life that touched him most jealously, at times to the quick) was ever ready to his hand. No wonder he was almost morbidly critical of them, as though out of his tormented superiority he must forever laugh at them and bear them a grudge.

Yet the pleasure was as real as his flesh, for his position allowed him to indulge even the weaknesses of his humours royally. This life had its peculiar parallel to the past army life. And if it ever came to the point that he had to lead men, he knew that he would elect to lead these, and with a ferocious humour curse and dragoon them to victory. As though their hidden twists had twisted into his blood.

His blood—probably his Scotch blood! At least, thank God, he could honestly despise that. But certainly it was a thought that his insight might be a result not of an overdose of intelligence but of a Scotch ancestry!

But everything was humour to the Colonel in a certain mood. It had been sticky in bed and now it was stuffy. Because it wasn't yet raining! What a blasted apology for a climate! He wiped his forehead and turned round. At a slant below him in the glen he saw old Angie Sutherland, bent double with rheumatics, move across a green strip of pasture leading an old reluctant cow. Distance and the slope made the figures look curiously toylike, diminutive. The Colonel knew old Angie, and now regarded this thrilling spectacle of the old man and his cow with attention. The toy figures looked isolated and as if moved by fate. Philosophy moved the Colonel. What in the name of heaven, he marvelled, did they live for ? Of what use were they ? Not even able to support themselves! The old man would talk like a prophet—in Gaelic. ' *Och, och, la preea !* ' muttered the Colonel. ' *Hey flooch !* '

A spot of rain pricked his hot forehead. He hadn't taken his coat. Colin McKinnon's cottage was up the corrie there in front of him. He knew Colin and that pretty wench of his. The way she came on the village platform—countrified, but quality. The Colonel was always brightened by a good-looking young woman.

He started on again. Quite large drops of rain spattered his forehead. Curious hanging weather. Clouds heavy, motionless, blotting out the hill-tops. All at once it was raining. The Colonel quickened his pace. By the time he reached Colin's door he felt quite wet. He knocked, and opening the door came face to face with Colin, who smiled hospitably.

' Is it you, Colonel ? '

' Dashed wet! ' replied Colonel Hicks affably.

' Yes indeed, it's a heavy shower. Please to come in out of it—this way.'

He led the Colonel into the parlour, and the first thing that greeted them there was Ewan Macleod's unfinished bottle of whisky in solitary prominence on the round mahogany table. The Colonel eyed it jocularly, ' Ho! ho! ' The last part of his walk had quickened heart and breath, and his mouth was blown dry. As he moistened his mouth it clacked. Colin hardly appeared to hesitate.

132

' You would like a refreshment, Colonel ? '

' Why, I should, Colin, thanks.'

' I'll just get a glass for you.   You'll excuse me.'

As he entered the kitchen, Mary gave her father a quick look.

' Where's a glass ? ' he asked quietly.

' There—on the dresser.   You'll want some fresh water ? '

' It would be as well.'

When Mary returned with the jug of water, she found her father standing thoughtfully with the tumbler in his hand.

' That's it,' he said, laying hold of the jug.

She did not look at him.   He hesitated a moment, lifting his thoughtful face to the window through which his eyes travelled to a great distance.   Then he turned, saying ' That's fine,' and went through to the parlour.   Mary remained very still, her bright eyes to the window, listening acutely, lips apart.

' Thanks, Colin.   Good health! '

' Good health, Colonel! '

' Ah-h—that's better.   Didn't want to get wet. Not as young as I was! '

' No.'

' Do you think it's going to be much ? '

' I don't think it's going to be more than a shower.'

' Oh, well, in that case—if you don't mind— '

' It's a pleasure, Colonel.'

' Hm.   Feel dampish, though.   What about that kitchen fire of yours ? '

' Surely.   If you don't mind . . . '

Mary blew through the back door. The Colonel looked about him as he entered the kitchen; walked up to the hearth and stood with his back to it.

'This is better; what!' He straddled his legs and shook the ample folds of his grey-check plus-fours, then wriggled his shoulders and blew a breath, 'Pf-f-f!'

Colin stood by the dresser.

'Won't you sit down?' requested the Colonel. 'Don't mind me.'

'Ho, it's all right,' said Colin pleasantly. 'There's plenty of time for sitting.'

The Colonel regarded Colin with reflective humour. 'Do sit down!'

'Well,' smiled Colin, 'excuse me,' and he sat down.

The Colonel looked about him.

'Haven't you your daughter with you—what's her name?'

'Mary, is it? Oh yes. She'll be out about somewhere, I'm sure.'

'A good voice. I see she's to be singing at the concert.'

'Yes, so I believe.'

The Colonel shook his legs and turned his front to the fire.

You could take off your jacket and dry it,' suggested Colin.

'Oh—well—what?' The Colonel hesitated, then hunched his shoulders. 'Pf-f-f . . . nothing. Is the shower passing?'

'It's thinning,' said Colin. 'I'll go to the door and see.'

The Colonel looked about the kitchen. Trophies of the chase! The sight of Colin through the window leisurely regarding the heavens was bright as a joke. The way the blessed fellow looked this way and that as though he knew better than a weather-glass! What? As Colin came in the Colonel called to him with excellent good humour:

'Well, is it over?'

'Practically. It's clearing to the west and there will be a fair interval, but there's a lot of rain to come yet.'

'You're a prophet! I had better get going.'

'I'm sure there's no hurry,' said Colin hospitably.

'Well, I *am* in a bit of a hurry.'

'Oh, well . . .'

The Colonel laughed.

'You think no one should be in a hurry?'

Colin smiled before the Colonel's good humour.

'Indeed there are times when everyone must be in a hurry, I suppose.'

'But as seldom as possible, eh?'

'Oh, well . . .' murmured Colin, and remained perfectly still and faintly smiling.

The Colonel eyed him quizzically, then shook his shoulders.

'Pf-f-f, I am damp!' He stamped on the hearth, braced himself, and as he started for the door, said, 'Thanks for your refreshment. I needed it.'

'You're welcome,' replied Colin, and followed directly behind the stumping body, the red thick neck and exposed head before his eyes.

135

As they came out at the front door, Mary emerged from the hen-house on the near side of the byre. The Colonel stopped and called to her.

' Mary, how are you ? '

She had to come up, and her smile flashed from a quickening red, a stormy shyness. She was living flesh; she was a flame; soft flesh and red blood. The Colonel did not care for women much older. His face was welcoming, courteous, the flesh melting graciously . . . only the eyes could not help from staring a little and exposing a thin light.

' Very well, thank you,' Mary acknowledged.

' Been gathering eggs ? '

' One or two.' Her head was up to answer any remark, yet equally ready to retire. Light-coloured stockings, tweed skirt, and knitted jumper showing the swaying curves of a figure a little above middle height. Dusky hair and restless eyes under sweeping lashes. An ebb and flow of colour and light. Alive so disturbingly, against that background of hen-house, byre, and peeping dung-heap. The Colonel knew an internal disturbance. He mentioned the concert, the only thing he could think of. He paid her a compliment with a gallant air. He didn't much care for concerts as a rule, but now— they would have to turn up, eh Colin ? . . . But there was no way of keeping her there indefinitely; in fact, when he had said his few words about the concert he brusquely apostrophised the weather, shrugged, lifted his hat, smiled entrancingly again, and left them.

He was disturbed, quite deliciously, provocatively disturbed, on the way down.

Colin watched him for a little, then went into the kitchen, where Mary was busy banking up the fire with peat. Neither spoke. Colin turned and went into the parlour. Mary heard him pause. He would be staring at the empty glasses. His footsteps crossed the floor. She caught the click of the drone pipes; heard them being laid away again. Colin left the parlour and went out at the front door. Going to the window, Mary saw him drift over towards the byre and disappear from view. Down the glen the body of the Colonel stumped steadily on . . . drew to a halt . . . began flailing something with his walking-stick.

For the Colonel had reached the point where delightful provocation had increased to an uncomfortable warmth. Such sultry weather. There was the background of a hot East. There were memories of colour, of the close smell of human flesh. Not always unpleasant—that smell! He swung his walking stick, he paused, he wiped his forehead. A man was a man out there—harem an' all ! He gripped his stick convulsively. A tall thistle was growing at the roadside. He stopped and with one swipe unthinkingly beheaded it. . . . As his imagination grew active, he slew the thistle, branch by branch, to the ground. A certain spluttering humour came to his face as he went on. Colin's wench kept in front of him. Tugging at a trousers-leg, he eased the grip of his clothing about his body.

And that night the Colonel was in a splendid humour and gallant in a quiet way to Clare. When at last she bade him good-night, he remained in the lounge to finish his cigar, given over to vague but pleasant reflections. A feeling of well-being pervaded him, soothed and comforted his body to a certain reserve. The hotel grouped about him like his castle and in the silence he gazed through the window towards the dim dusk of the distant hillside. For a time there dwelt an odd reflectiveness in his eyes, lit by a glint of challenge. This was his home. There was no power to interdict him here. After all, he had more outlet here than many of those— those who *pitied* him—had on their polite lawns! It was a seductive mood. The sarcasm, faint as an evening haze, touched his mind to reverie, to a scarce discernible smile. He drew closer together; presently pulled his waistcoat down, blew specks off it, and got to his feet.

He seemed reluctant to leave the lounge, even if the dining-room would contain no more than lawyer Stansfield (for from ten p.m. it was tacitly understood to be their private den, a reminder of the old days when it carried the whole honour of ' public rooms '). Lighting a fresh cigar, he gazed for a moment through the smoke at Colin McKinnon's cottage so secretly remote on the edge of its corrie, then with a veiled air turned towards Stansfield's company. Outside his fishing—and his *Times*, yes!—Stansfield had no interests; no general sense of life, of culture. But at least he knew how to behave. Colonel Hicks appreciated the middle-class professional status. It had its limitations. It could never, so to speak, flower. But it was entrenched solidly and looked after the estates where the flowers grew! Naturally there were moments when Stansfield's quiet demeanour and efficiency irritated him. At moments, too, he had surprised a slight gleam of presumption in an attitude of studied indifference; and more than once a silent withdrawal into hostile criticism. All understandable manifestations. Stansfield was basically a decent fellow.

In this magnanimous mood the Colonel opened the door and, entering, was taken aback to find his own chair occupied by a stranger. The man was dressed in a blue lounge suit, had his dusty boots stretched out in front of him, his jacket loosely open disclosing a whole battery of fountain-pen tops and pencil tops in the left upper waistcoat pocket. His rather pale broad face was bent abstractedly on Stansfield who was making up a fishing cast. The face lifted to the Colonel and steadied, until the eyes came alive and the face drooped without any haste. The Colonel continued to regard the full body in the creased blue serge, then went to the sideboard.

That the stranger was neither a fisher nor a commercial traveller was clear from the first glance. Before the Colonel had poured out his drink he decided that this must be the Trade Union fellow come up about the raid in Ardbeg, where a few crofters had banded together and broken up for cultivation land belonging to the sheep-farmer. The sheep-farmer, not disposed to resign any of his rights, had naturally appealed for legal protection. Very naturally, the Colonel thought. Indeed the sheep-farmer's action was understood by all. Yet a certain vague popular sympathy went out to the crofters who complained that they could not get sufficient soil on which to grow what at the best would but provide the bare essentials of existence. There was, however, a

139

consideration that was vaguer even than the sympathy and yet took the shape of a claim to the land on the grounds that forefathers had cultivated it from time immemorial, or certainly from a time when under the tribal system the land had been held in common. In short, almost a claim that in the dark processes of history the land had been filched from them. And here, like a scavenging crow, prepared to caw still vaguer stuff, was a representative of Trade Unionism.

The Colonel looked around for a chair, for there were but two with arms, and at last drew up a stiff-backed one which poised him ridiculously between Stansfield and the intruder. His face reflected the firmness of his mind and he opened the newspaper which had been folded for him on the sideboard.

Stansfield, with flybooks and scissors, continued his delicate task of cast-making. The stranger took out a notebook, and the Colonel, as he arranged his paper, saw him writing in it. The sight annoyed him, and he turned to Stansfield.

Stansfield had had fair luck, ' but the trout on Ardbeg have gone down in weight.'

' Oh! Have they ? '

' Yes. That damming up of the loch—I was always a bit doubtful about it.' Then he added, ' Of course, it was a good experiment.'

The final note, as if excusing someone, was not lost on Colonel Hicks, who had driven McAlpine to the experiment. ' I don't follow you,' he said.

' In damming up the outlet the way they did they may have deepened the loch, but they also deepened the gravelly spawning beds at the intake. That's often fatal.'

140

'I see. But if they couldn't spawn how did you get a fair basket?'

'That looks difficult,' replied Stansfield with an inner humour on his weathered face.

'Quite,' agreed Colonel Hicks.

'Anyhow,' said Stansfield, forced to it, 'where spawning grounds have been affected for the worse, where the normal feeding depths and so on have been altered, and where the stock is definitely poorer, it is natural to assume that—well—that the higher water level has something to do with the weight.'

'Usual court evidence for hanging a man!'

'It's pretty good evidence,' said Stansfield, a shade firmly.

'I have heard better excuses for a doubtful basket. Hardly does your legal mind credit!' The Colonel chuckled, his eyes now alight.

Stansfield, smiling, concentrated on tying a fly.

'I'm afraid,' concluded the Colonel, 'I shall have to try it myself.'

'Do,' said Stansfield. 'I should like to have your opinion then.'

The Colonel looked at him. 'I shall—to-morrow.' And added, 'It might also let me see how the Ardbeg gentry are getting on. Any news?'

'No.' Raising his head, Stansfield unthinkingly glanced across at the stranger. The Colonel regarded him also. He had put his notebook in his pocket and though clearly conscious of their interest showed no embarrassment. Indeed for a moment he met the Colonel's eyes levelly—then removed his own, his face perceptibly hardening. The Colonel's annoyance deepened into a desire to draw him, to bait him.

' I heard to-day,' he remarked casually, ' that Trade Unionism is sending a fellow to egg the miserable devils on.'

' Oh,' said Stansfield.

' Yes,' nodded the Colonel. ' I suppose he'll stuff some more ideas into their heads—for which they'll have to pay. It shouldn't be allowed.'

' This is a free country,' Stansfield replied dryly.

' Quite. You can dam as much as you like—and spawn. But when they begin to lose weight—to run to seed— ' As he pregnantly paused, his eyes turned on the stranger, who finished the sentence, ' You could always let the loch revert to its original condition.'

The Colonel continued to look at him. But the stranger was not cowed. The pallor of his reserve held its own sarcasm as though he knew quite well how he had been spoken at.

' What do you mean ? ' asked the Colonel.

' That there may be something even in Trade Unionism, not to mention the lives of miserable crofters.' His tone was quite cool and edged with the sarcasm.

' So you're the Trade Union representative ? ' said the Colonel slowly, taking complete stock of him. ' I see.' Then he asked, ' Have you ever been a crofter ? '

' That doesn't arise.'

' Oh, doesn't it ? ' The Colonel raised heavy eyebrows. ' You are up here to egg on these fellows in a matter you know nothing about.'

' On the contrary, I know a lot about it,' replied Mr. James Duffy. ' Possibly more than you.'

' Seeing you don't know what I know, I consider that a damned impertinence.'

' It's been my business to study small holdings for years. That's all.'

To keep hold on himself, the Colonel turned on his chair and caught up his glass. This sort of fellow maddened him at a stroke. Having drunk, he carefully laid his glass aside, saying:

' Being paid to study small holdings, you naturally believe in them.'

' I don't.'

' You don't what ? '

' I don't believe in them—not as an economic proposition.'

The Colonel looked squarely at him. Mr. Duffy remained silent. This silence irritated the Colonel acutely.

' But if you don't believe in them, what the deuce are you up here about ? ' Then his voice narrowed: ' Or do I understand that you are advising them to clear off the land they've stolen ? '

' That's another matter,' observed Mr. Duffy.

The Colonel's lips closed slowly and tightly, his face darkening as it lowered.

' By gad,' he burst out, ' that's pretty cool! Eh, Stansfield ? He doesn't believe in small holdings as an economic proposition, but he comes up here to incite these ignorant crofters into smashing your law in order to become small holders! '

Stansfield snipped a piece of gut with a constrained smile.

The Colonel chuckled richly.

Mr. Duffy's face grew paler. ' Seeing you don't

143

know what I have come up here for,' he said, ' I consider your remarks a damned impertinence.' He spoke without any heat and, taking out his watch, got to his feet.

' You what?' spluttered Colonel Hicks, also rising.

' Oh nothing,' said Mr. Duffy, turning away.

' But yes, something!' rapped the Colonel. ' You come up here with your damned sewer poison and try to stuff it into the heads of—of— ' His voice was getting out of control. His flesh shook.

' Sewer poison nothing! You're more like a sewer yourself.' Mr. Duffy's pallor at last betrayed his intense excitement and his final words caught a broad Clydeside accent. Yet he turned away with a tolerable air of indifference and left the Colonel stationary and mute. When the door closed the Colonel followed for a stumbling step or two on stumbling oaths. Stansfield lifted a hidden look of acute interest wherein his humour glittered; then his head drooped as the Colonel came back.

The sight of the non-committal Stansfield steadied the Colonel's incoherence. He glared at him.

' Doesn't believe in small holdings. But when it comes to the Ardbeg small holdings he believes in them—because it gives him a chance to break the law. To break your law, Stansfield; your precious law!'

' Yes,' said Stansfield.

' And what's your law doing about it?'

' It'll get the crofters prison, I expect.'

' And what about this fellow?'

' Oh, he'll be all right.'

The Colonel's hand shook as it groped for his glass. But Stansfield murmured about having something to see to before turning in and walked out, leaving Colonel Hicks to the silent room.

The Colonel helped himself to another drink; lit a fresh cigar; felt the room half choking him. In a murderous mood he walked through the empty lounge, heard voices in the drawing-room. A Sandersonian ' Hee! hee! ' drew a smothered, ' Oh, shut up, you bitch! ' He went out on to the gravel, his cigar glowing, and met the night.

The air was cool and invigorating. Intensely he regretted having let Duffy escape. He should have twisted the fellow's filthy guts. He looked about him ardently. The pebbles pressed up through the thin soles of his slippers with an exasperating hurt. The figure of a woman noiselessly passed him going towards the back premises. It was undoubtedly the kitchen-maid Jean. Where the devil had *she* been ? . . . It was a place this, by God! He expelled great gusts of breath and smoke. Footsteps were approaching. And voices. Could he be mistaken ? . . . The voice of Clare ? Undoubtedly the voice of Clare—here beside him—with another shape—a man's.

' Is that you, uncle ? '

' Yes,' affirmed Colonel Hicks.

Clare laughed.

' And you thought I was in bed! '

But the Colonel had made out the person of her companion. It was Ewan Macleod. And he could find no more wind for any sort of words whatsoever.

' But I couldn't resist it, for far away some one was

playing such music,' continued Clare, ' I thought the night was bewitched!'

The Colonel cleared his throat heavily, and at that moment, and unobtrusively, Ewan Macleod muttered ' Good-night,' and walked off into the darkness, Clare's voice calling after him, ' Thank you so much, Ewan.'

' Somehow you do contrive to make me feel like a naughty girl who has stolen out after hours,' said Clare. Her voice trembled in its merriment.

' H n,' said Colonel Hicks. ' Ha. Yes.' His voice was thick, harsh; sounded as if he were in such a choking rage that he could hardly articulate.

' My window looks out across there. It is such a perfect night. I heard these pipes—they had quite a different sound from the sound in daylight. Positively unreal. They did bewitch me. So down I came and out!' Clare found herself talking rather rapidly and slightly at random. She stopped. She would presently be making palpable excuses—for being out alone—with Ewan Macleod . . . whence her dear old uncle's rage! . . . She laughed suddenly and, as it seemed to Colonel Hicks, more than irrelevantly. Yet her humour must be met.

' Huh!' said Colonel Hicks. Clare's voice rippled. She caught his arm. All this was a perfectly new experience to her. They moved back towards the hotel.

' But—look here, m'dear. You must remember I'm your guardian—while you're here.'

' I remember.'

' And your health—you must remember—you must remember your health.' Colonel Hicks was getting his agreeable voice again.

' Of course, my health! ' echoed Clare.

' And going out like this at night—dangerous— not knowing your way an' that.'

' Yes. I rather think I lost my way when I hailed footsteps that turned out to be Ewan's. So he was good enough to put me on the right path again.' That should finally appease him! ' I'm not used to the dark.' And she smiled more inwardly than ever.

' Hm, keep unused to it.'

Her smile came out.

' Clever of you, uncle! '

' Hm.' After all, one's company did make a difference. Street-corner gutter like Duffy and peat-bog muck like Macleod, what could anyone expect from them but their own oozings ? Yet he would forget it. Sometimes came precious near being an ass. Result of this one-eyed hole.

They entered the lounge and before sitting down the Colonel looked about him, his face fixed in an inflamed and bellicose dignity. Its warmth suggested a profound emotional stirring.

' There's a chap here,' he said curtly. ' He rather annoyed me to-night.'

' Oh ? '

' Yes.' His mouth closed. He crossed his legs, gripped the ends of his chair, and in the momentary silence threw a glance at Clare.

The light had been slightly turned down, and in the dim glow Clare looked radiant; all the more radiant for the hint of fragility, of an exquisite mantling of convalescence. And as this radiance now stilled in sympathetic enquiry, there came a final impression of purity. All in a moment the Colonel was glad he hadn't opened out on the road. He was immensely relieved, as if by a fluke he had fought back for his breeding and proved it. He might have disproved it so drenchingly. The last large whisky began to warm him softly, to incline him towards radiant sympathy.

'Yes,' he said. 'He's one of those fellows—absolutely uneducated—some sort of Trade Union job. I don't mind the men—but these fellows! . . . He's here about those crofters—over there in Ardbeg. You know, they've dug up some land and been ordered off by old Innes, who has the sheep-farm there, bought it, decent fellow. Well, unless we're going to go absolutely Bolshy, something's got to be done about it. And I know all about them here.' He turned to his elbow for a glass which wasn't there.

'Yes, you must,' murmured Clare.

'Into the dining-room, which old Stansfield and myself, you know, for years . . . in he comes and squats down in my chair and stretches his feet out. Well, damme, you expect a man at least to know how to behave. But not only that—he butts into our talk. And when I outargue him, he gets to his feet and is damned rude. Unmentionable.' His lips closed tightly for a moment. 'I'm afraid I was a bit ruffled—just when I met you.'

'You hid it well,' said Clare, with a friendly smile. 'I didn't think you were troubled so far out of the world with—that sort of thing. I think I know the type. It wants to be as good as anyone else. One needn't really be annoyed. Though at the moment —I know—it's difficult.'

148

' Hm. Very difficult. And, what's more, take an old experienced man's word for it, m'dear, what they need is not pity.' Brows gathered ruthlessly. As an old soldier he had knowledge and memories. He might be in a position to be pitied, but damnation. . . . He suddenly got up. He was under the influence of his feelings. He took a turn or two about the lounge. With his buttoned, close-fitting, dark jacket, his fingers in his pockets and thumbs out, he looked soldierly, carried a certain reminiscent dignity. . . .

But to Clare his appearance was quite suddenly extraordinarily pathetic. Something rose to her throat. The soldierly bearing, the vertical commanding eyebrow furrows, the restrained facial red . . . futile, lost. Something in the essence of him gone wrong. Landed here, stranded, upset by mere professional agitators, tortured in his dignity by the most trivial pinpricks, his half-corrupted flesh wallowing like a stranded mammal stung by any chance gnat. . . .

Her charity felt immense, suffused her with a melting glow. Life, the night outside, that strange mesmeric night of dark hidden earth and haunting sea, set deep in the heart of which something within her opened like a secret rose . . . life was leaving him, throwing him aside, half-corrupted. . . .

When he could bring himself to throw her a glance, he surprised the upwelling of her sympathy, her commiseration, warm, softly engulfing. Her tender eyes fell away to her finger-tips. She heard his chair creak as he sat down again. There was silence for several seconds. He turned once more to the drink which wasn't there; cleared his throat. ' Though

149

I'm no use any more for quelling anything —
much less the Bolshies!' His voice was bravely
ironic. It chuckled. 'There's nothing for me to
do but hang out here, among these cattle—until
I pop off.'

'I wouldn't say that, Uncle Jack.'

Her low voice moved him like a caress.

'Life, m'dear. Race is run. I know.' His throat
swelled in the surge of his feelings; he felt himself
uprising, breasting warm salt seas.

Divination moved in Clare. The drawing-room
was too near. He mustn't let himself go—not too
far. Her expression did not alter, but her voice rose
a tone, gathered understanding cheerfulness.

'No, no.' She smiled gently. 'You mustn't say
— ' But a sudden movement of feet and laughing
voices in the drawing-room made her pause. Presently the Sanderson girls and the English family
appeared. A last breath of fresh air was voted sound.
While they were trooping to the front door, Colonel
Hicks and Clare arose.

'Good-night, my dear,' said Colonel Hicks.

'Good-night, uncle.'

As she moved to the stairs he turned towards the
dining-room, and found he had it to himself. He
closed the door and walked with congested dignity
to his bottle. He poured himself a stiff one; took a
pull at it; sat down and let his eyes sink into the
fireplace. Gradually something welled and gleamed
in his eyes. He got to his feet, his face working convulsively. He finished his drink. He swore sense-
lessly. He dashed a hand across his eyes. Rage
mounted in him. He tugged the bell-pull so that it

slapped back into position with the sound of a pistol shot. A maid appeared.

' Tell your master I want to see him! '

While in her bedroom Clare stood before her mirror, her face pale and quite flawless. The eyes looked large and dreamily sombre—as though they were dark brown instead of summer blue. But she did not smile, wishing for a moment more to hold her flawlessness serene. She held it quite a few seconds; looked into the sombre eyes until the surrounding face went out of focus, and through its blurred pallor the eyes stared back. Staring eyes, holding her; disembodied eyes, penetrating. . . . She blinked her eyes into her pale face, looked at it critically, de-tachedly; then smiled slowly to it, slowly turning away, watching the face as it turned.

She went and sat on her bed, hands falling limply to her lap. What next ? This curious state of rest-lessness, of indecision—why ? Slowly her gaze be-came fixed on nothing, and she sat as though lost in profoundest reverie for minutes. Then her head perceptibly uptilted, her lips came apart, and she listened. Nothing. What was she listening for ? Holding her breath at it too. . . . Nothing. There had not been even reverie. But in a vague fathoming way, how restful . . . and how deliciously troubled by restlessness, satisfaction dying out in a sigh, sighing far and faint and sad. . . . Delicious ecstasy of the night. Why ? She listened. Nothing.

She began slowly to undress. She saw herself, in another mood, laughing at herself. But not in this enchanted mood now. Her uncle's face unable to speak—and Ewan's melting into the dark. An unreal picture of a meeting in a dark light. Ewan's face dying into the darkness as into its natural element; her uncle's coming into the lamplight, fleshy, disturbed, the blood congested as though anger gorged the veins. The face of Ewan, her gillie, leaving nothing but darkness. The darkness of peat and loch water. The warm, soft loch water. She felt it on her hands. The fingers stirred, caressing one another.

CHAPTER THREE

I

E WAN came into the kitchen a little before eight in the morning to find his mother cooking the porridge. 'Good morning, mother,' he said as he half-paused, passing her, on his way to the back door.

Her stout body straightened as she looked over her shoulder and returned his greeting. It was a good morning indeed and time she had the porridge dished. She got busy about it, her face concerned through the steam that rose from the plates as the porridge flowed into them.

The face had undergone a slight but distinct change in these seven years. It was still coarse in the grain and the hair seemed to have grown even coarser in turning from dark to dark-grey; but it had set upon itself a new seal. The forehead was more lined and yet seemed like a forehead that was perpetually smoothing itself out of its lines and might some day smooth its lines quite away. Or again might not. Who could say? Least of all could the face itself, caught up in a mood that balanced serenity against gloom. The coarse grain, the life grain, was gloom. Gloom, the despondency of a congested fatalism, irradiated by serenity; the dark stupor of the heart touched by light; self-indulgence stayed by a finger. Or by a voice. Say, Ewan's voice. The voice of her son. All that was left to her. Moving about the house, its bright tones, ' Good morning.' This new seal of a serenity that might become abiding, that in odd moments might even become glad, but that could never altogether forget the darkness, the sighing stupor.

As he went out at the back door, Ewan filled a basin from the water barrel. Turning his shirt back, he set to.

As he was towelling his neck, his face red from rubbing and his hair over his brows, Annabel came round the corner of the house carrying two buckets of water from the well.

She appeared tall because she was thin. Or was it because she was immature ? Or what suggestion was it of something over-grown and delicate ? Or was it that she had merely grown a little out of her skirt and out of her thin sleeves so that her wrists looked very thin indeed and her hands long ? Her face at least was all alive as she stepped out of the hoop that kept the buckets from her legs. Nor did her legs seem in any way awkward as her eyes gleamed and she mocked him elegantly.

' So you got up ! '

' Not so long after yourself,' he retorted, and whether from the rubbing of the towel or by design his features twisted into a face.

Immediately she stuck out a remarkably long tongue. He saw it to the root and swiped the towel at it.

154

Her lifted hand caught the towel and held it.

' What kept you out so late last night ? '

' Late ? ' He snatched the towel from her.

' Ah, you would be busy at the pipes—with her father! ' The last words were whispered and, dodging the towel, she stumbled into the kitchen.

' It's just Ewan, mother,' she explained in a loud voice. ' He's at me.'

' What's he at you for ? '

' I was just asking him—asking him where— '
She made threatening faces at Ewan from behind her mother's back as he came in.

' Sit down,' said their mother, giving no heed to their talk.

Ewan and Annabel started into their porridge, Annabel maidenly composed. Ewan, slanting a glance across the table at her innocent expression, twisted a lip scoffingly. She traded him a rapid grimace, accompanied by a slight kick on the shin; then quickly and triumphantly tucked her legs under her chair.

' Mother,' she said in the tone of the English gentry, ' Muthah, where was—ah—last night, where was—ah—Ewan—I mean Euphemia Ross ? '

' Up the glen,' said her mother quietly out of her own thought. ' Little Andrew came over with the milk this morning.'

Annabel laughed silently for Ewan's benefit. Her mother was gazing at the fire, waiting for the kettle to boil.

' You'll pay,' he mumbled. ' You'll be sorry.'
He nodded to himself, gratified at the prospect; scraped his plate with deliberate care. He ignored

Annabel. His mother poured out the tea. ' Be eating plenty,' she said to her son.

' I'm always telling you I can't take two eggs.'

' And you out all day ? '

' But you should see the sandwiches Jean makes for him, mother. Just the same as for the gentry.'

' I should think so,' said her mother.

' And when he comes back at night she gives him late dinner,' risked Annabel.

' A lot you know about late dinner! ' scoffed Ewan.

' I'll be knowing more than you about it very soon.'

That seemed to stump him. With an intense curiosity, she furtively attempted to fathom his expression. But she couldn't quite. It was as though the scoffing, the mockery, for one nasty moment became real. She was having her first season out at Sronlairg Lodge this autumn. Mrs. Beagley, the housekeeper, had called in person three days ago; had not exactly taken a cup of tea, but had been very nice; had actually sat down and chatted in a voice that was more Englishfied than the gentry's. The voice had filled the little kitchen, dropping its aitches and picking them up with an astonishing fluency. She had eyed Annabel directly, up and down, and after a minute had nodded, ' She'll do, I think.'

' I'm sure she'll be willing, Mrs. Beagley,' ventured Annabel's mother.

' Ow, yes,' judged Mrs. Beagley. ' For the scullery—m'yes. She'll learn.' Plainly Annabel needed some filling out. But no doubt decent food. . . . Fortunate she didn't need her for the table. Mrs.

Beagley had a trained eye for possibilities in the most unlikely girls. One might be doubtful from first looks, but it was her experience that 'ighland girls were specially designed by Providence for the duties of maidservants. Soft voices and quiet, shy ways. Men liked 'em. And they picked up their duties very quickly. The best of them couldn't be beat. Under capable hands they soon lost their shy gawky ways. Their speech didn't matter. In fact, it was a hasset. A butler had to speak as she herself spoke—class English. But these girls could speak their soft twang—were encouraged to. She had seen it bring a half-surprised reminiscent smile to a guest's face in London. When they were pretty, men tipped 'em heavily. And no nonsense about 'em. No feeling of Jack's as good as his master about them. They knew their place. Even if now and then one of them proved difficult—really moody. But not often. On the whole, the perfect article, reflecting credit on any housekeeper—just as their men were the perfect gillies. And Mrs. Beagley reckoned that a long experience entitled her to know what she was talking about. So she had engaged Annabel for the stag-shooting season at Sronlairg Lodge which would very soon now be under way, for Mr. Denver had written from London, where he was staying a few days after the journey from Pittsburg, his son being with him on this occasion, Mr. Harold Denver. And Mrs. Beagley, with her taut face, having fixed the terms and other details of Annabel's engagement, which was to start from Monday next, sailed forth, accompanied politely by Annabel on her mother's whispered instructions.

' Good-bye, Annabel,' nodded the great one, when she had at last negotiated the footbridge over the stream.

' Good-bye, ma'm,' mumbled Annabel.

Whereupon the chauffeur engaged gear and Mrs. Beagley drove royally away.

At night Ewan had been told about it all by Annabel rather excitedly, a flush on her face. She was going out to a ' place,' her first place, Sronlairg Lodge no less. Mr. Denver, American millionaire. ' I guess,' drawled Annabel, choking her nose.

And Ewan had looked at her a moment, a steady penetrating moment, then turned and hung up his cap without a word.

' Mrs. Beagley was very nice,' her mother then said. ' She sat in that chair and talked away. She was very nice.' Plainly Mrs. Beagley had been human, when she might have exercised her vast powers in less understandable ways. Had come herself, dressed like the perfect lady, motor car an' all. The visit had left an impression, not at all unflattering to Mrs. Beagley. Not that Annabel's mother had been blind to certain possible firmnesses in Mrs. Beagley's character. But ' in her position,' that was manifestly to be expected. ' So precise she was! ' she remembered, with quiet interest.

And Ewan had scarcely said a word. An ' Oh,' ' I see,' a small smile, a nod, and presently, after tea, he had gone out and had not come home until very late, leaving Annabel seriously troubled, even miserable, at something horribly puzzling in his silence, as though he had not wanted her to go; even worse than that, something almost like a hidden sneer.

Nor had she had a chance of tackling him about it since, he had so persistently remained away at night.

And here this morning, when she was over-acting a little because she was feeling excited, and mentioned late dinner to test him, his expression took on that hardening that was a way of hiding his feelings. And he wouldn't look like that even for a moment, if the feelings he wished to hide were pleasant and friendly.

Now at breakfast he was saying in a business tone to his mother:

'Are you needing anything special?'

His mother rightly understood him to refer to the fitting-out of Annabel for her new post and answered, 'No, we'll do. She has her nice black dress, and Mrs. Beagley said that they wear special caps and aprons and that that would be all right.'

Ewan returned to his egg, ate steadily, and getting up said he must have a look at the boat as John McAlpine was at him last night about getting some white fish. 'What they get by car has not been keeping well with this thundery weather. I might have a turn at the ripper to-night if it keeps up.'

'You're doing enough,' said his mother.

He paused a moment, looking out of the window; then went into his bedroom. Presently they heard him go out at the front door. Annabel began to gather the dishes, her eyes downcast, troubled. From the moment he had turned and spoken to her mother it had become impossible to open her mouth, as though something had come into the room that killed all light-heartedness, that had the harshness of real life. Yet nothing had been said. She stole a look at her mother. Clearly enough her mother had felt nothing. Yet everything was wrong. And this wrongness was strong and brutal. She divined it uneasily. Yet—why? Why should it be? And what had her going to Sronlairg got to do with it? Why was life always like that? Always coming in from outside, cold and harsh, shrivelling up the fun and the warmth, as if they were the play of children. . .

'Mother, I don't think Ewan likes me going to Sronlairg,' came from her suddenly.

'What makes you think that?' asked her mother, setting peats on the stone hearth.

'I don't know,' she muttered.

'Surely it's natural he wouldn't like you to be going away from home.' And her mother laid down the tongs and lifted the steaming kettle off the crook.

Annabel looked up quickly.

'Do you think that's it?'

'What else?' Her mother, turning with the kettle, looked at her.

'Oh,' said Annabel, shifting her eyes to the window. 'I didn't think of that.'

'What were you thinking?'

'I don't know,' said Annabel, and, lifting the dishes, preceded her mother to the back door, whence presently, her mother having gone inside, she stole along past the end of the house to see what Ewan was doing down below with the small boat. He was standing beside it, looking out to sea. He was standing so still that the horrid sense of insecurity caught her up again worse than ever. What was he standing like that for? . . . The cold blue, the colder white, the sucking sounds . . . where her father and Ewan, so long ago. . . . Oh, what was he thinking of, gazing out like that ? . . .

Ewan suddenly turned and looked up at her. But he did not wave a hand or pretend to throw a stone. Embarrassed and vexed at having been seen by him, she returned quickly to the house, her mind hurt, in a turmoil, suffering.

Presently she heard him come round the gable-end, and looked up. He smiled, gave her a half-sarcastic, half-inviting wink. But she could not rise to it, and, turning away from him, poked the fire beneath the old black pot in which she was boiling some of her white clothing. But her ears, become extraordinarily acute, heard him tiptoe on the grass behind. Suddenly one of her hands was caught, and into its palm was pressed a piece of crinkly paper. Without looking at him, she opened her hand and examined the paper. It was a one-pound note.

' Case you need something,' he nodded, backing away from her.

For several seconds she stood unmoving, over-come, then started after him. He went through the action of picking up a stone and flinging it at her. But nothing could stop her advance. He turned and took to his heels, throwing a mocking laugh over his shoulder. She stumbled on a grassy hump and sat down. Through the tears and laughter on her face came a gulping sob.

As Ewan paused to draw breath, he looked down upon the swing-bridge and the amusement on his face faded out, leaving in its place a perceptible darkening, a reality of shadow curiously character-istic. It was not exactly that the face was less alive, but in some way that the light had sunk inward out of it, leaving its apparent normality more perfect because less arresting than any mask, and the more perfect in that the process was unconscious.

He turned upon the steep ascent, thinking to himself that it was folly to show Annabel that he was not pleased about her going to Sronlairg. What right had he to be pleased or otherwise ? To be vexed or bitter about it might be well enough as a matter of personal indulgence, but what had that to do with Annabel ? And not only so, but here he was himself going off to gillie. . . . He could be a philosopher about it, of course! The smile made his face darker than ever.

This bloody menial service ! He looked around— at the croft houses rotting down the road to perdition; the heirs of the heroes (whom he had recently heard accused of eating the potatoes the Board of Agriculture supplied at a charitable rate for seed)!

Hang, here he would go at it! As if he had not reasoned the whole thing out clearly enough to be tired of it long ago, to forget it, not to bother about it. . . . Breathing heavily, he crested the ridge. He did not make enough money to run a house in affluence! Scarcely! And she had to learn a trade to earn a living. It wasn't the actual scullery work— let him be honest—it was. . . . Oh, choke it!

Finally there was something about Annabel that warmed him, that crept into his heart.

Difficult to pretend to her that all was fine and splendid. Only the conscious serf suffered. The hotel front came in sight.

There was Donald. He wasn't going to have

turned out again! Never another step was he going to have gone with the Colonel! . . . He would have been waiting to have been asked, of course; and now he was going. And glad of the chance. Ewan's spirit lightened at sight of him.

'Morning, Donald,' he greeted. 'What's in the wind?'

'Och,' said Donald largely, 'it's that John McAlpine.'

'What now?'

'Och, didn't he send for me this morning, and prigged with me to come or he didn't know what would happen to him at all.'

'Are you telling me that?'

'Yes. And I had a good mind just not to come for him. But he has always been a decent man to me and—and what could I do?' He looked about him and added in a knowing whisper, 'Between you and me and the corner of the dyke, he's as frightened of the Colonel as a rabbit of a weasel.' He tossed his head, wrinkling his nose in humorous contempt.

Ewan laughed. Donald's eyes twinkled with pleasure, and he went on confidentially, 'But if the Colonel tries any of his nonsense with some of the rest of us, he'll know what he'll be getting.'

'That's the stuff!' encouraged Ewan.

'That's all right,' said Donald, nodding and winking. 'Leave it to me. It won't be the first time. To hell with him!' Donald was in fine feather, and rather pleased with the neat way in which he had turned his own presence to account. Plainly there was every possibility of the Colonel's having to rebuke Donald's tongue before the day was over.

163

' Where are you going ? ' asked Ewan.

' Ardbeg.'

' Ardbeg ? '

' Yes.' Donald chuckled.

' But what's the Colonel wanting so suddenly on Ardbeg ? '

' Ah,' replied Donald, ' I don't know, I'm sure, but I'm hearing there's to be a meeting up there to-day and that there's a man arrived from the Trade Unions. I saw him last night myself.'

Ewan regarded Donald with thoughtful surprise. ' So I heard,' he prompted.

' Yes,' proceeded Donald, who appreciated the importance of news, ' and I'm wondering if it's only for the fishing he'll be going. I'm not saying anything. I'm only wondering.'

' Ay, ay,' nodded Ewan.

' Yes, I'm just wondering,' repeated Donald.

' You'll have to watch out that they don't turn on him and throw him in the loch.'

Donald chewed this possibility. ' I wouldn't say that I would let them throw him in the loch exactly. I'll see whatever that he gets fair play. The Colonel may be this or that—but he's a gentleman born.'

' There speaks the true Highlander,' nodded Ewan.

' Yes, the Highlander knows a gentleman,' reckoned Donald.

' Serves him right,' smiled Ewan.

While Donald smiled too in order to cover the effort at finding out what exactly Ewan might mean, the Colonel in person walked round the hotel corner and approached the garage door. The sudden sight

164

of his grey-clad fleshiness so affected Ewan that of
its own accord his body turned and walked into the
garage gloom.

'So you have turned up?' came the Colonel's
voice.

'Yes, sir,' answered Donald.

'Why didn't you come for orders last night?'

'I didn't know that you might be wanting me.'

'You didn't what?'

'I was saying, sir, that——'

'Saying, be damned! Don't you know your job
yet?'

'Yes, sir.'

'Well, then——get ready. And see you have no
holes in that blasted net to-day!'

'Very good, sir.'

Ewan emerged to find Donald chuckling to himself.

'He was trying to be coorse,' explained Donald,
'because he knows he has the wrong of it. But he
won't get me to thaw as easily as all that! No. He's
a mistaken gentleman if he thinks that.'

'Ay,' said Ewan.

'He shouts away like yon,' proceeded Donald,
'thinking it will——'

'He's at the corner there,' remarked Ewan.

Donald twisted quickly and saw his gentleman and
Clare talking together on the gravel before the hotel.
Clare, turning, saw Ewan, and after a final remark to
the Colonel came walking, half-smiling, towards the
garage. The free easy grace of her body in a hot
splash of morning sun was very attractive, very
beautiful. He waited.

The flies discussed, she seated herself in the stern; he pushed off and vaulted the bows. They were afloat.

On Loch Cruach, with the great stack towering over the other shore. A good fishing wind, and towards the primeval rock, broadside on, oars shipped, their blue-painted boat drifted to the glucking of the water, Clare standing astern, Ewan sitting on the rowing seat, body leaning forward, eyes on the stretch that the flies covered. By mid loch they had diminished in size, looked from the shore more of a unity, of a craft adrift on waters running on and on to grey rock faces, inscrutable, immense. No sound came back, no disillusioning accent of the human voice. Only now and then there rose the thin scream of the reel, startling the boat and its occupants to a slight commotion, which ended in Clare's sitting down, so that no body showed against the grey rock, only bowed heads bending towards each other as in a final conspiracy of understanding in a final drift, where the dark loch marge, ever drawing near, hid the lost cavern to the final secret guarded with such menace by that grey eternity above.

Then Ewan rowed back, Clare sitting in the stern; and turning his craft broadside, drifted again. Rowed back and drifted again. Finally rowed back precipitately and beached at a rush. 'That hot sun in the morning,' he said.

Clare lifted her face. The raindrops were big and soft. One fell right in her eye, so that she suddenly exclaimed, blinded; then lifted an amused expression and looked about her and looked at Ewan.

' You think it's going to be much ? '

' It will be very heavy while it lasts,' he said, and handed her her rain-coat.

' But aren't we as well here ? '

' It's lunch time anyway,' said Ewan; ' and it's going to be very heavy.' He waited, however, manifestly prepared for any decision.

' But wouldn't we be as well in the boat ? '

' Very good,' said Ewan.

' But what do *you* think ? '

' There is a sheltered place along there,' and he indicated a narrow ravine where the feeding stream entered the loch. ' You could have your lunch there —and by that time it might be over.'

In a couple of minutes they were running for the mouth of the stream where an overhanging lip of moss and rock made a narrow but perfect roof. The downpour was torrential.

' This is jolly ! ' declared Clare, tucking in her feet. The thought came to her that he might have made no further reference to this place if she had merely continued the suggestion of their staying in the boat ! She turned to put her thought to him, curious to see. . . . But another thought took its place. Having displayed her luncheon basket, he was getting to his feet.

' Surely you're not going out in that ? ' She looked at him in amazement. He had no coat.

' Go along and see the boat,' he muttered, the rain already drenching one shoulder. ' My sandwiches. . . .'

167

' But I have sandwiches. Will you please lunch with me ? '

He hesitated, but politely. She faintly coloured.

' You would rather not ? Very well. Please take my coat and run.'

' No, thanks. Nothing.'

' Ewan! '

He waited.

' If you get soaked through,' she said calmly, ' it will simply mean that I can't keep you here all the afternoon.' Her tone was final. It was not a conversation one wished to continue needlessly.

' Have a coat,' he murmured; his feet crunched over the stones; gone.

And she knew he wouldn't come back.

She stared a moment, a glint in her eyes. The momentary tension eased; she smiled thoughtfully. It was really rather extraordinary. Two human beings—one going out into that—because . . . because what, really ? A midge pinged so suddenly in her ear that she hurt the side of her face with the slap she gave it. Another one on her wrist. She looked about her; up at the overhanging roof; at the tiny ferns and grasses in the rock cracks behind; at the stones scattered about; at the gravelly bottom of the stream, a blurred golden brown; at the miniature ravine face opposite, with coloured lichen splayed about in odd shapes on smooth slabs, one foot-high patch near the ridge like a fantastic yellow dragon. There were some midges about. With the coming of the heavy rain the wind seemed to have dropped. The sandwiches tasted good—roast beef—better than chicken. Like to bubbles when rain pelteth,

she munched at the stream. The submerged golden
brown grew less blurred; the fierceness of the downpour was abating. So he was definitely not coming
back. A midge stung her brow. No wind. A puff
of wind passed across her face like a cool breath. The
stones were cold. In picking up her coat she also
picked up the game-bag, which was lying under it and
which must have been grabbed up somehow in the
rush for shelter. It would make an excellent seat.
But on inserting a hand to remove the tackle, she
found an unexpected packet which proved on examination to contain sandwiches. Her gillie's lunch!
She smiled as she carefully laid bare the sandwiches
and sat on the bag.

But her gillie put in no appearance. It suddenly
occurred to her that of course he would be hunting
for the bag! Slipping on her coat, she stepped round
the corner and bespoke the boat. His head appeared
above its off side. Plainly he wasn't hunting.
Having returned to her seat, she presently observed
his legs come to rest before her, looked up and
caught his eyes as they found the exposed lunch
packet.

' Did you think you'd lost it ? '

' Oh yes,' he answered. It might as well have been
' Oh no,' for all it conveyed. But his expression
darkened self-consciously.

She took one of her own sandwiches—and wondered what he would do. He stooped with the
manifest intention of removing his little pile, when
she said:

' I wonder why they put more meat in yours than
in mine ? Do you think that's fair ? ' And she

169

looked from one packet to the other contrastingly. He did not move. She waited his answer.

' Would you— ? ' he mumbled.

' I would—if you don't mind.' She flashed him a charming look, the least trifle shy. ' Won't you sit down ? ' She lifted his top sandwich. Jean had certainly been kind to her brother, even if John McAlpine didn't know much about it. Clare Marlowe stuck her fine teeth in a mouthful. It was certainly juicy. ' Better,' she judged, a trifle indistinctly.

They sat eating sandwiches, gazing at the water on the opposite bank, Clare appearing absolutely unconcerned, occasionally indeed somewhat abstracted, as though her gaze were held. Only once or twice did she, between mouthfuls, say something of the rain or of the afternoon prospects, and then not with particular conviction. She suddenly sighed.

' Eating sandwiches always makes my jaws ache. Do you find that ? ' She fished out her flask of claret. ' And dry.' Then her brows contracted. ' We seem to have only this one cup,' she said, regarding the silver heel of her flask.

He said nothing.

She looked up at him. ' If you don't mind, I'll have my drink first. Then you'll be ready for yours.'

' No, thanks,' he insisted quickly.

' No ? ' And she suddenly thought of the student turned home on account of wine and women and raised her eyebrows blandly. ' Are you—don't you believe— '

' No, but— '

She removed her eyes, a faint excitement behind

170

her cool look. His face was the masked face of something caged. And what was caged was twisting on itself like a heather adder. She had seen a dead one on the road, killed by a passing tyre, its head flattened. Something different in his nature from anything within her experience—but possibly re-acting to pretty much the same old stimuli! And masked very well; oh, very well! She took two lingering sips and one draught. 'There you are.' She handed him the drained cup and nodded towards the stream.

After a moment's hesitation, he went to the water and rinsed the cup.

It was with difficulty she refrained from smiling to her apple.

'Like it?'

'Yes, thank you.' His gillie's face was agreeably solemn. Then he went to the stream and carefully rinsed the cup afresh.

'Sure you won't have more?'

'No, thanks.'

'Then I'll just finish it.' A single drop spilled from her lip to the napkin, leaving a red stain on white. She looked at it and looked up at him, right into black eyes that flicked from her to the stream, to the weather; dark windows to a nest of adders! Excitement became a pleasant warmth in her breast. She had to exercise distinct restraint over a desire to be amused aloud. If she did laugh outright—what on earth could he do?

'These midges,' she murmured, hunting her cigarettes. 'Do smoke.'

CHAPTER FOUR

I

THE following morning Clare realised that the sheer pleasure she got from watching the white curtain of drifting rain, as it crossed from Colin McKinnon the piper's house over the hill-face, blurring the lonely cottages and the little green fields, to vanish beyond the sea-precipices, had something to do with the mere state of her health. She was getting stronger, physically and nervously. When she got tired out she slept. But there was something more than that. . . . Her mind took a long drift, and presently began answering the letter under her hand, her chief's letter. . . . 'The rain here is surely the wettest rain in the world. It penetrates. I sometimes think it penetrates so far in that it waters the old arid mud in which the primal serpents have been so long baked by all our modern electrical improvements, so dazed by jazz lights. The mud softens. They stretch themselves sluggishly. They lift their diamond heads and their awful inscrutable eyes keep looking while they yawn. They love the dark because their deeds are—unconscious. They come to the light to coil their dark beauty in the sun, which they love most of all in spite of the prophets. I sit at my bedroom window in this enchanted land watching the rain—and taking great care—not to get wet! ' And so on. She could see his smile. That momentary flicker of hesitation while he wondered just precisely how much she meant.

How much she meant ?

She pondered. The mud and the serpent really meant—sex. He would see that. The symbols. But also of the unconscious, the vital. Therefore veiled. He would see that, too, the delicacy of it, and hesitate, with that odd considering smile.

Her face grew still and her eyes transparent with light. The pale cheeks had a faint underflush.

Sex after all meant life, came out of life. And this growing towards health and colour was warm and inviting. It made the body feel a lovely thing as if a lily had got flushed with rose.

And slightly restless.

Humanity—or was it puritanism ?—was like that: it would kill anything lovely by giving it a ' real ' name. . . .

But. . . .

She wondered.

Though secretly and in the clean ways of her heart she knew how lovely it was. And this awakening towards health—how exquisite among these hills, by loch edges, with the wind, the sea. The wind from the hills went round the body, rippled the skin. She had never quite felt like this before.

Before it had been too obviously an intellectual recognition of a sex emotion.

A faint smile shone deep in her eyes.

173

Her lips moved as if the flying mist had touched and softened them.

Her face was fair and slightly veiled.

But behind the veil—the playfulness, the hidden certainty, that life glowed and was iridescent. The body was in a condition of love . . . health struck a note in it like an under-sea bell . . . with whom ? . . . with what ? . . .

The flying mists that veiled the hillsides veiled her eyes, veiled her thought from herself. Or did it ? Yes. She withdrew her eyes. They regarded her pale fine fingers that straightened themselves measuring each against each, and slowly rocked over, glistening in their nails.

Her elbow touched an open poetry book, which the artist's wife had given her. She drew it in front of her.

' *Eilidh, Eilidh, Eilidh, dear to me, dear and sweet,*
  In dreams I am hearing the sound of your little running feet—
  The sound of your running feet that like the sea-hoofs beat
  A music by day an' night, Eilidh, on the sands of my heart, my Sweet! '

She read the three verses.

Her mind stirred; a smile trembled to her eyes, daringly. What about these verses—as the conclusion to the primal serpents stirring in the mud ? To work it out without any apparent logical development—one verse, say. ' Here is the Gaelic jazz, beating on sand.' With a final nicely baffling remark, ' Perhaps the primal serpents are sea-serpents after

174

all.' And then, ' Anyway, a walk one must have—
even in the rain. So good-bye. The glass has
decided not to go any lower! '

But she sat looking at the rain and didn't write
a word. . . . ' *that like the sea hoofs beat a music by
day and night, Eilidh, on the sands of my heart, my
Sweet ! . . .*'

Romantic sentiment; weak; had its day; done.
Art now looking to the classical or sculptural. What
was the phrase in the latest highbrow criticism of the
romantic ? . . . ' emotive fragments ' . . . that was it.
An amused flicker passed over her eyes. They were
clever, these men critics. They were positive
scientists. They were so sure they knew—everything.

The letter she would write certainly wouldn't be
an ' emotive fragment.' She felt suddenly tired and
pushed the writing material from her. Not quite so
strong yet as she fancied. Her head fell on her arms.
Closed eyes found the world dark. And sculptural
art becomes invisible in a dark where is only the
sound of sea-hoofs beating on sand.

After lunch, she escaped. The clouds were hanging lower down than ever, but the rain had lessened
and was now drifting in a soft smother of tiny drops.
As she swung down to the stone bridge she was
delighted to find this outside world warm and tender.
The near hill-slopes faded away mysteriously; even
things quite close at hand became blurred and
freighted and fragrant; while enveloping, all-per-
vasive, was the sense of strangeness, as of things under
a wild spell; under, say, the crying of wild geese and
wild swans.

When she crossed the bridge and came on the mouth of the road leading down to the sea, she turned into it at once. Faintly already she could hear the sea-hoofs beat. But very faintly, as though freighted also, and under a spell. Muffled hoofs—or muffled sand ? . . . No. Muffled was the wrong word. How to describe it ? How to tell of the heart listening, of the gaiety of mysterious mystical things ? Here was escape indeed! Sitting inside thinking about it . . . like the wise critics in their studies . . . these human spiders, spinning so industriously, with such design! Here was a sense of relief, of being caught up, that was joyous, intoxicating; and when she suddenly saw a real spider's web on a whin bush, beaded and beautiful in the small rain, she smiled. She hoped the poor fellow didn't get wet; but she felt pretty sure he wouldn't catch a wild swan, not even a wild goose! . . . Then she passed the two-plank bridge, down by the rock to the beach where by their sea boat stood Ewan and his sister Annabel.

Clare came on them so unexpectedly that they stared at her as she approached.

Where so much was mere card-playing and disgruntled moods, they at least were of this land, were genuine. And the girl rather looked like a wild swan.

She greeted Ewan with a disarming friendliness. He touched his cap. Annabel hovered painfully on the point of flight, but Clare caught her with a smile.

' Is this your sister ? '

Annabel's face was a flag of shy distress; her glancing eyes were very bright; her thin hand responded to Clare's clasp with a nervous uncertainty.

It required no great imaginative effort to hear the fluttering of her heart. Something in Clare instantly responded to this vivid, sensitive being here on the sea edge.

She turned to Ewan, who had an old black oilskin about his shoulders. 'You're not going out, are you?'

'Yes.'

'Really!' She faced Annabel. 'You're not?'

'No,' said Annabel, with a start of astonishment.

Clare looked at the boat, the coiled brown fishing line with lead and hooks.

'Going fishing?'

'Yes.'

'I say. Really. That does sound rather exciting.' She looked past the spit where the foam swirled, to the heaving planes of the sea, dying into grey mist. 'Rather a huge loch, isn't it?' Her teeth flashed; her eyes flashed, daring the sea. But in her heart she felt these two were hostile, were shutting her out. She turned to Ewan hesitatingly. 'You wouldn't— you don't take— ?'

'The boat is always for hire,' stated Ewan simply.

'Oh.' She felt pulled up. 'You mean—I could hire it now?'

'Yes . . . although I promised to get fish.' He was plainly uncomfortable. 'It's not very nice to-day.'

'I should like to go to-day, I think,' she mused.

Ewan gave a sidelong glance at her clothing, at her face.

'I think we'd better arrange a day,' he suggested. 'I have only one fishing line at the moment.'

'And you must catch fish! '

The awkwardness persisted. Clare could not break through to them. Ewan slid away.

'Do you always see him off ? ' she asked Annabel.

'Nearly always.'

'And do you never go out yourself ? '

'Oh no! '

Clare watched the body in its black oilskin swing to the oars, the boat rise and dip. As it rounded the boiling point to the right it heaved tumultuously, the black body a heaving part of it, the face a pale blur. She suddenly remembered her uncle's story of Ewan and his father; of Ewan who had managed to save himself anyhow. . . .

When the boat had disappeared she still remained looking at the waters. Annabel stole a glance at her and saw blue eyes flashing through a mist of thought or feeling. Clare turned and surprised her glance, smiled.

'The women never go, of course.'

'No.'

Clare saw that she wanted to be off.

'You go up that way ? '

'Yes.'

'Could I go that way—back to the hotel ? '

Annabel hesitated.

'Yes. But it's very steep and the grass is wet.'

Presently Clare asked, 'Do you ever think of leaving here ? '

'I don't know,' murmured Annabel. 'My mother. . . .'

'Ah, you have your mother.'

'Yes.'

Clare decided she would not take to the hillside after all.

'Good-bye. I'll see you again, I hope.' She paused. 'If ever you did think of taking a post away from home, I hope you would give me the chance— '

'Thank you,' murmured Annabel, embarrassed, edging away.

Clare gave a final greeting and turned. As she crossed the bridge, she thought how splendid it would be having a personal maid, like Annabel, in London. How Annabel would, at trying moments, bring back all this land with her soft voice, her flashing timid eyes, her vivid mind. . . .

As she went up the road there came the vision of Ewan in his boat, adrift on that tumbling waste. She saw his face gone a little grey, cold and expressionless as the sea, and as fearless. . . .

That was the note of this place: beauty and elemental strength and fate. In their songs, their poetry. . . . That note of fate. She looked about her. No wonder.

Something stirred in her heart like a poem.

2

Ewan followed up that same road in the evening, a fish wrapped in brown paper under his arm, while Clare in the lounge was pondering some remarks that had been made at dinner about the palatableness of really fresh white fish, remarks which had led to the question of transport in the Highlands, though it was not lost sight of that the introduction of the tripper would affect disastrously the combined attractions of charm and exclusiveness; a sporadic but rather illuminating discussion in which, however, her table had taken no part, though the Colonel had manifestly restrained himself with difficulty. Clare thought mostly of the fish, and had a rather morbid vision of the mouths consuming it.

But while Clare was anxious to escape again, to go out for a final breath of air, possibly as far as Cladach sands, Ewan was heading for Colin McKinnon's. He wanted to have a talk with Colin, to get some music, to have something cleared out of his mind that was growing sour there and bitter. He did not want to be going too often to Colin's. But he needed to go sometimes. He had hurt Annabel again. They wouldn't leave her alone. She would suffer yet. She was cut out for suffering. The suffering in the mind. He knew.

And no good blaming Miss Marlowe. She was trying to confer a favour, to be kind. He saw Annabel's enthusiastic eyes again. She had thought Miss Marlowe the perfect lady, wonderful, her expression full of kindness, of understanding, and so cool and beautiful and distinguished. Annabel had wondered if ever she would know enough to be her personal maid. But she had been watching his face; she had stopped; she had said no more about it; had gone out at the back door. . . .

The degradation of poverty in a world where money was the supreme power. The old spirit had had its day; was being squeezed to death; the old land existed for the hotels and the shooting lodges, where money gathered; and what sort of money it was didn't matter.

At it again! He would always be like this now; a chronic! They were too much for him, the Colonel and his kind. Why should a man lose his sense of dignity by acting as a gillie, any more than by acting as a bank clerk or even as a colonel? No reason. And, in the beginning, he might not. But in the end, he did. The thing wore him down. Money has the power to insult, and poverty (with mouths to feed) must have the silence to accept. If not at first, then always in the long run. The end was certain. Regarded philosophically, one might say that it would be impossible to be insulted by the Colonel. But it wasn't impossible. On the contrary, it was most maddeningly possible, as though one would rather accept it from anybody than from him. And the local saying, ' Och, never mind him! ' with its fatalism and dry humour wasn't anything but a way of giving in, a sort of inverted superiority in which there was nothing but the acceptance that damns. And when these people smiled at the Highlander and imitated his ' speech,' ' Ach put it will be a ferry fine day whateffer,' and laughed at his English solecisms and generally found him a source of humour, the Highlander himself would laugh with them, or perhaps, like Donald, flare into a sort of wordy temper which afterwards afforded these one-tongued snob-hunters the best fun of any. There had been that fellow from Edinburgh last year, with his diced stockings and goggle-eyes and ' humour.' They say that Stansfield had quietly insulted him. Stansfield would, because he was an Englishman with the decent manners of his own race. McAskill had been going with him for years and gave perfect service for good money. Though even there. . . . Hang, he would keep at it! . . .

A voice came to relieve him. In the half-dark, in a still rain-drenched world, it came with a stirring magic, floating out from the old schoolhouse, from the centuries, from the spirit of beauty long ago. It affected him like a knuckle at his throat. His weary body shivered, and all his smothered desires rose in him like ghosts. The ghosts of past lives in past generations; of men and women of his blood; of all the old unnameable desires, the great ways of joy and sorrow, the deep sad ways of death, to echoings of ancient heroism and tingling in the heart's blood.

When the Gaelic song had ended, the thought of Mary McKinnon the singer came in with his breath. And after a little he looked at the grey schoolhouse. And when logic came, he reckoned that she would be in there going over her songs for the concert with the old schoolmistress. But he kept looking at the schoolhouse as though it might vanish.

Then Mary McKinnon came out. He heard her soft laugh on the doorstep; heard the schoolmistress saying, ' And haven't you one waiting for you at all ? ' And Mary laughed, ' Not one! ' And the schoolmistress said, ' Well, well; but when they'll be hearing you singing, my dear, maybe one of the young gentlemen from the Lodge itself will. . . .' ' You never know! ' Kindly leave-taking, and now she was coming. He moved slowly along the road. As she came up, he turned.

' Hallo! ' he said quietly.

She started.

' I heard you singing.   I was just taking a turn up your way.'

' Father will be glad to see you.'

' There's no one in ? '

' No.   He was alone when I left.'

' Were you going over your songs for the concert ? '

' Yes.'

They walked on.

' It's a fine night now after all the rain.'

' Yes, isn't it ? '   And Ewan looked about him. But he found a slight difficulty with his breathing and could think of nothing worth saying. He added, listening to himself, ' It was very wet in the morning.'

' It was.   You wouldn't have been fishing, of course ? '

' No.   I took a turn at the sea in the afternoon.'

' Wasn't it stormy ? '

' No.   The wind was off the land.'

It was a long time since Mary and himself had walked together on a dark road.   He had deliberately taken care that it should not happen. This had been easy, with the possibility always in his mind.   And when it had chanced that Mary and himself had been thrown together for a moment, he had always been amused and jocular, in excellent spirits.

Mary could thus come to her own conclusions. She could throw over all thought of him.   It would have been an exquisite relief if she had, an exquisite torment.   He could gnaw at this torment till he had got his fill of it.   A black dog gnawing at it in secret, sucking its marrow of defeat.

That was it, of course; he had been defeated.   His spirit had been whipped into him and whipped down.

And he kept it there with a sure pride. If there could be nothing for him henceforward, then assuredly he was asking nothing.

Pride can be amused, jocularly; it can cover itself with flashing lights—from the passes of invisible steel.

Or—it can be silent.

He was silent now. He could have kept a conversation going—but, at the moment, after the singing, the dark road, Mary here walking so that every movement of her body was like a movement within his own flesh, why should he?

Her body walked through his own. The soft stir of her clothes filled his ears, gave her over to his senses till they brimmed.

They had not yet walked a score of paces. A pulse started somewhere in which pride and sensitiveness tremored and blurred. He threw her a look, swiftly lifting his eyes from her face to the night. Her face was set in front. There was no one in the night, no one but themselves.

The tremoring lightness passed to his feet. They scarcely touched the road at all. His walking became at once airy and awkward. He could stumble with the utmost ease, almost in spite of himself. And all at once he lurched towards her and bumped her shoulder.

She gave way instantly. But no more quickly than he drew straight.

An exclamation had slipped out of her; a tiny sound sheathed in a nervous laugh. Before it had gone he knew her feelings. They were his own, but a woman's.

He exclaimed, too; but the sound he made was

184

idiotic. It tortured him in its futility. ' Excuse me! '
Excuse me! He stumbled again.

Why not ? A reckless mutiny whirled in him, a
dark flame. Strength from it gripped round his
mouth. All his flesh gripped. In the darkness, the
two of them, sweeping and clashing, crushing together.

He stumbled to a pause, uncertain still. From a
step in front, she half turned. His taut muscles at
last squeezed from the brown paper parcel under his
arm the large codling it contained, so that it fell with
a noisy flop on the roadway.

' What is it ? ' asked Mary in a scared voice.

He stood fixed in an intense dismay.

A curse formed in the heart of laughter. He
stooped and put his fingers in the gills. As he
straightened himself, Mary, who had half-stooped
also, drew erect. They looked at each other, then
Ewan leant forward and kissed her fair on the mouth.

She started back.

They stared at each other for a second, then Ewan's
strangled laugh came through.

' It's a small cod,' he said.

She did not speak.

' I was taking it along to the house,' he explained.
His voice seemed large and full of merriment. His
feet hit the road, grinding the small stones. He felt
sure, he said, that they would like a bit of fresh fish.
' Won't you ? '

She did not answer. Her steps seemed to be going
more quickly.

He knew why she did not answer—precisely.
That was his perverted power.

185

But the surge from his dismay was passing. Merriment was its froth. They were coming near her house. In this walking, step by step—there was no power. They would soon be there. Desire grew in him. A craving came upon him. This craving became urgent and shackled each footstep. He walked more slowly. Her face seemed turned away from him—as she walked more slowly.

He must have her, he must have her alone.

'I say,' he began and choked and came to a halt by the dark byre door. His voice was little more than a whisper. She stood still. A voice sang out:

'Is that you, Mary?'

She heard the hiss of Ewan's breath; then his forced laugh:

'Is it you, Colin?'

'Well, now, is it yourself, Ewan? Isn't that lucky?' Colin had been leaning against the black peat stack and stepped out to meet them.

Ewan presented the fish and explained how he had fallen in with Mary as he came up the road.

He rose into a laughing voluble mood.

When they were in the kitchen Colin saw that Ewan's eyes sparkled. Colin felt his own spirit growing light. He was a capital fellow this Ewan. 'What's the news?' he asked, settling comfortably.

'Stirring times!' said Ewan. 'Ardbeg is in the papers, and the Colonel is busy!'

Colin plied him with questions and followed the Colonel who, 'by way of it,' had gone to fish at Ardbeg and had come on this Duffy fellow holding a meeting in a barn.

'You remember how it came down at lunch time

in buckets,' Ewan rattled on. 'We were on Loch Cruach and had to run for it.'

'Yes. It fairly came down. We were thinking about you. But there's shelter yonder at the mouth of the burn.'

'Yes.' Ewan suddenly remembered the burn— and Clare. 'Yes.' But in a moment he was off again. The Colonel had been refused admission to the barn on the hospitable score that he had better go to the kitchen to get dry. 'It's just a little private meeting,' old Homer the Red had said to him. Oh, ever so politely—and, with his best wishes that the Colonel would be dry soon, closed the barn door again!

Colin chuckled.

But the Colonel worked himself up into such a steaming heat in the kitchen that he stalked down to the barn again—to meet the men coming out. He held up an arm. 'Look here, men; I have had Highlanders in my regiment. Most of them were gentlemen. You can behave as you like, but you can behave as gentlemen. Anyway, I'd be damned before I'd take instructions from any rascally Bolshevist. *You* may have to go to prison: it's dead certain *he* won't.' With that the Colonel choked and glowered at Duffy, and walked on, with Donald bringing up the rear in the heavy rain. As they came to the boat, the Colonel exploded—'Gentlemen!'—and spat in the loch.

'That's like him,' said Colin smoothly.

Ewan threw him a glance. Mary was in the out-kitchen cleaning the fish. He heard the sounds she was making. Colin's smoothness! Ewan laughed.

187

He explained how the real joke of the thing was that this Duffy fellow was of no use to them. Colin wanted to know how that could be.

'The farm servants who work on the big farms have a Union. The crofters, of course, haven't: they are employers.'

'Employers of what?'

'Themselves! The farm servant is supposed to say, If we encourage the small-holder we'll merely lower our own standard of living and wages. If a small-holder will live in destitution, then a farm servant will be expected to do the same, for we are all in the same line of business.'

'Is that it? And what was that one coming up here for then?'

'To get first-hand knowledge—and to offer advice.'

'Well, now,' said Colin.

Ewan laughed, twisting in his chair.

Mary came in and Ewan threw her a quick glance. But she did not meet his eyes. She wore a jumper of some silken material with a bright 'art' design, which he had never seen before. It threw up her fresh skin and dusky hair in a striking way. Her eyelashes swept her eyes as she became aware of his glance steadying; then, the lashes lifting, she looked at him a moment. Stormy, shy, lovely eyes, they gleamed and passed. But that look with its half-veiled smile, its indescribable glimmer of something welling up and dying in a faint flush, affected him profoundly; so that he swooped on Colin, who had asked:

'And what do you think about it yourself?'

'About what?'

' About the raiders at Ardbeg.'

' Oh. The raid is illegal. To the sheep-farmer, it's a matter of theft. To the crofters, a matter of life.' His mouth closed.

' Tell me this,' said Colin, after a moment. ' Have you ever done anything to help them ? '

' No.'

' Why, now ? '

' What could I do ? '

Colin glanced at him. Ewan's smile held a waiting satire.

' Oh I don't know. I merely thought that with your education maybe you could write a letter for them or something.'

' Write a letter ? ' Ewan's restraint gleamed.

' Well ? '

Ewan flashed him a look. ' And in any case,' he said, ' there's no fight left in us—no *real* fight. We have so recently won the British Empire.'

' I see,' said Colin.

' Donald MacCrimmon,' pursued Ewan, ' was telling me about an argument they had at the hotel the other day over getting married. The conclusion they came to was that a man could hardly ask any decent woman to share his lot nowadays unless he had a thousand a year—with prospects.'

' I've heard them at that,' said Colin.

' They had been watching Hector McGruther cutting his hay. It came out that he was getting married and bringing his wife there, where his father and mother are also. The remarks were good! When John McAlpine happened along they appealed to him, and he said in his slow way, " Indeed he

189

won't be so badly off, because the old people are both independent, getting the Old Age Pension." . . . It was a sunny day, and one woman gushed, " All the same, I do think there's something idyllic in it! " The Colonel, who apparently did not think much of the lady, growled " Cattle! " And there's something in what the Colonel said.'

Colin turned slowly and looked at him, but Ewan was concentrating his amused reflections on the fire.

' I think Hector and Hughina will pull well enough there,' observed Colin.

' Oh, no doubt,' smiled Ewan. ' All the same . . . I don't think I would like to tackle it—if I was Hector.' And his smile held artificially. Then he stretched himself with clever laziness and grinned at Colin. ' You're surely full of politics to-night,' he probed.

' I'm full of nothing,' said Colin.

Ewan got abruptly to his feet. ' Come on, let us have a tune.'

' Och— '

' Come on! '

Colin got up. Ewan followed him. As he was passing out of the kitchen his body hung an instant in desperate hesitation, then went on without looking back. While Colin stumbled into the parlour for his pipes, Ewan stepped outside and gazed rigid on the night.

Nor when the music was over would he go into the house again.

Colin stood looking after him until he vanished. Usually he caught the drift of Ewan's mind, but all along to-night he had been uncertain.

As he entered the kitchen, he saw Mary lighting her candle at the fire.

' You're for bed early surely,' he said, looking suspiciously at her.

' It's not so early,' she observed evenly.

He could not see her face. It seemed as though there were two of them at it!

He sat down for a final draw at his pipe. He sat very still and thought over what Ewan had not said to him.

After a time he got to his feet, his face firm and set. He stood gazing at the blind window. Then he turned inconsequently and looked at the clock, his eyebrows wrinkling, his lips puckering a toneless tune, which gradually passed on a whistled under-breath into the tune that Ewan had played so queerly.

3

The following day Ewan, the gillie, was told on reporting at the hotel that he was not required. Humour flashed in his face as he returned by the steep path above his home. His had all the exciting uncertainties of a luxury trade in a restricted season. To compensate for which, the profits were large! For if he wasn't exactly saving a penny, still there was the penny to spend.

And, anyway, a day off meant a day about the sea. Coming down on a sparkling morning upon a glittering sea was a luxury in itself. It lightened the spirit and banished time. The body came into freedom.

About the beach he moved in quiet leisure, handling odds and ends of gear with an easy strength,

191

his lips whistling a few notes softly, then closing of their own will to let the throat carry the melody in an inner humming, again to pass the melody to the lips as the hands finished and the eyes appraised the completed act. When he lifted his head, there was the sea, glittering and uncoiling with an aimlessness that was entrancing. What a perfect command of leisure the sea had! Men wondered what they would do if they had nothing to do. And here the inanimate sea, with nothing to do for all eternity, doing it with a charm that varied eternally, that was forever fresh and vivid and full of flashing colour . . . and at moments positively suave in its brimming courtesy.

Annabel appeared upon the rock and gave him a wave. He laughed; and when she mocked him, the stone he threw hit the rock-face and bounded back through the air in a high singing curve. Whereafter, whistling an intricate tune rapidly, he boarded his boat and pushed off.

As he drew away from the spit, Annabel came round the base of the rock—and stopped, disappointed. He waved airily. Her thin body twisted ludicrously as it threw a pebble that didn't even reach the water. But by the way she hurried back, she might have had a golden moment.

Upon the sea, the ease of his mind was still haunted by Colin's question as to what he was doing for the Ardbeg men. It had haunted him through the night, just as though it had never interfered with his sleep before!

It's not that he could do nothing for them. That was certain; for he could hardly persuade them to give in; and if he egged them on to fight then he was merely egging *them* on to prison. This was their affair. And it could be his affair also only if he with other men was prepared for some form of 'direct action.' Was he? Were they? The question had only to be asked for mockery to answer.

And yet for one good old flare-up, not for any Prince Charlie or other anthropomorphic conception, but for their own land and sea! His mind flashed across the 'interests' from factors and ground agents to the local press, from political agents who boasted that the only things the Highlands exported were men and women to the typical 'correspondent' who proved in himself that the only thing they exported was brains!

Yes, there might be some satisfaction in having a smash-up. Besides, something would be bound to come out of it. For wherever the spirit is alive, the spirit flowers—in the body.

This preoccupation with the spirit! Very amusing. In a way a sort of self-indulgence in a perverted flattery. As if his spirit was the spirit of race and land! But then probably it was, for after all wasn't it underground and defeated?

And who anyhow could believe that a spirit should move anybody? And *such* a spirit! As if it were as important as any of the minor parts in the real human drama, not to mention major parts—like love and death and murder and money and success. Particularly success!

'Och, never mind them!' As he rowed past the fatal spit on the Black Rock, with its memory of that dreadful night when his father had been drowned, there came like a blasphemy on his mind, '*I should put up a tablet there!* '

The sea-sparkle darkened a moment. He lay over his oars, breathing through his teeth. The spit darkened. The water licked about it. As his thought held him, the spit slid out of focus and wavered and deepened—to an opening. He could not break the stare. He felt himself being drawn to the brink of revelation. The still sea water was beginning to lick like dark flames. The flame-waves curved upward, they increased in size and violence, they spouted and broke, flinging far curtains, while the rock beneath, like the back of a maddened beast, heaved tumultuously, water scudding over it in clash and welter of spume. . . . The sea, the raging, maddened sea . . . and now upon it, so that the eyes were held in horror, a small boat, with one struggling figure, tossed and driven towards that black opening. As boat and figure were swallowed up, the mist passed from Ewan's eyes and he broke away in violent agitation, his skin shivering with cold, his stomach sick with excitement. He pulled fiercely. His mind rushing out to grasp reality landed on the kiss he had given Mary on the dark road. And the kiss, like that dark picture, was dark and fatal, a final act of lonely betrayal.

A moment or two, and he changed the fierce rowing into a strong, steady pull, so that any watching eyes might be deceived.

Then a smile formed. Had he, for the first time, got a touch of second sight ? . . . Or was it merely the subconscious reconstructing what had already happened ? He looked about the rock-crests to see if he could spot anyone. He didn't often indulge in physical outbursts! Then he wiped his forehead. His hands were trembling and his face was deathly pale.

Slowly he pulled along, letting the blue and silver and the quiet sea's rhythm heal his agitation, so that presently he knew he had been merely indulging in a daydream. Often enough he slid into daydream. He had to face and remember the tragedy of the Black Rock, were it only to keep his mind and the sea healthy and clean. Until at last indeed an intimacy had grown out of it—which, for the first time, had betrayed him, as though the daydream had taken the one step further into the horrible realm of second-sight.

It hadn't, of course. But still . . . and he smiled speculatively and started fishing again. As his hand worked up and down, he looked abroad upon the face of the sea and got a new vision of its immensity, upon which he was cast, which his spirit rose to counter and to receive, until loneliness that might have been terrifying became a quiet strength, at the heart of which was peace.

Then in the evening he decided to go to the hotel, for it was as well to find out if possible what was in the wind for to-morrow.

' If you see Jean, ask her why she's never coming down,' his mother called to him.

' All right,' he answered.

But there was no hurry. So he took the road up the burn side to the stone bridge, where he ran into Ronnie McAndrew, now a fourth year's English Honours student in Glasgow.

Ronnie had always appeared a trifle shy of Ewan. There was a trace of it still in the sensitiveness that showed through an effort at assurance. He rarely came down the glen. Ewan had not seen him for many months, and now suddenly rather liked him. This came as a slight revelation to Ewan himself as showing how far he had travelled his own road. There seemed to be no longer that odd twist of emotion arising out of involuntary comparisons. Ronnie was expecting some friends, he said, by car.

' In that case, why not come up above ? '

Ronnie hesitated a moment. ' All right,' he said. They began walking up the steep road.

' Busy at home ? '

' Oh, giving my father a hand.'

' Stalking this year ? '

' I believe I am,' said Ronnie, after a moment. ' I'll probably go out with Mr. Harold.'

' Mr. Harold ? '

' Oh, he's Mr. Denver's son,' explained Ronnie quickly.

' I see.' Ewan caught the tone. Ronnie would not like going stalking with anybody. But if he had to go, then it would be rather fun going with the proprietor's young son. Not that Ronnie would mention even ' Mr. Harold ' abroad. Ewan rather liked his delicate evasiveness. Besides, there was just this one little extra note in it: when Ronnie was fifteen and Ewan twenty, Ewan must have appeared rather a terrible fellow to him; now . . . well, Ronnie had his new standards, and Ewan the gillie, sinking back into the soil, was something to feel uncomfortable about, to shrink from. Even Ronnie's clothes

196

were smartly cut. Ewan understood all this exquisitely.

Yet when he parted from Ronnie, who for some reason seemed anxious to avoid the hotel and walked hurriedly on towards the post office, his humour had grown the least trifle warped, and he had to make a slight effort to keep it in check.

Alastair bàn helped him. He had that day driven the Colonel and Clare almost to Cape Wrath. Near home the old Ford had developed a cough, and he was now busy with the magneto. 'Your one,' said Alastair bàn, 'seemed to enjoy the trip all right.'

'Did she?'

'She did that. And old Bubblyjock gabbled away in great form. She knows exactly how to take him. She's good at it. It's in her all right.'

'You seem impressed.'

'Don't mention it. She didn't forget you anyway.'

'Oh. She was confidential?'

'She was.'

'Don't mention it,' waited Ewan.

'I won't. Hold that—like that,' ordered Alastair bàn. 'She put her arm round my shoulder. She bit my ear. Then I woke up.'

'Too shy even in your dreams.'

'Right first go,' said Alastair bàn. 'No, but honestly, I heard her ask, "How does a gillie get paid when he's not actually out fishing with one?" That was you.'

'How thoughtful of her!'

'Won't you get a whacker of a tip to-morrow!' chuckled Alastair.

They talked and worked until the light began to fail

within the garage. As Ewan came to the door he saw his sister Jean leave the back premises. At once he drew up and secretly watched her reach the road and turn down to the bridge. If she had been going home she would simply have crossed the road and taken the short cut along the top. Alastair bàn came forward wiping his hands.

' Let's go in and have a glass of beer before you go. As a matter of fact, your lady remembered me to-day.'

Ewan smiled. ' Poaching! Well I'm hanged! And then you hold your offer—until it's too late.' Against Alastair bàn's entreaties, Ewan walked off laughing. He had helped him too long as it was, he said.

He reached the bridge. There was no sign of Jean. The home road was vacant. So she had gone up the glen ! He filled his pipe and started off after her.

There was a strained speculative expression on his face. His eyes were quick and watchful. His pipe went out in no time and he put it in his pocket. Then he put it back in his mouth again but did not light it. Now and then he carried it in his hand as if he were listening intently. Coming to a bend in the road, he saw her ahead walking alone. He waited until she was out of sight, then went on. From the next bend, however, he could not see her and after he had walked about a mile he knew that she must have given him the slip by going into the trees. At that he pulled up. She would have watched him going past, walking quickly, as if he were anxious. He screwed the mouthpiece out of his pipe and blew through it violently. ' Blast it! ' he thought, feeling self-conscious about the whole thing. ' What the devil is she up to?' He walked on slowly a few yards, lit his pipe, then suddenly turned and began coming back.

The dusk was falling now, but in off the road he saw by an odd chance her legs to the knees. It was a mute and extraordinary sight. His heart began to beat heavily. His instinct was not to look at them, to look away, to go on. As he came abreast, however, he stopped.

'Is that you, Jean?'

There was no answer, no movement.

He brushed his way in and rounding a low-spreading thicket confronted her. She was standing quite still and her pale face met his.

'What are you doing here?' he asked. His voice was thick and nervous.

'Nothing,' she said moodily, and slowly turned her face away.

He took a step nearer

'Look here, Jean, is there anything wrong with you?'

'No,' she said. Then she added, 'Leave me alone.'

He saw that his coming distressed her.

'Mother is wondering why you never come down.' He tried to speak evenly.

Her moodiness looked as if it might break, as if his presence tortured her. 'I'll be down soon. I'm just taking a walk.'

He turned away, saying 'All right,' in as cheerful a tone as he could. He even paused to light his pipe before turning down the road. But immediately he had gone out of sight, he went into hiding.

About half an hour later Jean came down alone.

She walked slowly as if she were worn out and her face in the gloom was set in a misery so profound that it was vacant.

When she had passed, Ewan sat up, his mouth slightly open, his face drawn and staring. Then he got nimbly to his feet and went after her. He saw her go up the road from the bridge to the hotel. After hesitating a moment, he followed.

Over against the hotel door, he caught the Colonel's glowing cigar. Someone was with him. He did not look, lest it be Clare. Leaving the road, he went along the valley crest, but not down to his own home. His body disappeared to the right and got swallowed up by the cliff-heads.

3

That greenness of the mountains where Clare had expected to find heather . . . sudden glimpses of the sea caught in winding inlets, flashes of colour drawing the eye to the blue unknown . . . between mountain and sea, the land in myriad shape, fantastic, ancient, grey, brooding in peat black, jewelled in loch blue, unexpected in goblin green, dreaming in brown . . . not lonely but withdrawn . . . the wind passing over it, touching it . . . touching it. A day of escape . . . more than escape—penetration. . . .

Before her reflective eyes, Ewan passed going towards the cliff-heads. He faded behind her uncle's cigar smoke. Bidding her uncle a pleasant good-night, she turned from the hotel doorway and went up to her bedroom, where, however, she could not reconcile herself to the day's end.

Even this trick of the wind's dropping in the evening and leaving the world so still that one involuntarily listened for—one knew not what, and had frighted sensations of something at once imminent and far, left one restless and vaguely craving. If one listened too closely the dark laughter of the hills came down through the hollow of the mind, pursuing and mocking, with a black strength.

Turning from the window, she regarded her reflection in the glass without thinking about it. Presently she paused before the wardrobe, took out her warm travelling coat and, after considering it a moment, put it on. She would see McAlpine and go for a short stroll.

There was the relief of meeting no one in the lounge, and, deciding she would see McAlpine when she came back, she slipped quietly out. This business of escaping! She smiled doubtfully.

But she did not take the road down to the stone bridge; instead, she turned to her right round the garage in the direction of the post office. A quarter of a mile farther on, she entered a cart track. This track, irregularly bounded by grey croft dykes, faded out in a grassy path which zigzagged steeply to the sands of Cladach whereon slow waves creamed in the finest weather. Her desire became clear. She would go right down to the very sea-edge.

In the last of the evening the sands held a strange fascination. Dead pale they spread below her, the sea weaving upon them its broidery of arabesque with a slow, long, hissing caress, creating and blotting out and creating, as if all the time its intense heart lay coiled like a sea-serpent in deepest ocean, while its children crept forth to play in the only way they knew with their forbidden mother, the earth.

Clare walked on the sand, which was quite firm, and stood for a time watching the mesmeric game. Then lifting her eyes, she looked about her and had an involuntary vision of herself as an infinitely lonely figure on a remote shore. . . . To her left were low dark rocks. She would go there and sit for a little. As she approached, a figure suddenly uprose, the figure of a man . . . of her gillie, Ewan Macleod.

Clare stopped short, her heart thudding. He had risen out of the low weeded rocks, his face to the sea, like an apparition. Then she went over to him.

' Is it you, Ewan ? '

He did not speak.

' I'm glad I've seen you. About to-morrow—it will be all right ? '

' Yes.'

The unexpectedness of the encounter did not lose in excitement by what she saw. He had no longer the air of a gillie. His face seemed grey-dark as graven rock. She looked over her shoulder at the sea and at once became aware of his eyes. Before discomfort could get the better of her, she met his look, her brows slightly arched, ' Thanks,' faintly smiling.

His eyes simply lifted off her face.

There was silence for several seconds. It cost her a real effort to say, ' We had such a lovely run to-day,' and even the words were trivial. She was looking again at the sea.

Her woman's intuition knew all at once that he was considering her. She felt it in a slight burning all over her body. Something forceful and black, and, perhaps, brutal.

She resented this, particularly resented its getting the better of her.

' Well, I think I will go up.' But her tongue added, ' Are you coming ? '

Once he gripped her elbow as she stumbled going up the steep zigzag. His fingers were so strong that they quivered nervously.

In his voice, when she got him to answer, she detected a restrained excitement. His words slid out on a breath that stopped.

On top of the declivity, they paused a moment. She was breathing heavily.

' I go this way,' he said. ' Good-night.' And touching his cap, he immediately walked off, as though contact had to be broken.

Really! she thought, going on a few paces to a cairn of stones on which she sat down, feeling weak, as if an immense virtue had been drained out of her.

Really this was—too amusing. She tried to give her body comfort, her lips wide for air. Her body was so warm. Good heavens! The whole thing was so—coming all at once—humiliating. Really she.... But a thought was forcing its way in as to what would happen—what might happen . . . she pulled her coat open at the neck . . . the next time.

4

Ewan, who had thrown himself down farther along the rocks, was thinking the same thing. The agitation in his body made his breath quick in his teeth.

He plucked grass in slow iron fistfuls. The excitement increased and his flesh grew warm and tremulous. A dark lust of life swam behind his eyes.

In this lust was an underswirl of triumph, so that his wide-open look did not waver but stared steadily, letting realisation seep about the inner retina, letting the full possibility rise up and flood hotly the mind.

She was fair and beautiful. She was so fair and beautiful that she was a cold pillar. She was distinct from him, untouchable, alien as a statue in a garden of evening dews. And she had come to life beside him, her flesh flushing warm, and looked at him— or not looked at him. He had caught the hidden pause in her thought.

The possibility faintly distorted his face with a power out of which the eyes gleamed. The distortion held like a smile, lingering and relentless, as if his recent meditations were behind it and the enigma of his sister, Jean, and the Black Rock he had gazed at.

Slowly he began to throw the fistfuls of grass from him and the smile on his face spread, the eyes holding. The smile spread to a silent satyr laugh and the eyes snapped. He sat up and looked about him, breath held and listening.

He got to his feet and started for home.

But in the kitchen with his mother he felt trapped. An inner restlessness increased, as if there was a wild and reckless fire in his blood. His mother watched him staring over his open book into the fire.

' What are you thinking of, Ewan ? '

' Oh, nothing!' he said, his body breaking instantly. A slight colour came to his face of impatience or surprise.

When his mother bowed her head to her knitting again, he looked at her with a cold appraising glimmer. He knew what she would like to say, to do, and his spirit revolted at the mere manner of it.

'Did you see Jean?' she asked.

'Yes,' he answered.

'Where did you see her?'

'Up by the hotel.' The vision came back of his sister's legs beneath the trees. His restlessness became intolerable, and he had to get up. He went towards the back door.

'What are you wanting?' she asked, almost with dismay.

'It's all right,' he said coldly and went out.

A convulsion of feeling gripped him as he stood by the back door. Muttering, he ground his teeth. He did not know what was wrong with him.

He walked away as if by action he could burst the strands about him. His spirit grew harsh and ruthless but with no more direction than a curse.

'This is what it's come to!' he said. That last night in his Edinburgh room slid before him. He saw Lothian's face. He thought of his own attitude before all their faces. His spirit writhed. 'O God!' it laughed.

He threw himself down and pressed his face into the grass, pressed it until his mind flattened and emptied, then slowly he turned over, sat up, and gazed at the sea.

The dream is for failure, the simple life an escape for the weak spirit, the past a delusion and its brave ways a snare. Behold the marsh lights leading the sensitive spirit through darkness to tragedy!

It was hardly worth a laugh—with tragedy ahead. Hardly. Ewan's face grew very still. His life was like something that a dark blade severed, the future, on its hither side, caught in its own fatality. It was something at least to be committed to that! With no going back. Not now.

The hopeless challenge caught the pride of stone. Before him the sea glimmered in the night. He could just see the Black Rock, low to the water, crouching. There came upon him his vision of the figure in the boat being driven through the leaping flame-like waves to the fatal opening and engulfed. There had always been something about that figure disturbingly familiar. Now in a moment he realised who the figure was.

Incredulity crept over him in a chill shudder. The world drained, leaving it thin and fine and cold. He got to his feet like one who has witnessed a dreadful entertainment and with a white look over his shoulder passes on.

The figure had been his own.

As he went on his spirit was uplifted with the incredulity which is so often but the veil of belief. The tragic end being known, he was freed! His head rose, his mind flickering in the chill gaiety. Within this fateful pattern he could quest hither and thither at liberty. . . . Clare Marlowe entered his mind again and possessed it. Far behind her stood Colonel Hicks. Ewan hung on his steps. He was freed now from all obligation—except the pagan need to right the balance, to satisfy the manhood that had been repressed—before he passed out. He stood thinking of Clare Marlowe, watching her image as it approached.

INTERLUDE

THE concert was a great success.

The local doctor, in dinner jacket, introduced the chairman, Mr. Denver, whose residence amongst them was of such great benefit to the community. He also referred happily to Mr. Denver's son, Mr. Harold Denver, whom the committee had had the signal courage to approach for a song. Finally he alluded in felicitous terms to the honour of the talk which they were to have from one whom he would dare to call the Grand Lady of Scottish Literature. In face of such a distinguished programme, clearly our Highland initiative was not waning.

Mr. Denver, rising through the applause, was pleased (a little more than very, a little less than vury) to preside on such an interesting occasion. The Highlander was known all the world over, and he didn't mind boasting right now that if not his main ancestral stream then certainly one of its not unimportant tributaries had had the tinge of the peat and the fragrance of the heather. He was bound to admit that some of his friends said the tributary was so far back that it was lost in the mists of uncertainty. But he had replied to that by saying that such a tributary would be lost in mists in any case—Scotch mists! (Laughter.) That was the right spirit, wasn't it? And, anyhow, if the spirit was right it could always come through a good lot of

water. (Loud laughter.) But it was his business
not to stand between them and their enjoyment. He
would therefore call on number one on the programme—Bagpipe Selections by Mr. Charles Macdonald.

Enter (left) Mr. Charles Macdonald in full piper's
regalia and with silver-mounted pipes playing the
' Cowal Gathering.' Down the platform, slow-marching . . . and up the platform towards Mr. Denver
and doctor. Mr. Denver's eyes and ears are shocked
into amazed concentration at extraordinary volume
of sound; short-cropped grey hair upstands as in
amazed concentration also; he edges back in chair
as piper approaches and slow-turns near his knees.
Subtle discomfort shows on sensitive faces in audience
concentrated on Mr. Denver's face.

Gathering them down the glens went the pipes . . .
gathering them; swinging down the glens, in sunlight and wind, in darkness and small rain . . . the
flick of the tartan about the knees of a man turning
to look back . . . down the glens, gathering them,
went the pipes. . . .

Mr. Denver looks at the roof. All eyes see Mr.
Denver look apprehensively at the roof, follow Mr.
Denver from the roof to the eyes of his friends in the
front row; discreet, smile-suppressed eyes of Mr.
Denver's friends appreciating with perfect taste the
joke of the invasion of Mr. Denver's ears and knees.
The doctor, also appreciating, leans to Mr. Denver
and whispers. Both nod and come erect, looking
at Mr. Charles Macdonald playing the ' Cowal
Gathering.'

With the polite light of their mutual smile still in

their eyes, Mr. Denver leans to doctor who holds sideways a ready ear. Lips break away from ear and doctor looks at drones, turns to Mr. Denver, shakes his head negatively. Mr. Denver nods, smilingly accepting doctor's ignorance of that which appertains to drones.

Audience follows with sensitive interest the discreet performance of Mr. Denver and doctor; regards Mr. Charles Macdonald, slow-marching in full piper's regalia, with mixed feelings, throwing up here and there a twist in facial sensitivity indicative of inexpressible wrongness in inexplicable ways. The 'Cowal Gathering' dies, having gathered no phantoms. (Applause.)

'The next item on the programme is a duet entitled "Life's Dream is O'er," by the Misses Macdonald.' Enter (right) the two Misses Macdonald in white schoolgirl frocks and golden corkscrew curls, followed by old schoolmistress in black. Both advance in proper formation to front left of accompanist's chair, halt, nod, and remain unmoving, eyes front. Schoolmistress half-turns on prearranged signal, stoops rhythmically until aged ivory is reached and tinkles in response. Sweet childish voices upraised in approximate harmony, solemn, girl-angel voices, pure. Life's dream is o'er. Audience, with an eye for chairman's face, notes the complacent smile of elderliness towards sweetly pretty children. Curls lie over each shoulder, gold-gleaming in perfection's corkscrew; faces waxen-pure and solemn; mouths with small white teeth round-opening and uplifted. Life's dream is o'er. (Applause.)

Applauding, the chairman uprises. ' At the same

time I shouldn't mind laying a bet that life's dream isn't exactly all over for them (laughter)—not with these curls! ' (Renewed laughter.)

' We are now to have some Violin Selections from Mr. Thomas Urquhart.'

Mr. Thomas Urquhart is small, wizened, hairy, and at the schoolmistress's tinkling impact, he proceeds to bite the gut of the Laird of Drumblair into three-inch lengths and, coming from a little north of the East Neuk, hauds at it conscientiously until the operation is complete. This classic accounted for, Mr. Urquhart changes into the ' Deil among the Tailors,' snuggles over the varnish, when the three inches contrive to knock sparks out of the brimstone. ' Hooch! ' By those of a certain age, looking forward to Mr. Urquhart and his dance fiddle at a later hour, Mr. Denver is momentarily forgotten. Tirrie-um, tirrie-um, tirrie-ow, tirrie-iddle. . . .

The admirable chairman beams upon applause. ' We have a long programme and I understand you will have an opportunity later—at the dance. . . . And now we are going to have Mr. Norman Shaw in that famous song—" The McGregors' Gathering." ' '

Mr. Shaw, of medium height, is carefully dressed in navy blue suit, gold watch chain, and small military moustache. He holds pendant from gold chain in left hand and, small-round-eyed, fat-cheeked, looks over heads of audience during introduction. Coughs, kuhum, as introduction ceases, and in a slightly husky tenor uplifts voice of unexpectedly small volume considering tightness of waistcoat under gold chain whence voice seems to be upward pressed. We are landless, landless, landless, Gregalach—

landless, landless, la-a-a-andless. It is a polite voice.
Mr. Shaw, who learnt the drapery business in the
south, can always be depended upon to shed his
acquired hielant manners. Mr. Denver decorously
watches him, legs crossed. The audience watches
him with anything but hidden fear. The small boys
in the back rows of the back seats stoop out of sight
and open their yawing mouths at each other to
bursting point, presumably in emulation of the effort
made by Mr. Shaw, which effort at its widest
succeeds in carrying the small moustache upon it
with the winged lightness of a black butterfly. Then
Mr. Shaw reaches to the leaves in the forest by
pressing forward and upward on his toes, and hangs
there, assuring whom it concerns that Mr. McGregor,
despite them, shall flourish for ever.

The small boys with the choked mouths at last
find relief, and Mr. Shaw from behind the stage door
(left) eases his collar with complacency.

A member of committee, issuing left, whispers to
doctor, who whispers to Mr. Denver, who nods and
arises.

' We regret that the little sketch, " English as she
is spoke," will have to be postponed to the second
half. Perhaps the accent got lost in the mist! . . .
And now— ' He smiles, picking out with his programme Mr. Harold Denver from the front row.

In dinner jacket and white front Mr. Harold Denver lightly leaps on to platform, half turns in a flash
of blue eyes, and strides to piano. The piano backs
away before him, growing dingy, visibly cowering.
Mr. Harold Denver athletically connects with
strangle-hold and swings it half-round towards

audience. Piano shakes to its foundation, emitting inner plaintive thrummings. Then rubbing his palms and throwing a sudden flash of smiling teeth at his audience, Mr. Harold Denver sits down and hits the aged ivory a right and left in quick succession. The piano jumps. The audience jumps. The electric current is linked up. The yellow ivories are hit and rattled in a manner without precedent in their half century. And suddenly is let loose in the hall the resonant voice of a whole college crowd:

> I wanta be
> I wanta be
> I wanta be down home in Dixie. . . .

Smiling head beckons the college crowd. They charge. Attaboy! Smash—bash—wallop! Come on you chaps! The hall rocks. Smiling head turns to audience through the scrum; challenging blue eyes flash in clear-cut face; fair hair back-brushed threatens invasion of chiselled forehead. Where the old. . . . What you waiting for? Come on you! Smash—bash—wallop. I wanta be—yes—I wanta be—ho—I wanta be down home in Dixie. . . . Steady you chaps! . . . where the hens are dog-gone glad to lay scrambled eggs in new-mown hay. . . .

Spellbound faces of breathless audience carried by storm, by dinner jacket and white front and flashing commanding face, by yells of whole corporate body of dinner jackets and white fronts and flashing commanding faces carrying on with blood and vim. What you sticking in the mud for? This is life! Here is life! Bang—smash—wallop! I wanta be. . .

So that whirlwind Mr. Harold Denver has resumed his seat in the front row before audience has sucked its forgotten wind. Thereupon, from the three-and-sixpennies—clappings and suppressed laughter; from the two-and-fourpennies—clappings, laughter and sporadic outbursts of 'Encore'; while the small boys fill their mouths with thumb and forefinger and whistle on a thousand sheep-dogs. Overwhelming triumph of Mr. Harold Denver.

Mr. Denver, from the chair, smiles, cheeks gathering unusual tinge. Doctor turns to Mr. Denver, bespeaks him, and sways back in his mirth. Splendid!

Mr. Denver arises. Mr. Denver waits. At last Mr. Denver holds up his programme. But the applause continues. The sheep-dogs are still upon the hills a thousand strong. But with smiling patience and shaking an admonishing head upon the front row, Mr. Denver waits. Already has he demurred to encores. Not now for his own son. Good-humouredly the trial of strength continues. Then Mr. Denver pleasantly has his way. 'I was advised that we must not have any encores in the first half. There's a second half! And now we proceed to the next item. A song—I regret that I have no Gaelic—*as yet* (cheers)—I shall just call it a song, by Miss Martha McRae.'

The last rumble in the audience dies, the bright faces withdraw and from the cover of their shells regard with shrinking the appearance of Miss Martha McRae preceded by schoolmistress carrying small book of music. Here and there a sardonic face and veiled eyes; a mouth-twist in a back seat. *Dhè!* (*God!*)

A small limp has Miss Martha McRae and her body is under-sized. Her eyes shine darkly in her face which is smooth and pale. Quietly she stands until the schoolmistress stoops, then quietly she sings a Gaelic song, her voice threading pitifully sweet the awful stilled spaces of the hall.

Small voice, thinly sweet, going on smoothly, crooningly, telling in the Gaelic its old story. Going on, always the same, telling its old story, on and on, smoothly, rising and falling, changelessly. Her face in its smooth twenties, her large soft eyes, her under-sized body, standing there, Martha, the gentle kind one, singing her endless Gaelic song with its old sadness—*Dhè!*

Out of shell corners eyes steal glances at Mr. Denver, who sits with attentive interest, faint-smiling. The doctor faint-smiling also, but in a certain way.

She starts on the sixth verse. *Thighearna!* She will sing the whole damn twelve verses that are in it. She has sung them before (when they were short enough with everyone joining in the refrain). . . . She hasn't the sense in her to—choke it.

She starts on the seventh verse.

A faint squirming sound rises from out of the floor. Someone should have told her. Trotting that out now—showing . . . standing there, singing like that . . . after what went before. *Dhiabhuil!*

But at the end of the seventh verse she gives her little bow and smiles—and limps—followed by schoolmistress. Immediate outpouring of applause, with faces gathering laughter of relief.

Mr. Denver, applauding with backs of right fingers on left palm, arises. If he was in the dark as to the actual words, he had a feeling that what lay behind the words struck an answering chord. O admirable Mr. Denver, receiving ready response! 'And we are now to have a humorous recitation by Mr. Duncan Morrison.'

Enter Mr. Duncan Morrison quietly, in kilt, smiling. Eet wass six or five years ago when I wass courting Peeg Annie that it happened. I wass in the kitchen with Peeg Annie because her father and her mother wass bose gone to a prayer-meeting. Ones will be laffing at me because they will be sinking I am speaking the English aaful proken, but Peeg Annie was not troubled wis me after a leetle time for giving her too much speaking at all. It's not the speaking I would be giving to Peeg Annie after a leetle. She had yellow hair on her. It wass as yellow as the barley that they will be making the speerit out of in the bothies long ago at one time. And maybe it wass as yellow as the barley that they will be after making the speerit out of in the bothies to-day away in that queer countries where they will be that dry whateffer. . . .

Mr. Denver sees the point. Splendid! He listens with expectancy, following the reciter as he climbs aloft to the rafters when Peeg Annie's father too suddenly returns from the prayer-meeting. As the county press reported: 'It was particularly gratifying to note that some of the distinguished visitors present followed Mr. Morrison's inimitable humour, so deftly interpretive of many Highland characteristics, with obvious appreciation. As an interpreter of the humble scene touched with the true pathos and sublime we have always maintained that Mr.

217

Morrison is an artist, and judging by the hearty applause accorded his performance, we are not alone in that opinion.'

' And now we are to be favoured with a song from Miss Mary McKinnon, entitled " Horo Mhairi dhubh "—(" how's that ? " and applause)—" Turn ye to me." '

Enter Miss Mary McKinnon, walking with un-hurried grace. Stormy dark lashes look over front row, over all heads. Dark prideful beauty trying not to be conscious of countrified self on platform before front row. Head up; delicate texture of smooth throat exhibits involuntary swallowing. Dark lashes on stormy eyes, waiting, while antique schoolmistress introductorily caresses battered ivory.

Then opens the red-lipped mouth of Miss Mairi McKinnon and a voice of such sudden beauty issues therefrom that Mr. Denver is seen visibly to be arrested. . . .

> ' *Cold is the storm-wind that ruffles his breast,*
> *Warm are the downy plumes lining his nest;*
> *Cold blows the tempest there, dark is the snowy air,*
> *Horo Mhairi dhubh, turn ye to me.*' . . .

Unhurriedly she sings, and the rhythm in her voice is the slow rhythm of seas on western shores; the swell of the wave, its fullness of suspense, its fall . . . Horo Mhairi dhubh . . . gliding downward to despair.

The untutored throat of Miss Mairi McKinnon palpitates with the surge of her song, golden-rich; stormy eyes flash like stormy seas . . . like stormy seas, O Mhairi McKinnon, who art Mairi dhubh of the song and thy voice thy lover's voice calling Turn ye to me. Turn ye to me, horo Mhairi dhubh. . . . And she sings for him in the rhythm of the dark wave, rising to surcharged crests of longing, slipping backward to spent valleys of sorrow, rising and falling, O song, in the gold-grey shell of their despair. Mr. Denver is forgotten and Mr. Denver forgets.

Mr. Denver arises, hesitates, cannot find what to say, yet, having hesitated, must say; reaches for his chairman's smile, nods, 'Very nice too!'

Not so admirable, O chairman. Glittering from the cold crest of the cold shudder of the wave of Mairi's song, eyes are measuring you. The jealous eyes of the hidden ones of the closed lips.

'And now we are going to finish the first part of our programme with an address on Our Highland Heritage from—' Front seat applause very properly drowns the unnecessary introduction and Mr. Denver, also applauding, resumes his seat beside applauding doctor.

A fur coat is unsheathed in the front row, and gallantly assisted by front-row gentleman up the three platform steps arrives before them an old lady with evening-bare throat and chest upon which rises and falls a star of jewelled gold. (Applause, with eyes regarding the phenomenon of aged bare chest.)

What a pleasure it is to stand on a real Highland platform and speak to real Highland people! In these days we are all in such a dreadful hurry that we never seem to have time to pause and look around us and do a little stock-taking. The spirit of unrest is loose amongst us. Our minds are upset and are too often feverishly excited pursuing vain things. All the values of life are being measured against money. And so we hurry on and hurry on and hurry on. How fine it is, then, with what a sense of repose, of becoming, as the poet says, captain of one's soul once more, does one come back to the glorious age that is Ardnacloich! It is such a glorious thought that one can only treat of it a little seriously. For here money is not everything. Not that money of course isn't a great deal! Money in the big sense represents the wheels of industry, and it is to the great captains of industry manipulating those wheels that we owe the running of civilisation itself. Without them, without their Herculean labours, the world would rapidly revert to a state of barbarism. To them we owe our World Heritage. These men are the Caesars and to them must be rendered the things that are theirs. But because of the divine justice which has illuminated the world since the days of the old imperial Caesars of Rome, we have now happily reached that stage where our modern Caesars of Finance can be at once Caesar and humble worshipper of the True Being. It is truly a blessed consummation and one which has not made His sacrifice a vain one. But it is the place in this World Heritage of our Highland Heritage of which one would speak particularly to-night, for that place has been—and one would venture to say still is—a great one. No domain of world-thought or world-action but has been signally affected by our Highland contribution. Take, first, the arts. Take music. It is recognised the world over that the folk-music of the Highlands is the finest, the most distinctive, the world has ever

.known. We have had examples to-night. It would be invidious to pick one, but take, let us say, ' Horo Mhairi dhubh.' What depth of human emotion is in that melody! You see the sea, and the white sea-gulls gliding so realistically. A wonderful picture that touches the strings of the heart. A beautiful song. One feels it. It gets there—in a way that many more popular songs do not. But that is only one. They all pluck at the very strings of the heart. And they were composed and sung at a time when surely the golden age must have been on earth. In these days there was no haste. There was the ceilidh round the peat fire. There were songs. There were stories. There were great long poems recited by wonderful old men with such memories as are not amongst us nowadays. . . . (In similar vein the speaker addressed herself to Letters, War (the Empire), Religion (Columba to the Great Divines), ' and the same with every other pre-occupation of man since the history of these Islands had a beginning '). That was our Highland Heritage, culminating now—in this hall and in this audience! So that it was more than a pleasure to stand on a real Highland platform and talk to real Highland people—*it was a privilege*. When one arrives in the midst of these great hills, when one stands in the peace of these great glens, when one looks upon the smiling security and dignity of your simple homes caught away from the world, one feels that one is coming from the fretfulness of the artificial, of the untrue, back to the source—to the most hospitable source—of all reality and truth. No wonder that Highland institutions spring up all over

221

the world, where men will persist in wearing the tartan, if only for a night, and in reminding themselves in heart-stirring speeches of—Our Highland Heritage.   (Noble applause.)

Whereafter followed the second half of the programme, where the same artistes appeared again— with the exception of Mr. Charles Macdonald and his Highland bagpipe.

PART THREE

CHAPTER ONE

I

OUTSIDE the concert hall (officially, the Drill Hall)
were dark groups of people laughing and talking,
calling greetings to one another, dissolving, eddying
away into the night. Colin McKinnon and Ewan
Macleod lingered, looking back over the heads into
the open hall doors. The hotel visitors, with the
exception of Stansfield, had filled the second row
from the front, the first having been reserved for the
chief of Sronlairg Lodge and his distinguished guests.
This exclusive reservation of a front row of chairs for
those from Sronlairg who had only paid their three-
and-sixpence like anyone else occupied the close
attention of Colonel Hicks's thought. To know that
the local concert committee had done it off their own
bat as a slavish tribute to the Yankee super-quality
was the sort of thing one might expect from (the
label being ready-made) ' hielant crawlers.' ... Not
until Mary McKinnon's voice caught the heart of
the hall did Colonel Hicks quite forget.

From the front chairs he had heard her sing last
winter. But she had not sung like this then, not
with such golden volume, such stormy restraint.
The Colonel had felt his heart come alive in a distinct

225

palpitation; had heard his breath and cunningly suppressed the sound; had been conscious of withdrawing behind Clare's shining tribute of applause. He had not much of an ear for music.

Colin and Ewan saw the Colonel and his niece, the fair hatless head rising cool and distinguished out of a fur-trimmed wrap, hesitate on the doorstep against the lamplight; then make their way outward. Ewan turned a shoulder to the door; and at that instant his arm was clutched.

'Ewan!'

It was Annabel.

'Annabel—you!' he said, surprise and delight in his voice.

Her eyes were shining. She clung to his arm.

'Oh Ewan! I—I saw you all the time in the concert.' She was breathless with the excitement of seeing him after her first nights away from home. Her voice trembled.

'How did you get down?'

'The brake—the hill brake—nearly all the servants got off. Oh, Ewan, how is mother?'

'Why—' Then he looked closely at her and smiled; pinched her waist. She was impulsive as ever, now even more unreal than ever, like a wisp of the moon, and really rather remarkable, was Annabel.

'I'm dying to see mother. You're sure—'

'What?'

Eyes regarded him soberly, face uplifted.

'That she's missing you?' he added.

'Ewan, tell me though—you're sure she's all right?' She pinched his arm.

226

He lifted his head to the rising moon, sniffed sarcastically—and observed, hovering at Annabel's back, Ronnie McAndrew. His eyes returned to Annabel's face and stayed there. She shifted her head from side to side, tugged at his coat excitedly.

' Well, I'm off down to see mother! '

' Oh, Annabel! ' he whispered, holding her arm.

She tried to meet his eyes, but failed, and her face flamed. Then she made out Mary McKinnon talking to her father at Ewan's back. A reckless, mocking look invaded the face she turned to her brother; a tongue flicked out; she suddenly pushed him up against Colin, and with a laugh fled. With the tail of his eye Ewan saw young McAndrew begin to slip through the crowd. Laughingly he started excusing himself to Colin—and saw Mary. For a moment he stood quite still. Then in lively tones he said:

' Hullo! You fairly gave it to them to-night! '

' Oh, I don't know.' Her voice was slightly embarrassed, her body withdrawn within its dark coat.

' You sure did,' he guessed, and Colin gave a quiet chuckle.

' Was that Annabel ? ' she asked.

' Yes. Quite excited at getting down again. She wants to see her mother! '

' I'm sure she will,' agreed Mary simply. ' What did you think of the concert ? ' she asked.

' Oh, splendid! '

Dazzling headlights swept them and in the instant's glare Ewan's eyes glittered. The Sronlairg party came from the entrance door, the crowd

227

quickly falling into two lines. Mr. Denver's ' Good-night! ' was rewarded with a loud cheer as the cars drove off.

' You'll be waiting for the dance, I suppose ? ' said Colin to Mary.

' Yes, I think so,' she replied indefinitely.

' What are you doing yourself, Ewan ? ' Colin asked.

' I don't know,' returned Ewan. ' You're not thinking of dancing a step or two ? '

' No, now,' reckoned Colin. ' Scarcely! I'll just be going up the road home.'

' It's early enough, man,' said Ewan.

' Yes, yes; never mind me. I'll just be putting my best foot foremost.'

' What's all your hurry ? Wait till they get the seats cleared away at least and you'll hear Charlie Macdonald at the first reel.'

' Indeed, Charlie didn't play bad at all once he got settled. . . .' A girl caught Mary by the arm and swung her aside, her voice bubbling with suppressed giggles. Immediately Colin finished what he had to say about Charlie's piping, Ewan drew him casually out of the crowd the better, he said, to have a smoke. Then he added, ' I may as well walk a bit of the road with you. They always take a time clearing the hall.'

' Very good,' said Colin, and they set out.

Ewan was immediately in excellent spirits, and his head rose laughing as though it had cleverly slipped a halter.

' Did you see Mr. Denver and the doctor ? ' he asked.

' I saw them.'

' Good, wasn't it ? '

Colin said nothing.

' A real stage turn, yon, Colin! ' He laughed, thinking of how he had given Mary the slip. ' How a concert like that reveals us! And the old woman! ' It was rich! ' I knew a fellow at college—MacTaggart was his name—who pretended that he couldn't speak Gaelic. To say that he had come out of a black croft, that he had had the pipes played about his bare legs in a kitchen where you couldn't swing a cat—why, nevah! ' The excitement of having escaped Mary ran riot in his blood.

' Hmff! '

' No, not exactly! He merely wanted to be upsides with the other fellow! '

' Oh,' said Colin.

' We think the fellow with the money a better fellow than ourselves. And yet at the same time we think a fair amount of ourselves! We feel we *should* be, we *are*—and yet it would seem that we *aren't*. And the funny thing is that I am almost convinced that we *are!* So you take your change out of that.'

' Well, well; perhaps they are,' said Colin smoothly.

Ewan laughed (inwardly crying Why ? Why ? to his desertion) and rushed on rhetorically, ' When we look upon these rich foreigners lording it over our creation, we are overcome with wonder. They must be the great people! They must have had great and splendid gifts to have become so successful. And then to complicate things, right on the back of that, a sort of pride of heritage gets us, our sensitive crafty minds go to work, and we know that the real difference between these people and ourselves is the difference of worldly possession and power; they have the sign on us; but yet and on, when it comes to the real sensitive acuteness of the living mind— well, many of them are more like that dead cat! '

' What dead cat was that ? '

' The one I swung in the kitchen.'

' Oh,' said Colin.

Ewan laughed till he shut himself up.

And Colin that night out of an unfathomable perversity of his own, played the lovely healing ' Lost Glen.' Perhaps it purged his mind. It did not purge Ewan's, who wandered down through the night—whither ? Pursued by a torturing restlessness. He knew what was going on in the hall. Against himself, the revelry drew him, calling to his instincts. He would go as far as the door; no farther. Then perhaps he could go home. . . . Not less than a thousand a year—with prospects! Almighty father, it was good that! Oh good! good! He laughed. However, as it happened, he was leaving Mary alone. Had been on the mad verge that other night though! Their hearts went on fire when they were together with no one near. Their bodies burst into flames! Could not speak naturally even. Their very laughter was pain! Heaven and heaven above! Enough to make the dead cat turn in its grave. Unless, of course, he ran two establishments ? He looked at the sickly hunchback moon and grinned.

He approached the door of the dance hall with casual care. A dark figure or two smoking; a couple of young girls came out arm in arm and slipped past him, talking and giggling. The music stopped. He could not hang back, but luck ran Alastair bàn into him.

'Phew, it's hot!' Alastair wiped his neck, advancing from the crush in the doorway. 'Ewan! Where have you been?'

'Went back with Colin. There's a crush surely?'

'Yes. I wish you could wring my shirt. Aren't you coming in?'

'I don't think so.'

'Come away, man! Annabel was asking me if I saw you. Have a cigarette. That one of yours is there too—Miss Marlowe.'

'Is she? And the Colonel?'

'No. But the artist and his wife are in, and the two fellows with the car. They seem to be enjoying it too! Miss Marlowe is a hot dancer.'

'Is she? Were you having a go with her?'

'I was.'

'Weren't you nervous?'.

'Nervous! What would I be nervous for?' Alastair laughed and lowered his voice. 'To tell the heavenly truth, I was, and bedam if I didn't tramp on her toe. I could have cut my foot off!'

Ewan laughed. Alastair had a secretly chivalrous heart.

'Look here, Alastair—you ask to see her home. And then, you know, just when you're saying goodnight. . . .'

'Oh, boil your fat head!'

'Anyway, you'd have to wring your shirt again if you did.'

' No blasted fear! ' swore Alastair. He wiped the inside of his collar. ' But there's these two young bloods with the artist people. They're falling over each other to dance with her. Doing all the latest glides and slides—showing off like blazes.'

' Does she like it ? '

' How should I know ? All the same. . . .'

' A regular connoisseur! '

' You take a running jump at yourself. There's hairy Urquhart tuning up. Come on, man! '

' I'll see.'

' Well, I'm off.' He threw his cigarette away. ' Come on! ' And vanished.

Alastair bàn becoming the deuce of a chap and a man of the world! Feeling almost equal—to the best! The very thought of it stirred a reckless humour. When the dance was in full swing, Ewan walked into the little entrance hall.

Standing in the shadow of the ante-room door, he got a view of half of the dancing floor which was well lit by hanging round-wicked paraffin lamps with white shades, and, as it happened, the very first couple he recognised was Mary McKinnon and Ronnie McAndrew, dancing a waltz in the latest fashion that Mary wasn't at all sure of but that Ronnie was smilingly anxious she should learn. Mary was smiling also, embarrassment in her cheeks, eyes glancing. Ronnie was piloting her with a firm hold, talking, instructing her, and obviously delighted with the result of his work. As he might well be, for Mary McKinnon as a schoolgirl, perfectly trained by her father, had danced Sword Dance and Highland Fling many a time on the village platform. That she

232

was the best dancer in the district no one would think
of disputing. And she was finely made, breast curves
definite and firm, a clean waist, and the dancer's
rather slender hips; with a final lasting impression of
a texture rich and warm; swept by smiling eyes,
with black lashes that appeared slightly wet as
if they had flicked the wells they guarded. Ewan
had the odd sensation of his sight flickering the
least trifle dizzily so that he could just hear it in his
ears like the sound of a remote moth on a white lamp-
shade. Alastair bàn came swinging Annabel in the
old joyful fashion, but with due courtesy. Annabel
on her tiptoes looked a hovering wisp of girlhood,
ready at a moment's alarm to take off, an excited light
in her eyes. But once those eyes shot a look over her
partner's shoulder at two dancers in front, one of
whom was Ronnie. Ewan saw that look, and his lips
crept apart in a dry humour. They, too, swung out
of sight—and here, unmistakably, came one of the
two bloods with Miss Clare Marlowe in his arms.
They slid through the dance, glided and paused,
reversed, hesitated, pursuing like moths whatever
they were after. Local dancers in passing shot them
surreptitious glances, the girls critically, the men
amusedly, both with a slightly humiliating sensation
perfectly hidden. The ' blood ' was a trifle too
earnest, too exquisitely careful, and his healthy
shoulders drooped forward; Clare, with perfect ease
and unconcern, glided flawlessly. When they, too,
had passed, Ewan reckoned that it was time to go.
But somehow he could not move, though deep down
he was conscious of no desire beyond an empty bitter
hunger to see the cycle again. A hulking shape

came in upon him, looked at him. 'Hullo, Ewan! Not dancing?'

Ewan drew the back of an obliterating hand across his mouth. 'No.' He smiled.

'Why not? Eh?' Lachlan Mackenzie was a great-shouldered, full-faced, pretty man, with a reddish moustache and colour in his cheeks. He worked on the Sronlairg forest making and repairing drains and pony tracks, gillieing in the season, and doing winter work about the Lodge.

'Can't be bothered,' said Ewan. 'Aren't you dancing yourself?'

'Yes. I was dancing. It's a good dance.' He winked mysteriously, and whispered, 'I was just down round the corner—you know? Would you like one?'

Ewan hesitated, looking at the dancers.

Lachlan, following his glance, asked:

'Who is she that one?'

'Visitor in the hotel.'

'Wait till I see the next dance.' He consulted a typed programme on the wall. 'Pas de quatre. Strip the Willow. Polka.' His smooth face held husky conspiracy. He winked again. He was out for the night, and Ewan's dark lean face looked like a devil's.

But when the dance ended Ewan slipped away before the usual crush of young men who never sat it out with their partners on the seats round the walls of the hall. With the desire to be free of them altogether, he walked down the short grass-bordered path to the road. There, leaning against a corner of the dyke, he began to fill his pipe slowly. It was no use going home. He would last out the whole thing somehow, so that he would not have to feel about it and imagine it from a distance. The whole night, until it was over, so that it would be over for everybody; the whole aching thing broken up and made normal once more. He wouldn't strike a match to attract anyone; would wait till the music started up. . . . He peered about him, at the shadows, the crooked moon. A figure slid out of hiding quite close to him and began moving off. It might be any woman, but he knew in a moment that it was Jean. Long after she had disappeared, he kept staring as if his mind had been touched by the thin finger of hidden sorrow or hidden crime.

As the music started, with clamour and hurrahs, he struck a match and lit his pipe. Through the last splutter of the flame he was aware of a noiseless shadow bearing down upon him. He threw the match away carelessly, intent on his pipe. The shadow had stopped. He looked up. It was Miss Marlowe.

' Ewan ? '

He took his pipe out of his mouth, stood up, touched his cap.

' You're not dancing ? '

' No.'

' Why ? ' she asked.

' Oh, I don't know.'

Her voice was soft and clear, very kind, almost shy.

' Don't you dance ? '

' Not much.'

' I should imagine— ' She paused. They both stood quite still, silent. Her head, hatless, sleekly round, rose out of the fur neck-wrap, pale-faced, suave. She smiled, and her shoulders made a scarce perceptible gesture. ' I thought I'd come out to see the moon! It's just a little hot in there.'

' I'm sure.' Suddenly he felt awkward, witless.

' Is this the way down—down, you know, above the sands ? '

' If you go down there until you come—no, if you go up this way to the main road first and then— ' Excitement crept into his voice.

' Yes, I know that way. But can't I go down there and along by the cliff-heads ? '

' Yes. But you couldn't follow the path in the dark.'

She appeared to consider this a moment, and then said quietly, ' But I should like to go that way.'

Some persons were coming down on them from the hall. Instinctively they both took a step or two down the narrow road.

' You're sure you don't mind ? ' asked Clare as their footsteps continued.

' No,' replied Ewan. ' It's a pleasure.'

She could hardly smile even to herself. The roofs of thatched cottages curved here and there beyond the stone dykes. It was very quiet down this way, and the sound of the music and the dancing already sounded far off, the echo of a human skirmish, high, forlorn, presently dying out altogether.

' I always think this land of yours beautiful at night; don't you ? ' And she turned her head and looked at him.

' I suppose so.' His thought, too, was ravelled, but he instinctively repressed the awkward half-laugh.

236

' I can understand of course in a way that when you live always amongst it, naturally you cannot see it with the eyes of a stranger. I know. But— ' She hesitated.

' We see it in our own way.'

' Yes, that's just it! ' she returned expectantly.

' We see it so often that perhaps we don't see it at all,' he said, getting hold of his thought.

' That's just it,' declared Clare. ' If you don't see it—what do you see ? '

' What does a city person see when he looks at a street of houses that he passes every day ? '

' Is it—like that ? ' she reflected slowly.

' Yes.'

' I agree: it cannot be, of course.' It was as though at a stroke she penetrated to the secret sceptical core of his mind and answered that. There came a confused pricking to his skin.

' But, of course— ' Her tone implied a faint shrug.

He saw in a moment that he was not equal to her. He might think what he liked, and decide what he liked, when alone; but actually in her company everything was remotely different, and she herself a personality cool and aloof, interested in him precisely as she was interested in the place, in the people. Their relationship was eternally defined, and could be invaded only by assault! Even her divination of his repressed thought had been as nothing, an imperceptible shrug, while she retained her own dignity, her restful charm, unaffected. He saw her look about her at the night, at the dim grass, the dark dykes, the humped cottages, over the approaching cliff-heads to the far fusing of sea and sky. His nerves winced.

'You have been—you have studied—' Her voice came wandering out of the night.

'I was at Edinburgh University—for a time.'

It left her for the moment without a word. He smiled. So she knew all about that too!

'Oh,' she murmured. 'I was, however, actually thinking about the men who have written about your land here. It is difficult for a person like myself, who has no one with whom to discuss it—I mean, no one who *knows*. There is something in it that eludes me. You speak Gaelic?'

'Yes.'

'And—I think—you play bagpipes?'

'Well, I wouldn't—'

'Was it you I heard to-night?'

'When?'

'After the concert—away up the hillside?'

Ewan remembered Colin and his 'Lost Glen' and gave a half-laugh. 'No.'

'Why do you laugh?'

'At the idea that I— No, that was great playing.' His tone unconsciously hardened. 'It was also a great piece of music played by the man who composed it.'

'You seem to think I couldn't understand that?'

'I didn't say—'

'Didn't you? Difficult to penetrate your scepticism, isn't it?'

He looked at her. Her face turned and held his glance a moment, smiling, dim and pale in the thin moonlight. Then she looked away.

238

Excitement started low down in him again, giving to his body that uncertain loss of control which craves a physical act to restore its poise. The moment of assault has its triumph.

They came to the place where the zigzag path went down. The sands lay beneath them and on the sea-verge the foam shone ghostly white and died. They stood looking at it, till her voice stirred:

' What was the tune he played ? '

' " The Lost Glen." '

' " The Lost Glen," ' she repeated, her voice awakening curiously.

' Yes,' he answered. And then in the silence, ' Would you like to hear why he named it that ? ' His voice sounded quiet and pleasant. Before this sea, it was folly to be moved! His mind rose clear.

' Yes.' But she did not look at him.

He began talking at once. ' He told me himself . . . but I doubt if he has told anyone else. The Lost Glen is a real glen. At least, it was more real to him than any other glen. But you may see for yourself. Or perhaps you won't, because it is really fantastic...'

' Thanks,' she encouraged.

He found himself almost at ease. The excitement which had left his body and passed to his mind was so fine and so controlled that it had a prompting to mastery, as though he were speaking not directly and personally but at one remove. Her ' Thanks,' too, was a delicate thrust. The dance hall and what he had come through were behind him. There was nothing in front—nothing, that is, but the sea. He knew the sea! The sea could be cool and suave enough!

' I don't remember his actual words,' he said, his tone acknowledging the thrust, ' but this is something like the story. When he was about eighteen years of age, he once lost his way in the wilds away back there. After walking miles and miles in a mist and more miles in the dark, he became exhausted. He lay down and fell asleep. When he awoke in the morning the sun was shining in a little glen, and he knew when he looked at it that it was not only a lost glen or a glen at the back of beyond, but that it was a glen where never a human foot had been before. He emphasised that it wasn't a queer or uncanny glen. It was simply innocent of the human being. Rather odd, I thought.'

' Rather,' said Clare. The undernote was tonic again. It excited him to a detachment that was complete.

' Yet the oddest thing was perhaps that after getting this impression in a moment, in one long glance, he had thought nothing more about it. He started for the nearest hill and soon got a bearing on Ben Loyal. Then he struck out for home as hard as he could. That's all that happened. But—from that day—he began to see the lost glen in his mind more and more. When his friends found him absent-minded and would ask for her name, he would pass it off with a smile. It was little they knew! he thought.' Ewan paused and drew breath. This touching on the human relationship was not so easy.

' Quite,' she said.

' Well, from that day onward,' Ewan resumed, freed in a moment, ' he could turn in his mind into the little glen and sit down and look at it. It had, according to him, the sweet fresh feeling of a first morning in creation. It lay under the sun in fairy green and aspen silver. Looking at it and listening, he could imagine it having ears, long hidden ears like a hare's that might prick up. Though he admitted that that was no doubt merely what one imagined afterwards. For it was not easy to command the first impression, which had been so vivid and inhuman.'

This time Clare did not speak.

'Anyway,' Ewan smiled, 'he hunted the impression for about thirty years. Snatches of the theme, odd variations—perhaps; but the whole vision itself was recaptured one October night. His wife had been ill. Things had been going wrong with him. He had been depressed for a long time. Then suddenly, out of the pain of all that, his composition was born white and shining. From that moment, believe him or believe him not, the cloud began to lift and the illness of his wife to cure itself.'

'I am inclined to believe him,' said Clare to the silence. Her tone was so simple that its meaning pierced him. For clearly she found everything right but Ewan's attitude with its self-preserving irony; the more clearly in that the story itself was so extraordinary—and beautiful.

'There's just one thing I omitted,' said Ewan, reacting at once. 'He could not leave the glen's innocence alone; that first inhuman innocence. He had to people it with his fancy. Poets seem fond of doing that. They can't leave an exquisite thing alone. He said, however, that it is the mood to create life and that it leaves us helpless. Anyway, he assured me that she would come walking down by the little birch trees in that glen, walking down towards him where he stood—or was it sat?—waiting. Her beauty—he put it in the tune—was more wonderful than anything else in the world—except perhaps the look in her eyes.'

These words, however, carried him just beyond what he could command. And though a half-laugh might have eased, he could make no sound.

Clare turned to him. He saw the moonlight in her eyes. It was in a way as if in their shining regard there was something faintly distressed. Nor did they wander. He could neither hold them nor turn from them. The surge rose up within him. And all at once, maddened by her eyes, he caught her and kissed her. He must have hurt her physically, for she cried out with a curious choked cry. Instantly he released her and stumbled back.

She, however, said nothing. When she had settled her wrap, she hung a moment looking at the sea. They were both breathing heavily. Then she turned and regarded him mutely.

' I'm sorry,' he said. In another moment he said it again. His voice stuttered slightly in its sudden abasement. He could not look at her. He had not been a pagan, he had merely been an ill-mannered fool. Dogged all the accursed night.

' Shall we go back ? ' she suggested calmly.

There was no way in which she could have so perfectly tortured him. As if his crude behaviour had simply never been!

Nor did she speak to him all the way to the gate of the dance hall, where she paused.

'Good-night,' she said clearly, almost gently, as if she were sorry for him.

He touched his cap. 'Good-night.' As she walked away, he thought, 'I should have said, "Good-night, m'am"!' His face twisted in a bitter humour. A man came down on him from the hall. It was Lachlan Mackenzie. He was staggering slightly. 'I have been looking for you,' he said thickly. 'Come 'way round here where they won't see us.' Ewan stared at him a moment, then with a sudden black elation, followed.

Clare, back in the hotel, was also invited to a drink. The Colonel, with glowing cigar, assured her he had just been coming for her; was surprised at her appearance, 'What—come back alone?'

'I was beginning to feel tired.'

'I should think so! And didn't anyone—'

'I didn't tell them,' said Clare, 'that I was going home. Didn't want to—'

'Hm. Quite. I agree. They're not. . . . Quite. I warned you that you would get tired.'

'But I really did enjoy it.'

They were in the lounge lamplight.

'All the same, you do look a trifle hectic, m'dear. I hope you haven't overdone it.' The Colonel was in courtesy's most excellent humour. His fingers rose towards her chin as if to tip it up for proper avuncular inspection. His face was rich as his breath. Before his fingers quite touched her chin, however, Clare removed it with a lazy little laugh.

'Hectic?' She raised amused eyebrows, and looked over her shoulder at the stairs.

She could make a man feel civilised.

' Won't you have something ?   Glass of port, eh ? '
Her eyes returned, hesitated.

' No,' she decided.   ' I'm going to bed.   So please
don't tempt me.'

' Oh, come on!   One glass—one teeny-weeny
glass.   You must.'

' No, please don't go for it.'   She put out a de-
taining hand;   touched his sleeve.   ' I'm really off.'

He caught her hand;   patted it.

' But one—just the smallest one.'

' No, really.   Thanks so much.   You're very kind.
But—no.'

' Oh well—so long as you are enjoying yourself.'

She looked at him with the queerest little smile.
' I am,' she said.   ' Good-night.'

' Good-night, m'dear.   God bless you.'   As she
gave a last look over the stair-rail, he saluted from
his brow.   By the way he behaved, he might have
been moved to-night by memories of music, by a
golden voice, a very siren voice, in his ears.

2

Whereas Stansfield fished every day, Colonel
Hicks took many days off.   He was not the slave of
any hobby and could look upon life regally.   In the
freedom of his moods there was often a kingly
humour.   There were moments, for example, when,
standing in front of the hotel of an afternoon, he
experienced a rich satisfaction and blew smoke with
slow ease, his eyes now and then lifting as though to
find something to tease and subdue.

On one such afternoon, the Colonel beheld Colin McKinnon coming down the road from his house to the stone bridge, his stick in his hand, clearly dressed for an outing. The Colonel was moved to have him in for a drink, to return hospitality to the accompaniment of friendly talk! The thought of such good fellowship was a diversion in itself. It was a pleasant warm afternoon. His recent bodily continence, in honour of his niece's presence, induced a feeling of physical well-being that was at once delightful and needed an outlet. There would be some fun in this talk with Colin!

But Colin never appeared and at last the Colonel was forced to conclude that, after crossing the bridge, he must have turned up the glen to Torbuie.

That was a pity, decided the Colonel—thoughtfully. He became restless and getting stick and cap declared for a walk. So away he went towards the stone bridge, crossed the bridge, and began to ascend the road that Colin had come down.

Being in no great hurry, he could pause for his wind and survey his territory. He saw how he was withdrawing from his world on this upward path, could command all the approaches and as it were make sure of his dominion. No actions of crofter or cow called for the flick of a humoured sarcasm this afternoon. On the contrary, a certain elation, almost an undercurrent of excitement, gave his glance a fine breadth, his eye the gleam of adventure.

On he went in his grey tweeds, body braced, warmth contending with imperiousness in his face. Removing his cap once, he wiped his brow, the hand passing upward and drawing the hair damply from the forehead in that smooth sweep of intelligence and breeding. His jaws moved, moistening his mouth which was getting blown dry. He could do with a drink, a drink of water even. He looked at Colin's house, now slightly above him and to the right. Why not ? he thought, regarding its stillness.

As though to discount the increase of excitement, his face grew distinctly imperious. The slight tremor in his flesh need not occupy his attention. It was a warm day for climbing this hill; a beastly warm day, he thought, with an oddly pleasurable sensation. The colour deepened in his face and courtesy's smile came to no more than glints in his eyes. When at last he reached the door, he knocked, and in accordance with the customs of a friendly people, as he knocked he opened the door and hesitatingly entered.

There was a rush of feet, and Mary, with a blue wrap round her shoulders, her face glowing from the rubbing of a towel, stood before him at the kitchen entrance, her eyes widening in shocked surprise.

'Good afternoon, Mary!' greeted the Colonel, smiling profoundly.

'Oh!' exclaimed Mary weakly.

The Colonel advanced naturally, as if invitation were understood and he did not see her clutching at the inadequate blue wrap which was no more than an apron of sorts. 'Sorry if I intrude.'

'My father's not in,' Mary managed at last, shrinking towards the rear exit.

'Isn't he ?' said the Colonel, pausing a surprised moment at mid floor.

'No.'

'Oh, he isn't?' Then he added gallantly, 'But you can satisfy my thirst even better!' and smiled, his eyes observing the fissures in the inadequate apron. 'That hill would make anyone dry.' He lifted his eyes to her face.

'A drink?' And she turned and vanished through the back door, pushing it shut behind her.

The Colonel filled and emptied his lungs. He had little or no finesse. He felt his madness coming upon him. He knew the symptoms quite well. The last vestige of caution would get carried away and drowned in recklessness. But that final stage was all right, it had a royal sanction. The worst moments were always those that preceded the outburst. It was the holding himself in while the whirling was proceeding internally that was the devil. Now she would be dressing herself. . . . In the first flush at the door, she had been glowing like a Venus, then—in a moment—was conscious of him, shrinking, hardly able to speak, her whole body moving and twisting, clutching the apron over her breasts. . . . He listened all ears until the holding of his breath hurt his chest. The veins congested in his face. On the verge of being carried away towards the blinding door, he rocked, as she entered—her hair combed, the 'art' jumper where the apron had been, and a glass of water in her hand.

His head inclined perceptibly as if in tribute, his eyes passing to the glass of which he took hold. The glass shook slightly. For the moment he could not look at her directly without giving himself away. And the affair required of him something more than brute force, something more than an enveloping

247

sweep. The instinct of ingratiation needed satisfaction. He looked up from the glass, smiling. Her eyes were drawn to his—before they swept downward and sideways in swift uncomfortable avoidance. Her colour flushed and waned. She stood waiting until he would drink so that she might relieve him of the glass. He did not drink. Time held in a tension that became acute. Under his gaze the self-consciousness of her delicate flesh was extraordinarily potent. It flooded his mind with his real desires. His eyelids lowered; he raised the glass and murmured to it, ' Beautiful, clear,' as in an idiotic secret toast. He saw her body writhe just perceptibly, a sort of captive shudder of fear. The silk jumper over her breast began to heave noticeably. The expression on her face became strained, artificial, painful; her nostrils flexed as if they sniffed something . . . like the heat of his body. He tried an intimate little laugh, ' So your father is not in! '

She swallowed, hovering on dizzy flight.

Instinct had come alive between them. He could not stand the strain of doing nothing a moment longer. His left hand went out to chuck her under the chin, playfully, his head stooping forward, his breathing become a trifle heavy, his eyes hot. Instantly she staggered back. The sudden movement snapped the tension; snapped also the thin glass which fell smashing to the floor. As at a signal, full action was released.

She fled into the back premises, closing the door behind her and leaning against it, gasping. Her surcharged mind could not hold the thought that he would follow her. The full impact of the Colonel's body, however, sent her staggering into a corner so that pots and pans clattered and were upset. By the time she had regained her balance and swung round, the Colonel had the doors of escape at his back, and was slowly advancing upon her, hemming her in. His face was now not only charged with desire but charged with the desire to dominate. He had gone too far to draw back. He had committed himself and was in to the end. His presence before her grew vast and terrifying, while still in the broad dominion of his face was that red lingering male effort at ingratiation. Horror whitened her face, sent her cowering against the low shelves, head leaning back, palms coming up. But as the Colonel's hands were about to clutch, she gave a scream and smashed through them with all the frenzied strength of her young body. He got a grip, tried to hold on, but she tore free, leaving in his right fist a strip of the ' art ' jumper ripped from shoulder to waist.

Maddened unbearably, he hung a moment, then with an oath was after her through the back door.

But already she was not to be seen. The still hillside looked down upon his inflamed body crushing with blasphemous haste along the back of the house towards the gable next the byre. Still no sight of her. Damn her! where had she gone ? On towards the byre, the door of which was shut. He put his shoulder to it. It gave slightly. He heard her breathing. He burst the door open and entered, closing it behind him.

He had her now. At that moment it was not so much perhaps the satisfying of the instinct of lust as the gratifying of the instinct of dominance; male dominance, a man's final pride. He stood against the door, watching her through the faint gloom; saw her panting breasts, the feverish hands that clutched the torn revealing jumper. All the animal scents of the byre assailed his nostrils, the infesting smell of dung, of secretive bodily acts. Lust itself became the incense of dominance. He had her—cornered in the cow's stall. His body surged up in a harmony of power. The concentration of his advance fascinated her. The dreadful intention that sat in his face weakened her. His mouth moved and the lower jaw set. His shoulders hunched a trifle. Her body fluttered to weak acts of mimetic rejection. ' Go away! Go away!' screamed her golden voice, gone thin, ugly.

At his final enfolding lunge she thrust out blindly, but he was more careful this time and, meeting her squarely, his sheer weight bore her down and she fell backwards in the straw, his heavy body tumbling on top of her. Immediately she became frantic. Her screaming maddened him. He crushed a hand on her mouth. For a moment she choked, then bit clean through the lobe of his palm. He swore in a savage astonishment, snatching his hand away. At the swing back of his weight, she rolled over. The weakness of her initial fear had given way to an abnormal strength, and though he grabbed at her he could not quite hold her. She was too pliant for his set muscles and, rolling free, leapt to her feet, leaving in his hands the remainder of her ' art ' jumper. In her wild scramble, she hit into the wall, rebounded, and thrust for the door, which she swung open with such a crash that it slowly quivered shut after her, leaving him on all fours in the stall.

His mouth was gibbering in a fierce incoherence, his whole face plethoric; then carried away by his madness, he staggered to his feet and made for the door, tripping over the jumper and stamping it in the liquid runnel.

She was rushing away from the steading, upwards over the slight rise that was the rim of the corrie and that brought the crofts into view. . . . They would see her! Was she mad? He looked about him. Damn her, was she mad? She disappeared.

He glared about him again. The still hillside looked down upon his palpitation. A chill breath touched his hot gorged face. Damn her; the bitch! This was a place to get out of.

He reached the roadway with a sense of relief; lifted his hands to fix his tie and found them bloodied. He stared at them and laughed thickly. A shallow cut in the right palm . . . broken glass. Tooth marks in the left. He looked about him once more. No life moved anywhere . . . nothing except a red cow in the corrie that lifted its head, bellowed reverberatingly, and remained with out-thrust neck gaping down at him. From where he stood no other house was visible—except the hotel with its white walls on the edge of the valley. And anyone could hardly have observed the business from the hotel. He took out his handkerchief and wiped his wounds. No need to get hydrophobia! He began looking for a trickle of clean water and, when he found it, washed his trembling hands carefully, wiped his face, and assured himself that all traces of the amorous combat had been removed.

On the way down his blood began to cool. He

grew sick of the whole filthy affair. God alone knew what forced him into degrading stunts of this sort. He was amazed at himself. A pewling crofter's wench at that! Gargantuan mockeries assailed him. Things had always gone wrong with him. A broken colossus, to be jeered at, to be pitied! It was true; damn it, they could *pity* him. His emotion swirled up and stung his eyes maddeningly. He hated *them* at that moment intensely. They left him with nothing even to crush. A shell, a husk. After a man had given of his best. . . . His mouth closed firmly. Vertical lines grooved intolerantly between the eyebrows. He wasn't cute enough, wasn't underhand enough, was too straightforward. He shouldn't have lowered himself, shouldn't have gone near the squawking, fighting bitch. Result of living in a place like this—rotten, poverty-stricken, stinking hole. . . .

He went on solidly, uncaring what was behind this resurgent egoism. Yet now and then a glance swept the hillside, crossed the bridge, ran along the hotel ridge. Colin . . . the people of the place . . . a queer twisted lot . . . never knew what they would be up to . . . like the crofters of Ardbeg. . . .

But he didn't consider the crofters of Ardbeg. He didn't give a curse for them. And she wasn't such a fool as to give herself away. Who would believe her that he hadn't gone the whole hog? Trust a woman for that! They weren't the sort to invoke the law of assault. He laughed in his nostrils. They ought to be bloody well honoured. As he approached the bridge a tall thistle by the roadside attracted his eye—and reminded him that he must have left his stick in the cottage.

It was the last straw. As he drew up, the treacherous emotions he had denied assailed him. In their
fierce ardour they blotted out all control. His jaws
ground, his fists clenched. He became inarticulate.
Both fists rose up and crushed down violently. His
feet stamped the rotten earth. Beads of saliva
spluttered from his mouth. His eyes shot fiercely
hither and thither—and saw Donald, his gillie, going
up beyond the bridge.

In an instant he realised that Donald had been
watching him. By God!

He rocked, and in a voice that lacerated his throat
shouted, ' Donald! '

But Donald did not appear to hear, and in a few
moments rounded the upward bend and passed from
sight.

3

But that evening when the Colonel, before dinner,
chanced to go round the hotel corner, he was witness
to a diverting pantomime in the garage door. Donald
was all wound up before Ewan Macleod and Alastair
bàn, who were following him with the closest attention. Donald finally raised both arms and crashed
an imaginary body downwards and then proceeded
to stamp the ground. Ewan laughed. Alastair bàn,
pivoting on the heel of his mirth—saw the Colonel.

Colonel Hicks observed their arrested faces, and
remembering what Donald had witnessed that afternoon, felt at once that they had been talking about
him, and began his advance. Alastair drifted into
the garage behind the cars. Donald, after a swift
guttural imprecation in Gaelic, started laughing and

253

talking at large to Ewan in English . . . ' so I said
to him,' he continued in a loud clear voice, ' if that's
what you did on Saturday night, what about Sunday
when you would be going to church and lifting your
eyes above ? ' He appeared to hear the Colonel
at his back—' But I'll tell you the rest again.' And
he turned to face the Colonel with innocent expectancy. Ewan also looked at Colonel Hicks levelly,
and turned away after Alastair bàn.

' What's the joke ? ' enquired the Colonel.

' Och, it was just a little story I was telling them.'

' Seems to have been amusing.'

' It was amusing enough in its way,' admitted
Donald, bashfully taking credit for his small powers.

' Oh,' pierced the Colonel.

' Och yes, sir.' In his genial bashfulness, Donald
looked about him.

The Colonel's mouth closed.

' About the fishing in the morning, sir ? It would
save me coming back.'

' It will save you nothing,' said the Colonel. His
eyes had never left Donald's face. He appeared to
be on the point of saying something final, when
Clare came from the post office where she had been
buying postage stamps.

' Anything wrong ? ' she smiled, as her uncle
accompanied her to the hotel.

' Oh, only these. . . .'

' What have they. . . . ? '

' You don't know them,' he observed. A profound and unmentionable knowledge seemed to
prompt his peculiar smile. She got a whiff of his
breath. He had been drinking heavily.

Her intuitive understanding of his mental attitudes usually drew forth her sympathy. At odd times her fancy even caught glimpses of the lost cavalier. At the moment, however, her sympathy was clouded by a slight shudder of the skin as though something clammy had touched it. Her eyes turned away to the golden afterwarmth of the vanished sun, to the corrie lying still as a dream high to the left, with the piper's cottage like a jewel at its throat. If only now and then her uncle could glimpse that ineffable peace. . . . A faint smile dawned and died.

But over coffee she had to be more direct. His humour, grown broad and intimate, drew her within its destructive conspiracy. What he implied about the Sandersons, especially one of them; how he ' touched off ' old Stansfield; and particularly the way in which he referred to the local people, began to fix her smile painfully. Clearly some trifle had pricked his dignity during the day, and now his egoism, worked upon by drink, was transforming it secretly into a full poisoned lance.

' But, after all,' smiled Clare, ' you must make allowances! '

' Allowances ? ' His humour thickened.

' These local people, anyhow—they haven't had the opportunities. They haven't seen anything different.'

' You mean they haven't seen anything beyond their mud huts—apart from those who went to the University—and came back.' Ewan's cool level look from the garage door had penetrated. The memory of it so flushed in an instant the Colonel's inmost

255

attention that he did not perceive the quickening flick in Clare's eyes.

'Perhaps they had to come back . . . who knows?' she suggested coolly.

'Oh?'

'Well, you can't keep attending a University without cash.'

'Has he found a supporter?' suggested the Colonel.

Clare gave a half-wearied smile.

'He had the cash all right,' the Colonel added. 'Though I agree the subject isn't worth—' he searched for the right word, but all at once concluded —'stinking one's thoughts with.'

Clare made no response. The Colonel knew his expression was too strong, his whole attitude over-done, from Clare's point of view. But he could hardly help himself. He wanted to make a clean sweep. The whole afternoon had been damnable.

'I think you're hardly fair,' said Clare at last.

'You what?'

'Oh, I don't know, but—' and she gave her imperceptible shrug.

Feeling himself judged did not help the Colonel.

'So you, too—' He stopped deliberately.

'No. But the cultivated mind should make allowances. And, perhaps, for all we know, their minds may be as sensitive as ours. It's difficult.'

'Difficult, rot!' said the Colonel.

'Oh, well, in that case. . . .'

There was silence.

The dining-room began to empty into the lounge. Presently Clare got to her feet.

'Some letters to write,' she murmured.

The Colonel was silent, blew his cigar smoke. Clare turned to him and smiled.

The Colonel arose and bowed.

'Good-night, m'dear.'

In her bedroom she felt suddenly wearied. She quite understood her uncle. She could make every allowance up to complete absolution. It wasn't that. It was in some way his attitude of mind coming between one and the sweet freedom of life, like a shadow, tinging things, tainting them, in spite of oneself. It was bigger than that; in some way it transcended the personal altogether; as if it were not merely her uncle's mind, but an altogether bigger mind, the mind of a world, a manifestation of life everywhere, always, tainting the 'golden apples of the sun, the silver apples of the moon.' It was at work here, all about her, and in a certain way in its most objectionable form because it was right up against sun and moon in their naked gold and silver. In the city, with the artificial writhing in electric design, it was different; money, power, fashion, wit, ambition, made a glittering show in high lights and black shadows.

But to carry it here was wrong; a sort of human motley in the sunlight; grotesque. Yet though one might use words like these, one wasn't defining the violence itself; for it was no more than a shadow on thought at best, an insidious destruction of humour, a corrosive taint. One wanted to escape from it, to get out of its condition of mind, so that the freed eyes might look on the silver and golden apples in their purity, and then look downward on the ancient

257

necromantic earth, look long and nakedly, and penetrate to where the antique stirred bronze shapes in a fluid darkness . . . and excitement passed from the intellect to the blood, and with the warm rush of the blood the heart stirred, and out of the heart leapt strength, mounting to the spirit, that trembled like a naked flame . . . and one stood poised in laughing, swift-limbed immortality. . . .

She moved to the window, troubled by the burden of undefined thought. The intellect wasn't enough; the definable was safe and paltry; commonsense was the pride of bores. It was what lay beyond, the almost unimaginable, the thrill that never was on sea or land . . . but might be *in* them! . . .

She regarded the evening world with a vague smile, a curling lip, a doubting clouded eye. Was she going off the rails ? How amusing! She slowly scorned the world. An access of cruelty like a small chill wave went over her heart. She felt cold and cruel, her mind in an under-sea chill light, her hands clean and thin and cold, hands pitiless. She hated with a slow scorning all the safe assured worldly people, the cocksure complacency of ' superior ' lives, the mottled flesh of her uncle's face, his imaginary ' dignities,' all their ' dignities ' . . . like his face—except that for the most part they were paler, more correct, unconscious leprosy lording it in the daylight. . . .

Turning from the window, she brushed the small writing-table. It reminded her of her chief's letter, which she must answer. Unlocking a suitcase, she picked up the letter and began to read it.

Without moving from where she stood she read

it all through, her eyes gathering a more concentrated light. From the last word she looked up, looked at the image and the thought in her mind, remained looking at them for quite a time.

He was clever, this chief of hers. He was very clever, with a mental grace and nimbleness almost feminine, so full of elusive understandings, of half-expressed humour, of raillery, of gossip twisting through personalities into a web of amusement in which the mind got caught up and laughed in lingering astonishments. Only Clare did not laugh now. She saw his face behind the writing, his clever man's face, with the eyes searching out her thought in glances, slanting glances wherein he veiled his meanings, glances that she as a woman could understand and answer, that were amusingly intimate, a half-exciting second language. . . .

Clare smiled and dropped the letter in the suit-case. She had an hour. She would answer him. She was as clever as he was; knew his mind better than her own. And she could be far more elusive. The smile in her eyes grew hard. She would plait quite a fantastic crown of thorns for his faultless forehead. She would bring red-flicked pain into his intelligent eyes. His handsome face with its neat-cropped moustache and coloured cheeks, its military distinction in such interesting contrast to the acute political brain behind, would twist up, doubting her, and yet not be quite sure.

He was so careful to be careful; always so invisibly careful not to compromise himself. And the attitude was in a way such an insult with its destructive implication that she might take advantage of him if he

let go. But he would now understand that she would
take advantage of him just because he wouldn't. She
would weave the fantasy of leprosy in the daylight
and the other fantasy of the silver and golden apples;
and in the light of her cool amused detachment he
would be left doubting, doubting her intention and
his own understanding. For his peculiarity was that
he imagined himself capable of understanding all
things. And if he thought that she was looking into
him, penetrating into blank recesses, and archly
mocking . . . with just something in her look, her
tone, that was within a mile of being real mockery
. . . and that yet smiled to him, receding. . . .

She had an hour. She could do it.

But she found she could not do it. Not a word.
Her hands lay on the writing-table, heavy as lead.
An hour—before she went out, down to the sands,
to meet Ewan, perhaps. A heart-flush of nameless
excitement wearied her. Possibly he would not be
there at all. In discussing the weather prospects and
the evening outlook, she had made accidental reference to the sands. He had, of course, said nothing.
But he had heard.

She lit a cigarette and lay back in the room's basket
chair. The hour drove its minutes across a hinter-
land she no longer made any effort to see or understand. The room gathered darkness; became very
still.

Presently, wrapped in her travelling coat, she
stood a dim figure on the centre of the floor. Opening the door silently, she passed out.

Her light footsteps went down the carpeted stairs
and through the empty lounge. No one seemed to

see her. She rounded the hotel. The moon was risen somewhere, but was not yet visible.

This ' escaping '—to see the moon on sand!

4

Two hours later, she found the outer door shut. But it was not locked, and with a breath of relief she slipped quietly in, her coat collar about her ears. The booming of half-smothered voices reached her from the dining-room. The drawing-room door stood half-open and dark. Everyone was in bed—except her uncle and someone with whom he was manifestly in a towering passion. She went quickly to the stairs, mounted them, walked the few yards of corridor, opened her bedroom door, shut it after her, then moved slowly towards the bed, upsetting the wooden towel-rail at its foot and letting it lie. She sat down on the bed, her eyes on the grey window. She lay down on her side; finally turned over and pressed her face into the pillow, her dark body motionless on the white bedspread.

While all the time the row continued in the dining-room, at the door of which John McAlpine was now inclining an ear, fumbling at the same time with the loose neckband of his shirt.

The Colonel had had Donald in shortly before Stansfield had retired. The Colonel had been hospitable to Donald, had given him a drink with robust humour, had even pulled his hielant leg in the accepted manner, had finally sent him for all the fishing tackle so that they might prepare for the morrow were it only to prove that lawyers and business men and artists were not the only people in the world who could catch fish, however much they fancied themselves, eh Tonald ? At that, Stansfield had gone.

And Stansfield was right, for the inspection of the fishing tackle wasn't even an excuse. The Colonel waved the stuff aside. The bottle of whisky shook and gushed into Donald's glass.

' Hold! ' cried the respectful gillie.

' Hold what ? ' enquired the Colonel. Then he laughed. ' Sit down, you— ' He checked himself. ' Drink! ' he commanded.

' Good health to you, sir.'

The Colonel, pouring a drink for himself, ignored the salutation. When he had got seated once more, he pointed to Stansfield's chair.

' Sit down there! '

' I'm all right here, sir.' And Donald occupied the edge of a stiff chair.

' Sit down there! Don't you hear me ? '

The sight of Donald in Stansfield's armchair prompted the Colonel to a splutter of laughter. ' Lie back! ' he ordered. ' And now light up that filthy pipe of yours.'

But Donald felt this was going too far. The Colonel's hospitality was, however, inexorable, and Donald lit his pipe. Then for quite a long time the Colonel said nothing and appeared gradually to sink into a heavy-breathing semi-stupor, out of which his eyes stared firewards with a glazed malignancy. In order to reassure his own discomfort, Donald quietly finished his drink.

' Fill up,' muttered the Colonel.

' Oh no, sir.'

' Fill up ! '

Donald charged his glass.

' Put chair under my feet.'

Donald lifted the podgy legs on to the seat of a chair.

' Drink ! ' commanded the Colonel. . . . ' Lie back.' The glassy eye, gathering fire again, surveyed with brutal sarcasm the relaxed figure of Donald in Stansfield's chair, then ignored him once more.

Time passed. To Donald the Colonel's inactivity was something entirely new, and he reflected that for the first time he found his patron in a condition approaching complete helplessness; and reflected further that the attainment of such a happy state implied a good bucket and maybe two good buckets. The Colonel's generosity was never his strong point. It was a long time since Donald himself had had anything approaching half a bucket. . . . The whisky stirred warmly in his stomach, warmly and ever more confidently. Why shouldn't he lie back and smoke, whatever ? He might know his place, but otherwise he was as good as the next and maybe better. The old boy was ' paralytic.' The rank was but the guinea stamp, as the minister said at the Burns social last winter. Donald took a sip at his whisky.

Time passed. Donald finished his whisky. The minutes went over the room like slow black birds. He coughed. But the extended figure of Colonel Hicks breathed labouringly on, lost to the world, glazed eyes fixed and malignant. Donald decided he would slip away quietly, pass a word to John McAlpine, then go home.

'Drink,' said the Colonel.

'Oh no, sir,' deprecated Donald, politely startled.

The Colonel's eyes fixed on him in blasting mockery.

'Frightened of it, uh?'

'I'm not frightened of anything,' smiled Donald.

'No?' The Colonel moved, but his eyes never left Donald's face. A clock struck eleven. Voices and laughter came from the drawing-room. The exodus to bed. As if this were what the Colonel had been waiting for, his face came burningly alive. 'Take away that damned chair.'

Donald obeyed; handed the Colonel his drink.

'Sit down on it,' commanded the Colonel.

Donald seated himself where the Colonel's feet had been.

'Look me in the eye. . . . Dammit, don't you know how to look a man in the eye?'

'I'm not afraid to look any man in the eye.'

'Well, *look*, blast you!'

Donald smiled.

'You will have your little joke,' he suspected. His politely evasive eyes glistened.

'Little tchoke! . . . You simple ass!'

'I may be an ass——'

'Oh, shut up! Look me in the eye.'

Donald looked the Colonel in the eye, but with his head set back in a glancing sensitive attitude like a stag's.

'Now,' began the Colonel, 'I want you to tell me. . . . Damn your blasted face! In the eye!'

Donald concentrated again.

'Now then, tell me,' proceeded the Colonel.

264

' exactly—you understand ? *exactly*—what you were telling them in the garage door. . . . No, blast you, *in the eye!* '

Donald arose.

' Sit down.'

' I'll sit down if I like— '

' Sit—down ! '

' Now,' said the Colonel, drawing the back of his hand across his wet mouth, ' in the eye. . . . *Now*— you will inform me exactly—you understand ?— *exactly* your story at the garage.'

' Och, it was just a comical story,' said Donald, giving a toss to his head.

The Colonel's chest swelled. He was doing his best to project his mind to a certain end. It was being made difficult for him. His passion, like his voice, wanted to burst through, to rocket upwards. Destructive desires swirlingly assailed him.

' Your eyes ! ' he hissed. ' Can't you look a man in the eyes ? Do you always lie ? The whole blasted pack of you, twisters and liars. You think I don't know your breed. Gentlemen ! . . . ladies ! . . . Misery-ridden lousy crofters, with their bloody women ! thinking that they. . . .' He choked. The thought of Mary McKinnon would not leave him. Like a secret poison it had inflamed him the whole evening. There was that uncertainty about its publicity and maddening humiliation. Now even in his extremely drunken condition he knew he was going too far, yet was fatally drawn by the chance to throw up his venom. He could drown them with it, blot them out . . . only he had to get Donald's story, had to be dead certain precisely how much he knew—or

265

others knew—while at the same time it gave him countenance to make the miserable fellow keep eyes front as a mere point in personal subjection.

But Donald had got to his feet, head up, eyes flashing hither and thither, his doubtful smile gone at last.

' Sit down ! '

' I will not sit down.'

' Sit—down ! '

' No.'

The Colonel staggered to his feet, put out a hand to grab Donald, who, however, retreated a pace in orderly fashion. The Colonel swore at him and followed. Donald continued the retreat, his face to the enemy. In this way they circled the small table. Then the Colonel, who was more drunk than he knew, made a reckless forward lunge, and Donald, retreating too precipitately, stumbled backwards and fell his length, the Colonel's jaws coming to rest between his upturned toes.

They got to their feet.

' You mind your own business,' said Donald angrily.

The Colonel's jaws shut like a bulldog's, and with baleful eye he advanced. Donald, holding his ground, put out a hand and gave the Colonel a push. The Colonel sat with a staggering thud in his chair, and remained there a moment glaring with such intensity that Donald felt himself rushed into speech.

' What are you wanting to be making a fool of me for ? I will not be made a fool of by you or anyone else. That's not why I'm here. And what's more,

266

if you don't like the Highlands you can leave them. You think you can come here and order us about like dogs as though we were dirt. But we won't be ordered like dogs by you or anyone like you. And if you don't like it you can be going to the devil. To hell with you!' concluded Donald hotly.

The Colonel was again on the advance, but now more warily and with a speechless madness in his eye. Involuntarily Donald retreated a pace or two before him, his mind still under the imaginative handicap of seeing all round the affair, aware exactly of what was going on, of his own position as gillie, of the privileged social position of Colonel Hicks, of the theatrical unreality in his own wordy attitude; yet with these growing less and less, becoming fused into the heat of a real anger, beginning to blaze back at the Colonel. At last he stood his ground, hands by his side. The Colonel gripped his arms below the shoulders, sunk his fingers into them, drew himself up against Donald's face. Donald tried to shake him off. The Colonel hung on. Donald tried to worry himself free. They staggered about the floor.

'Don't be a fool!' shouted Donald.

The Colonel bored in.

'Oh, to hell with you!' exclaimed Donald, getting his hands on the Colonel's chest and flinging him backwards against the table, which crashed to the floor sending the monogrammed whisky bottle spinning and smashing.

John McAlpine entered, peering about him.

'What's this, Donald?' he asked in his soft voice.

' Oh, it's that damn fool of a man, thinking he can do what he likes. But he's mistaken if he thinks he can do what he likes with me. He can go to blazes. I'm finished with the b—.'

' You go home, Donald.'

' I'm going. Don't worry yourself. I'm off.'

' Go on, then.'

' I'm going.' But he still hovered, breathing battle, over the fallen enemy. Then he pulled himself together, snorted, and walked out. The house shook under the crash of the front door.

The reverberation awakened Clare Marlowe. She sat up in bed, listening. Found herself clothed; remembered.

After a time she got to her feet; went to the window. Clouds had won into the sky. A small wind wandered in a diffused moonlight. Her warm newly awakened body gave an involuntary shiver. The breasts of the hills. The dark hollows of the earth. A profound everlastingness. Nothing fretful or fearful. The wandering dark wind passing over all things like a secret caress, old as the hills and the hollows. Her own body had become nearly the last hollow of all. But not quite. But nearly. . . . A faint excitement stirred in her breast. She felt Ewan's breath. He was caught in a strange madness of his own. She could not fathom it. That swift speechless action of burying his head had been an involuntary spasm of black contrition. For what ? Why ? . . . It did not matter. He was merely caught in his own dark web. As she was caught in . . . what ? She smiled a doubtful, lingering smile on moonstruck hill and hollow and turned from them.

The candlelight showed her face pale and the lingering smile taking on a new aspect of self-consciousness, as she slantingly glimpsed her face in the mirror. But she avoided the mirror thereafter and slowly began undressing. About the curves of her mouth, grown soft and red, flickered something like the memory of a strange but not unpleasant dream . . . that might be dreamed again.

CHAPTER TWO

I

His mother was sitting by the fire as Ewan entered. She straightened herself, turned half-round, ' Is that you, Ewan ? ' and gathered some knitting from her lap. Her voice was friendly and inviting. ' I'm sure you're tired.'

' Don't move for me.' He gave her a sidelong look, vaguely troubled by the eagerness with which she made way for him. Clearly, with the evening coming on, she was glad to have him in about.

He sat opposite her and they talked about little things of the day, where he was going on the morrow, the trouble Alan Ross had with one of his cows, yet all the time he could not banish from his mind that first sight of her by the hearth, as if all the burden of her life had been there.

He began to feel the weight of it as their talk dribbled out. There grew within him the sense of what a whole lifetime meant. It made the stillness of the kitchen acute and the clicking of her needles sound like the clicking of dry pebbles on a worn shore. Its significance grew overpowering in a dumb fateful way. Alone—with her only son, upon whom her hopes had been built, whom she had striven to give to the world as a shining scholar and a minister of God, so that his light might be reflected even upon herself in her declining days . . . here by her hearth, a man rejected and of no substance, all that was left to her . . . with the drowning wave closing over.

She lit the lamp. ' You can't see to read.'

He regarded her face against the lamp-glass. Its prickly yellowish skin, so often vaguely loose, seemed firmed a little to-night. Again he had that strange almost cold sensation that he did not belong to her, that her face was something which moved him no way except curiously and to a dreadful clearness of detail. But instead of making him feel impatient or secretly hostile, this vision actually raised a responsibility that was silent and far-spreading and affectionate. As he lowered his eyes, he waited for her to utter some particular thing that he saw was on her mind.

' I can't help wondering,' she said at last, ' about Jean. She hasn't been near me for such a long time.' He noticed the effort to keep complaint out of her voice.

' They're very busy.'

' That must be it.'

' Often people pass in motor cars and have a meal. I thought she was down the other night ? '

' No. Annabel was that handy for running a message.'

' If there's anything you need from the shops, you've only got to ask me to get it.'

' It was only a little bit of clothing from Norman Shaw's. There's no great hurry.'

' All right. You tell me when you want it.' He

271

thought for a moment. ' You could write it on a bit of paper if you like.'

' Oh, it can wait meantime.'

He filled his pipe. Not being able to get Jean out of his head, he became restless. After a little, he laid his book aside.

' You're not going out again ? '

' I won't be long. I'll go as far as the hotel,' he said.

' You shouldn't go out again.'

' I won't be long.'

Against the dumb pull of her complaint, he closed the door, and stood still, affected by the darkening rocks and the restless sound of the sea. As he passed the window, he was aware of her face staring out.

Going up by the stream in the dusk, he saw a young woman whom all at once he was certain was Jean coming down the steep road from the hotel. He must head her off and talk to her directly. This mysterious dumbness of hers had gone too far. At the same moment, however, he saw a group of men on the bridge.

And he had grown wary of meeting people. These last few days he had deliberately avoided his neighbours. This desire not to touch the realities of life in his native place had something hidden, almost furtive, about it. He realised this quite clearly and enjoyed it as he might enjoy something withdrawn in time and space. It held the elements of a delicate revenge, not only on the life about him but on his own essential life, as though at one remove he mocked his defeated self and, shifting his glance, smiled at the world of which Clare Marlowe was the perfect emissary. She had given him the entrée there! True, it was no more than the circle about Clare Marlowe herself, as though she moved like a star carrying her own light. In contrast to the darkness of his mind with its twisting underways of thought and occasional escapes on empty seas, the light was a ring of whiteness moving with her, so that she was always at its centre, tall and slim—and waiting . . . until the desire to conquer the darkness moved her, as it always moves light, grown curious and attracted.

Attracted as though she instinctively felt that his darkness was equal and opposite to her light, and perhaps, in certain ways, more potent! Potent, for example, in the ways that the hills and the glens were potent, drawing her to some mystical secret source of life, of fertile life—which always works back to the source in oneself!

Light and darkness are forever different—and forever meeting. And the meeting in this case must have produced in her mind something not unlike a Celtic twilight! How glamorous—and how fatal!

That was the humour of revenge with which he amused his vanity when she was not there. When she was there—it was delicately otherwise, without being profoundly different—except at certain moments, when her light overcame him. At these moments she became wholly transparent because of some obscure doubt in her raised by a last honesty. Then he grew uncomfortable and his mind balked as at guilt. A disharmony that cried to be crushed, a sensitiveness that could be conquered only by an overriding roughness, and afterwards when alone, in reaction, by the strong brutal humour that laughs out of conquest, with always that remoter air of surprise that holds its own male delight.

For there was that between them, finally lacking in frankness. It could not be otherwise. They stepped out of such different worlds, with minds intricate and responsive to even imagined distinctions. Simplicity could not uncover itself and gaze. Certainly not in his case. She might have the illusion of simplicity, even of frankness, because from her world she was stepping down. So superb a movement of the freed spirit that she might feel uplifted. Probably she did. Even carried away. Forgetting that he could scarcely accept her in the same spirit— by stepping up!

Not so much a fine rapture as a fine torment. And therefore none the less fascinating. For the body can never get away from the mind, not anyhow for long, and when it does the mind re-enters, looking around for any new lumber in the way of shame. Certainly to begin with—which meant in his case, and clearly, for all her sophistication, in hers.

It was doubtful even if she was attracted by him so much as by what she imagined in him, as though she added to him all unconsciously a certain environmental or symbolical value! The odd things she said surprised him; she said them, too, so cleverly, taking for granted that no more than a hint was needed to call out the deepest meaning. And the meaning somehow centred in themselves, as if the mountains and glens were really in their own brains and bodies.

While always she knew so perfectly how to behave. In the morning she appeared again completely unself-conscious. There was added to her behaviour a certain lightness, an ease and grace, born surely of the daylight itself. What a relief, after the night before, and how it balanced his own effort at the gillie's mask! The excitement within him of a vague dread, of a disposition to face out anything (with its incipient hostility) had died down and he had answered her calmly. Nothing of the previous night was betrayed between them. Their secret world was sealed up. Her clear brow dismissed everything but the wind-wandered morning with its promise of a day's fishing. 'You think it's going to be a good day? How excellent!' She was delighted. And something of the freedom of that delight passed into him.

There was, too, in this delicate morning relationship a singular zest of life, particularly when finally they were left alone to the loch. It showed itself in an extra keenness of interest, a restrained merriment, as though perhaps she was excited after all. It was very definitely something to be alive. And she said as much, provoking him to talk, while she fished satisfactorily. 'That was a good rise!' he had interrupted her this morning. 'Yes!' she exclaimed, falling short with her next cast. 'I'll take you over it again.' The trout came once more and she hooked it. 'He's a monster!' she cried. 'Let him go!' he directed; and then 'wind in quickly, quickly—mustn't let the line slack.' The excitement increased until he netted it. Then she sat down heavily, breathing quickly, her skin flushed. 'It's the biggest one you've yet caught,' he said, as he released the fly and knocked the trout, which was all of a pound. She leaned forward, lips apart, then leaned back as he dipped his hands overboard. She made no effort to start fishing again, and though they had not completed the drift, he turned the boat to the wind and lay on the oars. That gave her a rest. She sat looking over the loch and at the hills with a curious deep quiescence. When he quietly put the boat broadside on again, she picked up her rod and said ' Thanks,' with unmistakable understanding.

After that she was silent for a time, but her eyes soon began to grow bright with merriment. It was good to be alive—and to be away from work. ' Though, of course, this *is* your work! '

' Yes.'

' Why ? ' she asked, but absently.

' Why not ? ' he answered, without stress.

After a moment her smile broke on a delicious chuckle. ' Why not indeed! ' as though hitting at her covered thought. He had felt himself flush and been aware of a quick glance.

' It seems ridiculous,' she explained, ' that I should be praising this life here and yet expecting you to go in for some other. I know. Only— ' And she held out her reservation. As he did not accept it, she added frankly, ' That sounds unfair. I suppose I meant that there is a difference between my position here and yours.'

' All the difference,' he said quietly.

' It must then be of your own choosing.'

' How ? ' He did not look at her.

' Because in a world of competition you should make your way better than I have made mine.'

' I don't think so.'

276

She looked at him. ' You are thinking of family influence ? '

' No, I wasn't.' He was speaking reluctantly.

' Well ? ' And she raised her eyebrows over her scepticism.

' It's perhaps the existence of that difference of mind or appearance—that the evolutionists pin their faith to.'

In her surprise all she could answer was ' Oh ? ' until she thrust back, ' For a young man who may not have been altogether ignored by the evolutionist theory—isn't your attitude rather defeatist ? '

' It may depend on how far one's been bludgeoned.'

' What about the bloody and unbowed ? '

' But he was an Englishman.'

As she laughed the cast whipped round his neck. He watched how her fingers behaved as she unloosed the flies.

But therein had been exposed their worldly relationship. The inevitable one, of course. What urged her to want him to be successful ? Did some obscure feminine instinct desire him more nearly on her own level ? An amusing line of reflection! . . .

For she was so honest. And when they landed and she jumped from the gunnel of the boat and bumped into him, he saw at once how she was affected. He was instantly affected himself and before he knew what he was doing he caught her strongly and kissed her. She yielded completely, with that powerful fascination of yielding against her judgment, as though this moment had been kept under all day.

When they stood apart they were both shaking

277

and blindly uncomfortable. He hauled the boat up unnecessarily. She walked slowly away to the heather and lay down, for strong emotion still exhausted her quickly. She turned her face over.

Presently he stood beside her and quietly dropped the game bag to the heather. Looking down on her, a cruel desire grew in him. Her long slim body and fine hair were abandoned to the earth. As if feeling his look, she turned over. Her eyes fluttered and she got to her feet.

'This is your lunch.'

'Thanks,' she replied coldly, and he walked away out of sight in the usual manner.

Then he had laughed to himself, knowing that the afternoon's fishing had been destroyed, that it would be a tormented afternoon, that it might go from one thing to another. Already he felt it closing in on him and his imagination became active. He could just see the wind's black laugh on the loch's face. They were shut off—into this world. Very well, very well, he laughed, tingling and tormented and clutching the wind.

But when he came back, he found her as he had found her in the morning, clear-eyed and smiling. It made him feel immensely awkward, and yet in a moment obscurely relieved.

'I have decided not to fish any more to-day. I should like,' she said, 'to climb that hill and see the world.'

'Very well.'

'Do you mean you won't come?'

'I'll wait for you.'

'I suppose,' she said at last, 'you are not paid to

278

climb mountains ? ' Her innocent voice was bright with mockery.

His awkwardness gathered an edge.

' Ewan,' she said slowly, ' you look like a shy boy. Alas,' she sighed, ' that you should be so adorable.' And with that she walked away, in complete command of the situation.

But a situation not so much against him—as against herself. And the male in him knew it.

It was certainly a world removed from this of the men on the bridge, of the place about him, of the crofts—a world with no conditions and no caring, full of its own tormented fascination. The only thing that was wrong with it, perhaps, was the fineness of Clare Marlowe, which, in his calm moments, was its added light. That afternoon, when she had returned tired from her hill walk she had approached him with a friendly simplicity. Her frankness had obviously not a thought behind it. She talked of the view. ' I wish you had come.'

All at once he had felt moved, very friendly, would have done her any service. She turned to say something else—and remained looking at him, eyes to eyes. . . .

He had avoided even asking for Jean when he had returned to the hotel. Nor would he have followed her farther now, were he not sure some of the men on the bridge had made him out. They would conclude he was going queer! And he would not give them that satisfaction quite yet!

Besides, the chances were that it was Fachie Williamson holding forth on the Ardbeg raid.

Fachie had been trying to get the men to answer the sheriff's summons. What about engaging him and blowing him up?—as something positive against them all! He kept an eye on Jean's bobbing head and shoulders and when she disappeared beyond the bridge—and therefore up the glen—his mind sharpened cruelly and he swore softly to himself.

Nor was his desire for an encounter lessened by his seeing Colin McKinnon on the edge of the company, speaking to no one and looking in the half-light rather like the menacing ghost of himself. Ewan did not let his eyes rest on him, did not appear to see him, and, after listening a moment, his heart beating uncomfortably, threw in his word against Fachie.

Fachie Williamson was the local agent for the sitting Member, full of talk of 'the House' and 'committees,' of words like 'lobbying' and 'private interviews.' What he couldn't do by a word in the ear of the Member! An important man, priding himself on his hard-headed common sense. There was no good of flying in the face of things as they are. Human nature was human nature, just as the law was the law. But—leave the trouble to him; he would see what he could do. 'You wait on—and you may be surprised.' A staunch Liberal, with a certain doctrinaire attitude towards Toryism, and a completely contemptuous one towards Labour which he always called Communism. But the Ardbeg raid was proving itself a snag. He had hoped to be able to 'work' things. He had told the men to hold on; they had a case; they had been promised the land before the estate was sold; they were willing to pay rent; their economic position was desperate. . . . But the

280

gallant Member apparently couldn't work the oracle this time. The man who owned part of the county as a sheep-farm had felt himself compelled to invite the attention of the law, and everyone perfectly understood his position. There was no general rancour against him. The sheriff on the East Coast had requested the attendance of the raiders at court, and the men, quite on their own initiative, had decided not to go. Fachie had sent a telegram that had cost all but half-a-crown. He had stormed at the men, telling them it would mean prison, until Red Homer had asked, ' Well ? ' a steady voice in a steady face. Fachie had blustered—and gone away.

Now to-night, to these men on the bridge, he was going over the whole position, making it clear how no human being on earth could help the raiders, and how no one was to blame for what was about to happen but themselves. It was against this desperate effort for assurance that Ewan thrust his word.

With his reserve and measuring eyes, added to what was known and (more especially) unknown in his past, Ewan did not make an easy, popular figure. Yet in the secret minds of his neighbours he undoubtedly had precisely what Fachie lacked, a sort of personal prestige, which they liked or didn't like according to their natures. His apparent indifference to the fate of the Ardbeg crofters and his refusal at one point to write letters which were to move the powers that be, naturally did not on this occasion attract the crowd's sympathy from Fachie.

And Fachie knew this. He was prepared to revel in it. ' What,' he challenged, ' could you do with these hills more than they are doing to them ? Do

281

you think you could grow potatoes on them, and corn?'

'And carrots,' piped a young wag.

'And monkey-nuts,' added Ewan, freed by the personal attack.

'Anyone can talk,' said Fachie. 'But how could you give men money and work to be doing anything to these hills? That's what I would like to know?'

'So therefore,' Ewan deduced, ' seeing we cannot grow corn and monkey-nuts on these hills, ought we not to be grateful to men who can grow them elsewhere, like Mr. Denver, and who come here and spend the proceeds in amusing themselves and feeding the local monkeys? That's the idea, isn't it?'

'The point is,' cried Fachie, ' that these men like Mr. Denver are here. If he wasn't here, there would be another here instead of him. That he's an American does not make any difference to the argument.'

'Quite. It merely makes the contemplation of our Highland heritage, which the lady spoke about so touchingly at the concert the other night, really romantic. But it makes no difference to the monkey-nuts. I grant you that.'

'You and your monkey-talk! A man like Mr. Denver at least brings money to the place. That means extra comfort to the place and to the people. That's the real truth, and a generous man would admit it. Any fool can open his mouth.'

A rare delight stirred in Ewan. He could drown Fachie with talk.

'That's what's called the common-sense view. I know. But if we are satisfied with things as they are, then why all this fuss? I know about our past, the

282

wonderful past of a great race, but—*the past.* I thought you were interested in the present. I'm sorry if I mistook you.'

'What do you mean?' cried Fachie. 'You know it's the present that's my life's work. I work for to-day; when others—' He pulled himself up, spittle at the lip.

'Very well. Take the present. Here's your wealthy outsider using your Highland heritage as a sports preserve. Such of the natives—that's us— as remain are his gamekeepers or his gillies or—ah— his handmaidens on the one side; and on the other— crofters, living in poverty on their small holdings, and glad of any chance of earning a pound or two from him to help to pay him their rent; no longer producing music or poetry or anything of the slightest consequence; a really first-class slave race. That's the state we have arrived at. If you're satisfied with it I can quite understand why you want territorial concerts to help to defend it. You were always logical.'

By their silence and the way they stood, Ewan saw that the folk were trying to steal into his mind. His talk had all the gaiety of an oblique revenge. It maddened Fachie, who shouted:

'Communism! Rubbish! And, anyway, if things were like that, what would *you* do?'

'No, you don't get me as easy as that! You've got to admit what I say—or show me where I'm wrong.'

'Go on!' probed a voice.

'Yes, tell him to go on!' cried Fachie.

So all at once Ewan did go on. He even found himself launched upon something like a speech, mounting from ' the futile little questions that Highland M.P.'s ask in an English House of Commons about decayed little piers and fences for deer, and so on ' to inspiring speeches ' by great Gaels dealing with the homes they've been driven out of or been very careful to leave behind them. One of them the other day, complete in kilt and sporran, was saying that " grandiose ideas " for dealing with the Highlands were nonsense; what was needed was " something practical." So he suggested tourists! Tourists! . . .'

' Well, what's wrong with tourists ? ' demanded Fachie.

' Who else,' cried Alastair bàn, ' would give a bun to the monkeys ? '

' I'm no' a tourist,' said the young wag, ' I'm a plumber.'

Fachie saw that the sarcastic fun appealed to them, and that beneath the fun they could be stirred. Perhaps he had a misgiving that deep in their hearts they mistrusted and were prepared to laugh at ' agents ' like himself. His humour gathered a certain ferocity as he insisted, ' So after all, there's nothing you *could* do ? '

' On the contrary,' replied Ewan, prepared to move him properly, ' I would do a lot. And the first small step would be getting possession of the sporting lands— '

' Ha! ha! ha! ' Fachie's body doubled up.

' Keep your irony,' Ewan suggested, ' to iron your kilt. Even to buy them out would cost less than a battleship— '

' Ach— '

284

'Yes,' Ewan laughed. ' It may hardly be worth it, I know. But at least it's not dear. Mr. Denver spends more on his works. It's dirt cheap. Woolworth wouldn't miss it out of his day's balance. It's a damned joke.'

Fachie waved his arms. Did ever anyone hear such rot ? But a voice ignoring him asked of Ewan with an odd interest:

' What would you do if you got the land ? '

In a moment this new voice made Ewan tired of the argument, but he had to go on now, and so in a bantering tone suggested, ' Then the fun would begin. According to the blue books there are nearly two million acres of arable land within the deer forests. That would have to be shared out, I'm afraid. The crofters would also be condemned to accept outruns to their holdings for cattle and sheep. Then there would be the sporting rights above a certain height and the fishing—as a pastime. Not to mention the only industry we have, the inshore sea fishing, at present handed over by the Government to foreign trawlers. There are people who even talk of afforestation, as though we had the intelligence of the Norwegians. But at the worst we could always import a Dane or a Swede, or even an Irishman, to show us how to run things. The only drawback would be that the man on the land would hardly be able to keep any buttermilk for himself, there would be such a run on it. His produce would be snapped up and he would have nothing but cash to show for it. He might even have to form himself into trading associations. However, he could always lament the good old days when the corn-beef kings and the sauce-makers (you need the one for the other) were in power and the crofters of Ardbeg, faced with prison— '

But here was the sore point and Fachie instantly lashed out:

' A lot you're doing for the crofters of Ardbeg! '

There was silence.

' And what have you done ? ' Ewan asked.

' At least we have tried to do all we could.'

' But if all you have done has amounted to nothing then you haven't done anything.'

' I see! Wonderful! And how do you know we could not have done anything ? ' Fachie's sarcasm scarcely covered his wrath.

' By what you said earlier. The law is the law. The men have no legal claim to the ground. Your M.P. can do nothing. The law is bound to tell the men to clear off the raided ground. Isn't it ? '

' Damn you, you stand there talking like that as if the police weren't here to take the men away like criminals in the morning.'

' Isn't it ? ' repeated Ewan, hit by this new intelligence, made suddenly cold by it. He had not known that things had gone so far.

' Shoving your nose in, with your university and all your orders! A lot you've done! '

' Isn't it ? ' persisted Ewan. ' You see, you can't answer. You're just talking away as if you were a great man who could work wonders. In a case of this sort you can work nothing. And you know it.'

In a moment the tension had become acute. Ewan found himself in a cold rage. The bystanders stood dead still, watching. This ruthless attitude of

Ewan's was quite new to them. The university taunt had apparently gone home.

'Who's the great man?' demanded Fachie. 'By God, we try and do something, whatever. We at least try to face up to it, to help where we can.' He took a step forward. 'That's what we do.'

But the first blind flush over, Ewan had command of himself.

'And I say that what you have done amounts to nothing—nothing but talk. If you had had your way, the men would have had to pay their own travelling expenses and legal fees with money they haven't got. Now, at least, the police will pay it for them. They are so much to the good in spite of you. They have also shown some guts. And I think any man with a decent stomach would in the circumstances keep his mouth shut.'

'You do, do you?'

'I do.'

'Oh, I see. You're a fine fellow, aren't you? You would stand and see your neighbours go to prison without lifting a finger to help them because —because your stomach is so dainty. You're the one!'

'Quite. The trouble is that even with the lifting of all your fingers you can't help them. Nothing short of turning up all your toes would be any use.' And he laughed shortly.

Fachie's head stooped forward threateningly to belie the menace of that laugh.

'And you would see them go to prison like criminals—and laugh. You would laugh,' he spluttered.

287

'Not at all. I merely laugh at you, and at your master, and at the sort of stuff that has never done a thing for the Highlands except slowly smother it with poultices. You would try to hush this thing up. Get the men to be agreeable and nice and not make a disturbance in the constituency. The Ardbeg men know all about it. They are going to stick to what they have taken, and be damned to you and the law. They are men, anyhow—even though they've been reduced to such circumstances by your rotten political jobberies that the food they'll get in prison will be better than anything they can afford in their own homes.'

There was complete silence for seconds. Ewan's words had for the first time a stinging reality. The feeling and bitterness touched the crowd on the bridge. Fachie knew in a moment they were moved.

'Political jobberies!' he cried at random. 'What political jobberies? Name them! Name them!'

'Name the hairs on your head,' said Ewan.

The young wag coughed, for it was many years since Fachie had trained long obscuring side hairs over a gleaming crown. Fachie could not believe that Ewan's thrust was unintentional. He lost his temper completely and went right up to him.

'I'll make you eat your words,' he hissed. He postured in front of Ewan's body. 'You may think you're a damn fine fellow. You may think you're a gentleman with your goings-on. We cannot all have the privilege of going sniffing about our betters all over the place.'

The dark innuendo blinded Ewan. Then his words came like a whip-lash:

288

'No. You can only sniff them in the one place like a dog.'

Alan Ross got his restraining hand on Fachie's shoulder.

'Now now, there's no need for anything more, boys.' He got in between them. Fachie was herded away, head high and muttering. Colin said to Ewan, 'Let us go up the road a bit.'

Ewan turned away with him.

'That was all damned silly,' he said. 'I know that. But somehow it came over me. I don't mean anything against Fachie, but—I don't know, there's something in the thing somewhere that I hate . . . it's so paltry, so rotten, crawling to every big bug, blowing about the famous Highlands. . . .'

'He needed it,' said Colin. 'He's always running with his tale here and his tale there, and thinking himself the great fellow with his kilt on him, representing the Highlands—the great Highlands,' remarked Colin smoothly.

But beneath Ewan's words to Colin was the dark innuendo: could folk possibly have seen Clare Marlowe and himself? . . . And when he had stopped talking and was listening to Colin, deeper than the dark innuendo came alive the aversion to touching his native world at any point, and particularly at that point represented by Colin and his daughter Mary. That's what he had been withdrawing himself from; what he had been avoiding; that was why he had been living in his precious secret world, building it out of the beauty and cleverness of Clare Marlowe, out of the resignation of his mother, out of the sea and the rocks.

289

' You haven't been near us for a long time,' said Colin, as they walked up the road to his house. But Ewan wasn't going into his house. That was absolutely certain. He wasn't going near it. His footsteps dragged hesitatingly, stopped.

' No,' Ewan answered, taking a deep breath, as though he were still ruffled by the bridge encounter, and turning round to look down upon the darkened scene. ' No. To tell the truth, my mother is all alone since Annabel went to Sronlairg. She's feeling it a bit. So I don't go out much at night.'

' Ay, she'll be all alone now. It generally comes to that.'

' Yes.'

' Though she has Jean near by in the hotel there.'

' Yes, that's so,' Ewan answered, ' but they're busy enough there, what with late dinner and that; it's not often she can run down.'

Colin agreed that it would be difficult for her.

' Aren't you coming up ? ' Colin asked.

' No. You'll excuse me, Colin. I said to my mother I would be back in a minute and I have something to see to at the hotel. I can never resist Fachie.' He laughed. ' For some reason I feel he always makes a dead set at me! '

' Ay. I think he has the feeling that you are laughing at him up your sleeve. A few people have that.'

' Have they ? No ? ' It sounded amusing.

' Yes,' said Colin mildly.

They stood in silence for a time during which Ewan grew more uncomfortable. There was some hidden thing in Colin's mind. He sensed it, and with a blinded premonition feared it. In a moment he realised that all along it had been there, quiet and deadly.

'Won't you come up just for a little ?' suggested Colin.

'No. I can't, man.' The refusal cost him a physical effort, went pricking at his forehead. But he couldn't go. He couldn't. 'I—I have to be over. I'm late as it is.'

'I see,' said Colin. 'All right.'

'Some night soon,' hoped Ewan.

'Yes. Some night soon.'

They stood unmoving.

'There wasn't anything—anything you wanted to say ?' Ewan forced himself to ask.

'Oh, nothing in particular.'

'You're sure ?' He had to find out now; must get it over. He could not carry about with him the burden of indecision; for he felt it had to do with himself, with Colin's attitude to him, and Mary's. And Colin was his greatest friend. And Mary. . . .

'Oh well,' hesitated Colin; and there was now no doubt about Colin's mind. It was quiet and cold like death. Colin was the only one who had ever been able to communicate to him this fatal sensation.

'Let us sit down a minute,' suggested Ewan.

'It's about the Colonel,' said Colin, almost pleasantly, when he had carefully seated himself.

Ewan waited.

'I thought if you happened to come up I would tell you, so that we might speak over it together, for maybe I know how you feel about the man, too. But if you didn't come up it wouldn't matter for I would

surely some time meet him myself. This is his stick
I have.'

' What is it, Colin ? ' Ewan coughed a dryness
out of his throat.

' Though why should I tell you, in any case, I
don't know. I think I had been expecting that you
would come up while it was fresh on my mind, and
I would be conspiring with you when you weren't
there, and that put the habit of telling you in me.
But. . . .'

Ewan waited.

' Anyway, having gone so far I may as well tell
you. I admit it's been bothering me. And Mary
up by—she gets that frightened now . . . she'll be
looking at me white as a sheet when I'll be going back
in at night. But it won't let me rest. And this is his
stick. She always sees me taking his stick. For if
I have a word with him, it must be alone, for her sake.
It's the thing that must be kept hidden, for her
reputation is in it, and you know what people like to
say when they get the chance. The only one I could
think of was yourself, for I don't see how I'm going
to come at the Colonel, and we cannot go on like this.
I can see it's telling on her that I should be going out
about in the darkening, looking for him to give him
his stick back.'

Ewan could not summon a single word.

' It was last Thursday,' proceeded Colin, with quiet
detachment. ' I walked up the glen in the afternoon
to see Rory Mackay about that young cow of his.
I had promised Rory I would go. I met him on this
side of his house, sitting looking at the beast, and I
examined her and told him what I thought, but I

wouldn't go into the house, because, as I said, Mary at home was wanting to go to the shop before it shut. So I stepped back in good time. . . . But when I got into my house there was Mary herself in the queer state, what with weeping and some of the clothes torn off her so that you could see great bruised marks on her arms. I had seemingly come in on her before she knew. I asked her what was wrong. But she wouldn't tell me. She looked that dazed and scared. Thinking on what she had come through had maybe got the better of her. But she came to herself quickly enough. I was kind to the lassie, and after a while she broke down and told me about it. I don't know whether the Colonel spotted me going up the glen or not. Anyway, shortly after I had left he knocked at the door of the house. Mary was washing herself in the back-place, and, hearing someone knocking and coming right in, she thought it was Jean from the Crioch with some piece of dress or other she was expecting, and throwing her apron over her shoulders, she came running into the kitchen. It was, however, the Colonel himself. I'll light my pipe.' Colin lit his pipe and puffed at it a moment, then put it back in his pocket. ' Yes, it was the Colonel himself. Mary told him I wasn't in. But it wasn't me he was wanting. He stood looking at her, and she with the scanty apron about her, until she nearly dropped from not knowing what to think at all. Then he said something about a drink, and that let her into the back-place where she dressed herself right enough. She came back to him with a glass of water. He took the glass but he didn't drink it at all. It's not water he was wanting. It was Mary herself. The glass indeed fell on the floor in a hundred bits. Mary ran into the back-place. She doesn't know why she didn't run out of the house. I think she sort of couldn't believe what was happening. She was leaning against the door, when he suddenly burst it open and sent her flying in amongst the pans and the dishes. He cornered her there and began to come at her. But she broke through him and went running round the house and into the byre, maybe because it was the first place she saw. Someway he found out she was in the byre. He got the door open with the full weight of him against it . . . and he had her cornered in the stall. He would try to make sure of her this time. But she's strong in herself and though he got her down she managed to fight her way from him, leaving nothing in his hands but that fancy blouse of hers. She was fond of it. I found it later on trampled into the sharn in the byre. Then she took to the hill; and indeed it's a wonder she didn't go as she was to Angie Cruban's. But she didn't. She climbed up a little and lay down. There she got worse than ever and vomited. After a while she came back home. The Colonel left his stick behind. This is it in my hand. As I say, I was looking for him to give it to him back. Take a draw of the pipe,' suggested Colin in friendly tones.

Ewan did not move. His jaws were clamped and Colin could not hear him breathing.

' I'm telling you this,' said Colin, forgetting to light his pipe, ' in a neighbourly way, as I've told you other things besides; but what I was thinking to myself, too, was that maybe you would know the Colonel's habits, being about the hotel as you are.

294

You don't know if he takes a walk to himself at all after his dinner?'

'I don't know,' said Ewan tonelessly.

'Then we're no further forward.'

They sat silent.

'I think I'll be getting down,' said Ewan, and quietly got to his feet.

Colin put his pipe back in his pocket and stood up. There was silence.

'You understand, Ewan?'

'Understand what?' asked Ewan, indifferently.

Colin stood very still, peering at him through the dark.

'Now don't you begin to make me sorry that I told you.'

'Sorry? How that?' returned Ewan, with the suspicion of a dry laugh.

'This is my business.'

'Of course! Whose else?'

'You have no reason, you understand—'

'Reason? I should think not!' said Ewan. 'No shadow of reason at all, Colin. I know.'

'Now, look you here, Ewan—'

'It's so dark, man, Colin, I can't see.'

'You're seeing well enough. And I'm seeing you.' Colin's tone hardened dangerously.

'You always had the good sight,' laughed Ewan.

Colin said nothing.

'Well, I'm off. Good-night to you, Colin.' And Ewan went lurching down the road, the suspicion of his satiric laughter left on the eddying air.

When his footsteps had died away, Colin started after him at a rapid pace. He had almost reached the

bridge when a figure rose out of the ditch behind him
and said:

' You're surely in a hurry, Colin.'

Colin turned round, came back a pace or two, and
faced Ewan. He was breathing heavily.

' What do you mean,' he demanded, ' carrying on
like that ? '

' How carrying on ? ' asked Ewan, with taunting
innocence.

' You will understand—that I won't have it.'

' Won't you ? Very well, whatever it is.'

Colin's fist came out and clutched a lapel of
Ewan's jacket. His cold rage was getting beside
itself.

' Don't you be a fool, Ewan Macleod. Don't
speak to me like that.'

' Like what ? '

Colin shook Ewan; a button of the jacket coming
undone, the lapel slipped through his fingers and
Ewan stumbled and fell. He got to his feet and faced
Colin as before.

' Why don't you use his stick ? ' he suggested.

' I'll use that too—if you're not careful.'

' Have a go at it! ' taunted Ewan.

Colin's hand went back. There was a moment's
dreadful pause, then Colin brought the dishonouring
stick sharply across Ewan's body.

' Go on! ' said Ewan.

Colin hit him a second time.

' Again,' prompted Ewan.

' Damn you! ' said Colin, and his voice broke.

' You could cut me on the face, Colin, man, and
I would take it from you with a smile and remember

it as a joke. There's nothing I wouldn't do for you between this and hell. But I was always bad at making promises.'

Colin did not speak. His shoulders sagged.

They stood in the grip of an understanding deeper than any affection, in their vision a cruel clear light. Colin wanted to utter a whisper of caution for the lad's sake, and Ewan wanted to tell Colin not to fear for his pride. But neither spoke, and Ewan turned down the road.

2

There was no one on the bridge now. Ewan crossed it and turned up the road to the left towards the hotel. Inwardly he was laughing over the affair with Colin, getting much mirth out of it. Colin would be wondering about him now, as Mary was wondering about Colin when he went out with the stick. The twist things get! Colin did not want Ewan to do anything. ' You have no reason.' ' No reason ' was good! It was flaming good! Colin naturally didn't tumble to the inwardness of the joke. Colin's pride, discernible behind the telling, was a beautiful thing, like a tune. But he had endangered it by telling Ewan; had implicated Ewan by the very telling, as if he had dragged him in—*with* a reason! He would be vexed now. Lord, but he would be vexed! What a repayment of the affection that had prompted him to speak out of his loneliness, his fatal anger. . . .

Suddenly, as though he had been keeping these thoughts in his mind with a purpose, the purpose of merely occupying it, they slid out of sight, and his mind rose up naked and cold. He listened. The hotel was now directly above him. By climbing the steep broken face he would avoid the road curving up to the gravelly front, and so would come out on the right of the hotel where tumbled ground was and the dining-room windows. Thus no one would by any chance see him. He started to climb. His muscles were extraordinarily expert. He experienced a certain cold pleasure in their use; was conscious of their sheathed strength as a man might be conscious of a rapier. Quite noiselessly and breathing lightly, he in time approached the dining-room windows. A half-drawn blind gave a clear view of the room. There was no one in the room but Stansfield lost in the pages of *The Times*. Ewan drew back; and after a moment's pause, crept noiselessly round towards the back premises. There was just that odd chance that the Colonel was out about—somewhere.

The foundations of the back part of the hotel had been dug out of an upward tumbled roll of ground, and from some warped pines Ewan emerged on to the ledge of the cutting which placed him on about a level with the top of the back-kitchen window and only some twelve feet from it. There was, however, no light in the window. Nor was there any light about the bar door farther along. It must be well after nine. There was an indistinct mutter of voices on towards the garage. He lay down flat. And quite suddenly there came before his inner vision, with vivid clarity, the torn clothing and bruised arms of Mary McKinnon, the face above, worn with emotion, haggard, and the eyes, the black eyes, looking straight at him. . . . He hit his face into the ground and his teeth tore at the grass.

The unreasoning spasm passed, leaving his mind cold and blank. He lay on the ground, resting himself, his face in the grass. . . . But every now and then his teeth would spasmodically bite the grass, the muscular action defeating thought. . . . Two dark eyes swam before him. He stared at them—and bowed his head deep, deep, crushing them out. . . . They would not leave him alone. They came swimming back. And if he allowed them to steady for a moment the face formed round them . . . the body below . . . the bruised bare arms . . . like an idol of tortured dreams. He laughed brutally within himself. He would get out of this. What the blazes was he lying here for anyhow ? What ? . . . All at once the question penetrated. It gripped him with an unexpectedness that was cramping in its mockery. Had his hidden mind been prompting him to expect to find the Colonel somewhere hereabouts with— Jean ? Had he been driven round here, because Jean and the Colonel. . . . His face uprose, nostrils taking the air quiveringly like an animal's. All the time, without knowing it, dogged by an impossible suspicion, which had sunk into the deeps of his being . . . his sister, the servant girl, approached by the Colonel, aware that she was hardly expected to defend herself . . . as Mary McKinnon had been approached! . . . Christ!

Footsteps, a woman's, came past the bar and on to the kitchen door, secretive, yet unhurried footsteps . . . Jean. Her dark figure fumbled about the door, which opened and quietly closed behind her. A match was struck, a small hand lamp lit. The window was white-screened only half way up, so that Ewan looked directly upon Jean's revealed face. Its worn pallor was incredible; ineffable weariness and spent grief. The eyes were dark hollows. He was shocked beyond thought, could do nothing but gaze upon what he saw as upon a vision of tragedy removed from him, and all the further in that it should be enacted by a sister of his. Jean, who was holding the lamp in her left hand, looked slowly about her working premises, listened for sounds beyond the inner door. A stab of pain seemed to twitch her body, and she brought her right hand under her heart and pressed it there. He saw her lips tighten and the expression on her face cloud and grow dour. Then she opened the inner door and, passing out, left the back premises dark once more.

A strange foundering sensation beset Ewan; he became a lightless husk, like the back premises he looked upon. His mouth began to mutter senseless oaths. His astonishment grew alert, as though at any moment defeated thought might commend revelation. . . . Very quietly and carefully he got up, retraced his steps, looked into the dining-room where Stansfield all alone was still lost in yesterday's *Times*, and worked his way round the slope, until his raised head commanded—a glowing cigar approaching the entrance door. The door rattled open, and a shaft of light smote the congested features of Colonel Hicks, who, entering, rattled the door shut behind him. . . . *Jean at one door and the Colonel at the other!* Ewan lay slowly back against the slope, his eyes

300

staring into the blackness over the valley, his hands clutching into the earth.

3

But Colonel Hicks' luck was merely out. He hung about the lounge a moment, quested here and there uncertainly, then took the stairs. Underneath Clare's bedroom door was no light. He passed on to his own bedroom, where he stalked up and down like a man possessed. His indecision became unbearable, and returning to Clare's door, he paused and warningly cleared his throat . . . listened, suddenly tapped . . . no response. He tried the door. It opened into darkness. ' Clare! ' No answer. He closed the door and returned to his bedroom. So that proved it—she was out! By God! He resumed his restless parade.

About an hour earlier, while taking the air, he had come by the garage door, unseen and unheard, upon voices. The mention of his niece's name had naturally arrested him. . . .

' Would you believe it ? '

' No, and I don't believe it now.'

' So you think I'm a liar ? '

' I'm not saying you are. I'm only saying that Miss Marlowe and Ewan Macleod—don't be a fool, man, talking like that. Drink—but for God's sake don't go talking like that. The thing is mad.'

' Look you now, you're a decent lad, Alastair bàn —and I will not get angry with you if I can help it. I tell you—and I swear it before my Maker—that I saw them through my glass kissing away like the

301

devil. I wasn't half a mile away—no, nor a quarter; they were that big in front of my glass that I could have put out my hand and touched them. Do you believe me ? '

There was no response.

' Don't think,' proceeded the tipsy voice, ready to take offence, ' that I'll go talking about it. Only I thought it such a damn good joke—between ourselves, uh ?—between ourselves—ha-hah—what ? There you go sticking up for him ! He's a dark one. Damn me, I always said he was a dark one. Dark. . . And I saw herself—what you call her ?—Miss Marlowe, yes, a few minutes ago, going along the road— alone—by herself. . . . Where's that Ewan whatever ? Did you see him about ? We had a drink or two—night of the dance. Look here, I'm saying, look here. D'you think I'm telling you a lie ? I don't like way you speak.'

' Oh, hang it, you know fine I don't mean anything against you personally, Lachlan.'

' Well, don't speak as if you did. You're trying to make out that I'm telling you a lie. . . . And not only that, not only that: you're making out that I— that I shouldn't have told you what I saw. That's going too far, Alastair bàn. I told you as a joke. Now you make out that I am—no, damn me, I won't stand it from you or anyone else.'

Alastair switched into urgent Gaelic.

' No, I don't care. I'll speak as I like in the King's English. I'm in the Lovat Scouts. And I'll speak as loud as I like. I'm saying I don't like it. I'm saying I don't like your tone. And I have a damn good mind to throw you— '

' I apologize, Lachlan. I know you meant it as a joke. And—it is a joke. I believe you now. It's a tremendous joke. It's the hell of a joke. Ha! ha! It's the devil's own joke.'

' What do you mean ? '

' Look here, Lachlan. You're a gentleman. If the thing had been the other way round I might have told you the joke then. Very well. Accept my apology, and think no more about it.'

' No, damn me, I don't like your tone.'

' Well, I can't help my tone. If you don't like it, you can stick it in — '

' Oh, so— '

' No, I won't quarrel with you either.' Their voices had risen angrily.

' Come on out of here. I must get home. . . .'

A heavy shambling figure followed slim Alastair bàn out of earshot of Colonel Hicks standing rigidly at the garage corner.

Even the Colonel had felt that he could not have interfered; for in the half-drunken speech of Lachlan Mackenzie was an obvious childlike honesty and hurt pride which no man—certainly no stranger—could have dared challenge at the moment. And to quarrel with a drunken gillie over Clare's name, to let them understand that he had heard, to have the blinding insult affirmed and driven home. . . .

It took the Colonel nearly two miles of road to get any clear reason in his mind, and then two miles back for reason to stare at its ' blinding insult.'

And now she wasn't in her room. Out—after having gone to bed! And there was that other night —two or three nights—letters to post, was it ?

303

Letters! . . . He felt dry. His tongue clacked against the roof of his mouth. As he neared the foot of the stairs, Clare came in at the front door, her coat about her ears. They met face to face in the lounge.

The Colonel went a dark purple that tried to smile. The pale blue eyes made a strained effort to support the courteous suggestion. The total effect of desperate, contorted awkwardness lifted Clare's face a questing inch.

'Where have you been?'

'I've been out for a walk.' Clare's faultless eyebrows perceptibly arched. She turned down her coat collar.

'Thought you'd gone to bed.' The Colonel could no more than articulate. His inflated chest looked as if it might burst.

'Did you?'

'Where were you?'

'Is this—a joke?'

'No, by God,' said the Colonel, his breath escaping like steam, 'it's not!'

Clare continued to regard him.

'Where were you?'

'Uncle Jack—what do you mean?'

'I want to know where you've been—that's all.'

'Why do you look at me like that?'

The pale cool face, the direct eyes, the unfaltering steadiness, beginning now to be touched with a crispness of hauteur, did not help the Colonel.

'I want to know where you've been,' he insisted.

She deliberated a calm moment and apparently decided to answer him.

'As I say, I've been for a walk.'

304

' Where ?   Past the post office ? '

' Yes.'

' I went miles along that road—just now.'

' Well ? '

' How didn't I see you ? '

' Presumably because I was not on the road.'

' Where were you ? '

' I'm afraid I don't understand you.   If you have anything to say, will you please say it ? '

' Were you alone ? ' persisted the Colonel.

' I was quite alone.'

' The whole time ? '

' The whole time.'

The Colonel could not dare disbelieve that face. He was in the wrong.   Yet, in some way, he was being tricked, being made a fool of.

' Is that all ? ' asked Clare.

' I—I don't understand,' blustered the Colonel. ' I don't understand this.'

' I'm afraid I'm equally in the dark.'

' Well, it's this,' burst out the Colonel, stung by her tone.   Then he took a step nearer her, lowered his voice to a wheezy breath, maddened by the further thought that ears might be overhearing them. ' Have you been—been carrying on—with that fellow ? '

' What fellow ? '

' That—that gillie of yours.'

' Do you mean Ewan Macleod ? '

' Yes.   Ewan Macleod.'   The name stuck in his throat.

She looked him coolly in the eyes and a half-wearied smile broke on her lips.

'Carrying on!' she repeated. But her eyes were hostile and dangerous.

'Yes,' he hissed out of the growing freedom of his madness.

'And what if I were?' she asked.

'If you were. . . .'

'Yes?'

But the Colonel had momentarily choked. He could not deal with this woman. Something in her cool, slightly contemptuous poise, her amused hostility, her pale perilous beauty, was a trifle too much even for his madness.

'If I thought you were,' he stuttered, 'I would—I would horsewhip him.'

'*Him?*'

He could not lay hands on her. Impotence sent a dark flush over his brain. He peered out from it right into her face.

'You would betray your—your class? If I thought you would have any dealings with—with—with that sort of—sort of muck, I would—I would—' His fists came up breast high.

She saw now that he was losing control of himself. Her faint air of amusement vanished. Very cool and direct she looked at him, and spoke with a penetrative slowness:

'You will please understand that I am accustomed to do as I please. Believe me, I am quite capable of looking after myself. I think this unnecessary talk has gone far enough. Good-night.' And she walked past him quite unhurriedly and mounted the stairs.

4

And in her attic bed, Jean, that other doubt of Ewan's, heard Clare's door close.

She lay quite still, thinking without any emotion of what she had gone through that evening, her body relaxed, spent, grateful for the release from over-lacing, her brain wearily clear and remote from sleep.

These visits up the glen in the early dark thinking she might meet Ronnie McAndrew had been too exhausting. They had always met there at that time without arrangement. When he ceased to come and yet was at home (as she knew), there could be only the one reason: he had grown tired of her, wanted to break off.

At first she had been revengeful and humiliated. But—it had gone on too long now; it had worn her down. And at the concert, at the dance, he had been looking after Annabel. After Annabel, her sister! She had gone through the last depths of humiliation over that. It had also hunted her with a dreadful fear. So at last she had done—what she had always mistrusted doing—she had written him. And to-night they had met.

Ronnie's face had been pale and full of shifting laughter when they came together. He did not know what to do, what to say. It was plainly an uncomfortable trial for him. 'Hullo, Jean!'—his tone over-affable as if he wanted to hide the decision that had been taken—and must remain.

Jean saw all this, and in a moment it gave her the quiet power of despair. Months ago she might have become assertive, flashing with underlights. Now she was fatal and her face looked dark and moody as she said:

'I want to tell you something.'

'Oh, do you?' He smiled pleasantly, unable to stand still. His smile was strained. She waited. He found himself, as he had always done, inviting her 'in here.' He caught her by the elbow. When they got behind the bushes, she sat down. Her strength was drained. He kissed her. His lips had gone cold in a moment.

'What's wrong, Jean?'

She told him.

His hands began to twist and pluck at things. All his body writhed away from the terror of what had come upon it. She had passionately loved his quick movements, his gay spirit, so different from her own slow ways, and now, in a moment, seeing him stripped, she had pity for him. Through all the terror she herself had gone already.

And her pity made her cruel. For suddenly, with him beside her, she had no feelings at all. She was at rest. She began to talk in short slow connected sentences. She had never been much good at talking. Now the words came of their own accord in a dreadful monotone.

She told him of the times when she used to take a run down to see her mother, and coming back late would steal along to the cliff-heads and look over. One night she had looked over and then instead of going away had lain there—and looked over again. She didn't know yet why she hadn't just let go.

His voice broke nervously out of his bodily

twistings. Tears came into it. He begged her to stop; spoke anxiously, urgently, his hands plucking away; said how terrible it was, how desperately sorry he was, incoherently, plucking away, almost crying.

But she went on. She found it a stupendous relief just to speak, to tell him about it, to let him understand what months meant, what people would now and then say about how she was looking, the way she would think over what they had said afterwards, to see if it meant anything, her fear, her mother—especially her mother, whom she hadn't dared visit now for a long time. And Ewan. There was always Ewan. . . .

Why hadn't she told him ? Oh, why hadn't she told him sooner ? . . .

She did not answer.

' Why didn't you tell me, Jean ? '

' When you went back at the Old New Year—do you remember you wrote me and said you would be so busy studying that you would have no time to write letters—even home ? '

He remembered it too well. The transparency of his intention now overwhelmed him, its sheer crudity.

And after a minute, sitting there in the withies, he began to realise, to see in a desperate light, the appalling nature of the catastrophe that had overtaken him. Yet with a fluttering thought for her, a surrounding warmth of emotional feeling, of sorrow, of desperately unavailing regret.

What—what next ? How ? . . .

She made no effort to answer him. She was surprised at her own quiet mind, as though the thing

weren't happening to her at all—happening very
soon—a few weeks.   It was such a sweet cruel comfort to have him.

' You'll have to go away, Jean.'

' Where ? '

' I don't know, but somewhere; you'll have to go
away somewhere.'

She did not answer for listening to the stir in his
mind behind the words, to the thought that pushed
the words out.

' Couldn't you go for a time—somewhere where
we could meet without—so that no one would know
and you would be all right ?   I would hate them to—
you know what they would say—and if you went—
but you must—somewhere.   Surely there's some
place, some one . . . you—you see what I mean ? '

' Yes.'

' Yes.   Well, isn't there some place ?   There must
be some place.'

' There is no place that I know—and no one.   No
place—except home.'

' Oh but—good lord— '   He took his head in his
hands to steady his thought.   But in a moment his
head rose again and his hands became restless.

' But how do you know ?   Couldn't you have. . . .'

' What ? ' asked Jean.   Then the questions came
slowly, fatally: ' Who would take me ?   What
situation could I take ?   How could I get over the
time ?   For that—where would I go ?   What would
I do afterwards . . . two of us ?   Where in the world ?
. . . unless there is a sort of pauper's place.   But we
are not paupers, and I am able-bodied.   I would have
to tell the doctor—even a pauper they say has to tell

her home parish. The word would come back just the same—only worse. I have no money. Where could I go?'

He was now staring before him.

'No,' she said in the same tone, 'I saw that I must go through with it all here. . . . or else not go through with it at all. There was no other way for me. It took me a long time to see all that. Many a long night it was hard. I would think of mother and Ewan. Mother—it will break my heart. Not but that now she will be kind enough. She will be resigned—even to that. Oh, I know. It's awful.' Her tears came, but her voice retained its terrible monotone. 'And then afterwards . . . you know how the people will look on me. I remember Annie Sutherland when it happened to her. I was about fifteen. I thought it was like the end of the world. I was almost frightened to look at her when she came outside again, and I hurried past her, trying to say a polite word.' She stopped.

And then Ronnie McAndrew, with the set face of the grown man staring deliberately on doom, said: 'We must get married. That's the only way.' His voice was firm, almost harsh with decision, almost weary.

It broke the last illusion in her heart. A small smile crept to her face, weary as his voice, but unimaginably more prescient of doom's dark core. She said nothing.

'That's it. We'll just get married.' The momentous words were spoken. He shoved his feet out; pushed his body back; braced himself. He looked the darkness of night in the eye. He laughed one

311

harsh challenging note; turned it into a forced gaiety, half-turning to Jean. 'What do you say? It's the only way. We'll do it. Why didn't you tell me sooner? Did you think I would go back on you?'

After a moment, she said: 'I thought of that way too.'

'What do you mean?' Her tone arrested him.

Then all at once she broke down. He pulled her head against his breast; patted her on the back. 'It's all right, Jean,' he reassured her . . . and stared over her head into the night.

She recovered presently and sat very still. After a time as if reciting a lesson, she began: 'We cannot, Ronnie. You see—' But she hesitated still; then, her last hope snapped, went on monotonously, 'We cannot; you can see that we cannot. If we got married, what would you do? How would we . . . there's no way. You know that. You would have to leave the university; all your aims, all that your mother and father would like you to be, would be ruined. It would be the end of you. You see,' she said, 'I know how it was with Ewan and with my own mother. I'll never forget that. Never. It destroyed my father; it destroyed our home. You cannot understand—what happened to us.'

Yet she waited when he made a gesture, a pushing gesture, as though he were putting objections to one side. But he did not speak.

She asked him: 'How could I do that to you? If I was the cause of that to you, how could I live with you, knowing that in your mind . . . you would hate me.' And in a moment her voice broke on a rush of feeling, 'Oh, Ronnie, in your heart for bringing this on you, you hate me now. I know. We cannot help our feelings. We cannot help them.'

' Now, Jean, what's the good of talking like that ? That's nonsense.'   There was a great swirl in his mind.

' So you must go on with your studies. You must finish at the college. I can go through with my trouble now. I am prepared. No one will know it is you, except my mother. I would have to tell her. But no one else. It would make it easier for her, I was thinking, if I said to her that I wouldn't let you marry me until you had finished at college. I could put it to her like that. She would understand that. She would understand because of what had happened to Ewan. I would say to her that you asked me to marry you, but I wouldn't let you, not until you were through. And perhaps by that time—it wouldn't matter.'

A sense of her extraordinary magnanimity swept his heart, overcame him. He buried his face in her breast and burst into tears. She soothed him, caressed him on the back, and stared over his head into the night. There was no light in that darkness, but within herself there was one glimmer of cold thin light, and in it she saw, with an awful inevitability, that she would have her way.

She saw it still, in her bed. In a day or two, he would give in. He would become full of hopes, of enthusiasms, about what would happen after he was through college. If she wouldn't let him bear it meantime, by goodness when he was through wouldn't he make it up to her! . . . And, almost in spite of herself, like a remote pinprick of light in the

313

outer dark, there was that hopeless hope. . . . Her
mind drifted. Anyway, she had saved Annabel. She
wished she could sleep. . . .

5.

But the whole brain of the hotel was awake above
that valley, each grey wriggle of matter burrowing
its own cell, eyes lit here and there on its shrouded
white face, suggesting other eyes that were dark but
perhaps not vacant, as if hidden thought peered
through.

Towards it the single eyes of remote scattered
cottages stared with the yellow unwinking fixity of
reserve and mysterious withdrawal, as though behind
each the light penetrated in a secret beam back into
far time.

The wind had lost its daylight strength but could
not rest, and in cool puffs eddied aimlessly, drawing
a rustling sigh from bushes, a faint suspiration from
the grass. But the glen, neither dreaming nor awake,
would not be disturbed. The dark heart of the
mountains lay still in its hollow. The open space of
the sea was its soundless ear. All its antique knowledge was heedless even of the beams that penetrated
from the cottages built of its grey boulders. Heart
and ear and beam and earth, heedless in the sad
immemorial harmony of night.

Yet all with that extra stillness, that air of reserve,
as though not utterly heedless, as though in truth the
glazed yellow eyes were directed towards and the
valley itself lay under this new bright crown set upon
the brow of the night.

With John McAlpine as its titular owner.   Into
him now a maid came:
  ' The Colonel wants you.'
  ' What's he wanting me for ? '
  ' He didn't say.'
Slowly he lifted his head from his task of counting
the drawings from the bar and stared before him.
  ' Is he bad ? '
  ' I think so.'
Slowly he turned his face to her, and turned it
away.   A glimmer of intelligence moved in her eyes,
which were dark in a fat pale face with coarse black
hair.   He began to scrape the money towards him
with counting fingers.
  ' Will I say you're engaged ? '
  ' No,' he replied at last.
  ' I'll say you're not in your room.'
Getting no answer, she closed the door.   When
she had gone, he lifted his head and appeared to
listen thoughtfully.   There was only the one light
burning.   He could take a rest to himself by putting
the light out and filling his pipe.   He did this and
sat in darkness where no one could find him.

But the Colonel did not even disturb him.   Indeed
by the time the maid reappeared to say that her
master was not in, the Colonel did not care whether
he was in or not.   The ringing of the bell had been
an involuntary action following the encounter with
Clare.

Stansfield had retired early and the Colonel had
the dining-room to himself, but to-night he did not
throw himself into his chair and, full of blustering
thought, help himself to a drink.   On the contrary

his thought was hard and distinct, and he walked the floor.

That Clare should have had anything to do with a gillie like Ewan Macleod affected the Colonel to his marrow as something vilely unclean. The very thought of this uncleanness braced his body away from it. It was not so much at the moment that she had forgotten herself, that she had sold her class, that she had betrayed him; it was the idea of her getting soiled that was so incredible. Yet there could be no doubt of it. The fellow had been pawing her. Good God!

In this amazed anger, fierce as jealousy, his elements cohered. Decision grew sharp and clear. He would not only interfere here; he would interfere finally. If she thought anything else, by heaven he would undeceive her! Wouldn't he ?

As he walked the floor, his muscles tautened under an impulse to whip and lash. He would take complete control of this, and if she showed any signs of rebellion then he would send her packing at once. She would not stay here and disgrace him. *They* could pity him if they liked—but at their distance.

His face was flushed but firm, the brows drawn and intolerant. As he came to a pause before the fireplace, to focus a final decision, his demeanour suggested a powerful restraint. All the laws of his caste were graved there. In their execution he might have to be brutal or worse, but execute them he would. Colonel Hicks was now no longer the ' outcast ' from his people; he was indeed the very keeper of their citadel, which his niece, that cool defiant emissary of the holders, had attempted to betray.

316

He sat down. This thing required working out . . . precisely.

Yet he could not quite master his mind and his thought, eluding him, completed the circle to its starting point of the incredible. Clare simply couldn't have let her body be touched by a fellow like that. Even if she were debased and of that type—and he had known some beauties in his time—still, dammit, her gorge would revolt at that. She could not ' go native '; she was too cool, too fine. There wasn't a yellow streak in her.

Unless the fellow had been trying monkey-tricks ? . . . The Colonel's jaws closed like his fists. A student of God—sent down for debauchery . . . wine and women. And *women*, considered the Colonel.

His mind narrowed murderously. If there had been presumption by a hair's breadth, then he, Colonel Hicks, would show the whole twisted pack how such a cur was destroyed.

As if the fierce intensity of his thought called Ewan into being, there was the vague ghostly movement of a face in the dark beyond the half-blinded window. The face steadied full on Colonel Hicks for a long time. Then it drew nearer, black eyes and drawn mouth.

The Colonel's head appeared perfectly still and directed towards the fire. His solid body had for the moment the immobility of stone, an implacable figure, so encompassing the subject of his thought that his wrath but hardened his judgment and sharpened its decisions. Some such moment was needed to show him at his best, when superiority functioned like an instinct and ruthlessness searched for its just lash.

317

Against such embodied dignity, the face at the window was indeed ghostly. A dreadful pallor evoked on a dark screen. It came out of the night, or out of death, or out of the past, bodiless, yet with a fierce licking quality like flame. And it was *outside*.

In his throned armchair, the Colonel stirred and turned his head to the window, which was blank.

A flick of irritation whipped his face as he damned the girl who had not drawn the blind properly; the puffy-faced, coarse-haired, stupid —. He got up and stood with his back to the window looking down the room.

The ghostly face slid half into view. A hand went up the glass until it met wood. Half the body appeared and there was a sudden fierce straining upward. The window frame creaked loudly, but the latch was in position and held. The Colonel swung round as the figure disappeared.

The Colonel remained quite still while there surged up in him a sense of incredible outrage, then he strode to the window and, laying hold of the brass hooks in the bottom sash, heaved violently. The latch held. He cursed it in a fury of bewilderment; rattled the whole frame until the glass shivered.

Turning for the door to get outside, he drew it open upon the crowd making from the drawing-room for a last breath of air. He shut it at once. Returning to the window, he glared through it; then drew the blind with a slap.

Some one secretly peering in at him—had come against the glass. He had felt there had been some one or something. Spying upon his privacy! By God, what next ?

There was at the same time, however, an odd underlying feeling of insecurity. He could not say that he had seen the face, but yet it was like a face that he knew. And all at once he thought of the gillie, Ewan Macleod. Conviction that it was Ewan crept along his skin in a deadly enmity. His hand, which had closed on his tumbler, crushed round it, then slowly set it back on the table. His mouth grew narrow as his thought.

As the Colonel thus came at his final decision, the voices from outside barely reached him. Their merry easy talk hushed a little before the night. The contrast to the room and the card-playing was immense. It caressed them with a faint awe. It delighted them with the slightest shudder. ' What a size of a night! ' said the middle Miss Sanderson with a giggle. At that the artist moved away. His wife took his arm silently. The two bloods followed, one of them insisting, ' I always double four,' in a clear satisfied voice. The artist's wife laughed softly.

They moved about the hotel front filling their lungs, some with a vague desire to draw apart as if the night had an appeal secretive and individual. Miss Sanderson's giggle was a wrong note that jarred on this poetic superiority. The tacit condemnation of it was uplifting. Yet the night lent a singular sympathy to Miss Sanderson who was prepared openly to own up to its size. There was the echo of it in her voice—that had to giggle for assurance against tacit condemnation. ' What a size of a night! ' The wind whirled and broke amongst them. The elderly English gentleman said in a cool voice, ' It's going to blow.' Miss Sanderson shoved down her filmy skirts, choking back a throaty ripple. She wanted to laugh and be immensely silly, to let life spill its wanton excess. Her young sister kept looking about her as if a male presence might miraculously materialise. And all at once she saw a ghostly face go down beyond the grassy brink in front of her, where the thin light from the door died out. 'It's chilly!' she said. Darkness could attract her, but there was something menacing about it here. How she secretly hated the whole place!

They began to dribble back into the hotel and dribble to bed. Stansfield heard them and, closing a book on trout fishing in chalk streams, leisurely raised and filled his chest, which showed a growth of strong hair where the striped pyjama lapels fell apart. Methodically he put the bedclothes straight and turned to snuff the candle, accidentally upsetting the book from the small table as he did so.

Clare in the next room heard the thud of the book on the floor. She got up off the bed, still fully dressed. The encounter with her uncle had shaken her. Not that she greatly cared what he knew. And clearly he knew, and therefore all the people in the place knew, of Ewan and herself, and no doubt put the worst construction on the affair.

All that that did, however, was to raise the problem before her. She could now no longer evade it. She had to come to some sort of decision, not as to what she might do but as to what she ought to do. She had got to get at her mind and see exactly what she was after. This required some severe honesty.

But in this stillness of night it was difficult to make any effort. She went to the window and stared out.

There was a light in the piper's cottage away on the rim of the corrie. The sheer enchantment of this land, the rightness of desire, the joy of mere living, the freedom of the wind coming round a hill, the dark moving expression on a loch's face, the exquisite fatigue of the body that lay over open as a flower to sun and sky. Seductive. Sweet, sweet night, how seductive. The smiling whisper died out on a breath.

Evading again! She turned from the window. It was the eternal issue that women did evade, trusting to instinct. And probably rightly too. Why not? To have the mind made up, to go for what one wanted or to evade what one wanted from a standard of honesty, to perceive clearly, almost to intellectualise— was it not in the most passionate and exquisite sense to destroy? It was, of course. The long thought of it made her tired. Yet out of her very nature, within the virginal shaft of her body, she had to see clearly. In the last analysis her skin was white as her thought, as if in its fine English mould there was something of the cool beauty of the water nymph.

The water nymph that desired the source in the hills! Perhaps all this arising merely because she had been ill and was now in a state of convalescence— always a dangerous condition! And in any case, asked her mind quite suddenly, what would happen *afterwards*?

There was the whole question at last. There it was. . . . And in a moment and calmly she put it at arm's length, enquiring coldly, ' Well ? ' Nor did her eyes waver in their faint aristocratic enmity.

But it wasn't enough. The coolness was a deceit, an evasion. She sat down on her bed, lay quietly over, and then violently buried her face in the pillow. The truth was that she passionately desired Ewan. That was the truth. She passionately desired him. Her mind flooded.

Nor was it all desire, to do herself justice. There was something lost in him, as there was something lost in the hills, like this new darkness lost in herself, which so fatally attracted her, as if, beyond it, she would come on the source of light and life, out of which swiftness came and beauty, and without which life must be forever thin and sterile.

Whether one could go and live on a croft or another in a social city; whether indeed this might not be an adventure for the time being, taking what the gods give with the gods' carelessness. . . . But that's where she balked. She had not the courage. Even to-day had she not been wondering why he did not make his way in life ? If he did make his way and had money, did that mean ? . . . And then later, when she had returned from her climb and they had lain together and his face had gathered something of the hawk, had she not repelled him by subterfuge ? A double deceit!

She hated deceit. It brought her off the bed and as her fingers began to undo her clothes, her feet took her to the window. The croft lights always attracted her, but now there was only the piper's left. The stillness of the night soothed and uplifted her mind. To take life's supreme offer was the way of the great. Out of it, myth and drama and that high singing sense of the splendid pilgrimage. . . . A sound of sobbing, soft-dripping as water, fell on her ear; presently there was a padding of naked feet overhead in the attic room where Jean slept; then silence fell again.

The silence, extending into the immense world outside, was broken by a *click click* of stones upon the road to the stone bridge. The man's feet had grown careless as though immeasurably weary and the man himself swayed a trifle. Yet perhaps his mind rather than his body was exhausted. There had been that mad moment by the dining-room window when, had the frame been unlatched, heaven alone knows what would have happened. The sight of the Colonel, with all that he represented implicit in his very stance, had not so much bereft him of all reason as in a moment turned him into a hunting beast. He would have sprung on the Colonel and choked him. Every sense had whipped lean and keen as a fang. Completely unhuman—like a jungle cat!

He had stepped from the window all shaking, had had to lean against the wall. No emotion so decisive and merciless had ever possessed him before. Murdering would hardly have satisfied: he would have had to tear his throat out!

His trembling had made him feel slightly sick. Yet there was an odd satisfaction in the unconditional certainty of his emotion. I would have killed him, he had thought to the night.

So perfect a conclusion had almost allowed him to look with detachment on the battle between Mary and the Colonel. Then the pitiless smile faded out and, leaving the wall, he had slid over a bank to avoid the hotel guests coming out at the front door.

323

But the Colonel had not come out. And the night was empty now, was a hollow in which nothing moved but the wind. The croft lights were withdrawn. The fairness of night had gone from the sky. The wind had strengthened and become chill.

As he went down by the burnside towards his home his lonely figure gathered that dark glen about it. His mind became at last emotionless and clarified, held that curious still recognition of tragedy which is often indistinguishable from its acceptance, and in which murder can be apprehended as clearly as love.

He got lost in the hollow, his body drifting like a nucleus of the darkness, an emanation of the glen, its uneasy being, its core. Presently his feet sounded on the bridge, paused for the sea, then went on and up to the plateau. The light in the kitchen window was there but turned down. Turned down. His face, now by the door, hesitated, giving the smile of a confederate to the night, then withdrew and the door closed.

CHAPTER THREE

I

THE day broke in a dark wind.

When Clare Marlowe was knocked out of a short but deep sleep, she heard the wind like the dying underswell of a past night's thoughts. It blew about her window eaves, and had an intermittent whine about some near chimney gable. The morning light in her room, too, was dim. Her mind, leaping awake, instantly suspected a wet driving mist—and no fishing. She slipped out of bed and went to the window. There was, however, no rain. She knew a thrill of relief. A dark-grey formless sky quite good for fishing. There was wind, of course; certainly a breeze—but surely not too strong. Mr. Stansfield, for example, would fish, one could depend on it. The thought of Mr. Stansfield at that moment was very agreeable. She was going to fish, whatever happened. Her being cried out for it; a whole day away from the hotel. Ewan and the boat. The wind and the sky and the loch and the old earth. The craving this morning was deep as for some secret cleansing act.

She was down in good time for breakfast—but not before Stansfield, who was already finishing his porridge in assured style. She gave him her most pleasant smile, hesitating to ask: 'All right for fishing to-day?'

She saw his eyelids flicker a moment under her morning brightness.

'Oh, yes,' he answered. 'Or, well, at least,' he smiled, 'there's always some place or other, in any weather.'

She showed her appreciation of such excellent wisdom: 'That's what I'm beginning to think'; and passed on to her chair.

When Stansfield had finished his breakfast, he got up, stood a doubtful moment, pulling down his waistcoat, feeling in his pockets; then went towards the door, suddenly stopped half-way, came back to Clare.

'The upper half of Lochglas will be sheltered to-day. I don't expect these people'—nodding towards an unoccupied table—'will go out. And it's quite a good spot. An ordinary grouse-and-claret is as good as anything.'

'Oh, thanks,' said Clare. 'I'll find out if they're going. Thanks very much. Grouse-and-claret.'

'Yes—as a rule. But to-day, it's pretty dull. There's a new fly I have got; it's doing rather well; something like a wasp and not too small. There will be enough water for it to-day with this wind.' He took an aluminium case from his pocket and, opening it, revealed serried rows of flies from which he extracted one. 'That's it. You have a shot at it,' and he laid it on the table beside her.

'Really, that's too much!'

'Nothing,' he said negligently. 'Good morning —and good luck!'

'Good luck!' she responded warmly. It was decent of him. And, besides, he so obviously lived here for nothing else but his fishing, had no side interests, didn't care for anybody or anything, beyond being away all day on a loch with his gillie and his perfect tackle, catching trout. Something almost austere in this concentration touched Clare for a moment. He was even so sure of himself that he could afford a quiet, lawyerlike humour over his concentration. He had once chanced to point out to her in passing the verses which were hung up in a dark-edged frame just behind the dining-room door about the fisherman on a green bank who ' looked it ' and ' hooked it ' and so on. There could be no doubt but that he would go back to London with stories of what his gillie said and what the weather did, retailed quietly round a club fire, with one or two intimates impatiently waiting to tell *their* stories negligently! The sound middle-class concentrated on its job, washed and fairly satisfied, well-mannered and not without humour, and quite free from the distressing handicap of an imagination. Very sound. Clare felt immensely tolerant and (rather more obscurely) grateful. She would be specially nice to Stansfield some time. Nor might he be exactly indifferent! She discovered herself smiling at the way his eyes had brightened and flickered.

Breakfast over, she was very soon on her way to the garage. It was blowing, all the same; steadily and yet with extra dark lumps of wind now and then. She could almost see these eddying swirls. And there was Ewan crossing over to the garage door. He was alone. Alastair was not back yet. That was all right. She would put Stansfield's suggestion before him and exhibit the new fly.

As she came up, Ewan's face gave her a shock. But she did not hesitate to greet him happily. His invariably polite answering smile was ghastly. There was no humour in it or dark shyness. It was simply automatic. Instead of immediately broaching Stansfield's suggestion she found herself asking him what he thought of the day.

' It won't be much use for fishing.'

' Don't you think so ? '

' It's going to blow a gale.'

' Is it ? ' She looked about her, at the sky. There was something dim and uncanny in the wind. Or was it in his face ? It was the face of one to whom some secretive appalling thing had happened. She observed a knot of men by the roadside over towards the post office. On the wind came the low-gear roar of a heavy car mounting the hotel brae. It rounded into view, came abreast of them, a small closed-in charabanc, with men inside. Ewan saluted, and one or two of the men nodded to him with a dry grin. Was that the policeman beside the driver ? In a flash she knew that these were the Ardbeg crofters being taken to prison for contempt of court. She now observed several persons standing about here and there. The charabanc roared on, disappeared, the people looking after it, unmoving. She turned to Ewan, and found him politely waiting her pleasure.

' Are these ? . . .' she stammered, lost for words.

' Yes,' he answered; ' off for their joy ride.' Yet there was no real irony in his voice. She had never seen any face quite like this. It was empty of all

328

emotion, drained, and yet with a still, cruel quality of menace in its drawn passionless flesh.

' I'm sorry,' she murmured. And then after a moment, ' So the fishing is off ? '

' If you think so.'

' All right. Shall we wait and see what to-morrow is like ? '

' Very good.'

For she knew quite well that no power on earth would make him fish that day.

There was no more to be said, yet he stood beside her in the awkward silence showing no slightest trace of the discomfort that she herself experienced acutely. Her back was to the hotel, and raising her head in a parting word, she surprised in his expression an eye-narrowing that was not merely hostile but utterly pitiless. She involuntarily half-turned and saw her uncle arrested in his stride by the hotel corner.

Clare's own mind hardened. She turned her back on the hotel again.

' Ewan.'

' Yes.' He looked at her.

' I'm sorry. . . .' She tried to search his eyes.

' Yes, I know,' he nodded, gazing past her at nothing.

' We cannot talk here.'

' No.'

' It's going to be a long day—until night. But— I should like to talk with you then.' And she gave him her eyes frankly. He met them, and in his own for a moment glimmered fugitively something that faded and died.

' Very well,' she concluded.

But just as he was turning away, he paused, and gave her a lingering look, and said, ' You have been very kind.' Some of the hidden man she had never before seen came out in that look; it was a brightness of revelation from something very deep in him and kind and loyal, and yet in a moment with a nameless air about it of courtesy and withdrawal and farewell. A warmth went over her. She felt her eyes shining and giving themselves like a lover's. When he turned away he did not touch his cap: he lifted it. The trivial distinction was like a gesture of gaiety to her spirit, and she prepared herself to meet her uncle with more than belief in her powers, with some of Ewan's pitilessness happily in her own soul.

But her uncle had merely been waiting to see that she did not go fishing. Satisfied on that point, he ignored her by appearing to attend to affairs of his own. Even at his worst he was jealous of their correct relations before the crowd. He would not, if he could help it, give anything away there. All this she realised, and not until lunch-time did she come into contact with him. Then his self-control rather unsettled her. The bloodshot filaments in his eyes were less noticeable than their reserved expression. He had in fact all the reticent air of a man remorselessly acquiring evidence. And as lunch went on, no trace of awkwardness or distress came into his bearing. His body on closer inspection seemed positively more compact of basic dignity, of personal decison. His politeness grew cold and inimical. She began to feel it more and more, to suspect some inner cohering of the final elements of the man under a sense of assault on the very significance of what his

330

existence stood for. He had been struck at in his foundations.

The more she sensed his feelings the more inimical she herself became, the more wounded in her own dignity. The whole thing at this time of day was utterly preposterous. It was exasperating; it made one angry. Nor would she have cared if he had been imaginatively capable of understanding. He wasn't. Nor was Stansfield. No one like that could understand. They were not merely dated: they were stupid; they were maddening. The Colonel stood at attention by his chair till she got up, and then followed her. But in the lounge they parted without a word.

She was certain now that he was merely gathering his forces. He would, when the right moment came, crush her mercilessly, or—if driven to the last extremity—expose her Then what an exposing would be there! With the temper that would destroy before casting the body to the native dogs! Social prestige and power are maintained by treating thus the betrayer.

There is, however, at least relief in open warfare. The afternoon was ahead—and then the evening. She would wander through the afternoon, waiting on evening. This class-baiting by her uncle merely confirmed her in her own wisdom. And in her wisdom was a dark loveliness, which she experienced with a rush when once more alone.

The wind had increased to a gale. Stansfield returned by four o'clock. He hadn't many trout and sent them round to the back. Clare greeted him cheerfully and after tea went through to inspect. The trout were in a dish beside Jean who was peeling potatoes in the sink. Only a day or two before had she learned quite by chance that Jean was Ewan's sister.

'Well, Jean, you're busy?'

Jean started, then lowered her head.

'Yes, m'am.'

'That's rather a fine one,' murmured Clare with a sidelong look. There was something about Jean's face that disturbed her.

'How is your sister?' she asked, lingering.

Jean looked up.

'I met her some time ago—down at your home,' explained Clare with a friendly smile.

'She's very well, thank you,' said Jean politely, and stood looking at the window.

But Clare had nothing more to say without being personal, and this girl's face with its curious veiled apathy, its haunting suggestion of something unseen and fateful, touched her with a nameless apprehension. Some deep impulse in her woman's heart suddenly moved her to draw near to Jean. In a moment this impulse made her feel detached and alien. The whole experience quite ridiculous—yet unmistakably there! Perhaps they were all extraordinary, these people! Had looked on the dark wind and seen the 'hosting of the sidhe'!

At dinner the Colonel was still more powerfully entrenched within himself, his face a shade warmer, as with conviction, a grosser certainty. He was much nearer the moment of decisive action; had less concern for her feelings.

When they parted in the lounge Clare went

332

immediately to her room. The nearness of his outburst excited her. But, far more than that, she realised that he had made up his mind to watch her. He would prefer, as it were, to catch her in the act. Whereupon he would, as he had said, savage the gillie and then deal with her.

There was a wounding humour in this. It whipped her to an outraged flush. Her hands closed rigidly. She was caught in a deep humiliation. And all at once she realised her uncle's strength; the strength of what he stood for, what he meant. It was ridiculous, inflated, maddening, but utterly real.

When she found herself actually wondering if she could steal out by a back door she drew herself together, put on her coat, and intolerantly went down to the lounge and leisurely out at the front door. As it happened her uncle was not about and her heart began to beat strongly. He was not anywhere about the garage, not anywhere to be seen. She went past the post office unhurriedly with the feeling of walking on her toes. The excitement of escape mounted to her head. The wind bore her along. Had she been thinking about the sidhe ? She was not disinclined to be one of the sidhe herself! These fairy beings riding the wind! These claps and bursts . . . dark swirls . . . almost visible. Valkyries. . . . No, not Valkyries. More secretive, more intimate, the invisible beings and influences here; they came up to one on an eddy of wind, whispered, slid away. She laughed, and looked about her. A flattened world of streaming hair in the deepening dusk. The cottages and the dykes crouched close. They knew. She lay back against the strong invisible arms and let them

333

carry her on. The skirt of her travelling coat clapped before her legs. Her body began to tremble with laughter and fear . . . not altogether of the wind, though the wind helped . . . the mad, ravaging wind and its nameless riders—with their secret knowledge. . . .

She felt herself growing rosy with laughter, with tinglings of ancient mirth, of liberating mirth, cutting her adrift from all that had been and rushing her upon the unknown that was forever.

She owed an amende to Ewan, the swift amende of one human soul to another. His face had been with her all day, the drawn flesh, the unconquerable pride, the pitiless cruelty . . . these crofters, the bitterness . . . the crushing of a people . . . and something deeper than all that in the inmost defeated places of his being. . . . Followed by that look he had given her, that lingering look of self-revelation, making her realise in a moment that hitherto she had never seen the real man, the incorruptible integrity, with the air intimate and aloof. . . . For had not the parallel to what her uncle thought of him always been subconsciously in her own mind ? It was hateful to have that thought, but there it was. . . . Even after they had kissed, if he had called her ' Clare ' readily she would have heard it as a false note. ' Miss Marlowe ' or ' Ma'm ' would have been too cold an insult to her yielding. ' Clare ' would have been a rather warm presumption on account of it. And he had sensed her vague snobbery perfectly and called her nothing! An amende for that; oh, a swift amende! But why torture herself about it now, as though the duality were in her yet, inescapable and

334

of her paltry essence forever ? Was it ? cried her heart urgently to the wind. ' Not to-night! Not to-night! ' She passionately wanted freedom to-night, come what would of to-morrow. . . . And all at once, before her, the Cladach sands, a boiling, thunderous sea, and outward to the left a black sea-rock spouting foam in ghostly streamers. She started, and suddenly shivered.

2

And at that moment Colonel Hicks, having satisfied himself that his niece must have eluded him while he was having a preparatory stiffener, caught from his bedroom window the deceitful flicker in the gloom of a dress disappearing down towards the stone bridge. He visualised the road by the burn-side ending at the sea, where doubtless were hidden places and rocky caverns.

His mind was made up. He knew what he was going to do. As guardian of his class, of the eternal fitness of its regnancy, for which a man fought as a matter of instinct, he was definitely implacable rather than blusteringly in a rage. For the issue transcended the personal. Clare had done more than forgotten herself. It was his business to remind her. And he would, by God! In such a moment he had no doubt of his power. And every stroke at the gillie would be a lash at Clare. A shepherd's hazel crook belonging to John McAlpine, and shortened to a gentleman's use, became his staff.

He stumped the ground sharply with it between his strides as he went down to the stone bridge. Pride had drawn his features till they bore the old imperious look. Out of its flabbiness his body had braced itself and caught at the soldier's dignity so long lost.

All about him in the dusk came this northern land. No longer did he jeer at it; nor did it unroll before him with evasive humility. It was at once watchful and heedless, with something strange and inimical in its eyeless regard.

The power of the immemorial that remains and that may be jealous. Colonel Hicks was affected by it, as a man could not be who neither loved nor hated. By so much was he upheld and redeemed. The land rose about him. And his head rose. By the burnside, through the storm's hollow, he led—and was led with an unheeding and final cruelty. For Clare had gone the opposite way towards Cladach, but doom had made its appointment with the Colonel.

3

In that same hour Ewan Macleod was seated, as he had been most of the afternoon, on one or two crushed lobster-pots within the black shed by the sea. He had won to a state of quiescence that to an onlooker might have been taken for despair. As, perhaps, despair it was, in that ultimate sense, where all things are seen with an effect of final truth in an inner light of no colour. A bleak light in which all the emotions wither, except, perhaps, the emotion of mockery at the revelation vouchsafed. And Ewan could hardly be bothered even with mockery, as though its features were too intimately known to do anything except weary one.

The Colonel's attack on Mary had at a stroke stripped away the phantasy he had been weaving about life. The lure of solitariness, the smiling detachment, the play with Clare Marlowe, all the hidden compensations fell from him.

Tragedy may have its great moments, but there is a futility of tragedy that is sterile—perhaps the most terrible form of tragedy, for there can be no purgation, with the cleansed spirit going on.

Over against Colonel Hicks, Ewan felt this futility. No matter what he did, it would be there. Were he to destroy him. . . .

His face grew stone-still again.

Upon a plane of shadow and negation, one positive act cries with life.

And he had already worked out that act to its logical conclusion: destroying the Colonel meant destroying himself. For in a small place like this the chance of not having the deed brought home was negligible. But if on some such dark night as this they both disappeared, then at least there would be mystery and his own people would never know, would never have the awful certainty of what the end had been. Death by his own hand would save his mother and Annabel and Jean the terrifying suspense and final dread act of the law. There was no other way.

But that was not the point here and now. For even if, by some unimaginable chance, he could cover up his killing, yet how was he to stand up to its denial? Denial would sear his soul black. The Colonel would laugh at him in hell. No, he could not deny destroying a thing like the Colonel. He might be a liar for anything else, for everything else, but not for this now. For this included more than himself. . . .

Ewan's thought stilled to ultimate vision where he saw his spirit as the spirit of his people. The vision was so clear that irony could raise no clouding ripple. Indeed in a moment he saw not his own spirit but the spirit of his people. He saw something so fine and sure that its betrayal would live on through eternity. All who had gone before him would be bowed under it.

It was a terrible vision and the burden of its honour was so heavy upon him that he dare not evade it by saying he was making himself important. He was not making himself important: he was making himself one of the condemned.

The light was large and bright, and yet small and narrow as a receding loneliness.

Its truth was beyond sound, there was no shadow in it, and its beauty was calm as evening and terrible as an idle sword.

Ewan's body crushed away from it, making the lobster-pots writhe. His heels dug into the ground, his face lifted, he heard the storm. He listened to its smashing fury, his cheeks drawn pale, his eyes glistening. Flash and smash of rock-held seas. To fight the sea, oar by oar, in a last battle, and then, like that vision of the second-sight, to be swallowed up by the dark gateway whither his father had already passed; to cleanse and be cleansed, going down under. . . .

He forgot the Colonel.

His face drew back.

And because this picture of his own end had a strange and satisfying appeal, there descended upon him again the old feeling of evading life. He had always as it were been turning back and finding his place—and his hands—empty. . . . Why, when he came back, had he not in due course settled down and married Mary and supported his mother and gone on gillieing? It was not that any foiled part of him craved the world's success which he had repudiated how many years ago in Edinburgh! It was not that the place wasn't 'good enough' for him or that he was afraid of bodily work. His mind was far too cunning to be deceived there. What was wrong was that his spirit could not now find in this place an easy home. As though not his spirit but the place had been betrayed. And in this betrayed place his spirit moved like an uneasy ghost.

But what then did he expect? Was he merely a visionary, with no understanding of what Fachie called the 'practical proposition'? Fachie! 'You wait on—and you may be surprised!' The Highlander at his age-long game of climbing the political backstairs!

No wonder the ghost of the race walked!

The old Gaelic music, the pipe tunes, the long heave of the sea, the green glens, the mountains, the brown moors. On a dim winter's day, with raw smothering rain from a lowering sky, when the world looked a desolation of gloom and he would curse it, yet behind speech, deeper than the stir of thought, lay a profound awareness of that covering world as a fitting cloak. And even in the young girls and lads who showed an eagerness to be away into the wide

world, into the ' gay ' cities (not yet knowing the
' backlands ') arose a hatred of their poverty-stricken
lonely surroundings, but a hatred of something *alive*
at their core.

Fachie did not get hold there!

Any more than he got hold of the new dream of
the larger crofts, the outrun for sheep and cattle,
co-operative marketing, the forest communities, the
roads and steamers, the fishing creeks, loch and river
and hill for those whom they drew. . . . Not a revival of the old, but the old carried forward, evolved,
into the new, and the creative instinct at work once
more, and all the more powerfully for being free of
the increasing nightmare of city civilisations.

The ghost might put on flesh and blood. And
humanity be given a new vision.

Might! In this place now a man grew satanic over
his dreams . . . and thought of Colonel Hicks!

No, he would not murder Colonel Hicks. It
would be to make too important a burnt offering!
Last night he had merely seen how very easily he
might murder him. That had haunted his mind.
Nothing more. Yet he was going to deal with him,
to brand him in some way. That was the problem
he had come here to solve. And his muscles would
persist in gripping every now and then as if they had
Colonel Hicks under them and a knife-point was
snicking a cross on the imperial forehead!

In the gloom Ewan's black eyes flickered with fire
while his face gathered a slow thraldom of fatigue
that yet held a listening smile through which the
storm smashed delectably. As his lips slowly com-
pressed, his mind slid over the Colonel to Clare.

340

He liked Clare. There was something free and clean and fine about her, the flower of her race, charming and detached. Whatever might have happened, he would always see her, as it were, at a little distance. From that distance she had had to approach, consciously, troubled.

Through this white vision, the dark sea now curled over and smashed. He listened to it.

Slowly from its elemental thunder the Colonel and Clare were withdrawn, became two alien figures on a strange shore. In this land there dreams and drama finally did not matter. Love, marriage, death— roving, it did not matter *where* to them. But love and marriage here to the young and death to the old mattered profoundly because it was the right place. True environment gives to a man's actions an eternal significance. A native's natural movement is part of land and sea and sky; it has in it the history of his race; it is authentic. What others do or suffer may be touching or beautiful or sad, but finally does not matter.

Ewan's smile became disintegrating. It turned on himself its slow laceration. It was in the case of Mary McKinnon that this matter of race and environment got its point, its most barbed and poisonous point. Her singing voice had touched things in him forgotten for a thousand years. They went back together, side by side, every flicker of instinct or mind, every silence or listening, every thrill or despair, known most subtly each to each in a way dreadful and inescapable and ageless. . . . He got to his feet; his mouth stayed slightly open and his face slightly disfigured. . . . The unconscious held in

341

common—that was race. . . . He stepped to the
door. Thought was the weakling's disease! How
magnificent the sea, how stupendous the storm! His
body ran over cold and his face winced and drew
tense. He went out a few paces till he saw the
water spouting on the Black Rock. Its sheets died
away in far-flung fronds. The Black Rock—with
its black opening.

All his being paused.

Lifting his head, he saw the roof of his home,
where his mother would be waiting. His quickened
breathing eased, and the hidden smile flowered to his
face, lingering and enigmatic.

He had not been near the house since midday. He
would look in and see his mother; say that he had
been hauling the boat up a bit from the storm; tell
her not to sit up for him as he had promised to go
out and might be late.

Not that she would guess he was going out after
Colonel Hicks!

He was hardly surprised to see no light in the
window. She would be in all right for she never
went out to visit a neighbour. Often in the first of
the night she would sit over the fire by herself.
When she heard him opening the door she would
bestir herself and light the lamp, saying, ' You would
think I was saving the light! ' Saving the light!

When he opened the door, he saw that she was
sitting by the fire before the red glow and flickering
flame of the banked peat; but she did not bestir
herself. She did not move at all. Her stillness
caught his breath. He came into the kitchen quietly,
his eyes fixed on her; came up beside her. She

342

lifted her face to him with a worn smile; ' Is that you, Ewan ? ' and turned to the fire again. Her dry pitted face was haggard from weeping.

' Jean was down,' she said after a little.

His heart stood still.

' She's in trouble.'

For a time he lost the feel of his body, and then his feet were taking him along the kitchen floor towards the door. The cold knob touched his hand. He looked back. Her dark bent body against the red glow and the still gloom of the kitchen listening. Softly he closed the door behind him and stood un-moving, his heart listening, unbreathing.

4

He walked away quietly, that last vision of his mother filling some inner chamber of his mind, that was not his mind only, but all mind, as if the chamber were set apart in the immutable places of destiny— yet still the kitchen and the body of his mother.

Thought, with a dreadful jerk, obliterated pure vision, muttering, ' Jean at one door and the Colonel at the other!' The Colonel had tried it on Mary McKinnon, but he had succeeded with Jean! The whole of Jean's mysterious and moody behaviour became clear to him in a flash. She was having a child! The laugh guttered in his throat. All his body drew fine as steel and his lean hands curled strangling fingers. He did not look where his feet went, and if he stumbled on the uneven downward path he was scarcely conscious of it and caught him-self up without effort. When the sound of the laugh had died, the laugh itself remained about his lips and in his far-staring, hardening eyes; stole all over his body in a cold crepitation. He had little more than crossed the crazy bridge when, with the naturalness of a happening in a dream, he came face to face with Colonel Hicks.

Possibly it was Ewan's face that choked the Colonel's utterance. The Colonel was near enough to it in the fading light to see its convincing lineaments and its concentrated eyes, in which a faint surprise as of incredulity passed to something perilously like a welcome, as though some ultimate hunger had unexpectedly come upon its choicest food. It was not insolence, even the Colonel could see; it was far more devastating than any army superior's look, and he had known a few; there was no evasiveness in it, most unsettling of all; it was without any show of heat, lingeringly steady, and slightly inhuman. And the Colonel's instinct, as though he had come upon a human snake-head, was to hit it. His throat gurgled and raked 'Damn you!' and John McAlpine's crook for gentlemen whirled aloft and came down.

Ewan's head, of its own accord, dodged. The blow went glancing off his body. He scarcely felt it. But he took a step nearer the Colonel. The Colonel backed, his face now a working fury, his throat raking filthy sound. Through flailing arms and stick Ewan walked right into the Colonel's throat, and his lean hands encircled it, his thumbs meeting on the windpipe and keeping their hold as the Colonel toppled backwards on to the broad of his back.

Ewan brought prisoning knees to bear and pressed steadily on the windpipe, his fingers gripping like

344

ivory hooks into the flabby flesh of the neck. The great body heaved and squirmed under him. Then into the eyes came a hot maddened fear as they glared into the pitiless face above. And quite suddenly, in the very moment of the dawn of dreadful realisation, the glare fixed and the body lay still, for the Colonel's heart was a much weaker vessel than his lungs.

Ewan knew he was dead, yet the thumbs continued to compress the windpipe, as if actuated by the instinct that keeps an animal immersed in the drowning water for a much longer period than is necessary to defeat the ends of life, the spectacle of a crawling back to existence being offensive and intolerable.

It was clear the Colonel was not going to crawl back to existence. Ewan got off his chest with a smile at the goggling eyes and splayed body. Merely to have branded the noble forehead would have been rather a theatrical pretension.

5

As Ewan stood up and looked about him, he was all at once intensely aware of the night, of the smallest sound, of the depth of the gloom. His body was poised so flawlessly that when he turned his head he heard his clothes rustle.

The night's fingers touched him. He swayed; then stooped swiftly and catching the dead body under the armpits dragged it off the road and in amongst the rushes, where he turned it over on its face. In a moment, yet without haste, he was back on the road.

345

The night grew even more attentive. No one would come from his own home; it was unlikely that anyone would descend the steep face to the swing-bridge. But it was just possible that someone, a strolling couple, might come down the road he stood on; might indeed at that very moment be approaching.

All at once he started up the road, at first walking firmly, but his feet made such an infernal clatter that they tiptoed of themselves to the broad grassy verge where they strode swiftly and silently. If he met anyone he would ease up and talk laughingly. If they asked him where he was bound for, he would say for the bridge, in the hope that Fachie might be there! That would interest and amuse them. Unless they were lovers, when they would see nothing. *But if there was a dog!. . .*

He drew up, listening acutely. He was at least half way to the bridge now. It was getting dark quickly under the rushing stormy sky. If he got ten clear minutes, he would throw the Colonel's body over the rocks.

Turning, he started running at full speed, picking himself up with amazing dexterity when he stumbled. But as he ran he began to see with his inner eye a crofter bending over the body that his dog was sniffing at, a crofter setting rabbit snares or taking a short cut to visit friends on the other side.

A spirt of anger shot up like a flame into his brain. He burned all over. His boot hit a loose stone and set it racketing along the roadway. He pulled up, listened, stepped on to the hard surface and began walking steadily. As he came opposite the rushes he

346

saw the black body like a gaping ditch. He went on a few yards before he stopped. There was not a soul about. Slipping off the road, he made quickly and quietly for the rushes. With an agile sinuous movement, he got under the body and heaved erect.

But he could not stand the smell of the lolling face by his cheek; no, damn, it sickened him. He manoeuvred the body on to his other shoulder so that the head hung down his back. There was a tinkle of coins. Things falling out of the pockets? He dropped the body and groped about. Could only have been money, but he could find none. He stamped the marshy spot with his feet and securely buttoned the Colonel's jacket; then got under his burden once more and started upward for the cliffheads.

It was steep going, every step giving the sensation of leg bones being pushed into the soles of his feet, until it ended in a dragging zigzag mostly on all fours. When he rolled the burden from him on the ridge above the sea, his wind was whistling in his teeth. Sitting up, he encountered fair across from him but on a lower level the lamp-lit window of his home. Its nearness astonished him, like an eye. In a moment what it stood for flared in his mind. The mother lamp in the encircling gloom, lead thou me on! His breath raked its heroics harshly. His laughter nearly came through. His teeth ground on an oath, and getting under his burden he set out strongly.

The idea of pushing the body over the first convenient spot had suddenly changed itself into the idea of pushing it over a place as far as possible from that

347

light. As he staggered on, the light was set inwardly upon the dark storm of life like a mute beacon that the eye could not avoid.

It was a quarter of a mile to the Crioch point, beyond which ran inward a narrow sea-inlet, where if anything were dropped it might reasonably be expected to stay. Anyway, the body would not come washing about the little creek beneath the old home. The light would be at least free of that horrible taint. And even if not for the light's sake but merely to keep the place clean in the eternities. There must remain a fitness in death. The Colonel could find his own way to hell and take all his clamour with him.

Anyway, he was prepared to give him the push-off!

That is if he did not first rupture muscle from bone, for this fleshly mass could be little short of two hundredweights.

And once the Colonel nearly got him as he slipped and pitched downward, the full weight crushing on to his neck and head and sticking there with smothering persistence. Trying to pull himself backward against the slope, he found his chin trapped by a ridge of stone that pressed on his throat. Nor could he heave the body forward when he arched his back, for it was caught at the knees against a boulder. He lay a few seconds quietly, and a sardonic humour crept over his crushed face. The old boy was certainly doing his damnedest! Then he carefully worked himself free.

The Crioch point was set high in the very eye of the gale, and a mighty world roared and whistled round it and streamed away into endless night. The thunder of the sea beneath made the earth tremble.

348

As Ewan heaved on to that point, the solid rock rumbled under his staggering feet. The speed of the wind choked him. Nothing mean in the black, destroying magnificence of this night! As the body slid from him, he fell on it.

Breath and energy returned quickly. Upon this trembling peak there was an invigorating sense of insecurity. Better get the job over.

He began carefully pushing the body in front of him, pausing now and then to peer ahead, rolling it over and over, until he hesitated upon a grassy verge sweeping downward to sheer cliff-edge. A perfect send-off! He squared the body to the line of descent and gave it a push. It trundled noiselessly from view.

For a long time he listened. But no betraying note came up out of that inferno of sound. Three hundred feet of it had swallowed the morsel without sign. Ewan kept staring at a deeper darkness on the very edge of the cliff. That was where it had disappeared. He continued to stare at it. Through that very spot it had rolled over. This deeper darkness was a certain length . . . a mere cleft in the rock's ridge . . . about the length of a man's body. He kept staring at it; began to make out the pale blob of a face. He winked and stared again. . . .

Then he started down, feet first. It was even steeper than he had thought. Lying flat upon his face, he had yet to hang on very carefully indeed. With every precaution, he backed down inch by inch. It was getting steeper. He lay still for a little, then very carefully turned his face over his right shoulder. It *was* a dark cleft after all, and not a body. He was

349

on the very brink, the left toe reaching into space.
All at once the tuft of grass in his right hand came
away at the roots, and earth trickled up his sleeve.
His body slewed over. Feeling himself going, he
clawed into the ground. He was anchored again but
unable to move. Weakness crawled over his flesh.
The holding muscles trembled excitedly. This was
reaction after bringing up two hundredweights
through black pathless night! A bit too much.
Better let go and be done with it. Let mind fade
away . . . soft-falling . . . nothing. Out of this mist
of flushing nausea and insidious desire, his mind
groped, his hands and his toes groped, pulling him
upward by sheer compulsion of will. He slithered
at last over the ridge and, face to the earth, slid into a
short unconsciousness.

6

On the way back along the cliffs his disencumbered
body enjoyed a sense of extraordinary freedom and
communion with the streaming night. His mind,
after its short respite, rose purged of all sense of
struggle and emotion and was blown with his body
upon the wind. A magnificent night, black and
phantasmal and winged. The roar of the seas ran
along the rocks like muffled thunder in stupendous
caverns of doom. The under-roll of the drums of
doom. Invigorating and august. For doom transcended life; vast in its eternal dimension beyond life.

His spirit rose up in its assurance and mastered
the night. His body, the dark storm-centre, swept
the cliffs. Nothing negative and suppressed in this

vast world. Here freedom was positive and strength superb. When a man had done what he must, he could enter in. How a man enters this gateway is he finally judged by the valiant souls of his race who have gone before him and who live forever.

When the yellow light came once more before his sight, he paused. As his head turned away, the black night was flecked by that window-light as by an underworld star. In the bodiless pause there came about his ears in thin wisps, in ethereal eddies, fragments of distant pipe music. It was Colin, at ' The Lost Glen.' Colin! He smiled, listening. On the flat space yonder, piping immortal defiance at the storm! Piping ' The Lost Glen ' . . . the glen that was lost . . . forever lost. The old adventure was over. Eddying little wisps . . . dying out . . . gone.

His mind remained high with his thought, smiling in gentleness and irony, as his body went of its own accord about its deathly business, down past the crazy bridge, under the rock that hid his home, until it came by the fishing boat. Hands untied the head-rope from the anchoring boulder and, coiling it, dropped it by the ring-bolt.

The oars were aboard. He threw a look at the obliterating seas that went smashing past the inlet down upon the Black Rock. Then he got his back to the breast-curve and heaved. The keel grated downward over the stones. Her stern took the water and he vaulted the bows.